Also by Linda Howard

A Lady of the West
Angel Creek
The Touch of Fire
Heart of Fire
Dream Man
After the Night
Shades of Twilight
Son of the Morning
Kill and Tell
Now You See Her
All the Queen's Men
Mr. Perfect

Published by POCKET BOOKS

LINDA HOWARD

OPEN SEASON

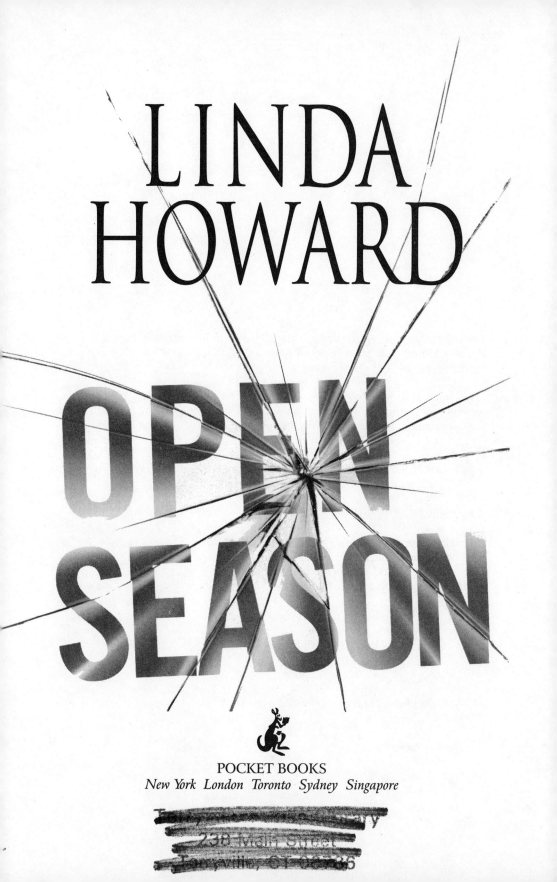

POCKET BOOKS

New York London Toronto Sydney Singapore

For information regarding special discounts for bulk purchases, please contact Simon & Schuster Special Sales at 1-800-456-6798 or business@simonandschuster.com

 POCKET BOOKS, a division of Simon & Schuster, Inc.
1230 Avenue of the Americas, New York, NY 10020

Copyright © 2001 by Linda Howington

ISBN: 0-671-03442-1

First Pocket Books hardcover printing August 2001

10 9 8 7 6 5 4 3 2 1

POCKET and colophon are registered trademarks of
Simon & Schuster, Inc.

Designed by Jaime Putorti

Printed in the U.S.A.

I'm blessed with many, many friends, without whom I couldn't operate. They aren't in any particular order, but they are:

Kate Collins, an editor who never let me see her sweat, even though everyone else around her was in panic mode; Robin Rue, agent and friend and number one cheerleader; Gayle Cochran, who is always there when I need her; Beverly Beaver, whose love shelters all of us; Linda Jones, with her steadiness and quirky sense of humor and good advice; Sabrah Agee, with her laughter and endless sources of legal information; Liz Cline, who literally makes it possible for me to function; Marilyn Elrod, whose friendship is always there, like a rock; my sister Joyce, who has been side-by-side with me since childhood. . . . Like I said, I'm blessed. Catherine Coulter, Iris Johansen, and Kay Hooper are irreplaceable in my life. And let's not forget the Clud Club—they know who they are.

By the way, there was a real Buffalo Club, though the only resemblance it bore to the one in the book was the name and the fact that it served alcohol. The real Buffalo Club burned to the ground many years ago, but it was the stuff of legends.

PROLOGUE

Carmela nervously clutched the burlap bag that held her other dress, some water, and the small package of food she had been able to save for the trip north, across the border. Orlando had told her that they wouldn't be able to stop, for food or water or anything, until they reached Los Angeles. She was locked in the back of an old truck that bounced and swayed, throwing her from side to side if she didn't manage to wedge herself into a corner and brace her back and legs in the small V, making sleep impossible because the moment she relaxed, she was sent tumbling across the rough wood bed of the truck.

Carmela was terrified, but determined. Enrique had gone across two years before, and he'd said he would send for her. Instead he had married an American, so he could never be deported, and she had been left with her dreams destroyed and her pride in shreds. There was nothing left for her in Mexico; if Enrique could marry an American, then so could she! And she would marry a rich one. She was very pretty; everyone said so. When she married her rich *norteamericano,* she would find Enrique and thumb her nose at him, and he would be sorry he had lied and betrayed her.

She had big dreams, but she felt very small, bouncing around in the back of the truck as it charged across uneven ground. She heard grinding metal as Orlando changed gears, and a soft exclamation of pain as one of the other girls banged into the side of the truck. There were three others, all young like her, all wanting something better than what they had left behind in Mexico. They hadn't exchanged names, hadn't talked much at all. They were too preoccupied with the danger of what they were doing, and both sad and excited: sad at what they were leaving behind, and excited at the prospect of a better life. Anything had to be better than nothing, and nothing was what Carmela had.

She thought about her mother, dead for seven months, worn out by a lifetime of hard work and having babies. "Never let Enrique touch you between your legs," her mother had lectured, time and again. "Not until you are his wife. If you do, then he won't marry you, and you'll be left with a baby while he finds another pretty girl." Well, she hadn't let Enrique touch her between the legs, but he had found another girl anyway. At least she hadn't been left with a baby.

She had understood what her mother meant, though: *Don't be like me.* Her mother had wanted Carmela to have more than she'd had. She hadn't wanted her to grow old before her time, forever laden with a baby in her arms and another in the womb, and dying before the age of forty.

Carmela was seventeen. By the time her mother had been seventeen, she'd already had two babies. Enrique had never understood Carmela's insistence on remaining a virgin; he'd been, by turns, angry and sullen at her steadfast refusal to let him make love to her. Perhaps the woman he had married had let him do that to her. If that was all he wanted, then he had never truly loved her at all, Carmela thought. Good riddance! She wasn't going to waste her life mourning a . . . a fool!

She tried to keep her spirits up by telling herself everything would be better in America; everyone said that in Los Angeles there were more jobs than there were people, that everyone had a car, and a television. She might even be in the movies, and become famous. Everyone said she was pretty, so perhaps it was possible. The fact, however, was that she was seventeen and alone, and she was frightened.

One of the other girls said something, her voice drowned out by the laboring engine, but the tension came through. In that moment, Carmela realized the other three were as frightened as she. So she wasn't alone, after all; the other three were just like her. It was a small thing, but she immediately felt braver.

Bracing herself against the lurching as the vehicle bounced from one rut to the next, she scooted across the rough wood of the truck bed until she was close enough to hear what the girl had said. It was daylight now, and enough light seeped through the cracks that she could make out the faces of the others. "What is it?" she asked.

The girl twisted her hands in the worn fabric of her skirt. "I have to relieve myself," she said, her voice thin with shame.

"We all do," Carmela said in sympathy. Her own bladder was full to the point of pain. She had been ignoring it as best she could, unwilling to do what she knew they would eventually be forced to do.

Tears rolled down the girl's face. "I must."

Carmela looked around, but the other two seemed as helpless as the weeping girl. "Then we will do what we must do," she said, because she seemed to be the only one capable of making a decision. "We will designate a corner . . . that one." She pointed at the right rear corner. "There is a crack there, so it will drain. We will each relieve ourselves."

The girl wiped her face. "What about the other?"

"I hope we stop before then." Now that the sun was up, the heat inside the truck would climb steadily. It was summer; if Orlando didn't stop and let them out, they might well die from the heat. He had said they wouldn't stop until they reached their destination, so surely they would be in Los Angeles soon. She had paid Orlando only half of his usual fee; if she died, he wouldn't be able to collect the other half. Normally everyone had to pay in full before the *coyote* would take them across the border, but because she was so pretty, Orlando said, he would make an exception.

The other girls were pretty, too, she realized. Perhaps he had made an exception for all of them.

Relieving themselves was a group effort, because of the bouncing of the truck, and Carmela organized that effort. In turn, with herself going last, each squatted in the corner while the others wedged themselves around her to hold her upright. At last, feeling exhausted but much better, they sank down on the truck bed to rest.

Abruptly, with one last bounce, the truck began rolling smoothly. They were on a highway, Carmela realized. A highway! Surely they were close to Los Angeles now.

But the morning hours ticked away, and the heat inside the truck grew stifling. Carmela tried to breathe normally, but the other girls were panting, as if drawing in extra air would help cool them. Since that air was hot, it didn't seem logical. At least, the way they were sweating, they wouldn't have to relieve themselves again very soon.

She waited as long as she could, because she had no idea how much farther they had to go, but finally her own thirst grew unbearable and she took her small flask of water from her burlap bag. "I have water," she said. "Just a little, so we must share equally." She gave each of them a hard look. "If you take more than one sip before passing the flask, I will slap you. And just a small sip, too."

Under her fierce dark gaze, each girl obediently took one small sip and passed the flask. Somehow, in organizing them to relieve themselves, she had gained the position of leader, and though she wasn't very tall, she had the force of will they all recognized. When the flask reached her, Carmela took her own one small sip, then passed the flask around again. When they had each had two sips, she capped the flask and put it back in her bag. "I know it isn't much," she said, "but I don't have much water and we must make it last."

There was, perhaps, enough water for them each to have another two sips. That wasn't much water, not when they were losing more than that in sweat every hour. Perhaps it would be enough to keep them alive. Why hadn't the other girls thought to bring food and water? she thought irritably, then forced the irritation away. It could be that they hadn't had anything to bring. As poor as she herself was, there were always others who had even less. She must be kind, in thought as well as deed.

The truck began slowing, the difference in the sound of the motor signaling the change. They looked at each other with hope bright in their eyes.

The truck pulled off the highway and stopped. The motor wasn't turned off, but they heard the slam of the door as Orlando got out. Quickly Carmela grabbed her bag and stood; since he had said they wouldn't stop for anything until they reached Los Angeles, then they must have arrived. She had expected more noise, though; she couldn't hear anything other than the sound of the truck's engine.

Then there came the sound of a chain rattling, and the roll-up door of the truck was shoved up on its tracks, letting in a blinding glare of sunlight and a blast of air that was both hot and fresh. Orlando was just a black shape, silhouetted against the white glare. Shielding their eyes, the girls all stumbled to the rear of the truck and awkwardly climbed out.

As her eyes adjusted to the sunlight, Carmela looked around, expecting . . . she didn't know quite what she expected, but at least a big city. There was nothing here but sky and sun and scrub bushes, and drifts of gritty gray soil. Her eyes wide, she looked at Orlando in question.

"This is as far as I take you," he announced. "The truck is too hot; you would die. My friend will take you the rest of the way. His truck has air-conditioning."

Air-conditioning! In Carmela's small village a few people had owned cars, but none of them had air-conditioning. Old Vasquez had pointed with pride to the controls on the dashboard of his car that had once made cold air come from the vents, but they no longer worked, and Carmela had never actually felt such a thing. She knew about it, though. She would ride in a truck with air-conditioning! Old Vasquez would be so jealous if he knew.

A tall, lean man wearing jeans and a plaid shirt came around the side of the truck. He carried four clear bottles of water, which he gave to the girls to drink. The water was cold, the bottles wet with condensation. The thirsty girls gulped the water while he talked to Orlando in English, which none of them spoke.

"This is Mitchell," Orlando finally said. "You are to do what he says. He speaks a little of our language, enough for you to understand what he wants you to do. If you disobey, the American policemen will find you, and throw you in jail, and you will never be freed. Do you understand?"

Solemnly, they all nodded. They were then swiftly hustled into the camper shell on Mitchell's large white pickup. There were two sleeping bags tossed on the truck bed, and a small stool with a hole on top, which on inspection turned out to be a toilet. There was no room to stand up; they had to either sit or lie, but after their sleepless night they didn't care. Cold air and music, both of which were incredibly soothing, were pouring into the camper shell through the open sliding rear window of the truck. After spreading out the two sleeping bags so they could all lie down, the four girls quickly fell asleep.

She hadn't imagined Los Angeles to be so very far away, Carmela thought two days later. She was tired of riding in the camper, of not being able to stand up and move around. Stretching kept her muscles as limber as possible, but what she really wanted was just to *walk*. She had always been an active girl, and this restriction, though necessary, was maddening.

They were fed regularly, and given water to drink. They hadn't been able to wash, however, and they all smelled really bad. Sometimes Mitchell would stop in a deserted area and raise the back gate of the camper shell, letting the camper air out, but the freshness was never complete, and never lasted long anyway.

Peeking through the rear window of the truck, Carmela had watched the empty desert turn into flat grasslands. Then, gradually, wooded areas had appeared, and finally, this last day, there were mountains: lush, green, rolling. There were pastures dotted with cattle, and pretty valleys, and dark green rivers. The air felt thick and humid, and perfumed with the scent of a thousand different varieties of trees and flowers. And cars! There were more cars than she had ever thought to see in her life. They had passed through a city that had seemed enormous to her, but when she had asked Mitchell if this was Los Angeles, he had replied that, no, it was called Memphis. They were still a long way from Los Angeles.

America was unbelievably huge, Carmela thought, for them to have traveled for days and still be a long way from Los Angeles!

But late at night on the second day, they finally stopped. When Mitchell opened the back of the camper and let them out, they could barely walk from having been cooped up for so long. He had parked in front of a long trailer; Carmela looked around, searching for anything that would indicate a city, but they still seemed to be far from any such thing. Stars twinkled overhead, and the night was alive with insect chirps and birdcalls. He unlocked the trailer door and led them inside, and all four girls sighed at the luxury. There was furniture, and the most amazing kitchen with appliances they had no idea how to work, and a bathroom such as they hadn't imagined in their dreams. Mitchell told them they were all to take a bath, and he gave them each a loose, lightweight dress that was pulled on over the head. The dresses were theirs, he said.

They were amazed at such kindness, and thrilled by their new dresses. Carmela smoothed her hand over the fabric, which was smooth and light. Her dress was white with little red flowers all over it, and she thought it was beautiful.

They took baths in water that sprayed out of the wall, and used soap that smelled like perfume. There was special soap for their hair, liquid soap that foamed into mountains of suds. And brushes for their teeth! By the time Carmela left the bathroom, having waited until last because the other girls seemed at the end of their strength, she was cleaner than she had ever been in her life. She had been so enthralled by the richness of the soap that she had bathed twice, and washed her hair twice. Warm water stopped coming out of the spray—there was just cold water now—but she didn't care. It felt so good to be *clean* again.

She was barefoot, and she had no underthings to wear because they were all so dirty, but she pulled on her clean new dress and twisted her damp hair into a knot at the back of her neck. Looking in the mirror, she saw a pretty girl with smooth brown skin, lustrous dark eyes, and a full red mouth, much different from the bedraggled creature who had looked back at her before.

The other girls were already asleep in the bedroom, snuggled under the covers, the air so cold that goose bumps raised on her arms. She went into the living room to tell Mitchell good night and thank him for all he had done for them. A television was on, and he was watching a game of American baseball. He looked up and smiled at her, and indicated two glasses filled with ice and a dark liquid, on the table beside him. "I fixed you something to drink," he said, or that was what she thought he said because his Spanish really wasn't very good. He picked up his own glass and sipped from it. "Coca-Cola."

Ah, that she understood! She took the glass he indicated and drank down the cold, sweet, biting cola. She loved the way it felt on the back of her throat. Mitchell indicated she should sit, so she did, but on the other end of the sofa the way her mother had taught her. She was very tired, but she would sit with him for a few minutes to be polite, and in truth she was grateful to him. He was a nice man, she thought, and he had sweet, faintly sad brown eyes.

He gave her some salty nuts to eat, and suddenly that was just what she wanted, as if her body needed to replace the salt she had lost during the first part of the trip. Then she needed more Coca-Cola, and he got up and fixed another one for her. It felt strange, to have a man bringing things to her, but perhaps that was the way things were in America. Perhaps it was the men who waited on the women. If so, she only regretted she hadn't come sooner!

Her fatigue grew greater. She yawned, then apologized to him, but he only laughed and said it was okay. She couldn't keep her eyes open, or her head up. Several times her head bobbed forward and she would jerk it up, but then her neck muscles just wouldn't work anymore and instead of lifting her head, she felt herself sliding sideways. Mitchell was there, helping her to lie down, settling her head on the cushion and stretching out her legs. He was still touching her legs, she thought dimly, and she tried to tell him to stop, but her tongue wouldn't form the words. And he was touching her between her legs, where she had never let anyone touch her.

No, she thought.

And then the blackness came, and she thought no more.

ONE

Daisy! Breakfast is ready!"

Her mother's voice yodeled up the stairwell, the intonation exactly the same as it had been since Daisy was in first grade and had to be cajoled into getting out of bed.

Instead of getting up, Daisy Ann Minor continued to lie in bed, listening to the sound of steady rain pounding on the roof and dripping from the eaves. It was the morning of her thirty-fourth birthday, and she didn't want to get up. A gray mood as dreary as the rain pressed down on her. She was thirty-four years old, and there was nothing about this particular day to which she looked forward with anticipation.

The rain wasn't even a thunderstorm, which she enjoyed, with all the drama and sound effects. Nope, it was just rain, steady and miserable. The dreary day mirrored her mood. As she lay in bed watching the raindrops slide down her bedroom win-

dow, the unavoidable reality of her birthday settled on her like a
wet quilt, heavy and clammy. She had been good all her life, and
what had it gotten her? Nothing.

She had to face the facts, and they weren't pretty.

She was thirty-four, had never been married, never even been
engaged. She had never had a hot love affair—or even a tepid
one. A brief fling in college, done mainly because everyone else
was doing it and she hadn't wanted to be an oddball, didn't even
qualify as a relationship. She lived with her mother and aunt,
both widowed. The last date she'd had was on September 13,
1993, with Aunt Joella's best friend's nephew, Wally—because *he*
hadn't had a date since at least 1988. What a hot date *that* had
been, the hopeless going on a mercy date with the pitiful. To her
intense relief, he hadn't even tried to kiss her. It had been the
most boring evening of her life.

Boring. The word hit home with unexpected force. If anyone
had to pick one word to describe her, she had a sinking feeling she
knew what that word would be. Her clothes were modest—and
boring. Her hair was boring, her face was boring, her entire *life* was
boring. She was a thirty-four-year-old, small-town, barely-been-
kissed spinster librarian, and she might as well be eighty-four for
all the action she saw.

Daisy switched her gaze from the window to the ceiling, too depressed to get up and go downstairs, where her mother and Aunt
Joella would wish her a happy birthday and she would have to smile
and pretend to be pleased. She knew she had to get up; she had to
be at work at nine. She just couldn't make herself do it, not yet.

Last night, as she did every night, she had laid out the outfit
she would wear the next day. She didn't have to look at the chair
to envision the navy skirt, which hovered a couple of inches
below her knee, both too long and too short to be either fashion-
able or flattering, or the white, short-sleeved blouse. She could

hardly have picked an outfit less exciting if she had tried—but then, she didn't have to try; her closet was full of clothes like that.

Abruptly she felt humiliated by her own lack of style. A woman should at least look a little sharper than usual on her birthday, shouldn't she? She would have to go shopping, then, because the word *sharp* didn't apply to anything in her entire wardrobe. She couldn't even take extra care with her makeup, because the only makeup she owned was a single tube of lipstick in an almost invisible shade called Blush. Most of the time she didn't bother with it. Why should she? A woman who had no need to shave her legs certainly didn't need lipstick. How on earth had she let herself get in this predicament?

Scowling, she sat up in bed and stared directly across the small room into her dresser mirror. Her mousy, limp, straight-as-a-board brown hair hung in her face, and she pushed it back so she could have a clear view of the loser in the mirror.

She didn't like what she saw. She looked like a lump, sitting there swathed in blue seersucker pajamas that were a size too big for her. Her mother had given her the pajamas for Christmas, and it would have hurt her feelings if Daisy had exchanged them. In retrospect, Daisy's feelings were hurt because she was the sort of woman to whom anyone would give seersucker pajamas. Seersucker, for God's sake! It said a lot that she was a seersucker-pajamas kind of woman. No Victoria's Secret sexy nighties for her, no sirree. Just give her seersucker.

Why not? Her hair was drab, her face was drab, *she* was drab.

The inescapable facts were that she was boring, she was thirty-four years old, and her biological clock was ticking. No, it wasn't just *ticking*, it was doing a countdown, like a space shuttle about to be launched: *ten . . . nine . . . eight . . .*

She was in big trouble.

All she had ever wanted out of life was . . . a life. A normal, traditional life. She wanted a husband, a baby, a house of her own. She wanted *SEX*. Hot, sweaty, grunting, rolling-around-naked-in-the-middle-of-the-afternoon sex. She wanted her breasts to be good for something besides supporting the makers of bras. She had nice breasts, she thought: firm, upright, pretty C-cups, and she was the only one who knew it because no one else ever saw them to appreciate them. It was sad.

What was even sadder was that she wasn't going to have any of those things she wanted. Plain, mousy, boring, spinster librarians weren't likely to have their breasts admired and appreciated. She was simply going to get older, and plainer, and more boring; her breasts would sag, and eventually she would *die* without ever sitting astride a naked man in the middle of the afternoon—unless something drastic happened . . . something like a miracle.

Daisy flopped back on her pillows and once more stared at the ceiling. A miracle? She might as well hope lightning would strike.

She waited expectantly, but there was no boom, no blinding flash of light. Evidently no help was coming from On High. Despair curled in her stomach. Okay, so it was up to her. After all, the Good Lord helped those who helped themselves. *She* had to do something. But *what?*

Desperation sparked inspiration, which came in the form of a revelation:

She had to stop being a good girl.

Her stomach clenched, and her heart started pounding. She began to breathe rapidly. The Good Lord couldn't have had *that* idea in mind when He/She/It decided to let her handle this on her own. Not only was it a very un-Good-Lord type of idea, but . . . she didn't know how. She had been a good girl her entire life; the rules and precepts were engraved on her DNA. Stop being a good girl? The idea was crazy. Logic dictated that if she wasn't going to be a good girl any longer, then she had to be a bad one, and that just wasn't in her. Bad girls smoked, drank, danced in bars, and slept around. She might be able to handle the dancing—she kind of liked the idea—but smoking was out, she didn't like the taste of alcohol, and as for sleeping around—No way. That would be monumentally stupid.

But—but bad girls get all the men! her subconscious whined, prodded by the urgency of her internal ticking clock.

"Not all of them," she said aloud. She knew plenty of good girls who had managed to marry and have kids: all her friends, in fact, plus her younger sister, Beth. It could be done. Unfortunately, they seemed to have taken all the men who were attracted to good girls in the first place.

So what was left?

Men who were attracted to bad girls, that's what.

The clenching in her stomach became a definite queasy feeling. Did she even *want* a man who liked bad girls?

Yeah! her hormones wailed, oblivious of common sense. They had a biological imperative going here, and nothing else mattered.

She, however, was a thinking woman. She definitely didn't want a man who spent more time in bars and honky-tonks than he did on the job or at home. She didn't want a man who slept with any road whore who came along.

But a man with experience . . . well, that was different. There was just something about an experienced man, a look in his eyes, a confidence in his walk, that gave her goose bumps at the thought of having a man like that all to herself. He might be an ordinary guy with an ordinary life, but he could still have that slightly wicked twinkle in his eyes, couldn't he?

Yes, of course he could. And that was just the kind of man she wanted, and she refused to believe there wasn't one somewhere out there for her.

Daisy sat up once more to stare at the woman in the mirror. If she was ever going to have what she wanted, then she had to act. She had to do something. Time was slipping away fast.

Okay, being a bad girl was out.

But what if she gave the *appearance* of being a bad girl? Or at least a party girl? Yeah, that sounded better: party girl. Someone who laughed and had fun, someone who flirted and danced and wore short skirts—she could handle that. Maybe.

Big maybe.

"Daisy!" her mother yodeled once more, the sound echoing up the stairs. This time her voice was arch with the tone that said she knew something Daisy didn't, as if there were any way on earth Daisy could have forgotten her own birthday. "You're going to be late!"

Daisy had never been late to work a day in her life. She sighed. A normal person with a normal life would be late at least once a year, right? Her unblemished record at the library was just one more indicator of how hopeless she was.

"I'm up!" she yelled back, which wasn't quite a lie. She was at least *sitting* up, even if she wasn't out of bed.

The lump in the mirror caught her eye, and she glared at it. "I'm never going to wear seersucker again," she vowed. Okay, so it wasn't quite as dramatic as Scarlett O'Hara's vow never to be hungry again, but she meant it just the same.

How did one go about being a bad girl—no, a *party* girl, the distinction was important—she wondered as she stripped off the hated seersucker pajamas and wadded them up, then defiantly stuffed them into the wastebasket. She hesitated a moment— what would she wear to bed tonight?—but forced herself to leave the pajamas in the trash. Thinking of her other sleepwear—seersucker for summer and flannel for winter—she had the wild thought of sleeping naked tonight. A little thrill ran through her. That was something a party girl would do, wasn't it? And there was nothing *wrong* with sleeping naked. She had never heard Reverend Bridges say anything at all about what one wore, or didn't wear, to bed.

She didn't have to shower, because she was one of those people who bathed at night. The world, she thought, was divided into two groups: those who showered at night, and those who showered in the morning. The latter group probably prided themselves on starting the day fresh and sparkling clean. She, on the other hand, didn't like the idea of crawling between sheets already dirtied by the previous day's accumulation of dust, germs, and dead skin cells. The only solution to that was to change the sheets every day, and while she was sure there were some people obsessive enough to do just that, she wasn't one of them. Changing the sheets once a week was good enough for her, which meant she had to be clean when she went to bed. Besides, showering at night saved time in the morning.

Like she was ever rushed for time anyway, she thought gloomily.

She stared in the bathroom mirror, which confirmed what she had seen in the dresser mirror. Her hair was dull and shapeless, without style. It was healthy but limp, without any body at all. She pulled a long brown strand in front of her eyes to study it. The color wasn't golden brown, or red brown, or even a rich chocolate brown. It was just brown, as in mud. Maybe there was something she could put on it to give it a little bounce, a little oomph. God knows there were zillions of bottles and tubes and sprays in the health-and-beauty section of the Wal-Mart over on the highway, but that was fifteen miles away and she usually just picked up a bottle of shampoo at the grocery store. She had no idea what the products in those zillions of bottles and tubes *did,* anyway.

But she could learn, couldn't she? She was a librarian, for heaven's sake. She was a champion researcher. The secrets of the earth were open books to those who knew where and how to dig. How difficult could hair products be?

Okay. Hair was number one on her list of improvements. Daisy went back into her bedroom and got a pad and pen from her purse. She wrote the number one at the top of a page, and beside it wrote: *HAIR*. Below that she quickly scrawled *MAKEUP*, and below that *CLOTHES*.

There, she thought with satisfaction. What she had was the blueprint for the making of a party girl.

Returning to the bathroom, she quickly washed her face, then did something she almost never did. Opening the jar of Oil of Olay Aunt Joella had given her for her birthday last year, she moisturized her face. Maybe it didn't do any good, but it felt good, she decided. When she was finished, she thought that her face did look smoother, and a little brighter. Of course, anything that had been greased looked smoother, and all that rubbing was bound to have reddened her complexion, but one had to start somewhere.

Now what?

Nothing, that was what. She had nothing else to do, no other ointments, none of the mysterious and sexy little squares of color or dark-colored pencils with which other women lined their eyes and darkened their lids. She could put on her lipstick, but why bother? It was virtually the same shade as her lips; the only way she could tell she had it on was by licking her lips and tasting. It had a slight bubble-gum flavor, just as it had when she was in junior high—"Oh, *God!*" she moaned aloud. She hadn't changed her shade of lipstick since junior high!

"You're pathetic," she told her reflection, and this time her tone was angry. Cosmetic changes weren't going to be enough.

She had to do something drastic.

* * *

Two gaily wrapped boxes were sitting on the kitchen table when Daisy went downstairs. Her mother had made Daisy's favorite breakfast, pecan pancakes; a cup of coffee gently steamed beside the plate, waiting for her, which meant her mother had listened for her footsteps on the stairs before pouring the coffee. Tears stung her eyes as she stared at her mother and aunt; they were really two of the sweetest people in the world, and she loved them dearly.

"Happy birthday!" they both chimed, beaming at her.

"Thank you," she said, managing a smile. At their urging, she sat down in her usual place and quickly opened the boxes. Please, God, not more seersucker, she silently prayed as she folded back the white tissue from her mother's gift. She was almost afraid to look, afraid she wouldn't be able to control her expression if it *was* seersucker—or flannel. Flannel was almost as bad.

It was . . . well, it wasn't seersucker. Relief escaped in a quiet little gasp. She pulled the garment out of the box and held it up. "It's a robe," said her mother, as if she couldn't see what it was.

"I . . . it's so pretty," Daisy said, getting teary-eyed again because it really was pretty—well, prettier than she had expected. It was just cotton, but it was a nice shade of pink, with a touch of lace around the collar and sleeves.

"I thought you needed something pretty," her mother said, folding her hands.

"Here," said Aunt Joella, pushing the other box toward Daisy. "Hurry up, or your pancakes will get cold."

"Thank you, Mama," Daisy said as she obediently opened the other box and peered at the contents. No seersucker here, either. She touched the fabric, lightly stroking her fingertips over the cool, sleek finish.

"Real silk," Aunt Joella said proudly as Daisy pulled out the full-length slip. "Like I saw Marilyn Monroe wear in a movie once."

The slip looked like something from the nineteen forties, both modest and sexy, the kind of thing daring young women wore as party dresses these days. Daisy had a mental image of herself sitting at a dressing table brushing her hair and wearing nothing but this elegant slip; a tall man came up behind her and put his hand on her bare shoulder. She tilted her head back and smiled at him, and he slowly moved his hand down under the silk, touching her breast as he bent to kiss her . . .

"Well, what do you think?" Aunt Joella asked, jerking Daisy out of her fantasy.

"It's beautiful," Daisy said, and one of the tears she had been blinking back escaped to slide down her cheek. "You two are so sweet—"

"Not *that* sweet," Aunt Joella interrupted, frowning at the tear. "Why are you crying?"

"Is something wrong?" her mother asked, reaching over to touch her hand.

Daisy drew a deep breath. "Not *wrong.* Just—I had an epiphany."

Aunt Jo, who was sharper than any tack, shot her a narrow-eyed look. "Boy, I bet that hurt."

"Jo." Sending her sister an admonishing glance, Daisy's mother took her daughter's hands in hers. "Tell us what's wrong, honey."

Daisy took a deep breath, both to work up her courage and to control her tears. "I want to get married."

The two sisters both blinked, and looked at each other, then back at her.

"Well, that's wonderful," her mother said. "To whom?"

"That's the problem," Daisy said. "No one wants to marry *me.*" Then the deep breath stopped working, and she had to bury her face in her hands to hide the way her unruly tear ducts were leaking.

There was a small silence, and she knew they were looking at each other again, communicating in that mental way sisters had.

Her mother cleared her throat. "I'm not quite certain I understand. Is there someone in particular to whom you're referring?"

Bless her mother's heart, she was an English teacher to the core. She was the only person Daisy knew who actually said *whom*—well, except for herself. The acorn hadn't fallen far from the mother oak. Even when her mother was upset, her phrasing remained exact.

Daisy shook her head, and wiped the tears away so she could face them again. "No, I'm not suffering from unrequited love. But I want to get married and have babies before I get too old, and the only way that's going to happen is if I make some major changes."

"What sort of major changes?" Aunt Jo asked warily.

"Look at me!" Daisy indicated herself from head to foot. "I'm boring, and I'm mousy. Who's going to look at me twice? Even poor Wally Herndon wasn't interested. I have to make some major changes to *me.*"

She took a deep breath. "I need to spruce myself up. I need to make men look at me. I need to start going places where I'm likely to meet single men, such as nightclubs and dances." She paused, expecting objections, but was met with only silence. She took another deep breath and blurted out the biggie: "I need to get my own place to live." Then she waited.

Another sisterly glance was exchanged. The moment stretched out, and Daisy's nerves stretched along with it. What would she do if they strenuously objected? Could she hold out against them? The problem was that she loved them and wanted them to be happy; she didn't want to upset them or make them ashamed of her.

They both turned back to her with identical broad smiles on their faces.

"Well, it's about time," Aunt Jo said.

"We'll help," her mother said, beaming.

TWO

Daisy drove to work on automatic pilot. Luckily she had no stop signs to worry about and only one traffic light: one of the benefits of small-town life. She lived only five blocks from the library and, to save the environment, often walked to work if the weather was good, but the rain was still pouring down and during the summer the heat always got the best of her conscience anyway.

Her brain fizzed with plans, and before she put her purse in the bottom drawer of her desk, she took out the sheet of paper on which she had scribbled the items she needed to tackle, to study them again. Her mother and Aunt Jo had been bubbling with excitement, adding their own ideas, and after careful thought they had all agreed that she should take care of the big-ticket items first. She had a healthy balance in her checking account, due to living with her mother and Aunt Jo and sharing expenses with them, not that the groceries and utilities ever amounted to that much, and the old house was long since paid for. Her car was an eight-year-old Ford, financed for three years, so she hadn't even had a car payment for the past five years. The salary of a small-town librarian wasn't great, even though she was director of the library, which was a glorified title that didn't amount to anything, since the mayor's office retained hiring and firing authority; she got to choose which books the library bought with its less-than-impressive budget, and that was about it. But when you put at least half, sometimes more, of even an unimpressive salary into savings every year, it added up. She had even begun investing in the stock market, after carefully researching her chosen companies on the Internet, and done very well, if she did say so herself. Not that Warren Buffett had any reason for jealousy, but she was proud of her nest egg.

The bottom line was, she could easily afford a place of her own. However, there weren't very many places available for rent in Hillsboro, Alabama. She could always move to one of the larger towns, Scottsboro or Fort Payne, but she wanted to stay close. Her sister had already moved to Huntsville, and though that wasn't really all that far, about an hour's drive, it still wasn't the same as living in the same town. Besides, Temple Nolan, the mayor, had a real obsession about hiring only Hillsboro citizens for municipal jobs, a policy that Daisy approved of. She could hardly ask him to make an exception in her case. She would just have to find some place here in Hillsboro to live.

Hillsboro had only a small weekly newspaper that came out every Friday, but last week's edition was still on her desk. She folded it open to the advertisement section—one page—and quickly scanned down the columns. She noticed that someone had found a calico cat over on Vine Street, and Mrs. Washburn was looking for someone to help take care of her father-in-law, who was ninety-eight and liked to take off his clothes at the oddest times, such as when anyone else was around. Rentals, rentals . . . She found the small section and quickly skimmed down it. There were eight listings, more than she had expected.

One address was familiar, and she dismissed that rental immediately; it was an upstairs room in Beulah Wilson's house, and everyone in town knew Beulah invaded her boarders' privacy whenever she liked, searching the rooms as if she were a drug dog sniffing out tons of cocaine, then gossiping with her cronies about whatever she found. That was how the whole town knew Miss Mavis Dixon had a box full of early *Playgirl* magazines, but Miss Mavis was so hateful and generally disliked that everyone agreed that the centerfolds were as close as she was ever likely to get to male genitalia.

No way would Daisy ever live in Beulah Wilson's house.

That left seven possibilities.

"Vine Street," she muttered, reading the next listing. That would probably be the Simmonses' small apartment over their detached garage. Hmm, that wouldn't be a bad choice at all. The rent would be *very* reasonable, it was a good neighborhood, and she would have privacy because Edith Simmons was a widow who had severe arthritis in her knees and could never climb the stairs to snoop. Everyone knew she hired someone to clean her house because she couldn't cope with all the stooping.

Daisy circled the ad, then quickly read the others. There were two empty condos in Forrest Hills over on the highway, but the rent was high and the condos were ugly. They were possibles, but she'd look at them only if Mrs. Simmons had already rented her garage apartment. There was a house on Lassiter Avenue, but the address wasn't familiar. She swiveled her chair to locate Lassiter Avenue on her city map, and immediately dropped that ad from consideration, because the address was in the rougher section of town. She didn't know exactly how rough, but imagined Hillsboro had its share of the criminal element.

The remaining three ads were also undesirable. One side of a duplex was available, but it was available on a regular basis, because the trashy Farris family lived in the other side and no one else could put up with the screaming and cussing for very long. Another house was too far away, almost at Fort Payne. The last ad was for a mobile home, and it, too, was on the bad side of town.

Quickly she dialed Mrs. Simmons's number, hoping the apartment was still available, since the newspaper was already four days old.

The phone rang and rang, but it took Mrs. Simmons a while to get anywhere, so Daisy was patient. Varney, the son, had given his mother a cordless phone once so she could keep it with her and wouldn't have to walk anywhere to answer it, but she was set in her ways and considered it a nuisance to carry the phone with her all day, so she accidentally dropped it in the toilet, and that was that. Mrs. Simmons resumed use of her land-line phone, and Varney saw the wisdom of not buying her another cordless to drown.

"Hello?" Mrs. Simmons's voice was as creaky as her knees.

"Hello, Mrs. Simmons. This is Daisy Minor. How are you today?"

"Just fine, dear. This rain makes my joints hurt, but we need it, so I guess I shouldn't complain. How's your mama, and your aunt Joella?"

"They're fine, too. They're busy canning tomatoes and okra from the garden."

"I don't do much canning anymore," Mrs. Simmons creaked. "Last year Timmie"—Timmie was Varney's wife—"brought me some pears and we made pear preserves, but I don't even try to have a garden. My old knees just aren't up to it."

"You might think about knee-replacement surgery," Daisy suggested. She felt honor-bound to try, though she knew Varney

25

and Timmie had been making the same suggestion for years, to no avail.

"Why, Mertis Bainbridge had that done, and she said she'd never go through that again. She's had nothing but trouble with it."

Mertis Bainbridge was a hypochondriac, and a general complainer to boot. If someone gave her a car, she'd complain about having to buy gas for it. Daisy refrained from pointing that out, because Mertis was one of Mrs. Simmons's best friends.

"Everyone is different," she said diplomatically. "You're much tougher than Mertis, so you might have better results." Mrs. Simmons liked being told how strong she was, to be able to endure such pain.

"Well, I'll think about it."

She wouldn't do any such thing, but Daisy had satisfied the social requirements; she moved on to the purpose to her call. "The reason I called was to see about the apartment over your garage. Have you rented it yet?"

"Not yet, dear. Do you know someone who might be interested?"

"I'm interested for myself. Would it be all right if I came over at lunch and looked at it?"

"Why, I suppose. Let me just check with your mother. I'll call you right back. You're at work, aren't you?"

Daisy blinked. Had she just heard what she thought she'd heard? "Excuse me?" she said politely. "Why do you need to check with my mother?"

"Why, to see if it's okay with her, of course. I couldn't let you rent my apartment without her permission."

The words slapped her in the face. "Her permission?" she choked. "I'm thirty-four years old. I don't need permission to live anywhere I choose."

"You may have argued with her, dear, but I couldn't hurt Evelyn's feelings that way."

"We didn't argue," Daisy protested. Her throat had grown so tight she could barely speak. My god, did the whole town consider her so hopeless that she couldn't do anything without her mother's permission? No wonder she never had any dates! Humiliation mingled with anger that Mrs. Simmons wouldn't even think Daisy would be insulted. "On second thought, Mrs. Simmons, I don't think the apartment would be right for me. I'm sorry to bother you." It was rude, but she hung up without the usual good-byes. Mrs. Simmons would probably tell all her friends how abrupt Daisy had been and that she was having a disagreement with her mother, but she couldn't help that. And Mrs. Simmons might not snoop in the apartment, but she would certainly monitor all of Daisy's comings and goings and feel obligated to report them back to her mother. Not that Daisy intended to do anything *bad,* but still . . . !

The humiliation burned inside her. Was this how all their friends and acquaintances saw her, as someone incapable of making a decision on her own? She had always considered herself an intelligent, responsible, self-supporting woman, but Mrs. Simmons, who had known her all her life, certainly didn't!

This move was way, way too late. She should have done it ten years ago. Back then, changing her image would have been easy. Now she felt as if she needed an act of Congress—and a permission slip from her mother!—to change the way people saw her.

Maybe it would work out better not to live in Mrs. Simmons's garage apartment, anyway. She would be out of her mother's house, yes, but still under "supervision." If she wanted to change her image, she had to give the impression of complete freedom.

The ugly condos were looking better by the minute.

She dialed the number in the ad. Again, the phone rang and rang. She wondered if the condo manager had arthritic knees, too.

"Hello." The voice was male, and sleepy.

"I'm sorry, did I wake you?" Daisy glanced at the clock over her desk; ten after nine. What kind of manager slept this late?

"S' all right."

"I'm calling about the rental listing—"

"Sorry. The last one was rented yesterday." The man hung up. Well, damn.

Frustrated, she stared down at the newspaper. She was left with the house on Lassiter Avenue, the duplex containing the Farrises, and the mobile home on the bad side of town. The duplex was unthinkable.

She couldn't back down now, or she'd never be able to face herself in the mirror again. She had to see this through. Maybe the mobile home or the Lassiter Avenue house wouldn't be *too* bad. She didn't mind a run-down neighborhood, so long as it wasn't dangerous, with drug dealers lurking on every corner and shots ringing out in the night.

She was pretty sure if there had been any shots ringing out in Hillsboro, night or day, she'd have heard about it.

The discreet little bell over the door rang as someone entered the library. Daisy got up and smoothed her skirt, not that the action would help its looks any. She was the only one working until noon, because they seldom had anyone in during the morning. Most of their traffic was in the afternoon, after school was out, though of course during the summer that pattern changed. The bulk of people still came in the afternoon, maybe because they were too busy doing other stuff during the relatively cool mornings. Kendra Owens came in at twelve and worked until the library closed at nine, plus Shannon Ivey worked part-time from five until nine, so Kendra was never alone there at night. The only one who was alone for any length of time was Daisy, but she figured the greater responsibility was hers.

"Anyone here?" a deep voice boomed, before she could step out of her small office behind the checkout desk.

Daisy took two hurried steps into view, a little outraged that anyone would shout in a library, even if there weren't any other patrons present at the moment. Seeing who the newcomer was, she checked briefly, then said briskly, "Yes, of course. There's no need to yell."

Chief of Police Jack Russo stood on the other side of the scarred, wooden checkout desk, looking impatient. Daisy knew him by sight, but had never spoken to him before, and she wished she wasn't doing so now. Frankly, she didn't think much of Mayor Nolan's choice for chief. Something about him made her uneasy, but she didn't know exactly what. Why couldn't the mayor have chosen someone local, someone already on the force? Chief Russo was an outsider, and from what she'd seen in town meetings, he wasn't averse to throwing his weight around. It was easy to dislike a bully.

"I wouldn't have yelled if anyone had been in sight," he said tersely.

"The door wouldn't have been unlocked unless someone was here," she replied just as tersely.

Stalemate.

Physically, Chief Russo was a good-looking man, if one liked jocks with thick necks and broad, sloping shoulders. She wasn't silly enough to automatically assume anyone athletic was also stupid; still, Daisy had never cared for the type. There had to be something basically narcissistic about a man who worked out enough to maintain that sort of muscularity, didn't there? She didn't know how old he was; his face was unlined except for a few squint lines around his eyes, but his short-cut hair, while still mostly dark on top, was gray everywhere else. At any rate, he was too old to be devoting hours to lifting weights. Nor did she care for the cocky arrogance in his eyes, or the way his full lips always seemed to be on the verge of sneering. Who did he think he was, Elvis? Moreover, he was a Yankee—he had been a cop in either Chicago or New York, she had heard both—with a brusque, abrasive manner. If he'd had to run for office, as the county sheriff did, he would never have been elected.

Daisy stifled a sigh. She was in the minority in her opinion of the chief. Mayor Nolan liked him, the city council liked him, and from what she heard around town, most of the single women thought he was the cat's pajamas. So maybe she was wrong in her instinctive dislike of him. Maybe. She reminded herself it was only neighborly to keep an open mind, but she was still glad she had the checkout desk between them.

"May I help you?" she asked in her best librarian's voice, both brisk and friendly. Working with the public was a science, especially in a library. One had to encourage people, because of course you wanted them to read, but at the same time you had to impart a sense of respect for the library and other patrons.

"Yeah. I want to sign up for the virtual library."

He couldn't have said anything more likely to bring a beaming smile to her face. His stock automatically went up a few points. She was justifiably proud of the state's virtual library; Alabama led the nation in that category. Any citizen of the state could register at any library and have on-line home access to thousands of newspapers, magazines, articles, encyclopedias, research material, medical journals, and the like. Some of the categories were targeted to specific age groups of children, for work in the classroom and for help with their homework, or as general interest. Other states had virtual libraries, but Alabama's was by far the most extensive.

"You'll love it," she said enthusiastically, lifting the hinged countertop that allowed her to step out from behind the security of the checkout desk. "Come with me."

She led him to the reference section, where their on-line computer sat quietly humming, always ready. She took the chair in front of the computer and gestured to him to pull up another. He hooked a chair over, positioning it much too close to hers, and settled his large frame on it. He immediately leaned back and hitched up one long leg, crossing his right knee with his left ankle. It was the automatic position of a dominant male, that of a man accustomed to physically commanding the space around him.

Daisy frowned and mentally deducted those points he had just gained. Didn't he know he shouldn't crowd people? She scooted her chair a couple of inches away and chalked up "bad manners" in his debit column.

She took the required information from him, entered it into the system, and gave him his password. All the time she was aware that he was *still* too close; she glanced several times at that muscular thigh right beside her. If she scooted any farther away, she wouldn't be able to reach the keyboard. Irritated, because he had to know he was crowding her personal space—cops in big cities studied things like that, didn't they?—she shot an exasperated look at him and almost jumped, because he was staring at her. He wasn't trying to hide it, either.

She felt a blush heating her face. Ordinarily she would have finished as soon as possible and scurried back to the safety of her office, but today was a new day, a turning point in her life, and she decided she'd be damned if she'd let herself be intimidated. She'd already been rude to Mrs. Simmons, so why not the chief of police, as well?

"You're staring," she said bluntly. "Do I have a smudge on my face, or do I look like a dangerous criminal?"

"Neither," he said. "Law enforcement officers stare at people; it's part of the job."

Oh. She supposed it was. She ratcheted her indignation down

a few notches—but just a few. "Stop it anyway," she ordered. "It's rude, and you're making me uncomfortable."

"I apologize." He still didn't look away from her, though; he probably didn't respond well to orders. His eyes were kind of an odd gray-green, more green than gray, and a tad out of place with his olive skin. Of course, she didn't have any room to comment on anyone else's strange eyes, since her own were two different colors. "I didn't mean to make you uncomfortable, Miss . . . Daisy, isn't it?" His full lips quirked. "May I drive you somewhere?"

Her face went way past blush, straight into tomato red. Since the movie *Driving Miss Daisy* had come out, countless people had thought it funny to make the same offer. She hadn't laughed yet. She gave him two more checks in the debit column, because making fun of someone's name was rude and deserved extra deductions.

"No, thank you," she said in such frigid tones he couldn't miss the fact that she didn't think he was amusing. She got to her feet and handed him his plastic card with his password written on it, then without another word marched back to the checkout desk and pulled down the countertop that closed her off from him. Thus barricaded, she faced him across the wooden expanse.

"Sorry," he said, which was the second time he had apologized in as many minutes. The problem was, she didn't think he'd meant it either time. He leaned on the checkout desk and flicked the plastic password card in his long fingers. "I guess you get that a lot, huh?"

"A lot," she echoed, keeping her tone deep in the arctic.

He flexed his shoulders, as if settling his shirt more comfortably, but she had read magazine articles about body language and thought he might be trying to impress her with his physique. If so, he had failed.

After a long moment in which she remained stubbornly silent, refusing to acknowledge or accept his apology, he gave another shrug and straightened. He tapped the plastic card on the desk—goodness, what kind of signal was that?; she tried to remember if tapping meant anything in body language—and said, "Thanks for your help."

Darn it, now she had to reply. "You're welcome," she muttered as she watched him leave. She was fairly certain she heard him snickering.

Damn Yankee! What was he doing down here, anyway? If he was such a hotshot big-city cop, why wasn't he in a big city? What was he doing here in Hillsboro, population nine thousand and something, tucked away in the north Alabama mountains? Maybe he was a dirty cop and had gotten caught. Maybe he'd made a terrible error in judgment and shot an unarmed innocent. She imagined he was capable of all sorts of things that would have gotten him sacked.

Well, she wouldn't waste any more time fretting about him. In the grand scheme of things, rude patrons weren't important. Mentally she settled her ruffled feathers. She was a woman with a mission, and she wasn't going home today until she had found a place of her own to live in.

She sighed as she remembered her short list of choices. If she kept that vow, she might be sleeping in her car tonight.

THREE

Mayor Temple Nolan loved his little town. Hillsboro was unusually compact for the south, where land was cheap and plentiful, and spreading out was easy. Hillsboro had never spread out much, but remained mostly nestled in a small valley, surrounded by the foothills of the Appalachians. He even loved the approach into town: the main road, lined with cedar trees, wound its way up a hill, then you rounded a curve and there was the town spread out before you, looking more like it belonged in New England than in the sunny south.

There were white church spires piercing the sky, big oaks and hickory trees spreading their enormous green canopies, lawns bright with flowers; hell, there was even a town square. There wasn't a courthouse, because Hillsboro wasn't the county seat, but they had a square. It was only one acre, and they'd made it into a pretty little park with well-tended flower beds and benches for sitting, as well as the requisite cannon from the War Between the States, with a pile of rusted cannonballs stacked at its base. Enough of the citizens actually used the little park that he felt the cost was justified.

City hall, a two-story yellow brick building, sat on one side of the square, flanked by the police department and the white-columned city library—the first ruled by Chief Jack Russo, a brusque, hard-nosed Yankee who kept the mayor's town squeaky clean, and the latter by Miss Daisy Minor, as starchy an old maid as ever lived. Not that she was all that old, but she was definitely starchy. She was one of the mayor's favorite characters in a small town filled with characters, because she was so very stereotypical.

Various stores faced on the rest of the square, like the dry cleaners, the hardware store, a clothing store, several antique shops, the feed store, the dime store, a hobby shop. Hillsboro didn't have fancy shopping, but the citizens could get everything they needed to survive and enjoy life right here. There were the usual assortment of fast food places in town, but none of them were on the square; they were all down the road toward Fort Payne. The only restaurant on the square was the Coffee Cup, which did a booming business for breakfast and lunch, but closed at six because the dinner business wasn't that great.

It was a peaceful town, as much as any gathering of more than nine thousand people could be peaceful. There weren't any bars or nightclubs in Hillsboro; the county was dry. If you wanted something alcoholic to drink—legally—then you had to go to either Scottsboro, which had separated itself from the rest of the county and voted wet, or over into Madison County. Oh, people were always trying to bring booze back home, and the police department tended to look the other way as long as they did indeed go home, but the department cracked down on people who wanted to do their drinking and driving at the same time, as well as kept a sharp eye out for teenagers who were trying to sneak cases of beer back for parties. And there were always people who wanted to smoke marijuana or pop some pills, but Temple Nolan worked hard to keep drugs out of Hillsboro.

That was one of the reasons he'd tapped Jack Russo as chief of police. Russo had worked in both Chicago and New York City; he had a lot of experience in the streets and alleys, and knew what to look for when it came to drug infestation. If his methods were sometimes a little rough for this part of the country . . . well, you had to take the bad with the good. The best thing about Russo was that he was an outsider. He could get the job done, but he wasn't hooked into the old-boy network by which an astonishing amount of information and favors were passed around. A favor received was a favor owed, and before you knew it, things were being done that shouldn't be done, information passed that should be kept quiet. By hiring an outsider, Temple had nipped that in the bud. Hillsboro was to stay peaceful and clean, the way he loved it, and the chief was too isolated to pick up on things he didn't need to know. So far, that had worked out well.

Temple had been mayor for nine years, having just won his third term of office the year before. He was only forty-five, a trim, good-looking man with blue eyes and neat dark hair. He'd grown up in Hillsboro, a popular boy who played all the sports—football, basketball, baseball—but never been the star of any of them. That hadn't affected his popularity, or his plans. He'd never dreamed of making it big in the major league of any sport. And the star quarterback hadn't been the one who married the head cheerleader; Temple had that honor. Jennifer Whitehead, lithe and blond, had become Mrs. Temple Nolan, in June, after he received his college degree in business administration. The next year had seen the arrival of Jason, and three years after that blond little Paige had been born. Their family portraits looked idealized, like a brochure for family planning.

His kids had kept their noses clean, too; Jason had turned out to have a decent throwing arm, and attended college on the strength of it. But a life in the majors wasn't his dream any more than it had been Temple's, and he was currently in medical school in North Carolina. Paige, at age twenty, was also in college, with double majors in math and science; she wanted to work in the space program. They were great kids; thank God neither of them took after their mother.

Yep, Jennifer was the fly in his ointment. Good old Jennifer; he should have realized that if she was easy in high school and college, marriage wasn't going to change her. He reckoned she'd crawl into bed with just about anyone. If both his kids hadn't resembled him so much, he'd have had their DNA tested. But at first Jennifer had at least tried to limit herself to his bed; he didn't think she'd begun steadily cheating on him until Paige was about two.

His political career would probably withstand the shock if he divorced her, but he had no intentions of doing so. For one thing, the kids loved their mother, and he didn't want them upset. For another, Jennifer had her uses. He was certain she gained him some sympathy votes—the "poor Nolan, he does his best to hold the family together" type of thing—plus if he needed her to close a deal or pay a favor, Jennifer was always willing to drop her drawers and lie down.

Of course, that meant he had to go elsewhere for relief. No way would he stick his dick in her again, not after some of the trash she'd let crawl on top of her. He could have set up a liaison with any one of several available women in town—as well as some who weren't supposed to be—had he been so inclined, but a wise man never fouled his own nest. No, it was best that he keep his urges out of town, and it wasn't as if he ever had any trouble finding a woman when he needed one.

His private number, distinguished from the other office lines by its distinctive tone, began ringing. After first glancing to make certain his door was closed, Temple answered the call. "Yes?" He never said his name, just in case—especially not on his cellular phone, but the habit had carried over to land lines, too.

"We have a little trouble with the shipment," said a voice he recognized.

"Will there be a delay in getting it out?"

"Yeah. You might want to see to this yourself."

Temple cursed to himself; he had a round of golf scheduled, if this damn rain ever let up. Now he had to drive almost to Huntsville. But Glenn Sykes was a capable man; he wouldn't have said Temple needed to oversee this problem personally if it wasn't something serious. "I'll take a long lunch," he said briefly.

"Come to the barn," said Sykes. "I'll be there waiting."

Both men disconnected, and Temple slowly replaced the receiver. So long as there hadn't been a successful escape, everything would be all right, and Glenn would have told him immediately if that had happened. But other problems sometimes cropped up, problems that had to be handled immediately before the situation became more complicated.

Three hours later, standing in a dilapidated old barn, he looked down at the problem and silently swore as he estimated the lost profits. "What happened?"

"Overdose," Glenn Sykes said succinctly.

It wasn't much of a stretch to guess what had happened, the mayor thought sourly. "GHB?"

"Yeah."

"Mitchell." Sykes didn't contradict him, and Temple sighed. "Mr. Mitchell is becoming a problem." This wasn't the first time Mitchell had dosed one of the girls with GHB. The sick bastard preferred them unconscious when he fucked them; Temple guessed it made him feel as if he was getting away with something. Or maybe he thought that if they didn't fight, then it wasn't rape. Whatever his reasoning, this was the second time he'd killed one of the girls with GHB. Using the merchandise was one thing, but when he started cutting into the profits, that was serious.

Sykes grunted. "Mitchell's *been* a problem. The fucking idiot's more trouble than he's worth."

"I agree."

"Want me to set something up?"

"I'm afraid we'll have to. Mitchell's fun and games are costing us money."

Sykes was relieved. He didn't like working with fuckups, and Mitchell was a Class-A fuckup. On the other hand, it was a pleasure working with a man like Temple Nolan; he never broke a sweat, but handled everything with a cool lack of emotion. Sykes indicated the bundle on the ground. "What do you want me to do with the body? Bury it? Or dump it?"

Temple considered. "How long has it been?"

"Almost four hours since I found out about it."

"Wait another couple of hours to be sure, then dump it." The chemical composition of GHB broke down after six hours, making it untraceable unless a body was found and tests were run within that time limit. After that, the authorities might suspect GHB, but there was no way of proving it.

"Any preferences as to where?"

"Not as long as there's no connection to us."

Sykes rubbed his jaw. "I think I'll take her to Marshall County, then; when she's found, they'll think she's just one of the migrant workers and no one will push very hard to identify her." He glanced up at the tin roof, where the steady rain was drumming. "The weather will help; there won't be any trace evidence left, even if the Marshall yahoos decide to make an effort."

"Good idea." He sighed, looking down at the small bundle. Death didn't just make a body motionless; it reduced it to a lump, devoid of the tension and inherent grace that the sheer force of life imparted to muscles. He didn't see how anyone could ever think a dead person was asleep, because the whole aspect of the body was so different. Alive, the girl had been a beauty, with an innocent spark that would have brought the money rolling in. Dead, she was nothing.

"I'll call Phillips, let him know what happened, and what we're doing about Mitchell." Temple didn't look forward to the call, because he hated to admit when he'd made a mistake, and the decision to hire Mitchell had been his.

Well, it was a mistake that would soon be rectified. Mitchell had dosed his last girl with GHB.

FOUR

Daisy stood in the rain and stared at the small, shabby house on Lassiter Avenue that was her last hope. The white paint was peeling, the few scraggly shrubs desperately needed trimming, the weed-choked yard looked as if it hadn't been mowed all summer, and the roof over the front porch sagged. The screen on the door was torn loose from the frame on one side, and one window sported a giant crack. On the plus side, the small backyard was fenced. She tried hard to find some more pluses, but came up blank. On the other hand, it was available.

"Let me find the key and we'll go inside," the owner, Mrs. Phipps, said as she dug in her voluminous shoulder bag. Mrs. Phipps wasn't quite five feet tall, was almost as big around, and her hair was arranged—or maybe it grew that way—in huge white puffs that looked like wispy clouds. She puffed as she made her way up the broken sidewalk, skirting one section that was completely gone.

"It's nothing fancy," she warned, though Daisy wondered why she thought any warning was necessary. "Just a living room, kitchen, two bedrooms, and a bathroom, but me and E. B. raised two kids here just fine. When E. B. passed on, my kids bought me a trailer and we put it in back of my oldest boy's house, so I have somebody close if I take sick or something. I didn't want to get rid of this old place, though. It was home for a long time. Plus the rent money helps out."

The sagging wooden porch seemed to give a little more under Mrs. Phipps's weight; Daisy hung back, in case she was needed to go for help in the event Mrs. Phipps fell through the floor. But she reached the door without incident, and wrestled with the recalcitrant lock. Finally the key turned, and Mrs. Phipps heaved a grunt of accomplishment. "Here we go. I cleaned up after the last bunch cleared out, so you don't have to worry about trash or anything like that."

The house *was* clean, Daisy saw with relief as she stepped inside. The smell was musty, of course, but it was the odor of emptiness, not of filth.

The rooms were small, the kitchen barely big enough to cram in a small table and two chairs, so she couldn't imagine how crowded it had been with a family of four. The floors were all cracked sheet linoleum, but they could be covered with area rugs. The bathroom was small, too, but at some point the tub had been replaced with a blue fiberglass tub and shower unit that didn't match the white toilet and sink. A small space heater jutted from the wall.

Silently she walked through the rooms again, trying to imagine them with lamps and curtains and cozy furniture. If she took the house, she would have to buy window units for air-conditioning, rugs for the floors, kitchen appliances, and furniture for the

living room. She already had her bedroom furniture, thank goodness, but unless she bought the cheapest stuff she could find, she
could expect to spend about six thousand dollars getting the place
habitable. Thank God she didn't live in a section of the country
where the cost of living was high, or she would be looking at an
expenditure of at least twice that amount. She had the money—
that wasn't a problem—but she'd never spent such a large sum in
her life. Her stomach clenched in panic at the very thought.

She could spend the money, or she could retreat to her
mother's house and live there until she grew old and died.
Alone.

"I'll take it," she said aloud, the words sounding strange and
faraway, as if someone else had said them.

Mrs. Phipps's chubby pink face brightened. "You will? I
didn't—that is, you didn't seem like the kind . . . This used to be
a right nice street, but the neighborhood's gone down, and . . ."
She ran out of steam, unable to express her astonishment.

Daisy could sympathize. Only a week ago—goodness, even
yesterday!—she couldn't have imagined herself living here, either.

She might be desperate, but she wasn't pathetic. She folded
her arms and put on her best librarian's face. "The front porch
badly needs repairs. I'll handle it for you, if you like, if you'll take
the amount of the repairs in lieu of the same amount of rent."

Mrs. Phipps crossed her arms, too. "Why would I do that?"

"You'll be out that amount of ready cash, true, but in the long
run your property will be worth more and you'll be able to charge
more rent the next time." Daisy hoped Mrs. Phipps was one who
could see the long-term benefit, rather than thinking of only the
rent money. Daisy had no idea how much the repairs would cost,
but the rent was just a hundred and twenty dollars a month, so
Mrs. Phipps could be looking at several months without any rent
income.

"I don't think I can go without the extra money for that long," Mrs. Phipps said doubtfully.

Daisy thought quickly. "How about every other month? Could you handle that? I pay for the repairs now; then I pay no rent every other month until I recoup my money. Or you pay for the repairs and raise the rent a little."

Mrs. Phipps shifted her weight. "I don't have that kind of cash to throw around. Okay, we'll do it your way. But I want it in writing. And I want the first month's rent; then we'll start that every-other-month thing. None of the utilities are included, either."

For a hundred and twenty dollars a month, Daisy hadn't assumed they were. She beamed and held out her hand. "It's a deal," she said, and they shook hands on it.

"Kinda small," Aunt Jo commented early that evening as she and Daisy's mother inspected Daisy's new digs.

"It'll do just fine," Evelyn said stoutly. "A coat of paint and some nice curtains will work wonders. Anyway, it isn't as if she's going to live here for very long. She'll find someone special in no time at all. Daisy, honey, if there's anything in the attic you want, just take it." She took another look around the little house. "Just what sort of decor do you have in mind?" she asked doubtfully, as if she couldn't think of anything that would truly help the looks of the house.

"Cozy and comfortable," Daisy said. "It's too small to try for anything else. You know, overstuffed chairs with afghans thrown across them, that kind of thing."

"Hmmph," Aunt Jo said. "Only afghan I ever saw wouldn't stay put unless you tied him down. Stupidest dog in the world."

They all began giggling. Aunt Jo's sense of humor tended to the absurd, and both Daisy and her mother greatly enjoyed the flights of fancy.

"You *will* need a dog," Evelyn said suddenly, looking around. "Or burglar bars on the windows and an alarm system."

Burglar bars and an alarm system would add another thousand to her growing expenses. Daisy said, "I'll start looking for a dog." Besides, a dog would be company. She had never lived alone, so a dog would help ease the transition. Having a pet again would be nice; it had been eight years—my goodness, that long!—since the last family pet had died of old age.

"When do you think you'll move in?" Aunt Jo asked.

"I don't know." Doubtfully, Daisy looked around. "The utilities have to be turned on, but that won't take long. I'll have to buy kitchen appliances and have them delivered, shop for furniture and rugs, put up curtains. And paint. It definitely needs a new coat of paint."

Evelyn sniffed. "A good landlady would have repainted after the last tenants left."

"The rent is a hundred and twenty a month. Fresh paint doesn't come with the deal."

"I heard Buck Latham is taking paint jobs on the weekends for extra money," said Aunt Jo. "I'll call him tonight and see when he can do it."

Daisy heard another cha-*ching* in her bank account. "I can do the painting myself."

"No, you can't," Aunt Jo said firmly. "You'll be busy."

"Well, yes, but I'll still have time—"

"No, you won't. You'll be busy."

"What Jo means, dear, is that we've been thinking, and we think you need to see a fashion-and-beauty consultant."

Daisy gaped at them, then smothered a laugh. "Where am I supposed to find one of those?" She didn't think Wal-Mart had a fashion-and-beauty consultant on staff. "And why do I need someone to tell me how I want to look? I've already been thinking about that. I want Wilma to cut my hair, and maybe put in some highlights, and I'll buy some makeup—"

Both Evelyn and Joella slowly shook their heads. "That won't get it," Aunt Jo said.

"Get what?"

Evelyn took over. "Dear, if you're going to do this, then do it right. Yes, you can get a different hairstyle and start wearing some makeup, but what you need is *style.* You need to have a presence, something that will make people turn and look at you. It's presentation as much as anything else, and you aren't going to find that in the health and beauty section of the drugstore."

"But I'm already going to be spending so much money—"

"Don't be penny wise and pound foolish. Do you think General Eisenhower could have established a beachhead on Normandy if he'd said, 'Wait, we're spending too much money; let's only send half as many ships'? You've saved your money all these years, but what good is money if you never use it? It isn't as if you'll be spending everything you've saved."

Daisy could be convinced, but she couldn't be bulldozed. She gave their proposition a moment's thought. "I want to try it my way, first. Then, if I'm not satisfied, I'll find a consultant."

Having known her all her life, both mother and aunt knew when she'd made up her mind. "All right. But don't let Wilma do anything to your hair just yet," Aunt Jo warned. "The damage could be irreversible."

"Wilma does your hair!" Daisy said indignantly.

"Honey, I don't let her anywhere near me with chemicals. The things I've seen in that beauty shop would make your blood run cold."

Daisy had a sudden vision of how she would look with green frizz, and decided she'd wait before booking an appointment with Wilma. Maybe she *should* go to one of the bigger cities to have her hair done, even though that would mean a trip every month for maintenance, and even more money. Wilma might be bad, but she was cheap.

On the other hand, Wilma might be cheap, but she was bad.

"Remember Normandy," she muttered.

"Exactly," said her mother in a tone of satisfaction.

Daisy was stubborn enough that she stopped by the drugstore on the way home and spent an astonishing amount on a small bag of makeup. Mascara, eyeshadow, blush, lip liner, and lipstick barely amounted to enough weight for her to feel them in the sack, but she was twenty-five dollars lighter in the pocket and she hadn't even bought the good stuff. This project of hers was turning into a real money pit.

She also spent some time researching the beauty magazines, and chose one that seemed to give the most instruction on makeup application. Anyone who could read could learn how to do this, she thought with satisfaction, and went home with her goody bag and instruction manual.

"What did you get?" Aunt Jo demanded as soon as Daisy walked into the house.

"Just the basics." Daisy listed the contents of the bag. "I don't want to try anything complicated, like eyeliner, until I get the hang of the other stuff. I'll put all of this on after supper, and we'll see how it looks."

Because it was her birthday, supper was one of her favorites: meatloaf, mashed potatoes, and green beans. She was too on-edge to do justice to the meal, though; a lot had happened that day, and her nerves wouldn't seem to settle down. After the kitchen was cleaned up, her mother and Aunt Jo settled down in front of the television to watch *Wheel of Fortune,* and Daisy went upstairs to put on her brave new face.

She studied the beauty magazine first, studying the correct

way to apply eyeshadow: lightest shade under the brow, medium on the lid, dark in the crease. That sounded simple enough. There were diagrams using Audrey Hepburn–type doe eyes as an example. Daisy opened the little container and stared at the four shades of shadow, in various shades of brown. Brown was so dull; maybe she should have gotten the blues or greens, or even the purples. But if she'd gotten the blue, it wouldn't have matched her green eye, and if she'd gotten the green, it wouldn't have matched her blue eye. She couldn't even imagine the purple, so she'd settled for brown.

It seemed as if she'd settled for brown a lot in her lifetime.

She carried her little trove into the bathroom and lined everything up on the vanity. The eyeshadow applicator was a tiny foam-tipped wand; she picked it out of the slot and swiped it across the lightest shade of shadow, then swabbed the color under her eyebrows as directed. She eyed the result in the mirror; well, that was practically unnoticeable. Relief warred with disappointment.

Okay, the next step was the medium shade. There were two medium shades, but she didn't suppose it mattered which one she chose. She swiped one of the medium shades across one lid and the other on her other lid, so she could compare the two. After a moment of critical examination, she decided she couldn't tell much difference between them. Her eyes looked more dramatic, though; kind of smoky. Feeling a little excited now, she used the darkest shade in the crease of her lids, but she misjudged the amount of shadow she needed; the resultant dark stripe looked like some kind of tribal marking. *Blend.* The magazine said to blend. Daisy blended for all she was worth, trying to spread that dark stuff around.

Okay, so now she looked more like Cleopatra than she did Audrey Hepburn. All in all, that had been fairly easy. She'd just take it easier with that dark shade the next time.

Mascara came next. Mascara, according to the magazine, gave eyes impact. Enthusiastically she twirled the wand around and around in the tube, then began swiping it on her lashes.

The end result looked as if caterpillars had crawled up on her eyelids and died.

"Oh, no!" she moaned, staring in the mirror. What had she done wrong? This didn't look anything like the models in the magazine! Her lashes stood out in thick, clumpy spikes, and whenever she blinked, her upper and lower lashes wanted to stick together. After she had pried them apart the second time, she did her best not to blink.

She would be a coward if she stopped now, wouldn't she? She had to see this through. Blusher couldn't be as bad as mascara. She swiped the small brush across the oblong of color, then carefully applied it to her cheeks.

"Gracious," she whispered, eyeing the little container of color. How could it look so much darker on her face than it did in the container? Her cheeks looked sunburned, except sunburn never attained that exact shade of hot pink.

Grimly she applied the remaining items, the lip liner and lipstick, but she couldn't tell if it helped the situation or made it worse. All she knew was that the end result was hideous; she looked like a cross between a rodeo clown and something from a horror movie.

She definitely needed help.

Grimly she went downstairs, where *Wheel of Fortune* still spun. Evelyn and Jo stared at her, eyes round and mouths agape, stricken into silence.

"Holy shit," Aunt Jo finally blurted.

Daisy's cheeks burned under the blusher, making the color even brighter. "There has to be a trick to it."

"Don't be upset," her mother begged, getting up to put a comforting arm around her. "Most young girls learn by trial and error in their teens. You just never bothered, that's all."

"I don't have time to learn by trial and error. I need to get this nailed down, now."

"That's why we suggested a beauty consultant. Think about it, honey; that'll be the fastest way."

"Beth could show me how," Daisy said, inspired. Her younger sister didn't slather on the makeup, but she knew how to make the most of her looks. Besides, Beth wouldn't charge her anything.

"I don't think so," Evelyn said gently.

Daisy blinked. Big mistake. Prying her lashes apart, she said, "Why not?"

Evelyn hesitated, then sighed. "Honey, you've always been the smart one, so Beth staked out being pretty as her territory. I don't think she'd handle it very well if you asked her to help you be pretty as well as smart. Not that you aren't pretty," Evelyn added hastily, in case she'd hurt Daisy's feelings. "You are. You've just never learned how to show yourself to advantage."

The idea that Beth might be even the teensiest bit jealous of her was so alien that Daisy couldn't take it in. "But Beth always got good grades in school. She isn't a dummy. She's both smart and pretty, so why wouldn't she help me?"

"Beth doesn't *feel* as if she's as intelligent as you. She finished high school, but you have a master's degree."

"She didn't go to college because she married her high school sweetheart when she was eighteen and settled down to raising a beautiful family," Daisy pointed out. In fact, Beth had what she herself had always wanted. "Not going was her choice."

"But you always wonder about the choice you didn't make," Aunt Jo pointed out, underlining Daisy's last thought. "Evelyn just means you shouldn't put Beth in that position. She'll feel bad if she turns you down, and if she helps you, it'll be like wearing wool during the summer: miserable and itchy."

So much for that idea. Luckily, she had another one. "I guess I could go to a department store in Chattanooga or Huntsville, and let them do my makeup."

"Actually," said Aunt Jo, "we thought of someone right here in Hillsboro."

"Here?" Puzzled, Daisy tried to think of anyone in Hillsboro who even remotely qualified as a beauty consultant. "Who? Has someone new moved into town?"

"Well, no." Aunt Jo cleared her throat. "We thought Todd Lawrence would do nicely."

"Todd Lawrence?" Daisy gaped at them. "Aunt Jo, just because a man's gay doesn't mean he qualifies as a beauty consultant. Besides, I don't know if Todd is 'out.' I'd hate to upset him by asking, if he isn't." Todd Lawrence was several years older than she, at least in his early forties, and a very dignified, reserved man. He had left Hillsboro when he was in his early twenties and, according to his doting widowed mother, did quite well for himself on Broadway, but since she never had any newspaper clippings or articles to show mentioning his name, everyone thought it was probably a mother's fond bias that led her to think he was so successful. Todd had returned to Hillsboro some fifteen years later, to take care of his mother during her last year of life, and since her death had lived quietly and alone in the old Victorian house on the edge of town.

"Oh, he's 'out,' " Evelyn replied. "For goodness' sake, he opened an antique and decorator store in Huntsville. And how many straight men know what color mauve is? At Easter, Todd told me how good I look in mauve; remember, that's what color my dress was this year? And he said it in front of several people. So he's out."

"I don't know," Aunt Jo said doubtfully. "Mauve isn't really a good test. What if a man's wife has had him looking at paint chips? He might know what mauve is. Now, *puce* would be a real test. Ask Todd about puce."

"I'm not asking him about puce!"

"Well, other than asking him outright if he's out, I don't see how else you're going to do it."

Daisy rubbed her forehead. "We're getting off track. Even if Todd is gay—"

"He is," both sisters said confidently.

"Okay, he is. That still doesn't mean he knows anything about makeup!"

"He was on Broadway, of course he knows about makeup. Everyone in the shows wears makeup, gay or not. Besides, I've already called him," Evelyn said.

Daisy groaned.

"Now, don't take on," her mother admonished. "He was as nice as he could be, and said of course he'd help you. Just give him a call when you're ready."

"I can't do it," Daisy said, shaking her head.

"Take another look in the mirror," Aunt Jo suggested.

Reluctantly Daisy turned her head to look in the mirror over the gas log fireplace. What she saw made her wince, and she surrendered without even another twinge of conscience. "I'll call him in the morning."

"Do it now," Evelyn urged.

FIVE

Daisy's insides jittered nonstop. Setting up an appointment with Todd Lawrence had been nerve-racking, even though he was just as nice as her mother had said. Not only was she still worried he was offended—though if he was, he hid it very well—but there was something so *humiliating* about having to ask for help in something as simple as applying a little bit of makeup. What had she done wrong? She knew she wasn't stupid, but was she so basically inept at this sort of thing that she was doomed to failure from the start? She could hear the jokes now: Daisy Minor get a husband? Hah-hah; she can't even put on mascara.

And did she really want a man who couldn't see the real her, just as she was, but who needed a layer of gloss before he even noticed her?

Well, yes. She'd tried the "real her" way and gained exactly nothing. Zippo. If she had to gloss herself in order to get what she wanted—namely, a family—then she would gloss as brightly as needed.

Her new awareness of how dowdy she was almost paralyzed her as she was getting ready for work. For once, she hadn't laid out her clothing the night before, and now she stood in front of the closet staring at the selection of boring skirts and blouses and dresses. She couldn't bear wearing those, not one more time. She dithered until, for the first time in her life, she ran the very real risk of being late to work. Finally she grabbed a pair of black slacks and pulled them on. She had never before worn pants to work, but that was because of her own stodginess, not any rule by the town council. This was yet another break with her old way of life, and her heart hammered in a combination of fear and excitement. She didn't have any stylish tops, of course, just her regular, boring white blouses, but she put one on and tucked the hem into the waistband of her slacks, then buckled the belt and slipped her feet into black loafers.

She didn't dare look in the mirror to check the result, just grabbed her purse and ran downstairs.

Aunt Jo raised her eyebrows when she saw her, but didn't say anything.

"Well?" Daisy demanded, even more nervous under that silent regard.

Evelyn came out of the kitchen and stared at her daughter. "Nice," she finally said, nodding her head. "Different. And the pants show the shape of your butt."

Ohmigod; now she wouldn't be able to turn her back to anyone all day long. Aghast, she swiftly checked her watch. There was no time to go change clothes. "Why did you have to say that?" she moaned.

Evelyn smiled. "It's okay, honey. If I remember correctly, men are partial to butts. See if you can remember to priss when you walk."

"Priss," Daisy repeated numbly, still unable to take in that her mother—her *mother!*—thought it was a good thing for her to show the shape of her butt.

"You know . . . back and forth." To demonstrate, her mother strolled across the room, her hips swaying in a gentle rhythm that drew attention to her own rear end. The movement was so astonishingly sexy that Daisy was shocked. Her *mother?* Her intellectual, unsophisticated mother?

"But not too much," Aunt Jo advised. "Or it'll look like two pigs fighting to get out of a sack."

That was all she could take. With a mumbled excuse about being late for work, Daisy fled.

She had barely got the key in the lock of the employees' door when a white car drove up behind her and Chief Russo got out. He might not be at the top of her list of people she didn't want to see that day, she thought in exasperation, but he was close. She tried to shift to the side so he couldn't see her butt, not that he was looking anyway. He was scowling as he strode up to her. "You're late."

Daisy checked her watch. It was twelve seconds to nine o'clock. "I'm right on time."

"You're always about half an hour early. Today, you aren't. Therefore you're late."

"How do you know what time I get to work?" she asked, feeling flushed and harassed. Just once she was almost late, and that *would* be the one day someone was waiting for her arrive. Besides, he was standing too close, crowding her again in that annoying way of his, as if he were trying to intimidate her with his size. Maybe it was working, since she felt flushed and harassed. She tried to squeeze closer to the door.

"The lights in the library are always on when I drive past."

Meaning she was always—well, almost always—at work before he was. She barely refrained from smirking and instead, with

·

an effort, assumed her librarian's expression and tone. "May I help you with something, Chief?"

"Yeah," he said in that brusque Yankee way. "I tried to get into the on-line library last night, but it wouldn't open. You wrote down the wrong password or something."

Why was it always the woman's fault? she wondered, mentally raising her eyes to heaven. "If the page won't display, then you probably need to upgrade your browser."

He stared at her as if she were speaking a foreign language.

"Your browser," she repeated. "How old is your system?"

He shrugged. "Two or three years."

"Have you upgraded at all since you bought it?" She knew the answer even before she asked the question. She would love to leave him to figure it out on his own, but good manners and a lifetime of being helpful prodded her conscience. She was a librarian; it was her duty to help him with the virtual library. "Do you have a laptop or a desktop?" She bet on the laptop. He was the impatient sort who would want to move his computer around to where it was most convenient for him.

"Laptop."

She awarded herself two points. "If you'll bring it by, I'll show you how to upgrade. If you have enough memory, of course." Let him decide if she was talking about his brain or his computer.

From the way his eyes narrowed, he must have suspected the former, but he let it pass. "It's in the car." He strode back to the city-owned Crown Victoria and got the laptop out of the front passenger seat, carrying it easily in one hand.

She unlocked the employees' entrance and turned to take the laptop. "You can pick it up at lunch," she said.

He retained possession of the machine. "Can't you do it now?"

"I intend to, but it'll take a few minutes."

"How many is a few?"

Her heart sinking, she realized he intended to wait. "Don't you have to go to work?"

He indicated the pager on his belt. "I'm always at work. How many is a few?" he repeated.

Damn modern electronics, she thought resentfully. The last thing she wanted was to have him *hovering*. "It depends." She tried to think how long might be too long. "Forty-five minutes or an hour."

"I'll wait."

Double damn. Her only consolation was that updating the browser wouldn't take nearly that long; then he'd be on his way.

"Fine. Meet me at the front door." She stepped inside and almost hit him in the nose with the door as he stepped forward. He slapped his free hand up just in time to stop it.

"I'll come in this way," he said, glaring at her.

Daisy squared her shoulders. "You can't."

"Why not?"

She thought that should have been obvious. She pointed to the sign on the door, just inches from his nose. "This is the employees' entrance. You aren't an employee."

"I'm a city employee."

"You aren't a library employee, and that's what counts."

"Hell, lady, what's it going to hurt?" he asked impatiently.

More points on the bad side. His demerits were rivaling the score of an NBA game. "No. Go to the front door."

Her stubborn expression must have finally registered. He eyed her, as if considering simply bullying his way past her, but with a muttered curse he turned on his heel and stormed around to the front of the building.

She was left standing there with her eyes as big as saucers. He'd said the F word. She was fairly certain that was what she'd heard. She'd heard it before, of course; one couldn't watch many movies these days without hearing it. She'd also gone to college, where young people tried to impress each other with how cool and sophisticated they were by using all the foul words they knew; she'd even said it herself. But Hillsboro was a small southern town, and it was still considered ill-mannered for men to use such language in front of women. Women who wouldn't turn a hair at hearing anything from their husbands or boyfriends in private would poker up like Queen Victoria if it were said in public. And to say such a thing to a woman you didn't know well was a total no-no, indicative of a total lack of manners and respect—

A thunderous banging on the front door interrupted her indignant reverie; the beast was already at the door. Muttering to herself, she hurried through the darkened library to unlock the front door.

"What took you so long?" he snapped as he stepped inside.

"I was frozen in shock by your language," she coolly replied, taking the laptop from him and carrying it to the library's on-line computer, turning on lights as she went.

He muttered something again, but this time, thankfully, she couldn't tell what it was. She wasn't as lucky with his next sentence. "You're a little young to have a stick up your ass like the blue-hairs in this town."

To her credit, she didn't falter. "Manners have nothing to do with age, and everything to do with upbringing." She set the laptop down and swiftly began hooking it up to the power source and telephone outlet.

It took him a minute. "Are you insulting my mother?" he finally growled.

"I don't know, am I? Or are you simply ignoring what she taught you?"

"Shit!" he said explosively, then blew out a deep breath. "Okay, I'm sorry. Sometimes I forget I'm living in Mayberry."

If they were so boring and restrictive, maybe he should think about going back to wherever he came from, she thought resentfully, but kept her thoughts to herself before the situation developed into a full-fledged argument. "Apology accepted," she forced herself to say, though she could have used a more gracious tone if she had really, really tried. She sat down and went on-line, then typed in the browser's web address and waited until the site was found and the page displayed. Then she clicked on the update bar, and let technology handle the rest.

"That's it?" he asked, watching the little timer.

"That's it. You should do this regularly, at least every six months."

"You're good at this."

"I've had to do it a lot since we got the virtual library," she said wryly.

He sat down beside her; too close, of course. She inched her chair away. "You know your way around computers."

"Not really. I know how to do this, but I had to learn. I can find my way around on the Web, I can hook up a system and load programs, but I'm not a computer geek or anything."

"City hall isn't even on-line. Water bills and payroll are computerized, but that's it."

He leaned forward, bracing his elbows on his knees as he watched the screen, as if he could hurry the process.

"The police department is, though, isn't it? Aren't you hooked up with all those police networks?"

He grunted. "Yeah. One line, one computer." He looked disgusted.

"Hillsboro *is* a small town," she pointed out. "The budget isn't very big. On the other hand, our crime rate is low." She paused, suddenly unsure. "Isn't it?"

"Low enough. There hasn't been a murder in the city limits

since I've been here. We have the usual burglaries and assaults, drunk driving, domestic troubles."

She would have loved to ask him who was having domestic trouble, but bit her tongue. He just might tell her, and then she'd tell her mother and Aunt Jo, and feel bad about gossiping.

Had he moved closer? She hadn't seen him do so, but she could feel his body heat, and smell him. What was it about men that made them smell different from women? Testosterone? More body hair? It wasn't an unpleasant smell; in fact, it was tantalizing. But it was *different,* as if he were an alien species. And he was definitely too darn close.

She had had enough. "You're crowding me," she pointed out, very politely.

Without moving, he glanced down; their chairs were separated by at least an inch. "I'm not touching you," he said just as politely.

"I didn't say you were touching me; I said you're too close."

He rolled his eyes and heaved a sigh, but hitched his chair another inch away. "Is this some other weird southern rule?"

"You're in law enforcement; you're supposed to have studied body language. Isn't that how you intimidate suspects, by invading their personal space?"

"No, I generally use a nine millimeter for intimidation purposes. Not much chance of missing the signal that way."

Oh, and wasn't that macho? He was such a typical man, bragging about the size of his weapon. She barely refrained from rolling her eyes, but he'd just done that and she didn't want to be a copycat.

A typical man . . . The conversation last night with her mother and Aunt Jo echoed in her mind, and a thought tickled her, but she pushed it away. No, she didn't want to get into that kind of discussion with him. She just wanted his browser to finish upgrading so he would go away—

"Do you know what color mauve is?" she blurted, the words leaping from her tongue before she could stop them.

The effect on him was almost electric. He jerked back, eyeing her as if she had suddenly sprouted fangs and tentacles. "What makes you ask?" he said warily.

"I just want to know." She paused. "Well, do you?"

"What makes you think I'd know?"

"I don't. I'm just asking."

"It sounds like one of those tests women use to find out if a man's gay or not. Why don't you just ask, if you're interested?"

"I'm not," she said, appalled that he might think she was. "It's just that someone else—never mind." She was blushing. She knew she was; her face felt hot. She stared very hard at the computer screen, trying to will the thing to go faster.

He scrubbed a rough hand over his short hair. "Pink," he mumbled.

"What?"

"Pink. Mauve is a fancy word for pink, right? I heard it often enough when my ex-wife was picking out stuff for our apartment, but it looked pink to me."

My goodness, Aunt Jo was right about mauve; it was no longer a definitive test. Wasn't that interesting? She couldn't wait to tell them.

"Puce," she said, and nearly smacked herself in the head. Why couldn't she leave well enough alone?

"What?" He acted as if he'd never heard the word before.

"Puce. What color is puce?"

"Spell it."

"P-u-c-e."

This time he scrubbed his hand over his face. "This is a trick question, right?"

"Why do you say that?"

"Puce. Who in hell would name a color 'puce'? It sounds like 'puke,' and nobody would want something colored like puke."

"Puce is a very pretty color," she said.

He gave her a disbelieving look. "If you say so."

"Do you know what color it is, or not?"

"Hell, no, I don't know what color puce is," he barked. "I know real colors; I know blue and green and red, things like that. Puce, my ass. You just made that up."

She smirked. "I did not. Go look it up in the dictionary." She pointed to the reference section. "There are several right over there."

He snorted, then shoved back in his chair and all but stomped over to the reference section. He leafed through a dictionary, ran his finger down a couple of pages, then briefly read. "Reddish brown," he scoffed, shaking his head. "Not that I've ever seen anything that's reddish brown, but if I did, you can be damn sure I wouldn't point at it and say, 'That looks like puce'!"

"What *would* you call it?" she taunted. "Something really imaginative, like 'reddish brown'? Though I've always thought puce was more of a purple brown than anything else."

"At least people would know what the hell I was talking about if I said reddish brown, or even purplish brown. And who needs a color like that, anyway? Who in his right mind would go into a store and ask the clerk for a puce shirt? Or buy a puce car? I worry about people who buy purple cars, but *puce?* Give me a break. Puce is only good as a gay test."

It probably was, but she wasn't going to admit that. "*You* know what color puce is now," she couldn't resist pointing out. "From now on, when you see any brown that has the least hint of red or purple, you're going to think: 'That's puce.'"

"Oh, Jesus." He pinched the bridge of his nose between his eyes. "You give me a headache," he muttered, then looked up, his eyes narrow and gaze dangerous. "If you mention this to anyone, I'll deny it, then I'll have you hauled in if you so much as jaywalk. Is that understood?"

"I don't jaywalk," she said triumphantly. "I'm so law-abiding I could be the poster child for responsible citizens. I wouldn't even let you come in through the employees' door, would I?"

"People like you need counseling." He glanced at the computer screen, then heaved a sigh of relief. "It's finished." He checked his watch. "That didn't take anywhere near forty-five minutes. More like fifteen. So I guess you do have a fault, Miss Daisy."

She felt her back teeth lock together at the "Miss Daisy." If he made another joke about her name, she might just smack him. "What's that?" she asked as she quickly unhooked the computer. The faster he left, the better.

He took the laptop from her. "You lie like hell," he said, leaving her speechless, and he strode out before she could think of a good reply.

SIX

Jack Russo was in a good mood when he left the library. Sparring with Miss Daisy was a lot of fun; she pokered up, blushed, but didn't back down an inch. She reminded him a lot of his great-aunt Bessie, with whom he had spent many of his summers right here in Hillsboro. Aunt Bessie had been as straitlaced and starchy as they came, but remarkably tolerant of having an energetic boy with her for at least two months every summer.

Though at first he'd been agonized at being stuck in the sticks—as he'd thought of Hillsboro back then—he had grown to love both his great-aunt and his time here. His parents had thought it would be good for him to get out of Chicago and find out there was another type of world out there, and they'd been right.

At first he'd been bored to tears; he was ten years old and away from his parents and all his friends, all his stuff. Aunt Bessie had been able to get a grand total of four—four!—channels on her television, and she did things like crochet every afternoon while she sat in front of the tube and watched her "stories." She went to church twice on Sunday, washed her sheets on Monday, mopped on Tuesday, shopped for groceries on Thursday because that was double-coupon day. He didn't need a clock to tell time; all he had to do was check what Aunt Bessie was doing.

And it had been hot. God, had it been hot. And Aunt Bessie hadn't had air-conditioning; she didn't believe in such foolishness. She had a window fan in each bedroom and a portable one she moved around the rest of the house as she needed it, and that was enough for her. Her screened windows were open to let breezes flow through the house.

But after he'd gotten over his tears and sullenness, he had gradually discovered the fun of lying in the sweet-smelling grass at sunset and watching the fireflies—or lightning bugs, as Aunt Bessie called them. He'd helped her in the small garden she tended every summer, learning to appreciate the taste of fresh vegetables and the work involved in getting them to the table. He had gradually gotten to know the neighborhood boys and spent many a long hot afternoon playing baseball or football; he had learned how to fish and hunt, taught by the dad of one of his new friends. Those six summers, beginning at age ten and ending when he was fifteen, became the best times of his life.

In a way, he had never become absorbed into Hillsboro culture; because he came only during the summer, he never met any of the kids other than the boys in the neighborhood. Since he'd been back in Hillsboro, he'd met only one man who remembered him, but over twenty years had passed since he'd stopped visiting Aunt Bessie except for lightning stops during the holidays, when people were busy with their own families and he hadn't had time to look up any of his old pals.

Aunt Bessie lived to be ninety-one, and when she died three

years ago, he'd been both startled and touched to find she'd willed her old house to him. Almost immediately he'd made up his mind to make the move from New York City to Hillsboro; he'd just gotten divorced, and though he'd been steadily moving up the ranks in the NYPD, he was getting tired of the stress and bustle of the job. The Special Weapons and Tactics team was fun, but the danger associated with it was one of the reasons behind his divorce. Not the big reason, but one of them, and on this issue he figured his ex-wife was at least half right. Being a cop's wife was tough; being the wife of someone who went to work only when the situations were the most dangerous took nerves of steel. Besides, he was thirty-six; he'd started at the age of twenty-one, in Chicago, then moved to New York. It was time to get out, look for something a little less edgy.

He made a couple of trips to Hillsboro, to look over the old Victorian house and see what repairs were needed, and at the same time put out some feelers for a job. Before he knew it, he was being interviewed for chief of police, and after that it was a done deal. He put in his notice—amid ribbing about being the Chief of Podunk—packed his stuff, and moved south. He had a staff of thirty, which was a joke compared to the size of the police force he'd just left, but Jack felt as if he'd found his niche.

Okay, so there wasn't a lot going on, but he liked protecting his adopted town. Hell, he even liked the city council meetings; he'd gotten a big kick out of the last one, with half the citizenry up in arms because the council had voted to install traffic lights around the square. It was ridiculous that a town of nine thousand people had only one traffic light, but to hear those people talk, all ten of the amendments in the Bill of Rights were being violated. If Jack had his way, traffic lights would be installed all over downtown, and at all the schools. Hillsboro lagged behind the times— he hadn't been joking when he called it Mayberry—but traffic was becoming more congested as people moved to the pretty little town, and he didn't want a schoolkid flattened by a car before the citizens woke up and decided maybe they did need more traffic lights.

Eva Fay Storie, his secretary, was on the phone when he entered his office, but she held up one finger to stop him, then handed him a cup of coffee and a sheaf of pink message slips. "Thanks," he said, sipping the coffee as he continued into his office. He didn't know how Eva Fay did it, but no matter what time he came into the office, she had a hot cup of fresh coffee waiting for him. Maybe she had his parking space wired, and a buzzer went off under her desk when he pulled in. One of these days he was going to park on the street just to see if he could throw her off. He'd inherited her from his predecessor, and both of them were satisfied with the status quo.

One of the calls was from a detective in Marshall County whom he'd become friendly with since moving to Hillsboro. Jack laid the other messages aside and immediately dialed the number on the slip.

"Petersen."

"What's up?" Jack knew he didn't have to identify himself. Even if Petersen didn't have Caller ID, Jack's accent was enough to give him away.

"Hey, Jack. Listen, we have an unidentified body on our hands, young, female, probably Mexican. Some kids found her last night."

Jack leaned back in his chair. There weren't any missing persons from Hillsboro who fit that description; they didn't have a large Hispanic population anyway, but no one at all had been reported missing in the past several months. "And?"

"Well, we don't have shit to go on. The rain washed away any tracks, and there's no obvious cause of death. No wounds, no strangulation marks, no lumps on the head, nothing."

"Overdose."

"Yeah, that's what I'm thinking. What has me worried, though, are the cases of GHB that've been cropping up in Huntsville, Birmingham, all over, with more every day."

"You think she was raped?"

"No way of knowing for certain until we get the autopsy report back from Montgomery, but I'd say so. She had on a dress, but no underwear. Anyway, I remembered a case Huntsville had a couple of months ago—"

"Yeah, I remember. It was pretty much the same."

They were both silent. If a guy was willing to slip one woman GHB so he could have sex with her, it was stupid to think he'd balk at doing it again. The problem was, GHB was so damn common and easy to get; it was a cleaning solvent, for God's sake. And guys took it, too; it was a high, and bodybuilders used it. The odds of finding any one guy weren't good, because too damn many women woke up without any memory of where they'd spent the night, or with whom, but with their bodies showing the evidence of sexual activity. To make it even harder to track the slimeballs down, very few of the women reported it to the police.

"How do you think I can help?" he finally asked, because Petersen had to have called him for a reason, and not just to tell him about the case. Jack would have found out about it when he read the reports, anyway.

"I was wondering, have you had any GHB cases in Hillsboro?"

"Not that I know of, but we're dry." GHB went hand-in-glove with the bar scene, because alcohol disguised the saltiness so well. Without any bars in Hillsboro, it wasn't unusual that he hadn't had any date-rape cases involving Ruffies or GHB—yet. Sooner or later, some local kid would die from it, or a bodybuilder would get caught with it, but so far his little town hadn't been hit. That didn't mean there weren't users in Hillsboro; it just meant that they'd been lucky in that none of them had died.

"I still don't know where you're going with this," he said.

"Do you hit many of the area bars? Off-duty, of course."

"Hell, I'm too busy and too old for that."

"You never get too old for it, buddy; just go in one someday and check out the gray hairs. Anyway, I was thinking: you're fairly new to the area, and if you don't wander up to Scottsboro or over to Madison County in search of a little entertainment, then you aren't likely to be known outside of Hillsboro, are you? So you could maybe cruise the clubs and bars, listen to what's being said, maybe keep any eye out for someone slipping that shit into women's drinks. Go undercover, I guess."

"And strictly off-record and on my own," Jack said wryly.

"Hell, buddy, it's better that way. Nothing official. You're a single man with an active social life, so what could be more natural? And if, in the course of a night's entertainment, you notice something or accidentally overhear something, why, I do believe we have probable cause. Whaddaya say?"

"It's a long shot."

"Granted. But, damn it, I don't like having girls' bodies dumped in my county. I can work my usual sources and get some busts around here for possession, but that isn't going to stop the bastards who cruise the bars. We need an edge, and I think you might be the sharpest knife available to us."

"We don't want to get crossways with the DEA, maybe foul up an operation they have going."

"Fuck 'em," Petersen said cheerfully.

Jack had to laugh, because it really was a pretty good setup. If he did step on some toes, it would be purely accidental. What the hell, it wouldn't hurt him to spend some time in some clubs. His experience was in SWAT, not narcotics, but he'd seen enough to know what to look for. "Who else is going to know about this?"

"About what?" Petersen asked, with an immediate case of amnesia.

"I don't guess you can tell me what some good clubs in the area are, can you?"

"Not speaking from personal experience, you understand, but I hear the Hot Wing in Scottsboro has some action. You might check out the Buffalo Club in Madison County, and the Sawdust Palace in Huntsville. I can come up with some more names if you're interested."

"Get me a list," Jack said, and hung up.

He leaned back in his chair, his eyes narrowed as he ran the plan in his mind again. There weren't any rules, because he was on his own. Hell, there really wasn't a plan, just a see-what-you-can-see mission. He'd have to play it by ear if he did happen to run across something, but his training had taught him how to act with initiative in fluid situations.

He felt the old surge of adrenaline through his veins, the tightening of anticipation. Maybe he missed the action more than he'd realized. This wasn't the same as a hostage situation or an armed standoff, but it was every bit as important. Women were getting raped and were sometimes dying because of GHB; if he could catch just one son of a bitch slipping it into someone's drink, he'd gladly nail his balls to the wall.

That night Daisy hesitantly knocked on Todd Lawrence's elaborate leaded-glass front door. The door itself was a work of art, painted a shade of blue that matched the shutters, with the detailing pinstriped in a dark green that made one think of a forest; given the number of potted plants on the wide porch, that analogy wasn't far off. The leaded glass gleamed as if it had just that day been cleaned with vinegar. Two antique bronze lamps bracketed the door, casting a soft light that made the entrance feel cozy and inviting.

Through the glass she saw a blurred figure approach; then the door opened and Todd Lawrence himself smiled down at her. "Hello, Daisy, how are you? Come on in." He stepped back and gestured with his hand. "It seems like ages since I've seen you. I don't get by the library as much as I should. Since I opened the store in Huntsville, it seems as if it takes up all my spare time."

Todd had always had a way about him that made you feel as if you were his best friend. Daisy's own contact with him had been limited, but his easy manner dissipated some of her nervousness. He was a slim, neat man, clad in tan chinos and a chambray shirt with the cuffs rolled back. Todd was about five-eleven in height, with brown hair and eyes and an easy smile, one that made you automatically want to smile in return.

"Successful businesses have a way of doing that," she said, following him into the front parlor and taking a seat on the overstuffed floral couch he indicated.

"Do they ever." He smiled ruefully. "I spend a lot of my free time going to auctions. A lot of nights there's nothing but junk and reproductions, but every so often a real gem will show up. The other night I bought a hand-painted Oriental screen for less than a hundred dollars, and sold it the next day for three thousand. I had a client who had been looking for something exactly like that."

"It takes a good eye to be able to tell real antiques from reproduction stuff," she said. "And years of study, I guess."

He shrugged. "I picked it up here and there. I like old furniture, so it was only natural that I paid attention." He put his hands on his hips and studied her, his head to the side. Normally such an examination would have made her uneasy, but Todd had a twinkle in his eyes that said, *Hey, isn't this fun?* "So, you want a makeover, do you?"

"An all-over makeover," Daisy said honestly. "I'm a mess, and I don't know what to do to correct it. I bought some makeup and tried it, but there has to be a trick to it or something, because I looked awful."

He laughed. "Actually, there are several tricks to it."

"I knew it," she muttered, indignant. Would it have been too much trouble for the companies to have printed the *real* proper way to apply their products?

"Most of it, though, is just practice, and learning not to use too much." He made a dismissive gesture with his hand. "Makeup's easy; I can show you that in less than an hour. What else are you planning to do?"

She felt her face heat up at having to catalog her faults. For goodness' sake, weren't they obvious? "Well, my hair. I was thinking about having Wilma put in some highlights—"

"Good God, no!" he exclaimed, horrified.

Daisy sighed. "That was pretty much the same reaction I got from my family."

"Listen to them," he advised. "They know whereof they speak. Wilma hasn't kept up with the trends or the new developments in chemicals. I doubt she's been to a hair show since she got her license forty years ago. There are some good stylists in either Huntsville or Chattanooga who won't burn your hair off at the scalp."

Daisy shuddered at the mental picture of herself bald. Todd lifted a strand of her hair and fingered it. "Your hair's in good shape," he said. "There's no discernable style, but it's healthy."

"It doesn't have any body." Now that she had gotten started, she was determined not to leave out the slightest flaw.

"That's no problem. Getting some of this length cut off will help, and there are some marvelous products available now to give hair more body and make it more manageable, too. Lightening it will give it more body, too." He studied her again. "Forget highlights. I think you should go blonde."

"B-blonde?" she squeaked. She couldn't even picture herself as a blonde. She could barely conceive of how she would look with a few highlights in her hair.

"Nothing brassy," he said. "We'll have the stylist put in several shades, so it will look natural."

For someone who had never even put a temporary rinse on her hair, bleaching her hair to several shades of blond seemed at least as difficult as putting a man on the moon. "H-how long would that take?"

"Oh, several hours, I'd think. Your hair will have to be double-processed."

"What's that?"

"Your own pigment will have to be bleached out, then blond pigment streaked in to replace it."

Well, at least that made sense. She didn't know if she'd ever have the nerve to do anything that drastic, but it was an option she could consider. "I'll think about it," she said dubiously.

"Think hard," he said. "What else?"

She sighed. "My clothes. I have no sense of style."

He looked at the skirt and blouse she wore. She had changed out of her pants as soon as she got home, because she couldn't stand another minute of worrying about whether or not people were looking at her butt. "Actually, you do," he drawled. "Unfortunately, it's all bad."

Her cheeks turned red, and he laughed. "Don't worry," he said kindly, extending a hand to help her to her feet. "You just never learned how to make the most of yourself. You have a lot of potential."

"I do?"

"You do." He made a circling motion with his finger. "Turn around. Slowly."

Self-consciously she did so.

"You have a good figure," he said. "You should show it, instead of hiding it inside those old-lady clothes. Your skin is excellent, you have good teeth, and I like those odd eyes you have. I'll bet you've been embarrassed by your eyes all your life, haven't you?"

She almost squirmed, because as a child she'd been hideously aware of her different-colored eyes and always tried to blend into the background so no one would notice them. "For God's sake, play them up," Todd said. "They're different, special. It isn't as if you have one brown eye and one blue, which would really look weird, and I don't know if it's genetically possible anyway. You'll never be a ravishing beauty, but you can definitely be very, very nice to look at."

"That's all I want, anyway," she said. "I don't think I could handle ravishing."

"I've heard it's a burden," he said, smiling at her. "The best light is in my bathroom. So step into my boudoir, if you dare, and let's get started on this transformation."

Daisy extracted a small bag from her purse. "I brought my makeup."

"Let's see what you have." He took the bag from her and opened it. He didn't make a *tsk*ing sound, but she got the feeling he barely refrained. "That will do for a start," he said with kind forbearance.

He lead the way through his bedroom to the bath, and if Daisy had ever harbored any doubts about Todd's sexual affiliation, his bedroom settled it. It was exquisitely furnished in Chippendale, with a huge four-poster bed that was swathed in graceful swags of netting, and with huge, lush potted plants artistically arranged around the room. She wished her own bedroom looked half as good.

My goodness, even his bathroom was decorated. He'd done it

in green and white, with touches of peach and dusty blues. She'd never been in a man's bathroom before, she realized. She was faintly disappointed to see an ordinary toilet, though of course there was no reason for him to have a urinal hanging on the wall. Besides, it wouldn't have gone with the decor.

"I don't have a vanity chair, sorry," he said, smiling again. "Men don't sit down to shave."

She'd never thought of it before, but he was right; shaving was something else men didn't sit down to do.

"Okay, first get your hair away from your face. Do you have a headband or anything?"

She shook her head.

"Then tuck it behind your ears and brush it away from your forehead."

She did as he said. That awful self-conscious feeling was back; her fingers were clumsy, unable to manage the simple act of tucking her hair behind her ears without fumbling. She suspected she'd stumble over her own feet if she had to walk anywhere right now.

He opened a drawer in the built-in vanity and took out a box, about ten inches wide and five inches thick. He flicked the clasp, raised the lid, and trays unfolded—trays filled with all sorts of brushes and lipsticks, arrays of colors for the eyes and cheeks all displayed in little containers. "My goodness," she blurted. "You have more makeup than Wal-Mart."

He laughed. "Not quite. This box brings back memories, though. I was on Broadway for a while, and you have to slather on layers of makeup to keep from looking like a ghost when the lights hit you."

"That sounds like fun. I've never been to New York. I've never done much of anything."

"It *was* fun."

"Why did you come back?"

"It wasn't home," he said simply. "Besides, Mother needed someone to take care of her. That's the way it works: they take care of you when you're young, you take care of them when they're old."

"Family," she said, smiling, because her own was so close.

"Exactly. Now," he said, his tone turning brisk, "let's get started."

Less than an hour later, entranced, Daisy stared into the mirror. Her lips parted in wonder. Oh, she wasn't a raving beauty, but the woman in the mirror was attractive, and she looked confident, lively. She didn't fade into the wallpaper. And most important, men would notice her!

The process hadn't been painless. First Todd had insisted she pluck her eyebrows: "You don't want Joan Crawford eyebrows, dear. She had one brow hair that grew to about three inches long, and she named it Oscar, or something like that." But thankfully he hadn't wanted her to have Bette Davis eyes, either, so she'd been able to limit the tweezing to a few stragglers.

Then he had walked her through the application of a full makeup job, and, to her relief, it wasn't very complicated. The main thing was not to use too much, and to always have a tissue and cotton tip at hand to repair any mistakes or wipe off excess. Even mascara was easy, once she had used the tissue to blot most of the goop off the little brush before applying it to her lashes.

"Heathens," she had muttered, surveying her lovely dark lashes in the mirror. There wasn't a caterpillar in sight.

"Beg pardon?"

"Mascara makers. They're heathens. Why don't they just tell you to blot most of the mascara off the brush before you start?"

"Honey, they have enough to worry about warning people not to poke it in their eyes, or eat it. I guess they figure if you really want to wear mascara, you'll learn how."

Well, she had wanted, and she had learned.

"I did it," she said numbly, staring at her reflection. Her complexion was smooth and bright, her cheeks softly flushed, her eyes mysterious and larger, her lips full and moist. It hadn't been difficult at all.

"Well, honey, of course you did. There's nothing to it; just practice and don't go overboard with the color. Now, let's think about style. Which would you rather shoot for: nature girl, old money, or sex kitten?"

Todd stood in his open front door and cheerfully waved a good-bye to Daisy. He couldn't help smiling. This was the first time he'd ever spent any time with her, though of course he'd known who she was, and he really liked her. She was touchingly naive for someone her age, but fresh and bright and honest, without a jaded bone in her body. She had absolutely no idea how to make the most of her looks, but, thank God, he did. When he was finished with her, she was going to be a knockout.

He strode to the phone and dialed a number. As soon as the call was answered on the other end, he said, "I have a candidate. Daisy Minor."

SEVEN

Glenn Sykes was a professional. He was careful, he paid attention to details, and he didn't let himself get emotionally involved. He'd never spent a day in jail; in fact, he even had a clean driving record, without so much as a speeding ticket to his name. Not that he hadn't had a speeding ticket, but the driver's license he'd presented had been in a different name, an alternate identity he'd prudently set up for himself some fifteen years previously.

One of the reasons he was successful was that he didn't draw attention to himself. He wasn't loud, he seldom drank—and never when he was working, only when he was alone—and he always kept himself neat and clean, on the theory that law-abiding people were more likely to keep an eagle eye on anyone hanging around who looked dirty and unkempt, as if dirt somehow translated into shiftiness. Anyone who saw him would automatically categorize him as Joe Average, with a wife and a couple of kids, and a three-bedroom house in an older subdivision. He didn't wear an earring, or a chain, or have a tattoo; all those, however small, were things that people noticed. He kept his sandy brown hair cut fairly short, he wore an ordinary thirty-dollar wristwatch even though he could afford much better, and he watched his mouth. He could and did go anywhere without drawing undue attention.

That was why he was so disgusted with Mitchell. The dead girl wasn't anyone important, but her body, when it was discovered, would still draw attention. The resultant investigation probably wouldn't amount to much, and he'd been careful to make certain the cops wouldn't have anything to go on, but mistakes happened and even cops got lucky occasionally. Mitchell was jeopardizing the entire enterprise; Sykes had no doubt that if Mitchell was ever arrested in connection with those girls' deaths, he'd drop every name he'd ever known in an effort to strike a deal with the D.A. Mitchell's stupidity could get every one of them a prison sentence.

The hell of it was, if Mitchell couldn't get it up with a conscious woman, there were other ways to do it. GHB was a crap shoot; you might take it one time and be okay, with just a gap in your memory. The next time, it could shut down your brain. There were other drugs that would work; hell, booze would work. But, no, Mitchell had to slip them GHB, like he was getting away with something and no one would notice when the girls didn't wake up.

So Mitchell had to go. If Mayor Nolan hadn't given the word, Sykes had already decided it was time for him to be moving on, before Mitchell brought them all down. But the mayor, for all his southern-fucking-gentleman manners, was as cold and ruthless as anyone Sykes had ever met; he didn't pretend that he couldn't sully his hands with murder—though Sykes didn't exactly call killing Mitchell *murder*. It was more of an extermination, like stepping on a cockroach.

First, though, he had to find the bastard. With a cockroach's talent for self-preservation, Mitchell had gone to ground and hadn't turned up at any of his usual haunts.

Since Mitchell was already spooked, Sykes decided to play this low-key. While it would have been satisfying to simply walk up to the bastard's trailer and put a hole between his eyes as soon as he opened the door, again, things like that tended to attract attention. For one thing, Mitchell had neighbors, and in Sykes's experience neighbors were always looking out the window just when they shouldn't. He could dispose of Mitchell in far less dramatic ways. With luck, he could even make it look like an accident.

Mitchell knew his car, so Sykes borrowed one from a pal and cruised through Mitchell's neighborhood, if you could call two ramshackle trailers and one dilapidated frame house, surrounded by junk, a neighborhood. They were the types of places inhabited by women with frizzy hair who wore tight, stained tank tops that showed their dirty bra straps, and by men with long, straggly hair, yellowed teeth, and an unshaken belief that life had done them wrong and owed them something. Sykes didn't openly look at any of the three places as he drove by; with his peripheral vision he searched for Mitchell's blue pickup, but it wasn't there. He'd drive by again after dark, see if any lights were on, but he didn't really expect the cockroach to turn up again so soon.

Seeing how Mitchell lived always reminded Sykes of how narrow his own escape had been. If he hadn't been smarter, made better decisions, he might *be* Mitchell. Now, that was a scary thought. But he came from the same trashy background; he knew exactly how Mitchell thought, how he operated. In his work that was a plus, but Sykes never wanted to actually live that way again. He wanted *more.* Hell, Mitchell probably wanted more, too, but he was never going to get more because he kept making those stupid decisions.

With an eye to the future, Sykes salted away every dollar he could. He lived simply, but cleanly. He had no expensive habits or vices. He even played the stock market a little, with conservative stocks that didn't perform spectacularly, but nevertheless always posted a gain. One day, when he had enough—though he wasn't certain exactly how much was enough—he would walk away from everything and move where no one knew him, start a small business, settle down as a respected member of the community. Hell, he might even get married, have a couple of rugrats. His imagination couldn't quite conjure up that picture, but nevertheless it was possible.

Mitchell wasn't jeopardizing just Sykes's immediate future, but all of his plans. Those plans were what had gotten him out of the trash dump of a house where he'd grown up, what had given him a goal when it would have been so much easier to just let himself drift in the sea of waste. It was always easier to do nothing. Don't worry about cleaning the house or cutting the grass, just drink another six-pack of beer and smoke another joint. Never mind there's no food in the house for the kids; when that monthly check comes in, first thing, you gotta get your booze and drugs, before the money gets gone. It was easy. It was always easier to blow the money rather than spend it on things like food and electricity. The tough ones, the smart ones like him, figured out that the hard road was the road out.

No matter what, Sykes would never go back.

Once he took on a project, Todd Lawrence was an unstoppable force. Between trying to get her house ready to move into and Todd commandeering every other spare minute she had, Daisy felt as if she had been caught up in a tornado that refused to let her drop. The only thing that kept her from collapsing was the visible change she could see in herself.

She didn't have the nerve to try for the sex kitten image, and she had no idea what "old money" entailed, so she opted for the nature girl. She could handle that, she thought. Todd, however, had other ideas.

"I think we'll go for old money," he said lazily when she presented herself at his house on Saturday for their shopping expedition and trip to a beauty salon in Huntsville. Hands on his hips, he looked her up and down. "Your face will look better with that kind of hairstyle."

"Old money has a hairstyle?" she asked incredulously.

"Of course. Simple, uncluttered, very good cut. Never too long, just to the top of your shoulders, I think. I have something in mind that you'll like. Oh, by the way, we're going to get your ears pierced today, too."

Protectively she grabbed her earlobes. "Why? I don't think a makeover should include bloodshed."

"Because clip-on earrings are hideously uncomfortable, darling. Don't worry, it won't hurt."

She peered at his own earlobes, hoping they were hole-free so she could refuse on the basis that he didn't know what he was talking about. No such luck; both lobes sported small indentations. He smiled and patted her hand. "Be brave," he said cheerfully. "Beauty always comes at a price."

Daisy didn't think she was brave so much as totally unable to stop this train she had started in motion. She was still trying to come up with a compelling reason why she didn't need any body parts pierced when Todd bundled her into his car and they set off for Huntsville.

Their first stop was a beauty salon. Daisy had only ever been in Wilma's beauty shop, and there was a definite difference between a "shop" and a "salon." For one thing, she was asked what she wanted to drink. All Wilma ever asked was if you were in a hurry. She started to ask for a cup of coffee, but Todd, with a twinkle in his eyes, said, "Wine. She needs to relax."

The receptionist, a striking woman with short platinum hair and a pleasant smile, laughed as she fetched the wine. It was delivered into Daisy's hand in a real wineglass, instead of the plastic disposable glass she had expected. On further reflection, though, she supposed Todd wouldn't give his patronage to any salon so gauche as to serve wine in plastic or Styrofoam.

The receptionist consulted her book. "Amie will be right with you. She's our top stylist, so you can just relax and put yourself in her hands. You'll look like a million dollars when she's finished."

"I'll just have a word with her before I leave," Todd said, and disappeared through a door.

Daisy gulped her wine. Leave? Todd was leaving her here alone? The bottom dropped out of her stomach. Oh, God, she couldn't do this.

She *had* to do this.

Three hours later, on her third glass of wine, she felt as if she had been tortured. Sharp-smelling chemicals had been swabbed on her hair, chemicals that bleached her a bright yellow-white and made her look like a punk rocker who had been frightened by a television evangelist. After that stuff was washed out, then more chemicals were applied with what looked like a paintbrush, on one strand at a time, and each strand was then wrapped to keep it from touching the other strands. She morphed from a punk rocker into something from outer space, wired to receive satellite transmissions.

While this was happening, her eyebrows were waxed—ouch— and she was kept busy receiving both a manicure and a pedicure. Her nails were now all the same length, polished a transparent rose with pale tips. Her toenails, though, sported a wicked shade of red. Daisy tried to remember if she had ever painted her toenails before; she didn't think so, and even if she had, she would have chosen some pale pink shade that was barely noticeable. She would never, never have chosen look-at-me red. The effect was startling—and wonderfully sexy. She kept holding her bare feet up and staring at her red-tipped toes, thinking they didn't even look like her feet now. Too bad she didn't have any sandals to show them off. She had some flip-flops, but she couldn't wear those to work.

At last the torture part was over. She was unwrapped, washed, and deposited in the stylist's chair once more. After three glasses of wine, Daisy didn't even wince as Amie set to work with her scissors, snipping industriously away. Long strands of hair slithered to the floor. Daisy finished the last of the wine in her glass and held it out for more.

"Oh, I think you can do without reinforcing, now," said Todd in a lazily amused voice. "How much wine have you had?"

"That's just the third glass," she said righteously.

"Darling, I hope you ate this morning."

"Of course. And Amie gave me a croissant. Three glasses in three hours isn't too much, is it?" Her righteousness changed to anxiety. "I'm not tipsy, am I?"

"Maybe a little. Thanks," he said in an aside to Amie.

Amie, a tall, thin young woman who wore her black hair in a crew cut, smiled at him. "It's been a pleasure. It would be worth two croissants to see this kind of a change in someone's appearance."

Todd lounged against the workstation, dapper in his customary khakis and a blue silk shirt, and watched as Amie used a round brush to shape Daisy's hair as she dried it. Daisy watched too, terrified because she was going to have to do this on her own the next time. It didn't look complicated, but then neither had mascara.

She had breathed a sigh of relief when the last washing had revealed hair that seemed dark, though she'd been a bit indignant that three hours of torture had had such little result. Why, even the lemon white had at least shown that *something* had been done to her. As Amie's hair dryer worked, though, Daisy watched her hair become lighter and lighter. It wasn't lemon white, but it was definitely blond. Different shades shimmered through it, catching the light with gold here, a pale beige there.

When Amie was finished, she whisked away the cape while Daisy stared openmouthed at her reflection. Her dull, mousy brown hair was a distant memory. This hair was glossy, full of body. It *swung* when she moved her head, then settled back into place as if it knew exactly where to go. The style was simple, as Todd had promised; the length barely reached her shoulders, the ends were turned under, and the top swept elegantly away from a short side part.

Amie looked incredibly smug. Todd hugged her and kissed her cheek. "You did it. That's classic."

"She has good hair," Amie said, accepting Todd's tribute and giving him a return kiss on the cheek. "Not much body, but nice strong hair with a smooth cuticle. With the right styling products, there's no reason she can't look like this every day."

It was a good thing Todd was along, because Daisy was in a trance. He made certain she had the styling products Amie recommended, he reminded her to write a check for services rendered—she was so dazed she would have walked out without thinking—and, thank God, he was driving. Daisy didn't know if it was the wine or just plain shock, but she wasn't certain her feet were touching the ground.

That was good, because their next stop was at a large mall where she got her ears pierced. It took only a minute—all she felt was a pinch—and the next thing she knew she was walking out with discreet gold hoops in her ears.

For the next four hours, Todd walked her into the ground.

She tried on clothes until she was exhausted, and began to see what he meant when he said "old money." The styles were simple, such as a plain beige skirt worn with a sleeveless white blouse. But the fit was slim, the skirt stopped at her knees, and a narrow belt drew attention to her waist. "Old money is never frou-frou," he said. "It's sleek and classic and understated." She bought shoes, graceful sandals that showed her sexy red toenails, and classic pumps with two-inch heels, in black and taupe. "Never white, darling," he said firmly. "White is for casual shoes, not pumps."

"But—"

"No buts. Trust me."

Because his taste so far had been infallible, in the end, she could do nothing else. And maybe her own tastes had something to do with it, because invariably her own preferences had been his, too. She had just never before had the nerve, or the incentive, to do anything about the way she looked. She had stayed with what was familiar, what was comfortable, what was easy. Looking good was a lot of work, plus she had never really seen herself as pretty or stylish. Beth had always been the pretty one, while Daisy had accepted her own role as the smart, studious one. Maybe she couldn't be pretty as effortlessly as Beth could, but she was definitely pretty, and it was her own fault she was only now discovering that.

She didn't even try to keep track of the money she spent. This was all for a good cause: her own. She didn't just buy clothes, though that was the majority of her purchases. She bought perfume, and a couple of chic handbags, and earrings she liked. Todd talked her into an anklet, telling her, with a sly look in his eyes, "There's nothing sexier, darling."

At last they were on their way home. Daisy sat quietly, still numb from the entire experience. If there was such a thing as cosmetic war, today she had waged it. From today on, her life was changed. It wasn't just the way other people would see her, but the way she saw herself. She had always been content with the background, thinking that it was all she deserved. No longer. From now on, regardless of what happened in her personal manhunt, she was going to make the most of herself for the sake of her own pride, if nothing else.

"If you don't mind my asking," Todd said after about ten miles of silence while she assimilated the day, "what was behind this sea change?"

Daisy sighed and rested her head against the seat, letting her eyes close. "My thirty-fourth birthday."

"Really? I would have guessed you're in your late twenties."

Despite her fatigue, that brought a smile to her face. "Really?"

"Cross my heart. Maybe it's your skin; you haven't been out in the sun much, have you?"

"Not a lot. I do tan, but I also burn easily." Plus she had always been inside with her nose in a book.

"That's good. You also have a charming air of innocence that makes you look younger."

Daisy opened her eyes, and felt her cheeks heat. "I don't get out much," she confessed. "That's another reason I wanted to change. I want to get married, and let's face it, the way I looked before no one paid any attention to me."

"That'll change now," he said, and smiled at her. "I guarantee it." He paused, then said, "Is there any certain man you're interested in?"

She shook her head, and felt the wonderful swing of her hair. Goodness, that was amazing! "No. I'm just going to go out looking. I've never been to a nightclub before, but I figure that's a good place to start. Do you know any good places?" Too late she realized that the clubs a gay man knew were probably not the clubs where she would have a good chance of success.

"I've heard the Buffalo Club is good," he said casually. "Do you dance?"

"I know how, though I haven't done it much since I took lessons. Dancing is a good way to break the ice, isn't it?"

"Very good." His tone was grave. "Do you think you might go out tonight?"

"I don't know." Going alone to a nightclub would take nerve, she thought, and after today she might have used up all her reserves.

Todd glanced at her, then returned his attention to the road. "Sometimes, once you get started, it's easier just to keep going than it is to stop and then start up again."

Meaning he thought she should go out tonight, after making the huge effort all day long to change her outward image.

"I'll think about it," she said. A thought occurred to her. "I don't know how to act like 'old money,' though. Is there anything special—"

"No," he interrupted. "Old money is just a style. Don't get presentation and personality confused. Just be yourself, and then you don't have to worry."

"Being myself never got me noticed before," she said ruefully.

He laughed. "It will now, honey. It will now."

EIGHT

Have you found Mitchell yet?" Temple Nolan asked.

"Not yet." Sykes was annoyed that the mayor had even asked. If Sykes had found him, he'd have said so, wouldn't he? "I figure he'll hide out for a week or so, but then he'll either figure it's no problem that the girl died, or he'll get antsy and figure it'll be safe for him to find some action as long as he doesn't go to his regular places. I've got it covered. When he shows, I'll know about it within five minutes."

"Mr. Phillips wasn't a happy man. There was a big buyer lined up for the girl. Now the guy has found another source, and we're out the money. Mr. Phillips wants Mitchell dead."

"He will be. Just be patient. If I start beating the bushes for him, he'll hear about it and bolt like a rabbit."

"Mr. Phillips isn't in the mood to be patient. It was a lot of money."

Sykes shrugged. Virgins always commanded a high initial price anyway, but sometimes there was a special demand from someone willing to pay big bucks. Sykes couldn't see anyone paying that much just to have sex with a virgin, so maybe they had another reason. He didn't think there were any ritualistic sacrifices going on, but he'd lived long enough and seen enough that he didn't put anything beyond some people. Whatever happened to the girls after they were delivered didn't concern him, anyway. They were merchandise, nothing more.

"Like I said, he'll turn up, and I'll be waiting when he does." Sykes had to make an effort to keep the impatience out of his voice. How often did he have to say it? Mitchell was as good as handled. And in the meantime, business continued. "We have another shipment scheduled to come in next Tuesday night, five girls. I'd rather not take them to the usual place, just in case Mitchell has already talked to the wrong people. That's another reason I don't want to push too hard in finding him; if he gets scared, he may go to the D.A. and try to cut a deal, our names in exchange for protection. You got any ideas for another holding pen, to be on the safe side?"

The mayor rubbed the back of his neck, frowning. The problem was that they had to find a place that was isolated enough to be private, but not so isolated that *some* traffic couldn't be expected. Rural folk were incurably nosy. If they saw headlights where there shouldn't be any, they'd investigate—and they'd usually be toting at least a .22 rifle. Neighbors looked out for neighbors. That was nice if you were one of the neighbors, but it was a pain in the ass when you were trying not to be noticed. The usual holding pen was an old travel trailer set well back from a dirt road. During dry weather, the road itself was a warning system, with any approaching vehicle sending up clouds of dust that could be seen well before any car came into sight.

"I'll find something," he said. "If nothing else, I'll rent a big U-Haul truck."

They'd done that before, in a pinch. It was amazing how little attention was paid to the rental trucks. The girls couldn't take a bath—and God knows they always needed a bath—the way they could in the travel trailer, but if the client had to take delivery of merchandise that was less than sweet-smelling, well, this wasn't exactly a dating service. But it was also a pain in the ass to use a rental, because if you parked the thing, sooner or later you could expect a deputy to come check it out. So you had to drive around until it was time for the clients to pick up the girls, then meet them somewhere and make a fast exchange. A rental just wasn't the best arrangement.

The mayor's pager began to beep. He silenced it and checked the number. "I have to go, but I'll get back to you about the alternate location. Just find Mitchell, for God's sake!"

Daisy paused at the closed double doors of the Buffalo Club. After much consideration, she had decided this was the place and now was the time to debut her new look and try her new approach to man-hunting. She was tired from the long day of shopping and being cosmetically tortured, but she was also still riding high on elation. When she had arrived home after the shopping trip, she hadn't called out a greeting as she usually did, just walked into the kitchen where her mother and Aunt Jo were busy putting up peach preserves for the winter. Her mother had glanced around, then whirled in alarm, sharply saying, "Who are you?"

Daisy had begun giggling. The other women had then squealed in delight and thrown themselves at her, exclaiming over the blond hair and the chic haircut. The peach preserves hadn't been able to wait, so while they continued with their canning,

Daisy had fetched all her shopping bags out of the car and displayed her take, which reached truly amazing proportions.

When she carted all of it upstairs to her room and began hanging the garments in her closet, she couldn't resist trying everything on again. And though she was tired, when she put on one of her trim new skirts and that classic white sleeveless shirt, then the taupe heels, a thrill ran through her. That stylish, pretty woman was really *her.* She wasn't gorgeous, she never would be, but the uncluttered hairstyle made the most of her rather unremarkable features and made her look . . . oh, reserved, maybe, instead of just mousy. And Todd was right: that anklet gleaming on her right ankle was downright sexy.

It was a shame to waste this look. She might not be able to get her hair in exactly this style again. And she was already made up . . .

With that in mind, she drew in a deep breath and made a decision:

It was now or never.

So here she was at the Buffalo Club, a large, sprawling country music nightclub just over the Madison County line. It had live bands, a big dance floor, and sort of a reputation. The occasional stabbing and fight had been known to happen, but it wasn't so far gone that women didn't feel comfortable attending. Another plus was that the cover charge was just two dollars; after the money she had spent that day, economy seemed prudent.

If she gave herself time to think, she knew she'd chicken out, so she just forged ahead. She took her two bucks out of the slim envelope purse swinging from her shoulder on a narrow strap. Her everyday purse was big enough to hold a month's rations, but Todd had insisted she carry something more elegant. "Don't carry a lot when you go out," he'd instructed. "Just enough cash to get by, a tissue, a lipstick, and stick a credit card in your bra."

That was good, because that was about all she could get in the slim little excuse for a purse anyway.

A big guy wearing blue jeans, boots, and a black T-shirt collected her two dollars at the door; then he allowed her to pass and she stepped into a din of colored lights, loud music, and even louder conversation. Voices competed with the band and each other to be heard. The place was jammed. She was bumped from behind, shoving her into a tall redhead with big hair who gave her an irritated look.

Daisy started to mumble an apology, then remembered that she didn't mumble anymore. Besides, a mumble couldn't possibly be heard in here. "Pardon me," she said clearly, her head high as she moved away. Her hair looked better than the redhead's, she thought with a little thrill. She couldn't remember ever thinking her hair looked better than someone else's before.

She squirmed her way to a relatively sheltered spot where she could take stock. The bar, a big square, was lined with stools, and people stood three deep around it. Couples swayed on the dance floor, with colored lights flickering around them, while the lead singer of the band crooned a love song. The band was situated on a small stage behind a protective netting of chicken wire.

The chicken wire worried her. Maybe the Buffalo Club was a little rougher than she'd heard.

There were a multitude of tables arranged willy-nilly around the dance floor, but they were all taken. Sawdust and peanut shells littered the floor, while jeans-clad waitresses dipped and wove with deftly balanced trays through the swarming crowd.

She was overdressed, Daisy thought. Jeans seemed to be the dress code, on men and women alike, though every now and then she spotted a short skirt paired with a halter and cowboy boots. Todd would have sniffed and pronounced such an ensemble "tacky."

Daisy had kept on the pumps and the khaki skirt, and the

sleeveless white shirt with the first two buttons unbuttoned. The gold anklet drew attention to her slim, bare legs. She looked cool and classic, not quite the usual thing at the Buffalo Club.

"Well, hello!" A hard male arm clasped around her waist and swung her around. She found herself blinking up at a smiling dark-haired man with a beer bottle in his hand.

"Hello," Daisy replied. She had to almost yell to make herself heard.

"Are you here with someone?" he asked, bending so his mouth was close to her ear.

Why, he was flirting. The realization zinged through her. This was a pickup! A man was actually trying to pick her up!

"Some friends," she lied, because it seemed prudent to do so. She didn't know him, after all.

"Would the friends mind if you danced with me?" he asked.

Because he was smiling and his eyes were friendly, she said, "Not at all," and with a grin he set down his beer, took her hand, and led her to the dance floor.

My goodness, that was easy! Daisy thought giddily as she slipped into the man's arms. He held her close, but not so close that she would have been embarrassed. For a moment she was terrified her dancing skills would desert her—after all, it wasn't as if she'd had a lot of practice—but he was fairly smooth and she found that, if she didn't think about it, her feet seemed to do what they were supposed to do.

"My name's Jeff," he said, again putting his mouth next to her ear so she could hear him.

"Daisy," she supplied.

"Have you been here before? I don't think I've seen you, and believe me, I would have noticed."

She shook her head, just to feel her hair swing and settle. "First time."

"Don't let it be the last—" He broke off, turning his head to glare in annoyance at a man who had tapped him on the shoulder.

"May I break in?"

"No," Jeff said rudely. "What the hell do you think this is, a prom? Go away. I saw her first."

The other man, lean and blond, also clad in the de rigueur jeans and T-shirt, grinned. "C'mon, Jeff, don't be selfish." Deftly he unhooked Daisy's hand from Jeff's and spun her away from him.

Daisy looked over her shoulder at Jeff, her eyes a little wide as she wondered what would happen. Jeff grinned and shrugged, then motioned to the table where he would be.

"Are you friends?" she asked the blond man.

"Yeah, we work together. I'm Denny, by the way."

"Daisy," she said again.

The love song ended and the band immediately swung into a foot-stomper. Lines formed, and Denny pulled Daisy into position. "Wait!" she protested frantically. "I don't know how to do this!"

"It's easy," he yelled back. "Just follow my lead."

The line dance involved some stomping and whirling, and she managed to stomp and whirl not too far behind the rest of them. She and Denny bumped into each other at one point and she began laughing at herself. She was *so* out of place here, in her old-money classic clothes, surrounded by jeans and tube tops, but this was fun. She hadn't been here ten minutes yet, and already two men had come on to her. That was more attention than she'd had in . . . oh, thirty-four years.

The line dance ended, and the band segued into another slow song, for a breather. Denny had barely gotten his arm around her waist when another guy cut in on him, and he surrendered her to yet another man. This one was older, probably in his fifties, with a close-cropped gray-and-brown beard, and not much taller than she was. He could dance, though. He grinned at her, said, "My name's Howard," and expertly twirled her. Daisy laughed, giddy with excitement and joy as their hands caught and he twirled her back into his arms.

Howard didn't mind showing off his expertise, so Daisy polished up her rusty skills as fast as possible and did a credible job, she thought. She was nowhere near as good as he was, but at least she didn't stumble, and she didn't step on his toes.

After Howard came Steven, and after Steven was a guy named Mitchell who had big brown eyes and a shy smile. By that time Daisy was breathless and more than a little warm. "I need to sit this one out," she gasped, fanning herself with her hand.

Mitchell slipped his hand under her elbow. "I'll get you something to drink," he said. "Beer? Wine?"

"Just water, for now," she said as she walked off the dance floor and looked around for a place to sit. The tables were just as crowded now as they had been five dances ago.

"Ah, c'mon, have some wine," Mitchell cajoled.

"Maybe later. I'm really thirsty now, and water's best for that." Besides, she had to drive home.

"A Coke, then."

His big brown eyes said he wanted to buy her a drink, and she was thwarting him by insisting on water. She relented. "Okay, a Coke."

His shy smile bloomed. "Wait right here," he said, and plunged into the crowd.

That was easier said than done. The swarming, shifting crowd constantly forced her to move this way and that, and within five minutes she was quite a distance from where Mitchell had left her. She peered toward the bar, trying to pick him out of the mass of bodies, but she didn't know him well enough to recognize him in a crowd and, besides, it might take him a long time to get the drinks. The new shoes fit very well, but they were still new, she had danced five dances, and her feet hurt. She wanted to sit down. She rose on tiptoe, trying to spot an empty chair.

"Looking for a place to sit?" a burly guy yelled, and looped a beefy arm around her waist before she could react, hauling her down on his lap.

Alarmed, Daisy immediately tried to jump up. He laughed and tightened his arm, pulling her back, and instinctively she put her hand down to brace herself. Unfortunately, she braced herself on his crotch, all of her weight bearing down on her hand.

He yelped, a high-pitched sound that rose above the din of music and voices. Suddenly aware of where her hand was and what she was feeling, Daisy squeaked and tried to leap up again, and her downward shove brought an even higher sound from the burly guy. Actually, it was now approaching a scream, one that brought heads turning their way.

Her face heated and she began struggling in earnest, but she couldn't find her balance or purchase, and wherever she put her hand seemed to be wrong. She felt something soft grind under her knuckles, and the burly guy turned purple.

My goodness, it was amazing how things escalated. Distracted by the steam-whistle noise coming from the burly guy, a man accidently walked into a woman and made her spill her drink down her dress. She screamed, and her boyfriend swung at the other man. A chair overturned, a table was shoved, and there was the sound of breaking glass. People scattered. Well, some people scattered; others seemed to leap in their eagerness to join in the fray.

The melee was like a tidal wave, sweeping toward her, and she couldn't get to her feet to escape it.

An iron clamp suddenly wrapped around her waist and hauled her off the poor guy's lap. He collapsed on the floor, wheezing and holding his privates with both hands. Daisy squealed and clutched at the clamp, surprised to find it was merely flesh, but there was no way she could wiggle free. Her feet didn't even touch the floor as she was swiftly carried away from the tangle of heaving bodies and swinging fists. The nightclub's bouncers were wading in now, cracking heads left and right and roughly restoring order, but Daisy didn't get to see what happened because the bouncer who carried her waded through the throng as if it were water, moving people out of his way with his free arm, and before she knew it she was bundled out the door and deposited on her feet with a thud.

How humiliating. Her first time in a nightclub, and she was thrown out.

Her face burning, she turned to apologize and found herself staring up at Chief Russo. The apology froze on her tongue.

There was the sound of more breaking glass inside, and a stream of people suddenly erupted out the door as the more prudent decided to leave while the leaving was good. The chief caught Daisy's wrist and hauled her to the side, out of the way. The yellow neon sign spelling out the club's name spilled light down on them, not even giving her the protection of darkness. Maybe he wouldn't recognize her, Daisy thought in panic. Her own mother hadn't even recognized her—

"Well, if it isn't Miss Daisy," he drawled, in a very good imitation of a southern accent, and her hope of not being recognized was blown out of the water. "Do you come here often?"

"No, this is my first time. I can explain," she blurted, feeling her face turn red.

He stared down at her with narrowed eyes. "I can't wait to hear it. In the space of thirty seconds you castrated a guy and started a brawl. Not bad for your first time here. Let me know when you're planning on coming back, and I'll stay home that night."

Well, no way was he going to make her the blame for that fiasco inside, she thought indignantly. "It wasn't my fault. That man grabbed me, and when I put my hand down to brace myself, I . . ." Her voice trailed off as she tried to find a delicate way to describe what had happened.

"Grabbed his balls and smashed them flat against the chair seat," Chief Russo finished for her. "I was about to step in, but when he began hitting those high notes, I figured you had the situation well in hand, so to speak."

"I didn't mean to! It was an accident."

Suddenly he grinned. "Forget about it. He'll think twice before he grabs a strange woman again. Come on, I'll walk you to your car."

She didn't want to be walked to her car. She didn't want to go to her car at all. Wistfully she looked at the door. "I don't suppose I could—"

"No, your dancing is over for the night, twinkle toes. You need to get out of here before the sheriff's deputies show up."

She sighed, because she had been having such fun—until she had accidentally castrated the burly guy, of course—but she supposed the chief was right. The deputies might just arrest everyone and sort things out later, and she could just imagine what everyone would say if she got arrested. He took her arm and forcefully turned her toward the parking lot. "Where's your car?"

She sighed again. "Over there." She crunched over the gravel to her car, with Chief Russo looming beside her and his hard hand never loosening its grip on her elbow, as if she were a prisoner he expected to bolt. She was glad he hadn't handcuffed her.

Cars were leaving the parking lot in every direction, and the two of them had to weave their way through the traffic. When they reached her car, he released her arm, and she got her keys out of her bag, then unlocked the car. The chief opened the door for her and Daisy slid behind the wheel. "Have you had anything to drink?" he asked suddenly.

"No, not even a Coke," she said, forlornly remembering the brown-eyed man who hadn't made it back to her in time. She was so thirsty; starting a brawl was almost as much exertion as dancing.

He braced one arm on the top of the open door and the other on car's roof, leaning down to study her in the glare of the dome light. "You've been sandbagging," he finally said, his eyes narrowed again. He seemed to be studying the open collar of her shirt. "Hiding under those god-awful granny clothes you usually wear."

Even the chief of police had noticed how unstylish her clothes were, Daisy thought. How humiliating. "I'm turning over a new leaf," she explained.

He grunted and straightened, stepping back so she could close the door. She started the car, hesitated, then lowered the window. "Thank you for getting me out of there," she said.

"It seemed the smart thing to do. The way you were going, that poor guy was looking at dismemberment." He lifted his head, listening intently. "I think I hear sirens. Go home before the deputies get here."

Still she hesitated. "What about you?"

"I'll help them sort things out."

That's right; he didn't have to worry about being arrested. She started to ask him to keep quiet about her being there, but realized she had just as much right to go to a nightclub as he did. Besides, maybe she *wanted* people to know she'd been at the Buffalo Club. That would certainly change the way people saw her. She wanted men to think of her as approachable and available, and just improving her appearance wouldn't accomplish that.

"Will I have to give a statement?" she asked.

Exasperated, he snapped, "Not unless you keep hanging around. Now get your ass out of here while you still can."

Well! Without another word, Daisy stomped on the gas pedal, slinging gravel and making her tires squall as she fishtailed out of

the parking lot. Startled, she fought the steering wheel for a panicked moment before she remembered to take her foot off the gas.
The tires stopped squalling as they gripped the road, and much
more sedately, she continued down the road. She had never made
her tires squall before in her life. Oh, my goodness, what if the
chief had been hit by some of the gravel? She started to go back
and apologize, but flashing lights appeared in her rearview mirror
and she decided it would be best to get her ass out of there, just
as he had said.

NINE

It wasn't everyone who could go out for a night of honky-tonking, dance until she was ready to drop, start a brawl, and be home by nine o'clock, Daisy told herself the next morning. So the night hadn't been an unqualified success; the first part of it had been *very* successful. What's more, she'd had fun and she was going to do it again. Not the brawl part—at least, she hoped not—but definitely the dancing and attracting men part.

After church, where she endured the blatant curiosity of all her fellow churchgoers—people who should have known better than to stare at someone—she ate a quick lunch and changed into one of her new pairs of jeans, intending to drive over to Lassiter Avenue to see how Buck Latham had progressed on painting her house. Now that she was well and truly launched on her new path, she was eager to move out on her own. As she walked out on the porch with her purse and car keys in hand, however, a white Crown Victoria pulled to the curb in front of the house.

Her heart sank as she watched Chief Russo unfold his big frame from the driver's seat. She had glossed over the previous night's episode to her mother, thinking it best not to let on that she'd smashed a man's testicles. She suspected Chief Russo was here to spill the beans and read her the riot act, as if he had any room to talk, because he certainly hadn't been at the Buffalo Club in any official capacity. He'd been out trolling, the same as she, but at least her intentions were honorable.

He was dressed in jeans, too, and a black T-shirt that clung to his broad, sloping shoulders. He looked more like a weight lifter than ever, she thought with a sniff. Remembering how easily, with one arm, he had carried her out of the Buffalo Club last night, she knew she had accurately pegged him.

"Going somewhere?" he asked, standing on their short, flower-lined sidewalk and looking up at her as she stood on the shady porch.

"Yes," she said baldly. Good manners dictated she should say something like, Oh, I was just going to run to the supermarket for a minute, but that can wait. Why don't you come in and have coffee? She limited her reply to that one word. There was just something about him that made her forget her raising.

"Aren't you going to ask me in?" he asked, eyes glinting in a way that said he was more amused than put out.

"No."

He jerked his head toward the car. "Then come for a ride with me. I don't think you want to have this discussion outside where all your neighbors can listen in."

Her heart lurched. "Oh, my God, are you taking me *down-town?*" She hurried down the steps as a horrible thought occurred to her. "That man last night—he didn't die, did he? It was an accident! And even if he did, wouldn't that be justifiable homi-cide?"

He scrubbed a hand down his face, and she stared suspiciously at him. It looked as if he'd been hiding a grin. For goodness' sake, this was nothing to laugh about!

"As far as I know, your boyfriend is all right; probably sore and walking a little funny, but alive."

She blew out a big breath. "Well, that's a relief. Then why are you taking me downtown?"

He did that face-rubbing thing again. No doubt about it, this time: he was laughing at her. Well!

He reached out and took her arm, his grip warm and too firm, as if he were accustomed to handling miscreants who didn't want to go with him. "Don't poker up on me, Miss Daisy," he said, stifling an audible snicker. "It's just . . . *Downtown* doesn't have quite the same ring to it in Hillsboro as it does in New York."

Well, that was true, considering they were already practically downtown, only a few blocks from the police station and the business section. He still could have been nicer about it.

As he opened the front passenger door of his car and put her inside, the front door opened again and Evelyn came out. "Chief Russo! Where are you taking Daisy?"

"Just for a ride, ma'am. We'll be back within an hour, I promise."

Evelyn hesitated, then smiled. "Y'all have a good time."

"Yes, ma'am," the chief said gravely.

"Oh, great," Daisy muttered as he got in the car. "Now she thinks we're *seeing* each other."

"We can go back and set her straight, tell her what's really going on," he offered as he pulled away from the curb, not even waiting for her answer. That was so annoying; of course she didn't want to do that, but he knew it before he even made the offer. He was just being a smart aleck.

"I had just as much right to be at that club as you did," she said, crossing her arms and sticking her nose in the air.

"Agreed."

She lowered her nose down to give him a startled look. "Then why are you interrogating me? I didn't do anything wrong. The brawl wasn't my fault, and I truly didn't mean to smash that man's testicles."

"I know." He was grinning again, darn him. Just what was so funny?

"Then what's wrong?"

"Nothing's wrong. And I'm not 'interrogating' you. I asked you to come for a ride; that's a helluva lot different from taking you to an interview room and grilling you for hours."

Relieved, she let out a whoosh of air and relaxed in the seat, then immediately sat upright again. "You didn't ask me, you *told* me, so what else was I to think? 'Let's take a ride.' Cops say that all the time on television, and it always means they're taking you downtown to be booked."

"So the scriptwriters need to learn some new dialogue."

A new thought, an appalling one, occurred to her. My goodness, the chief wasn't *courting* her, was he? Their encounters had always been bristly, but last night had shown her what a difference her new appearance made in the way men treated her. Her stomach knotted; she wasn't at all practiced in telling a man to shove off, she just wasn't interested. *He* couldn't be interested, could he? Maybe she didn't look as much better as she thought.

Swiftly she flipped down the sun visor and peered into the mirror attached there, then just as swiftly flipped it back up. Oh, dear.

"What was that about?" he asked curiously. "You didn't look long enough even to check your lipstick."

She'd forgotten all about her lipstick. Anyway, a quick peek was all it took to tell her that, no, she wasn't mistaken about the change.

"I was just wondering if cop cars had visor mirrors, too," she blurted. "It seems kind of . . . sissy."

"Sissy?" He looked as if he were biting the inside of his jaw.

"Not that I'm questioning your masculinity," she said hastily. The last thing she wanted was for him to feel he had to prove his masculinity to her. Men, she had read, tended to take such comments personally. Their egos were all tied up with their virility, or something like that.

He sighed. "No offense, Miss Daisy, but following your train of thought is like trying to catch a jackrabbit hopped up on speed."

She didn't take offense, because she was too thankful he hadn't been able to follow that particular train. Instead she said, "I wish you wouldn't call me Miss Daisy. It makes me sound like an—" She started to say *old maid,* but that description hit too close to home. "—a fuddy-duddy."

He was biting the inside of his jaw again. "If the hairnet fits . . ."

"I do *not* wear a hairnet!" she shouted, then sank back in the seat in surprise. She never shouted. She never lost her temper. She hadn't always been exactly polite to him, but neither had she *shouted* at him. She began to worry; was there a law against yelling at someone in law enforcement? Yelling at him wasn't the same as yelling at a cop who'd stopped her for speeding—if she had ever speeded, that is—but he was, after all, the chief of police, and it might be even worse—

"You've gone off into the ether again," he growled.

"I was just wondering if there was any law against yelling at a chief of police," she admitted.

"You thought you were going to be thrown in the pokey for yelling?"

"It *was* disrespectful. I apologize. I don't usually yell, but then I'm not usually accused of wearing a hairnet, either."

"I can see the provocation."

"If you keep biting your jaw," she observed, "you're going to need stitches."

"I'll try not to do it again. And for your information, I call you Miss Daisy as a sign of respect."

"Respect?" She didn't know if that was good or not. On the one hand, of course she wanted him to respect her; on the other, that wasn't exactly the kind of reaction she wanted from a man who was, after all, at least several years older than she. Maybe last night at the club had been a fluke, and she wasn't as attractive now as she'd thought. Maybe men would dance with anyone at a club.

"You remind me of my aunt Bessie," he said.

Daisy nearly moaned aloud. Oh, dear, it was worse than she'd thought. His aunt! Now she knew last night had been a fluke. Stricken, she flipped the visor mirror down again to see if she could possibly have made that big a mistake.

"I won't even ask," he sighed.

"I look like your *aunt?*" She almost moaned the word.

He began laughing. He actually laughed at her. Mortified, she raised the visor and crossed her arms again.

"Great-aunt, actually. And I didn't say you looked like her; I said you remind me of her. She wasn't very worldly, either."

Naive. He meant naive. Unfortunately, he wasn't wrong. That's what happened when you spent your life with your nose buried in a book. You might know a lot of interesting facts, but when it came to real-world experience, you were pretty much in the dark.

He turned down the highway toward Fort Payne. "Why are we going to Fort Payne?" Daisy asked, looking around at the cedar trees and green mountains. The drive was a nice one, but she couldn't think of any reason why they should go there.

"We aren't. I'm just driving."

"You mean we aren't going anywhere in particular?"

"I said we'd go for a ride. That means riding."

Now she was back to the awful suspicion that he might be courting her, though if he was, he went about it in a strange way, telling her she reminded him of his great-aunt and laughing at her. On the other hand, he was a Yankee; maybe that was the way they did it up North. "I'd rather ride in the other direction," she said uneasily. "Back toward home."

"Tough."

Well, *that* definitely wasn't very courteous, so he couldn't be courting her. Vastly relieved, she beamed at him.

"What?" he demanded, giving her a wary look.

"Oh, nothing."

"You're smiling at me. It's damn scary."

"My smile is scary?" The beam dimmed.

"No, the fact that you're smiling is scary. That tells me your train of thought has gone off track again."

"It has not. I know exactly which track it's on. I'm just relieved that *you* don't." Darn, she wished she hadn't told him that. She had to remember that he was a cop, and cops were notoriously nosy.

"Oh?" Just as she had feared, now he was interested.

"Private stuff," she informed him. A gentleman would leave it at that.

She should have remembered that he wasn't a gentleman. "What kind of private stuff?" he demanded. "Sexy stuff?"

"No!" she said, horrified. And because having him think she might want to do that was worse than what she really had been thinking, she said, "I was just afraid you might be courting me, and when you told me 'tough,' I was relieved, because you wouldn't have said that if you had been. Courting me, that is."

"Courting?" His shoulders started shaking a little.

"Yes, well, whatever it's called these days. 'Dating' seems a little too high-schoolish, and besides, this isn't a date. It's more like a kidnaping."

"You haven't been kidnaped. I just wanted to talk to you, privately, about last night."

"What about last night? If I haven't broken any laws—"

"Would you stop yammering about that? I have some things to tell you about going to nightclubs."

"I'll have you know I'm an adult and can go to any nightclub I want. What's more, I'm going to, so you can—"

"Would you shut up for a minute!" he yelled. "I'm not telling you not to go; I'm just trying to tell you some things to watch out for!"

She sat silently for a moment. "I'm sorry," she finally said. "You just make me feel defensive. Maybe it's because you're the chief of police."

"Well, stop it, and listen to me. With what you've done to your hair and the way you're dressing, men are going to come on to you."

"Yes," she said with satisfaction. "They did."

He sighed. "Did you know any of them?"

"No, of course not."

"Then you can't trust them."

"Well, I wasn't about to go home with any of them or anything, and I had my own car, so no one could drive me home—"

He interrupted. "Have you ever heard of date-rape drugs?"

That silenced her. Shocked, she stared at him. "You mean . . . those men—"

"I don't know, and you don't either. That's my point. When you go out like that, don't let anyone bring you a drink except the waitress. Better yet, go to the bar and get your own. Don't leave your drink on the table while you dance, or go to the bathroom, or for any reason. If you do, then don't drink out of it again. Order a fresh one."

"Wh-what would it taste like? If someone doctored my drink, I mean."

"You couldn't taste it, not mixed in a drink."

"My goodness." She put her hands in her lap, upset to think that one of those nice men she'd danced with the night before might have deliberately drugged her so they could take her some place and have sex with her while she was unconscious. "Then— how would I tell?"

"Generally, you can't. By the time you start feeling the effects, you aren't thinking straight. It's better to always go to a club with a friend, so you can look out for each other. If one of you starts acting sleepy or dizzy, then the best thing to do is get to an emergency room. And for God's sake, don't let any of the men you've met drive you anywhere."

Dismayed, Daisy tried to think of a friend who would go with her to nightclubs. None sprang to mind; not that she didn't have friends, but they were all married with families, and going out to a nightclub without their husbands so she could meet men just wasn't the type of thing any of them would do. Her mother and Aunt Jo were both single, but . . . no, that didn't bear thinking about.

"There are several date-rape drugs," he continued. "You've probably heard of Rohypnol, but the one that really has cops concerned is GHB."

"What's that?" She'd never heard of it.

He gave her a grim smile. "Floor stripper mixed with drain cleaner."

"Oh, my God!" Aghast, she stared at him. "That would kill you!"

"In a large enough amount, yeah. And it doesn't take all that much, sometimes, because you never know how hard it's going to hit you."

"But—wouldn't it burn your throat when you swallowed it?"

He shook his head. "Nope. With an overdose, what happens is you go to sleep and just don't wake up. If it's mixed with alcohol, the effect is enhanced and even more unpredictable. If a guy slips you GHB, basically he doesn't care if you die or not, so long as he can fu—ah, have sex with you while you're still warm."

Eyes wide, Daisy stared at the pretty countryside. To think things like that were going on in the world! He'd shone a far different light on the club scene, and she would never look at it the same way again. But if she didn't get out and mix, how would she ever meet single men? She chewed her lower lip while she pondered the situation, but the bottom line was, going out dancing at the clubs was the most efficient way to accomplish her aim. She would just have to be extra careful, and follow all his instructions.

"I'll be careful," she said fervently. "Thank you for warning me." It was very nice of him to go out of his way to warn her about the dangers she could face, nicer than she had expected of him. Maybe she'd been too harsh in her criticism, just because he was a bit brusque and too frank in his language.

He slowed down as they neared a church, then turned around in the parking lot and headed back toward Hillsboro. "When are you going out again?" he casually asked.

Gratitude only went so far. "Why?" she asked, her tone loaded with suspicion.

"So I can warn all the men to wear athletic cups, why else?" He sighed. "It was just a question, to make conversation."

"Oh. Well, of course I wouldn't go out on Sunday, or on a work night, so I suppose it'll be next weekend. I need to work on my house, anyway, so I can get moved in."

"You're moving?"

"I'm renting a place on Lassiter Avenue."

He slanted a quick look at her. "Lassiter? That isn't a great neighborhood."

"I know, but my choices were limited. And I'm going to get a dog."

"Get a big one. A German shepherd would be good. They're intelligent, loyal dogs, and would protect you from Godzilla himself."

German shepherds were the ones used in the K-9 units, so she supposed that was how he was acquainted with them. The dogs must be reliable and trustworthy, or police departments wouldn't use them.

She tried to form a picture of herself sitting in an easy chair reading while a big dog dozed at her feet, but the image just wouldn't form. She was more of a small-dog type person; a terrier, maybe, would be better than a huge German shepherd. She'd read that small dogs were just as likely to frighten away a burglar because they barked at the slightest noise, and really all she wanted was an alarm system, not an all-out counteroffensive. Terriers were good at sounding the alarm. Or maybe she'd get one of those cute little Maltese, with a little bow tied in its topknot.

She mentally debated the merits of various small dogs on the drive home, and was surprised when he pulled to the curb in front of the house. She blinked for a moment at the minivan parked behind her car in the driveway, then recognized it.

"You have company," Chief Russo observed.

"My sister Beth and her family," Daisy said. They visited at least twice a month, usually on Sunday after church. She should have been expecting them, but it had totally slipped her mind.

As she reached for the door handle, Aunt Jo came out on the porch. "Y'all come on in," she called. "You're just in time for homemade ice cream."

Chief Russo was out of the car before Daisy could tell him he didn't have to stay. When he opened the car door for her, she sat where she was, staring up at him with huge eyes. "Well, come on," he said impatiently. "The ice cream's melting."

"This isn't a good idea," she whispered.

"Why?" he whispered back, but his eyes were gleaming.

"They think you're . . . that we're . . ."

"Courting?" he helpfully supplied as he literally tugged her out of the car and began pushing her up the sidewalk.

"Don't joke about it! You know what gossip's like in a small town. Besides, I don't like misleading my family."

"Then tell them the truth, that I wanted to warn you about the dangers of date-rape drugs."

"And give my mother a heart attack?" Daisy said fiercely. "Don't you dare!"

"Then tell them we're just friends."

"Like they'd believe *that.*"

"Why's it so unbelievable?"

"It just is." By that time they had reached the front door, and he opened it for her, ushering her inside. There was a small foyer, with the big living room immediately opening off to the left. The tangle of voices died away as they came inside, and ice-cream bowls were set down with a clatter; Daisy felt as if a hundred people were staring at her, though of course it was only her mother and Aunt Jo, Beth and Nathan, and her two nephews, William and Wyatt. She was so seldom the focus of all eyes that even a little attention felt like a lot.

"Um . . . this is Chief Russo."

"Jack," he said, crossing to shake hands first with her mother, then Aunt Jo, as Daisy introduced them. Nathan rose to his feet when it was his turn, his hand extended, but his eyes narrowed in that expression men wore when they felt the need to protect their families. Why he should feel protective of *her,* Daisy had no idea.

Chief Russo must have been used to testosterone-driven displays, though, because he didn't acknowledge it by so much as the flicker of an eyelid.

"Let me get you some ice cream," Evelyn said. "It's just vanilla, but I can put some walnuts and fudge sauce on it if you like."

"Vanilla's my favorite," the chief said so sincerely that Daisy would have believed him even if she had known differently. He didn't seem like a vanilla type of person, but she wasn't about to argue. The faster he ate his ice cream and left, the better it suited her.

Beth wasn't paying any attention to the chief; she was staring at Daisy, her eyes wide and a little dazed. "You're blond," she said weakly. "Mama said you'd lightened your hair, but . . . but you're *blond.*"

"You're pretty," ten-year-old Wyatt said, almost accusingly. He was at the age when he didn't like girls, and finding his favorite aunt turning into one was upsetting.

"I'm sorry," she apologized. "I'll try to do better."

"I like it," eleven-year-old William said, giving her the shy smile that would slay female hearts in another few years.

"And you're wearing *jeans!*" Beth almost wailed. She herself was wearing very chic walking shorts with a matching top, but the Daisy she knew had seldom worn slacks and hadn't even owned a pair of jeans.

"I went shopping," Daisy said uncomfortably as everyone, including the chief, looked her up and down. "And I got my ears pierced." She indicated the small hoops, hoping to draw their attention upward.

"I think you look great," Nathan said, smiling at her. She loved her brother-in-law, but she wished that he were a little more sensitive to Beth's mood right now, because Beth was more than a little shocked by her sister's transformation.

Beth was not, however, a selfish person. She managed a smile, then got to her feet and hugged Daisy. "You look great," she said as Evelyn returned to the living room with two bowls rounded high with creamy white ice cream.

"Yes, she does," Evelyn said, smiling at both her daughters and handing the bowls to Daisy and the chief.

"So," Aunt Jo said brightly, "how long have you two been seeing each other?"

"We're not—" Daisy began, only to be overridden by a much deeper voice.

"A week or so," said the chief.

TEN

Jack laughed out loud as he drove away from the Minor residence; teasing Miss Daisy was becoming the highlight of his life. She responded to the least provocation as if he'd touched her with a cattle prod. When he'd said they'd been seeing each other for a week or so—which was, strictly speaking, true—she'd jumped and stared at him with undisguised horror before blurting, "We have *not*," in such appalled tones he'd had the urge to check his reflection in a mirror to see if he'd suddenly sprouted horns and a forked tail. Except for his ex-wife, he'd never had any complaints from a woman before, so Daisy's reaction pissed him off a little. And even his ex had never complained in bed. What was Miss Daisy's problem?

Then she'd turned beet red and began trying to explain things. "We're just friends—well, not really. I mean, he's a Yankee. He was at the club with me last night—not *with* me, just there at the same time—so when the fight started—"

"Fight?" A harmony of voices echoed the word. Her mother and aunt looked horrified, her sister looked stunned, her brother-in-law was alarmed, and the two nephews were fascinated.

"I didn't start it," Daisy said hastily. "Not exactly. It wasn't my fault. But the chief—"

"Jack," he put in.

She gave him a harried glance. "—Jack carried me out, and today he came by to tell me about date-rape drugs and . . . oh, dear," she finished, her odd-colored eyes widening as she realized her nephews were listening with sharp attention.

"Drugs," her mother said faintly, going pale. The bowl of ice cream wobbled in her hand.

Daisy took a deep breath and tried to be reassuring. "I didn't see any. And I'll be careful."

"What's wrong with being a Yankee?" Jack had demanded, his eyes shining with delight that he tried to hide.

She began spluttering again as she realized she'd been rude—in public, which seemed to be a big thing to her. "Well . . . nothing, except for—I mean, you aren't exactly . . ." Her thoughts evidently hit a wall, because her voice trailed off.

"I thought we were friends." He managed to keep a straight face and look solemn, even a little hurt. He wasn't exactly what? Her type? He'd go along with that. She was a naive prude, and he was a cop; enough said.

"You did?" she asked doubtfully, as he dug into his ice cream to distract himself. The cold, soft ice cream melted on his tongue, and he almost groaned with delight. There was nothing—*nothing*—like real homemade ice cream.

He swallowed and said, "Sure. You even gave me the mauve gay test. You don't do that to someone who isn't a friend."

Her family was listening in wide-eyed fascination. Both her

mother and aunt gasped. "Oh, my," her aunt Joella said faintly. "Did you pass?"

He rubbed his jaw to hide his grin. So this was where she got it from. "I don't know. If you know the answer, does that mean you pass or fail?"

Aunt Joella blinked. "Well—neither, I guess. It just means you're gay." She paused. "Are you?"

"Aunt Jo!" Daisy moaned, covering her eyes with her free hand.

"No, ma'am." He took another bite of ice cream. "But that isn't a good test, because I know what color mauve is."

Aunt Jo nodded decisively. "Just what I thought. How about puce?"

"Daisy made me look it up in the dictionary," he said, unable to hide his grin any longer. "I accused her of making it up."

Aunt Jo leaned back, satisfaction written on her face. "I told you," she said to Daisy's mother, Evelyn.

Poor Daisy had taken her hand down and was looking around as if searching for the best escape route. Jack forestalled her by grabbing her arm and pulling her down with him onto the love seat, which was the only free seating left in the room, making him wonder if her mother had arranged things so they'd have to sit side by side. If so, it was fine with him.

He stayed for almost an hour, making small talk and eating another bowl of ice cream while Daisy swirled her spoon in hers until it melted. She kept giving him wary looks and trying to inch away. Very protective of her personal space, was Miss Daisy. He deliberately intruded on it, letting his thigh brush hers, sometimes leaning so that his big shoulders crowded her, occasionally putting his hand on her bare arm. She couldn't tear a strip off his hide in front of her family the way she had in the library, and he took full advantage of what Aunt Bessie would have called her "company manners."

By the time he left, Miss Daisy was almost ready to explode.

Well, let her fume, he thought as he drove home. So she didn't like him, huh? She didn't consider him a friend, she'd been horrified at the idea that he might be "courting" her, and she was plainly appalled at the idea her family might think they were even going out together.

Too fucking bad, he thought cheerfully. Part of it was because he couldn't resist a challenge and part of it was because she was so damn much fun, but he'd made up his mind: this particular Yankee was going to get in her pants.

He had the feeling she'd be a real firecracker when she let go. Daisy wasn't frozen; she was just untried. If she'd ever had sex, she hadn't had much of it. He planned to change that state of affairs and really give her something to blush about.

He hadn't had a steady relationship since his divorce; he'd had sex, but been careful not to let a routine develop with any of the women. Relationships were a lot of work, and he hadn't been interested enough to make the effort. Until now, that is. Daisy was both innocent and complicated, naive and knowledgeable, sharp-tongued but without an ounce of malice in her—something that couldn't be said about many people. She appealed to him, with her different-colored eyes, old-fashioned ways, and utter openness. Daisy not only didn't play games, she didn't know what the games *were*. A man would always know where he stood with her. Right now he was on her shit list, but he planned to change that.

Unless he missed his guess, Daisy was looking for a man. All the signs were there: the sudden change in her hair and clothes, wearing makeup, and suddenly going to nightclubs. If a man was what she wanted, she needed to look no further. He volunteered for the job. Not that he was going to tell her; she'd likely run as fast as she could in the opposite direction. No, he'd have to play his cards close to the vest for a while, until she got over the idea he wasn't her type.

Until then, he'd have to keep her out of trouble, which could be a full-time job. Now he'd not only have to cruise the bars and nightclubs looking for some bastard who liked to slip women a drug that could kill them, he'd have to make certain Daisy didn't let some other man get too close to her, much less drug her. The way she'd spruced herself up, that might be a problem. She looked good as a blonde, especially with that sexy new haircut. As for her clothes—who would ever have suspected she'd been hiding a pair of breasts like that under those frumpy blouses she'd always worn before? Plus she had great legs; he wasn't the only one who'd noticed them the night before, either. He had plans for those legs; he bet they'd look fine draped over his shoulders.

He'd thought she was kind of cute even before, not that he'd ever have noticed her if he hadn't sat so close to her in the library. But that close he'd been able to tell how fine and translucent her skin was, almost like a baby's, and he'd noted those strange eyes, one blue and one green. It made her gaze oddly piercing, as if she saw deeper than others did. And she'd been downright pretty when she got angry, with color in her cheeks and her eyes snapping and sparkling. He'd planned to stop by the library more often—and then he'd recognized her at the Buffalo Club last night and damn near trampled several people in his rush to get to her before she got hurt in the brawl, not to mention get her out of that jerk's lap.

She was definitely going to be trouble, but he could handle it—with pleasure.

Sykes was pissed. Mitchell had been at the Buffalo Club over near Huntsville last night, but by the time Sykes had got there, he was long gone and sheriff's deputies were swarming the place, sorting things out after a brawl. It was just bad luck, but he was still pissed; if he'd gotten there half an hour sooner, everything would have been handled and Mitchell would be out of their hair.

At least he knew Mitchell was out moving around now, instead of staying holed up somewhere. That increased the chances of getting a line on him, but Sykes still wasn't having any luck. The bastard was slicker than he'd thought, though not slick enough not to kill the merchandise in the first place.

But the bartender at the Buffalo Club, who had called him in the first place, owed him more than one favor. When Sykes showed up on his doorstep on Sunday, he wasn't happy, but he wasn't surprised, either.

"Hey, I called you as soon as I saw him," Jimmy said, darting his eyes from side to side as if worried about someone seeing them together. "But some idiot started a fight just right after that, and everybody cleared out."

"No problem," said Sykes. He wasn't here to make things rough on Jimmy. "Did you notice if he was with someone?"

"Not that I saw, but he bought two drinks. A beer for himself, and a Coke."

So old Mitchell had already hooked up with a girl, or was at least trying to; and since he'd failed, presumably, because of the brawl, he'd be out looking again as soon as possible. Not tonight; bars were closed on Sunday. But tomorrow night, for certain. Would he go back to the Buffalo Club so soon? Maybe, if he wanted that particular girl, but what were the odds the same girl would be there on Monday night? She'd have to be real dedicated to the club scene. Still, it was possible.

"Keep an eye out for him tomorrow night," Sykes said. "I don't think he'll be there, but he might, and it should be easier to spot him than it was this weekend." That gave Jimmy an excuse for not seeing Mitchell earlier.

Jimmy grinned, at ease now that he knew Sykes wasn't mad.

"You think? We're pretty busy all the time, but, yeah, this past weekend was really crowded."

Sykes passed him a folded hundred-dollar bill, with Ben's face showing. "You were on your toes, but you can't predict when a fight will start." A little palm grease was always welcome. Of course, when Mitchell "disappeared," Jimmy would have to go too, but those were the breaks. A smart man didn't leave loose ends.

A black Ford Explorer pulled into Todd Lawrence's driveway, and an older man got out. He strode up the sidewalk and mounted the steps; the front door opened before he reached the porch. "So how'd it go last night?" Todd asked as he led the way to the kitchen, where a pot of strong coffee had been freshly brewed.

"She's a good dancer," the older man said neutrally. He had graying brown hair and brown eyes, and an average build. He could and did blend in almost anywhere.

"Anybody come on to her?"

The man snorted. "Men were all over her. They wouldn't have paid nearly as much attention to her if she'd been dressed like the others, in jeans and a tube top. It was like Grace Kelly had walked in." He opened a cabinet door and took down a coffee cup, then filled it.

Todd grinned. That was exactly the effect he'd aimed for in Daisy's makeover. He was rather proud of his work. "Anybody buy her a drink?"

"She didn't have time to drink anything. She hit the dance floor and danced several dances; then a fight started right after that and some big guy grabbed her and carried her outside."

Todd's eyes narrowed. "Did you follow them?"

"Of course I followed," the other man said testily. "That's the idea, right? But this guy just put her in her car, and she drove off alone."

"Did you recognize him?"

The man shook his head. "He hadn't danced with her, but they knew each other. They had a little argument outside. I couldn't hear what they were saying, but you could tell she was mad at him." Taking his cup to the table, he pulled out a chair and sat down. "This isn't a good idea," he said flatly.

"I agree." Todd picked up his own cup and leaned against the cabinet while he sipped. "But it's better than no idea at all. And she's perfect; she's so naive she won't be as careful as most women are."

"Most women *aren't*. Damn it, you can't keep tabs on every move she makes. What's she going to do, ask your permission every time she goes out?"

"I'll start calling every day, just to check on her. Girl talk." Todd gave a thin smile, and the other man snorted. "She'll tell me if she's going out, and I can guide her to the places we suspect."

"And you really expect to find out something?"

"It's like fishing. You can't see the fish, but you know they're there. You just throw out the bait and hope something bites. Look, she was going to do this anyway. At least this way, you can keep an eye on her."

"I do have a life, you know. Going out every night and stomping my way through line dances isn't something I'm crazy about. I might miss an episode of *Millionaire.*"

"I'll tape them for you."

"Fuck you."

"In your dreams, sweetheart."

The other man burst out laughing. "God, you're good! That was just right. Look, why don't we just concentrate on the job we were sent down here for, and leave your little private vendetta to the local cops?"

"Because they haven't accomplished shit. This isn't interfering with the job—"

"The hell it isn't. I'm not at top speed if I've been out dancing into the wee hours every night."

"It won't be every night; just the weekends, if I read her right. She's too responsible to go out on a work night. Besides, she'll be busy getting her house ready to move into; she tells me all about it."

"Any man who thinks he knows what a woman will do is a fool."

"I'll give you that, but I told you, I'm going to call her every afternoon about the time she gets home from the library, just to check. I don't want anything to happen to her, either."

"So what happens if we get contacted when she's going out, Pygmalion? Who's going to watch her then?"

"We've been working this job for, what, a year and a half? What are the odds it's going to break anytime soon, and on one of the two nights a week when Daisy is most likely to go out?"

"Look, buddy, there's this big pile of shit just flying around looking for a place to happen. Just be prepared for it to dump on us, is what I'm saying. And she'll be the one who's hurt."

ELEVEN

It occurred to Daisy she needed to do one last thing to change her image, so during her lunch hour on Monday she went to Clud's Pharmacy and bought some condoms.

Clud's was the best choice of the three pharmacies in town, because Cyrus Clud had lived in Hillsboro forever and knew everyone, and his wife, Barbara, worked as the cashier so he wouldn't have to pay anyone else a salary. Barbara Clud was at least as big a gossip as Beulah Wilson, and she didn't know what the word *discretion* meant; that was how it had become common knowledge that a certain city councilman took Viagra. The fact that Daisy Minor had bought condoms would spread far and wide to their circle of acquaintances.

Cruising nightclubs was fine, and nightclubs were probably the richest hunting ground, but Daisy didn't want to ignore the available men in Hillsboro, either; in fact, a local would be a much better choice for her, since she wanted to live near her family. The problem was, she didn't know that many single local men; the few in her church were all younger than she was, and she didn't find them particularly interesting anyway. Hank Farris was single, but the Farrises were trashy and there was a reason why Hank had never been married: he stank. Badly. So Daisy didn't count him as eligible, in any way.

But people talked, especially in a small town like Hillsboro with its spiderweb of acquaintances and kin. Just let someone say, "You know Evelyn Minor's daughter, Daisy? The librarian? I hear she went into Clud's and bought a whole *case* of condoms. My lands, what's that girl up to?" Before she knew it, interested men would be crawling out of the woodwork. She'd have to weed out the undesirables, of course, but she figured a big portion of them would disappear when they found out she had no intention of actually *using* any of the condoms. They were merely a conversation piece, as it were.

On the other hand, she had never suspected buying condoms would be complicated. She stood in aisle five and stared at the stacks and rows of boxes. Who on earth knew there were so many choices? And what did the sexually hip young woman buy these days?

For instance, was something called a Rough Rider desirable or not? Daisy thought probably not, because that sounded like something a motorcycle gang would buy, assuming Hell's Angels wore condoms. And what about ribs? Did it matter if a condom was ribbed or unribbed? Lubricated or not? On second thought, she opted for lubricated.

And on third thought, Cyrus Clud had an enormous selection of condoms, far more than she would have expected for a small, independent pharmacy. Surely condom sales couldn't be that brisk, since one could find them in so many other places.

She picked up a pack labeled "Tickle Her Fancy," read the back, and hurriedly returned it to the shelf. Maybe Cyrus had a niche clientele. Maybe she needed to warn Chief Russo to keep a close eye on aisle five at Clud's Pharmacy, because judging by the variety offered here, there were some hinky things going on in Hillsboro.

At last, desperate, she picked up a box called the PartyPak— that should cover all bases—and marched up to the register, where she plunked the PartyPak down on the counter in front of Barbara Clud.

"I hope everything's all right with Evelyn and Joella," Barbara said sweetly as she picked up the box, which was her way of priming the pump to find out if anything was wrong with anyone; then she noticed what she was holding and gasped. "Daisy Minor!"

Someone came up behind her. Daisy didn't look around to see who it was. "Cash," she said, as if Barbara had asked, and fished some bills out of her wallet to hurry along the process before half of Hillsboro lined up at the register. She had thought she would be able to accomplish this with an air of sangfroid, but she could feel her face heating. One would think Barbara had never sold condoms before, from her expression of shock.

Barbara began to turn red, too. "Does your mother know about this?" she whispered, leaning forward in an effort to keep their conversation private. Thank goodness for that much, at least, Daisy thought.

"Not yet, but she will," Daisy mumbled, thinking the phone lines would be burning as soon as she walked out of the store. She extended the money, trying again to just get this process completed.

"I'm in a hurry," said a deep, grumbly voice behind and above her, and Daisy froze. "Just ring the damn things up."

She couldn't have moved if she'd wanted to. She knew that voice; she'd heard it much too often lately. If she could have, she'd have vanished on the spot.

Barbara's face took on a purple hue as she scanned the bar

code, the register chirped, and a total appeared in the little window. She took Daisy's money, silently handed back the change, and shoved the PartyPak into a white paper sack emblazoned in red with the words *Clud's Pharmacy*. Daisy dropped the change into her purse, took the paper sack, and for the first time in her life left a store without saying thank you to the person who had waited on her.

To her absolute horror, Chief Russo didn't buy anything, just fell into step beside her. "What are you doing?" she hissed as they stepped onto the sidewalk. "Go back and buy something!" Maybe the redness of her face could be attributed to the heat rising in waves off the sidewalk. Maybe he wouldn't notice she was mortified.

"I don't need anything," he said.

"Then why did you go inside in the first place?"

"I saw you go in and I wanted to talk to you. Condoms, huh?" he said, eyeing the paper sack with interest. "That looks like a big box. How many are in it?"

"Go away!" Daisy moaned, marching down the sidewalk with the PartyPak clutched to her chest. When she had hit on the plan of buying condoms to get men to notice her, she hadn't meant *him* and she certainly hadn't meant *now*. She had a half-hysterical vision of a line of men following her down the street, trying to peek into her sack. "She thought I was buying them for you!" By now at least one person, perhaps two, had heard the news of Chief Russo and Daisy Minor buying a huge box of condoms. The chief had even said he was in a hurry! She swallowed another moan.

"I can buy my own condoms, thank you," he said.

"You know what I mean! She thought they were for *us*—that we . . ." She trailed off, unable to give voice to the idea.

"We'd have to be rabbits to use that many on our lunch hour," he observed. "I don't think it's possible. How many are in there, six dozen or so? That's seventy-two, so even if we had the entire hour, that means, roughly, using one about every fifty seconds." He paused and looked thoughtful. "That isn't the kind of record I want to set. One every hour, or every two hours, that would be different."

She actually felt faint with shock, though she supposed it could be from practically running in the noonday heat. With his longer legs, he was pretty much at his normal stride; he wasn't even panting.

Not that she was panting; she didn't want to even think about panting while he was talking about using a condom every hour. She was breathing fast, that was all.

"You're overheating," he said. "Let's stop in the Coffee Cup for something cold to drink, before you pass out on the sidewalk and I have to carry you."

Daisy whirled on him and said with muffled outrage, "She's probably already called my *mother,* and goodness knows who else, telling everyone that we bought a PartyPak of condoms on our lunch hour!"

"Then the best thing for you to do would be to go to the Coffee Cup with me so we'd have witnesses that we didn't go to my house and do our best to use them all. PartyPak, huh?" He grinned. "I bet there's an interesting variety. Let me see."

"No!" she shrieked, turning away when he reached for the sack.

He stroked his jaw. "There's probably an ordinance on the books against having pornographical items on the street."

"Condoms are not pornographical," she said, the bottom dropping out of her stomach. "They're birth control and health-aid items."

"Plain condoms, yeah, but there are probably some weird things in something called a PartyPak."

Daisy chewed her lip. He wouldn't arrest her; she was almost certain of it. On the other hand, this entire expedition had gotten out of hand so fast she was still reeling, and she wasn't ready to push her luck. Silently she handed over the sack.

He didn't just open the sack and look inside; he reached in and pulled out the PartyPak, right there on the street. Daisy looked around for a manhole to dive into, though any hole would have done. She'd made it half a step away from him before he seized her arm and hauled her back, all without looking up from the label on the back of the box.

" 'Ten different colors and flavors,' " he read aloud. "Including 'bubble gum, watermelon, and strawberry.' " He glanced up and clicked his tongue. "I'm surprised at you, Miss Daisy."

"I didn't know about the watermelon," she blurted, suddenly afraid there was a green-striped condom in the PartyPak box. This had been a terrible idea. Maybe Barbara would refund her money, unless there was a rule against letting people return condoms. You weren't supposed to return swimsuits and underwear, so Barbara might throw her out of the store if she tried to return the PartyPak.

"If I were you, I'd worry more about the bubble gum," he said absently, still reading.

She blinked, taken aback. "Oh, I wouldn't *blow* them," she said, then clapped her hand over her mouth and stared at him with wide, horrified eyes.

"Shut up," she said furiously a few minutes later, when he showed no signs of stopping laughing. He was all but *howling*, leaning weakly against a parked car and still clutching the box of condoms as he bent over to brace his hands on his knees. Tears were running down his face. She wished they were tears of pain.

No, she didn't; she didn't want to hurt anyone, even him. But enough was enough, and she wasn't going to put up with this another second. If he wanted to arrest her, he'd have to stop laughing to do it, because she was leaving, and taking her PartyPak with her.

He held up his left hand to ward her off as she approached, evidently thinking she was going to hit him, though that didn't stop the chortles and wheezes. Daisy snatched the box away from him and said, "Adolescent!" in her most freezing tones, and marched away.

"W-wait!" she heard him gasp. "Daisy!"

She didn't stop marching, or even turn around. Fury propelled her all the way across the square to the library and up the two marble steps to the front door. She paused there, taking deep breaths in an effort to appear composed, then breezed through the door and up to the checkout desk as if she were Miss America. It was only when she reached out to raise the counter barrier that she realized she held the PartyPak in her hand, and there was no white paper sack covering it.

Kendra was behind the desk, and of course she immediately looked at what Daisy was carrying. Her eyes popped open so wide, white showed all the way around the irises. "Daisy! What—" She stopped, remembering where they were and that she should lower her voice. She pointed mutely at the box.

Everything else had failed her, so Daisy tried for nonchalance. "This?" she asked, lifting the box as if she couldn't understand Kendra's reaction. "It's just a box of condoms." Then she sailed into her office, shut the door, and collapsed in her chair.

"I hear you bought some condoms," Todd said on the phone that evening, his amusement clear even through the telephone line.

"You, my mother and aunt, half the church, and all of the neighborhood," Daisy said, and sighed. After all, that had been her plan. Sort of.

"And that you and our illustrious chief used half the box during lunch hour."

"I went straight back to the library!" she wailed. "I *knew* that's what Barbara Clud would say, the gossiping busybody! He wasn't with me; he just came up while I was checking out."

"She also said he didn't buy anything, said he was in a hurry, and left with you."

"This is going to ruin everything." She sighed and sat down at the breakfast table, having taken the call in the kitchen. Her mother and Aunt Jo were watching television, as usual.

"How's that?"

"If everyone thinks Chief Russo and I are having a—a thing—"

"An affair," Todd supplied.

"—then no other men will come near me! How am I going to find a husband if no one will ask me out because they think the chief of police wouldn't like it?"

"I can see where that would be a problem. He's a big bruiser."

"Well, that takes care of all the local men, so I bought those condoms for nothing."

"I'm not certain I understand. Are you saying only local men could use them?"

"Oh, I'm not planning on *using* them. I knew Barbara would get the word out I'd bought them, and then some of the single men in town would find out I'm available, and modern, and things like that, and they'd be interested enough to at least check me out. That's how it worked in theory," she said glumly. "In reality, the chief ruined everything. Now I'll have to concentrate on the nightclub men."

"Are you going out tonight?" he asked.

"No, there's too much to do getting my house ready. Buck Latham is finished painting, so now I have to clean and look for furniture, buy appliances, that sort of thing."

"What style of furniture are you looking for?"

"Well, the house is small, so I'm aiming for cozy and comfortable. Whatever style that is, that's what I want."

"Does it have to be new? Or would you like some individual older pieces? We can pick those up at auctions for a fraction of what you would pay in a furniture store for something new."

The idea of saving money always interested Daisy. "I've never been to an auction. Where is one, and when?"

"Everywhere, and always," he drawled. "I'll find one for tomorrow night, and we'll have that house decorated before you know it."

Daisy moved into her little house on Friday, after a whirlwind of preparations that left her no time to fume about the way Chief Russo had sabotaged her condom plan. She was so busy she didn't really mind the way some people whispered behind their hands when they saw her. This was the twenty-first century, after all; it was no big deal to buy condoms, even in Hillsboro. A lot of people did, or Cyrus Clud wouldn't carry such a large supply.

For the most part, she didn't have time to think about anything except the herculean task of moving. She had never let herself buy things to put away for when she got married and had her own home, because that would have been like admitting she wasn't satisfied with her life. Well, she *wasn't* satisfied, but now she was admitting it—and doing something about it.

She still wasn't married, but she had her own house. So what if it was a tiny rental in a run-down neighborhood? It had a fenced backyard, she was going to get a dog, and it was her very own place. Unfortunately, because she'd never bought any household things beyond her own bed linens, that meant she had to endure some shopping marathons to get stocked up on the thousand and one items needed to set up housekeeping.

She bought curtains and cookware, stocked up on groceries and household items, bought brooms and a vacuum cleaner and a dust mop—her own vacuum cleaner! She was ecstatic—and worked every spare hour cleaning and getting things put away.

When she wasn't doing that, Todd kept her busy looking for furniture. She was a little surprised but deeply grateful that he exhibited such interest in her new life, because his aid was invaluable. He took her to a couple of auctions, and she discovered the joy of simply nodding her head until her competitors for any certain piece gave up and dropped out of the bidding; then she'd hold up a numbered card and the lamp or the rug or the end table would be hers. Winning gave her a thrill, so much so that Todd watched her with amusement whenever she decided to bid on a piece.

"You're like a shark going after raw bait," he said lazily, smiling at the color in her cheeks and the sparkle in her eyes.

She immediately blushed. "I am? My goodness." She folded her hands in her lap as if to keep them from flashing that little numbered card again.

He laughed. "Oh, don't stop. You're having more fun than I ever do."

"It *is* fun, isn't it?" She eyed the tea cart being offered for sale. She didn't have much room, and if she bought everything she liked, she wouldn't have room for the necessities, such as furniture. On the other hand, the tea cart would look wonderful in the corner of the living room, with plants on top of it and maybe photographs on the lower shelves . . .

Several minutes of furious bidding later, the tea cart was hers—along with a cozy little table and two chairs, a pair of lamps with translucent pink bases and creamy shades, a dark sage green rug, a big, squashy easy chair that rocked and was upholstered in dusty blue with cream pinstripes, and a small cabinet for her television. When they were ready to leave, Todd looked over her booty and said, "I'm glad we borrowed a pickup; that big chair would never wedge into the trunk of your car."

"It's wonderful, isn't it?" she said blissfully, already imagining herself curled up in it.

"It certainly is, and I know just the piece to go with it. It's new, I'm afraid," he said apologetically. "But it's a perfect sofa, I promise."

The perfect sofa was covered with the most impractical cabbage roses on a dusty blue background that very nearly matched the blue of her big chair. She considered the sofa outrageously expensive, but fell in love with it on sight. No drab brown upholstery for her, no sir! She wanted the cabbage roses. And when everything was arranged in her little house, the effect was even cozier than she had imagined.

Friday night, Daisy's little house was full of people and furniture and boxes.

Evelyn and Beth and Aunt Jo were sorting things out, putting boxes in the rooms where the contents would go but not unpacking them, because if they did, Daisy wouldn't know where anything was. Todd was putting the finishing touches on the decoration, hanging some prints, helping her arrange the furniture just so, and providing some much-needed muscle for the heavier pieces. Her clothes were in the closet, the curtains were all hung, her books were in the bookcase, food was in the refrigerator—everything was ready.

The house was a testament to what could be accomplished when some very determined women—and one antiques dealer—worked at it. Neighbors had been pressed into service moving her bedroom furniture over; the local appliance store had delivered and installed her stove, refrigerator, microwave, and washer and dryer the same day she bought them. She thought, considering the money she had spent, same-day delivery was the least they could do.

Evelyn had prepared a pot roast and brought it over for Daisy's first real meal in her own home. Daisy put her mother and Aunt Jo at the tiny table she'd bought, and she, Beth, and

Todd sat on the floor, laughing and talking the way people do when they've accomplished something herculean.

"I can't believe it," she said, unable to stop beaming as she looked around her kitchen. "All of this has happened in only two weeks!"

"What can I say?" Todd drawled. "You're a slave-driver." He took another bite of roast and sighed with delight. "Mrs. Minor, you should open a restaurant. You'd make a fortune."

"I already have a fortune," she said serenely. "I have my family, and I'm healthy. Everything else is just work."

"Besides," Beth said, "I'm just now getting over the shock of how Daisy's changed her looks. Give me a little while before you start turning my mother into a food mogul."

They all laughed, because after her stunned reaction on Sunday, Beth had been as enthusiastic as everyone else about Daisy's improvements. Evelyn had been greatly relieved, because she'd worried about her younger daughter's ego. Beth was a Minor, though, and the Minor women were made of stern stuff. Besides, Beth and Daisy truly loved each other and had always gotten along.

"I'll give you a few months to adjust," Todd said. "But I'm not giving up; food like this needs to be shared."

"And paid for," Aunt Jo said, pursing her mouth.

"That, too." He looked around, then said to Daisy, "I hope you changed the locks on the doors."

"That was the first thing I did. Actually, Buck Latham did it for me. I have two keys, Mother has an extra key, and the landlady has a key. I wasn't about to leave the old locks on the doors."

"And she's getting a dog," said Aunt Jo. "As a matter of fact, I have a friend whose dog had a litter several weeks ago. I'll check with her and see if she still has any of the puppies."

A puppy! Daisy felt a little spurt of delight. Somehow she'd only thought of finding a grown dog, but she'd love to have a puppy and raise it from babyhood.

"A puppy," Todd said, frowning a little. "Wouldn't a grown dog be better?"

"I want a puppy," Daisy said, already imagining the feel of the warm, wriggling little body in her arms. Okay, so it was probably transference from wanting a baby of her own, but for now a puppy would do just fine.

Todd lingered as the others were leaving, pausing on her front porch. "Are you going dancing tomorrow night?"

She thought of everything that needed to be done in the house; then she thought of the long hours she'd already put in this week. Last week at the Buffalo Club had been fun, at least until the fight started.

"I think I will. I really liked the dancing."

"Then be careful, and have fun."

"Thanks. I will." She smiled and waved at him as he drove away, thanking her lucky stars she'd found such a good friend as Todd Lawrence.

TWELVE

Saturday night was always the busiest night of the week at the Buffalo Club, so Jimmy, the bartender, wasn't sure how long Mitchell had been there before he saw him, holding a beer and leaning over a redhead with enough makeup on her face to cover the San Andreas Fault. The redhead didn't seem impressed; she kept turning back to her friend, an equally made-up platinum blonde, as if they were trying to carry on a conversation and Mitchell was intruding.

Jimmy didn't look at them again; the last thing he wanted was for Mitchell to notice he'd been noticed. Since Mitchell had a beer, he must have had one of the waitresses bring it to him, instead of bellying up to the bar the way he usually did. Jimmy picked up the phone under the bar, punched in the number, and said, "He's here."

"Well, damn," Sykes said genially on the other end of the line.

"I really need to talk to him, but I can't get away. Oh, well, another time."

"Sure," said Jimmy, and hung up.

Sykes broke the connection, then quickly called two men he knew and said, "Meet me at the Buffalo Club, forty minutes. Come prepared."

Then Sykes himself got prepared; he pulled on a baseball cap to hide his hair, boots to make himself seem taller, and stuffed a small pillow inside his shirt. In good light this effort at disguise would be obvious, but at night those small things would be enough to make it difficult to identify him if anything untoward happened at the club. Sykes didn't plan on doing anything at the club; he just wanted to get Mitchell and take him someplace where there weren't a couple of hundred potential witnesses, but something could always go wrong. That's why he wasn't driving his own car; he had borrowed one again, just in case, then replaced the license plate with one he'd taken off a car in Georgia.

Barring any unforseen occurrences, such as another brawl, their little problem with Mitchell should be taken care of tonight.

Daisy found that it took a lot of nerve to go back into a club where one had accidentally caused a brawl. There shouldn't be too many people who actually knew the cause: herself, Chief Russo, perhaps the guy whose testicles she had smashed—though she thought he hadn't been paying much attention to what was going on around him—and maybe one or two perceptive people who had been watching. So, five at the most. And what were the odds any of the four other people were here tonight? She should be perfectly safe; no one was going to point at her as soon as she walked in the door and shout, "That's her!"

That's what logic said. Logic, however, had also told her buying condoms would be no big deal, so logic obviously was not infallible.

So she sat in her car in the dark parking lot, watching couples and groups and singles enter the Buffalo Club, which was swinging. Music poured out every time the door was opened, and she could feel the heavy beat of the bass drum throb even through the walls. She was all gussied up, without the nerve to go inside.

But she was working on it; every time she gave herself a pep talk, she got a little closer to actually opening the car door. She was wearing red, the first red dress she'd ever owned in her life, and she knew she looked good. Her blond hair still swung in its simple, sophisticated style, her makeup was subtle but flattering, and the red dress would make all the tube-top wearers look low-class, which was kind of a redundancy. The dress was almost like a sundress Sandra Dee would have worn back in the early sixties, with two-inch wide straps holding it up, a scooped neckline—but not too scooped—a slim fitted waist, and a full skirt that stopped just above her knees and swung around her legs when she walked. She was wearing the taupe heels again, and the gold anklet glittered around her ankle. That and her earrings were the only jewelry she wore, making her look very cool and uncluttered.

She didn't just look good, she looked great, and if she didn't get out of the car and go inside, no one except herself would ever know it.

On the other hand, it might be best to let the place get completely full, to lessen the already small chance that someone might recognize her.

She drummed her fingers on the steering wheel. She could feel the music, calling her to get on the dance floor and just *dance*. She'd loved that part of the night, loved the rhythm and feeling her body move and knowing she was doing it right, that the lessons she'd taken in college had paid off because she still knew the steps and men evidently loved dancing with someone who could do something other than stand in one place and jerk. Not that country nightclubs were much into the jerking; they were more into line dances and slow-swaying stuff—

"I'm stalling," she announced to the car. "What's more, I'm very good at it."

On the other hand, she had also always been very good at obeying the time limits she set for herself. "Ten more minutes," she said, turning on the ignition to check the dash clock. "I'm going inside in ten minutes."

She turned the switch off again and checked the contents of her tiny purse. Driver's license, lipstick, tissue, and a twenty-dollar bill. Taking inventory didn't occupy more than, say, five seconds.

Three men came out of the club, the light from the overhead sign briefly illuminating their faces. The one in the middle looked familiar, but no name sprang to mind. She watched as they walked across the crowded parking lot, wending their way through the roughly formed lines of cars and trucks. Another man got out of a car as they neared, and the four of them headed toward a pickup truck parked under a tree.

Another car pulled into the parking lot, the lights slashing across the four standing near the pickup. Three of the men looked toward the new arrival, while the fourth turned to look at something in the bed of the pickup.

A man and a woman got out of the car and went inside. The music blared briefly as the door opened, then receded to a muffled throb when it closed. Except for the four men under the tree and herself, there was no one else in the parking lot.

Daisy turned on the ignition switch again to check the time. She had four minutes left. That was good; she didn't really want to get out of the car and walk across the parking lot by herself, not with those four men standing there. Maybe they would leave. She turned off the switch and glanced up.

One of the men must have been really, really drunk, because two of the men were now supporting him, one on each side, and as she watched, they hefted him into the bed of the pickup, supporting his head as they did so. That was good; they weren't letting him try to drive home in his condition, though from the looks of him, he'd already passed out. All three of them had seemed to be walking okay when they left the club, but she'd heard of people who walked and talked okay up until the very second they passed out. She'd always thought that was so much malarkey, but there was proof of it, right before her eyes.

The two men who had helped their friend into the bed of the pickup got into the cab and drove off. The fourth man turned and walked back to his car.

Daisy checked the time again. Her ten minutes were up. Taking a deep breath, she took the keys out of the ignition, dropped them into her little purse, and got out, automatically hitting the Lock button as she opened the door.

" 'Cannon to the right of them, cannon to the left . . .' " she quoted as she marched across the parking lot, then wished she had thought of something else, because the Light Brigade had perished.

Nothing happened to her, however. She wasn't shot out of the saddle, nor did anyone point at her as soon as she opened the door. She stepped inside, paid her two dollars, and was swallowed up by the music.

Glenn Sykes sat in his car, his eyes cold and burning as he watched the woman walk into the club. Where in hell had she come from? She had to have been sitting in one of the cars, and in the dark they hadn't noticed her.

It wasn't whether or not she had seen anything, but how much she had seen, and how much she realized. It was dark, details were difficult to make out, and there hadn't been any loud noises to alarm her. If Mitchell hadn't tried to call out to the couple who had driven up, there wouldn't have been anything for her to see. But, hell, as soon as he'd seen Sykes get out of the car, he'd known they were going to kill him, so what did he have to lose? Sykes didn't blame the bastard for giving it a try. Too bad Buddy was greased lightning with that knife; Mitchell hadn't gotten out more than a squeak.

She didn't know them; she evidently hadn't noticed anything unusual going on. But she was a loose end, and Sykes didn't like loose ends. His original plan had been to pour enough GHB down Mitchell's throat to kill three men, which had seemed like a fitting end to the bastard. He'd even decided to leave the body where it would be found before the GHB broke down so the cops would know exactly what killed him, and they'd think it was just another overdose. He couldn't do that now, not with that gash in Mitchell's throat, plus there was blood in the parking lot if anyone cared to look.

If she was a regular here, she might have recognized Mitchell, might know him—and might remember way too much when she heard his throat had been slashed.

He hadn't seen which car she got out of, but he could narrow it down. He got out of his car and walked over to that section of the parking lot, squatting down out of sight and quickly jotting down the tag numbers. He thought about going into the club and trying to find her. She had blond hair and had been wearing a red dress; he'd seen that much when the door opened. She should be easy to spot.

But he'd told Jimmy he couldn't get free tonight, and now that Mitchell was dead, he didn't want to show up after all, thereby placing himself at the scene of Mitchell's last known whereabouts.

Sykes sighed. He'd have to sit out here and wait for the

woman to leave, then follow her home. He needed to be overseeing the disposal of Mitchell's remains, but he couldn't be in both places at once. He'd just have to trust Buddy and his pal to be smart about where they dumped the body. After all, their asses were on the line, too. Taking care of the woman would have to be his priority.

The Buffalo Club was, if anything, even more crowded than it had been the week before. Daisy stood for a moment, letting her senses adjust to the overwhelming noise of voices and the band singing very loudly about someone named Earl needing to die, a song that a good many of the female customers were singing along with the band. Some man, probably named Earl, took exception to the song and hurled his beer at the band, which explained the chicken wire encircling the stage. Two very big men converged on the beer-hurler, and Daisy was pleased to see him escorted to the door. She'd just gotten here; she wanted to get in at least a few dances before a fight started.

"Hey, sweetheart, remember me?" a man said, appearing beside her. An arm went around her waist and she found herself being propelled toward the crowded dance floor.

She looked up at the tall blond man, who was trying to grow an Alan Jackson mustache. "No," she said.

"Aw, come on. We danced last week—"

"No," she said positively, "we didn't. I danced with Jeff, Denny, Howard, and Steven. You aren't any of them."

"You're right about that," he said cheerfully. "I'm Harley, as in the motorcycle. Well, if we didn't dance last week, let's dance this week."

Since they were already on the dance floor, that seemed like a good idea. Earl had died and the band was singing something else, which didn't require half the audience to shout the lines along with them. People were twirling and dipping, so Daisy twirled and dipped right along with them, her hand in Harley's, her sassy skirt swirling around her legs. Next came Elvis Presley's "Kentucky Rain," and Harley retained possession of her hand for that number.

"Say, what's your name?" he asked, finally remembering that he didn't know.

"Daisy."

"Are you with someone? Can I buy you a drink?"

Oh, gracious, was he one of those men about whom Chief Russo had warned her? "I'm with some friends." She gestured vaguely toward the tangled cluster of tables, because that still seemed like a safe lie. She added, "Thank you, but I don't want anything to drink right now. I came to dance."

He shrugged. "Fine with me. I think I'll sit this one out." He wandered off as abruptly as he had appeared, and Daisy looked around. So far, not counting the man whose testicles she had smashed, she had met six different men, and not one of them had really appealed to her. Maybe she was being too picky; though, really, she didn't see how; she had danced with everyone who had asked her.

She saw Howard on the dance floor, and he waved. Maybe he would ask her to dance again; he'd been the best dancer of the bunch.

Then—oh, no—she saw him: the burly guy who had pulled her down onto his lap. He spotted her at about the same time and a horrified expression crossed his face before he turned sharply away.

She wanted to do the same thing, turn away and pretend she hadn't seen him, but her conscience gave a sharp twinge. He shouldn't have grabbed her and she hadn't meant to hurt him, but nevertheless he had been in a great deal of pain and she owed him an apology.

Determinedly she began fighting her way through the crowd, trying not to lose sight of him. He seemed to be heading just as determinedly toward the men's room, for all the world as if he intended to hide from her, though of course she had to be mistaken in her impression. He was at a club, he'd probably been drinking beer, so it stood to reason he had to urinate.

He made it to the short hallway leading to the bathrooms before she caught up to him, however, and disappeared through the scarred door as if the hounds of hell were after him. Daisy sighed and squirmed through a knot of people, ignoring both a protest (female) and an invitation (male); she felt like a salmon fighting its way upstream. At last, though, she managed to reach the wall near the bathrooms, where she planted her feet against all the nudges and shoves, and waited.

It seemed to take forever, and she had to refuse three offers to dance, before her quarry peered out from the hallway.

Taking a deep breath, she stepped forward and tapped him on the shoulder.

For a big guy, he sure could jump.

He backed away from her as if she were the Antichrist, his beefy face turning red. "You stay away from me, lady."

Daisy was taken aback; the man honestly seemed afraid of her. She blinked, then tried to reassure him. "Don't be afraid," she said as soothingly as possible. "I won't hurt you. I just wanted to apologize."

Now it was his turn to blink. He stopped backpedaling. "Apologize?"

"I'm very sorry I hurt you. It was an accident. I was just trying to get out of your lap, and I put my hand in the wrong place. I truly didn't mean to crush your—" My goodness, she couldn't say *balls,* though that seemed to be the most popular term, and neither did she want to call them his *things,* because after all she was trying to be more sophisticated about such matters. "—testi-cles," she finished, with more emphasis on the word than she'd intended.

He flinched as if she'd hit him, and she realized she'd said the last word loudly enough that, despite the noise from the band, the people nearby had heard her and heads were turning.

His face turned redder. "Apology accepted," he mumbled. "Just go away."

Daisy felt he could have been a little more gracious, considering the entire episode was his fault anyway; if he hadn't grabbed her, as if he had the right to pull strange women down onto his lap, then none of it would have happened. A touch indignant, she opened her mouth to tell him so, but abruptly a tall form materialized by her side and a deep voice said, "I'll keep her away from you."

And just like that, willy-nilly, Chief Russo picked her up much as he had the last time she was here and carried her, not outside, but onto the dance floor.

"You are just like a heat rash," she said irritably as he set her down.

One eyebrow rose in query. "I bother you?" He took her right hand in his, set her left hand on his shoulder, and put his arm around her. "Dance."

"You turn up *everywhere.*" Automatically she followed his lead to the slow rhythm of another Elvis song. The band was very big on Elvis tonight, though perhaps this wasn't the same band that had been here the week before.

"Someone has to keep you out of trouble."

"Out of trouble? *Out* of trouble?" She tilted her head back and glared at him. Even though she was wearing heels, she still had to look up. As Todd had pointed out, Chief Russo was a big bruiser. "Thank you for getting me out of here last week, but other than that, you've been the *cause* of all the trouble I've had."

"Don't blame me. I wasn't the one buying a year's supply of rubbers. Used any of them yet?"

Words failed her. Or rather, polite words failed her. She thought of several she wanted to say, but was afraid God would strike her dead if she did.

He grinned. "If you could see your face . . ." His arm tightened around her and he swung her in a circle, forcing her to cling to his shoulder. Somehow she ended up much closer to him than she had been before, closer than she had danced with any of her other partners. Her breasts brushed his shirt, she felt the slide of his hip, and his legs moved against hers. They were—my goodness, one of his legs was between hers.

A rush of heat caught her unprepared. She felt as if she were melting on the inside, softening, her bones losing their stiffness and her muscles their tension. It was the most peculiar sensation, but also the most beguiling.

"Chief—"

"Jack." His arm tightened a little more, as if insisting she use his name.

"Jack." She really *was* melting. She was all but lying against him now, her feet still moving, following his lead, but he supported most of her weight. "You're holding me too close."

He bent his head so his breath fanned her ear when he said, "I think I'm holding you just right."

Well, he was, if he liked melty women. And perhaps her protest had been more pro forma than sincere, because she wasn't making any effort to pull away. It felt too good to lie against him, the softness of her body conforming to the hard contours of his. Her breasts were slightly flattened against his chest, and she liked it. She liked it a lot. To her bemusement, she found herself reveling in the hard strength of the shoulder under her left hand, in the warmth of the arm around her waist. Warm . . . God, yes, he was warm. His heat and musky scent enveloped her, making her want to rub her nose against him.

She wanted to rub her nose against *Jack Russo?*

The shock of the thought gave her the strength to lift her head. He was watching her with a strangely intent expression; he didn't look stern, but neither was he smiling.

"What's wrong?" she asked, her voice unaccountably low.

He shook his head. "Not one thing."

"But you look—"

"Daisy. Shut up and dance."

She shut up and danced. Without the distraction of conversation she started sinking against him again. He didn't seem to mind, though. If anything, he gathered her even closer, so close she could feel his belt buckle against her stomach.

That wasn't all she could feel.

Her mind was still reeling from the realization that she could feel the chief of police's penis when the dance ended and the band swung into a lively little number about Bubba shooting the jukebox. Jack grimaced and led her from the floor, keeping a tight grip on her as he maneuvered his way through the crowd to a spot near the back wall, almost behind the band, which was probably why there were a couple of empty seats there. He all but plunked her in one, looked around at the scurrying waitresses, and said, "Stay here. I'll get you something to drink. What do you want?"

"Ginger ale with lemon, please."

He grinned and shook his head, then left her there while he waded into the throng around the bar.

Daisy, in a slight state of shock, stayed. Perhaps she was even more naive than she'd suspected, because he didn't act as if there was anything unusual in his partner feeling his penis while they danced. Maybe that was *why* people danced together. But she hadn't noticed any other penises when she danced, just Jack's.

She would never again be able to think of him as chief.

She had no idea how long he was gone, because she was lost in her thoughts. As luck would have it, no one asked her to dance until she saw Jack approaching, a beer in one hand and a glass of sparkling ginger ale in the other.

"Want to dance?"

The question came from a man leaning over from her left. He was wearing a "Party Hearty" T-shirt, so she would have refused anyway, but she didn't get the chance. Jack set the ginger ale on the table in front of her and said, "She's with me."

"Okay." The guy immediately turned to another woman. "Want to dance?"

Jack settled into the chair beside her and tilted the beer to his mouth. She watched his strong throat work as he swallowed, and began to feel too warm again. Gratefully she seized the cold ginger ale.

After a moment she noticed how his gaze constantly moved over the crowd, occasionally pausing briefly while he studied someone, then moving on. She felt another little shock of awareness, of a completely different type. "You're working, aren't you?"

He shot her a quick glance, the gray-green of his eyes glittering. "I don't have any jurisdiction outside of Hillsboro."

"I know, but you're still watching the crowd."

He shrugged. "It's a habit."

"Don't you ever just relax?" Abruptly her whole outlook on law enforcement officers changed. Were they all always on guard, watchful, wary? Was constant vigilance, even when they were off duty, part of the price they paid for their jobs?

"Sure," he said, leaning back and hitching his right ankle onto his left knee. "When I'm at home."

She didn't know where he lived, couldn't picture his home. Hillsboro, though a small town, was still large enough that it was impossible to know everyone or be familiar with all the neighbor-hoods. "Where do you live?"

Again that quick glance. "Not all that far from your mother's house. Elmwood."

Elmwood was just four streets over. It was a section of Victorians, some in good repair and some not. She certainly hadn't pictured him in a Victorian, and said as much.

"I inherited the house, from my great-aunt. Aunt Bessie, the one I told you about."

She sat upright. She had known a Bessie on Elmwood. "Miss Bessie Childress?"

"That was her." He lifted his beer in salute to his dead great-aunt.

"You're Miss Bessie's nephew?"

"Great-nephew. I spent the best summers of my life with her when I was a kid."

"She brought over a coconut cake when Daddy died." Daisy was stunned; this was almost like going to Europe and running into your next-door neighbor. She had thought Jack a complete outsider, but instead when he was a boy he'd been spending summers just four streets away from her.

"Aunt Bessie made the best coconut cake in the world." He smiled, reminiscing about coconut cakes he had known.

"Why didn't I ever meet you?"

"For one, I only came during the summer, when school was out. For another, I'm older than you; we wouldn't have hung out with the same crowd. You would have been playing Barbie while I played baseball. And Aunt Bessie went to a different church."

That was true. Miss Bessie Childress had been solidly Methodist, while the Minors were Presbyterian. So it was logical they hadn't met when they were children, but it still gave her a jolt to realize he was . . . why, he was almost home-folk.

There was a sudden disruption in the flow on the dance floor. A man sprawled on the floor, making couples scatter. A woman screamed, "Danny, *no!*" Her shrill voice cut through the loud music, which crashed to a discordant stop. The man who had fallen—or been knocked down—jumped up, lowered his head, and plunged toward another man, who swiftly sidestepped and bumped into a woman, sending her sprawling. Her partner took immediate exception, and the dance floor erupted.

"Aw, shit." Jack heaved a sigh and grabbed her wrist, hauling her to her feet. "Here we go again. C'mon, we'll go out the back."

They joined the pack of bodies that was doing the same thing, but again Jack used his size and strength to bull his way through, and in just a moment they were in the humid night air, listening to the sound of shouts and breaking glass coming from inside.

"You're a catalyst," he said, shaking his head.

"This wasn't my fault," she said indignantly. "I wasn't anywhere near those people. I was sitting with *you.*"

"Yeah, but it's just something about you being here, like the universe is out of whack. Believe it or not, most nights there isn't any trouble at all. Where's your car?"

She led the way around the building to her car. People were pouring out of the front entrance, too. It was like an instant replay of the week before.

She sighed. She'd danced only three dances this week. At the rate things were going, next time she'd be lucky to get in one dance before the fight started.

When she got her car key out of her purse, he took it from her, unlocked the door, then opened it for her before returning the key. He watched, his expression inscrutable, as she buckled her seat belt and reached for the door handle to close the door.

He stood in the way, frowning a little now. "I'll follow you home."

"Why?" Her surprise was plain.

He shrugged. "Because I just got an itch between my shoulder blades. Because I heard you've moved and I don't like the street. Just because."

"Thanks, but it isn't necessary. I left the porch light on."

He bared his teeth in a grin that wasn't a grin. "Humor me," he said, and it wasn't a suggestion.

THIRTEEN

Son of a *bitch!* When people started pouring out of the club like ants, Sykes would have pounded the steering wheel in frustration if it wouldn't have gained him attention he didn't want. What was it with these people? Couldn't they go to a god-damn dance without fighting?

He didn't like getting out of the car, but he did it anyway, searching in the turmoil for blond hair and a red dress. The scurrying crowd blocked his view of the section of the lot where she'd parked, so he worked his way in that direction, craning his head for a glimpse of her. In the dark, with people darting in every direction and headlights briefly slicing across the scene as cars left, the effect was almost like having a strobe light flashing.

Then he saw her, walking calmly across the gravel as if she'd just left a wedding instead of a brawl. He sidestepped as a car went by just inches from his toes, but never took his gaze off his quarry. Then he halted, swearing to himself. She had gone inside alone, but she came out with company, in the form of a guy who looked like he ate rocks for breakfast. Sykes was close enough to hear him say, "I'll follow you home," and he immediately swerved away, lingering only long enough to note which car was hers, so he could match it to one of the tag numbers and makes of car he'd written down. Okay, so he couldn't follow her home tonight; three cars would make a damn parade. But he had her tag number now, so essentially he had *her*. Swiftly returning to his car, he glanced down the list and immediately saw the description he wanted: eight-year-old Ford sedan, beige—which was a pretty blah car for a woman with such sexy class—with a 39 prefix on the license plate, meaning the car was registered in Jackson County.

That made it easy. He'd give the number to Temple Nolan, who could have someone in his police department run it. He could have the woman's name and address within a matter of minutes from the time he talked to the mayor.

On the other hand, it was smarter to play it cool. If the mayor called his P.D. tonight, whoever he talked to would remember the license plate that was so important that the mayor had wanted it checked late on a Saturday night. It was always best not to call attention to yourself, even in the smallest detail. Monday morning would be plenty of time.

Everything was cool; nothing had to be done tonight. Waiting might even be better, give him time to make sure there were no mistakes. This really should be easy; the elements were already there. She did the bar scene, and he had a supply of GHB handy. She'd be just another overdose, and since he had no intention of having sex with her, the cops would write her off as a user who tossed the dice one too many times.

* * *

Daisy pursed her lips as she glanced in the rearview mirror. The headlights behind her were way too close: Jack was tailgating her. She might have known he would. The man was constantly crowding into her personal space, and she didn't know if he did it just to annoy her or if that was his working style, to keep people off balance. She did know she didn't like it.

She slowed, looking for a safe place to pull off the road, and turned on her blinker. By the time she got her car stopped, Jack's car was tucked in behind hers so closely she couldn't even see his headlights, and he was opening her car door before she could find the switch for the emergency flashers.

"What's wrong?" he demanded.

"I'll tell you what's wrong," she began, then said, "My goodness." He had a gun in his hand—a big one, held down against his leg. It was an automatic, probably a nine millimeter. She leaned over and peered at it. The night-sights on the barrel glowed despite the light coming from her car. "My goodness," she said again. "Those little suckers are bright, aren't they?"

He looked down. "What little suckers?" He was examining the ground as if he expected to find glow-in-the-dark ants.

"Your night-sights." She pointed at the weapon. "What kind is it? An H&K? A Sig?" In the dark, and with it in his big hand, she couldn't tell.

"It's a Sig, and what in hell do you know about handguns?"

He certainly was grouchy. "I helped Chief Beason research handguns when he wanted to upgrade the weapons the department carries. That was before your time," she added, just because she knew it would annoy him. Chief Beason was his predecessor.

Sure enough, she saw his jaw clench. She could almost hear his teeth grind. "I know who Chief Beason is," he growled.

"He was very thorough. We spent *months* looking at all the

models. In the end, though, the city council didn't vote the money to buy new weapons."

"I know." His teeth were definitely grinding. "I had to take care of that when I came on board, remember?" That had been his first act, to raise hell with the city council because they had let their police department become woefully outgunned. He'd gotten the weapons he wanted, too.

"To be fair," Daisy said, "at that time the city was spending a lot of money on the sewer system—"

"*I don't give a fuck about the sewer system!*" He shoved his hand through his hair—or he would have, if it had been long enough. Daisy thought he really should let it grow a little. He drew a deep breath, as if struggling for control. "What's wrong? Why did you stop?"

"You were tailgating me."

He stood frozen in her open car door. Another car went by, its tires whooshing on the pavement; then the red taillights disappeared around a curve and they were alone on the road again.

"What?" he finally said. He sounded as if he were strangling.

"You were tailgating me. It's dangerous."

There was another long moment of silence, then he stepped back. "Get out of the car."

"I will not." So long as the car was running and she had the steering wheel in her hands, she was in control. "You were wrong and you know—"

The sentence ended in a squeal as he leaned in, swiftly un-clipped her seat belt, and hauled her out of the car. Embarrassed by the squeal, because she thought she'd outgrown such noises, she was too distracted to be alarmed as he slammed the door and backed her against the car, his big body leaning in and pinning her to the cold metal. It was like being caught with fire on one side and ice on the other, and the fire was strongest because she immediately felt that peculiar internal melting again.

"I have two choices," he said conversationally. "I can either strangle you, or I can kiss you. Which one do you want?"

Alarmed at the prospect that he might kiss her, she said, "Those are your choices, not mine."

"Then you shouldn't have worn that red dress."

"What's wrong with my dress—*uummph.*"

The rest of her indignant sentence was smothered by his mouth on hers. Daisy went still, her entire system thrown into a weird kind of suspended animation as her mind struggled to adjust expectation with reality. No, not expectation, because she'd never expected Jack Russo to kiss her. Such a thing was not on her mental list of Possible Happenings. Yet he *was* kissing her, and it was the most amazing thing she'd ever felt.

His lips were soft in touch, and firm in application. She could taste the beer he'd drunk, and something else . . . something sweet. Honey. He tasted like honey. One big fist was twined in her hair, holding her head tilted back, while he leisurely kissed her deeper than she'd ever been kissed before, his tongue in her mouth, and the honey taste of him dissolved her bones and turned her internal organs to mush.

She slowly went limp, held upright only by the pressure of his body all along hers. Vaguely she was aware that nothing in her life had ever felt as good, or as comfortable. It shouldn't have been comfortable, not with the cold metal of the car behind her, but she lifted her arms and twined them around his neck, and her body fit to his as if they had been custom-made to go together. Curves and mounds, angles and planes—they fit. The heat of his body seared her all the way through, the scent of his skin permeated her, and his honey taste beguiled her into wanting more, needing, demanding more. And he gave her more, holding her even closer, so that her hips cradled his pelvis and the ridge of his erection rode hard against the juncture of her thighs.

Another car went by, horn blaring. Jack raised his head long enough to mutter, "Bastard"; then he kissed her again, more of those deep, hungry kisses that fed her own hunger. Her heartbeat hammered wildly against her breastbone. Part of her mind—a tiny, distant part—was astonished that this was happening to her, that she was actually standing beside a road in the dark letting a man kiss her as if he intended to strip her naked and take her right there, standing up, in public. And she wasn't just letting him kiss her, she was kissing him back, one hand clasped on the back of his head and the other slipped inside his collar to touch the back of his neck, that small touch of his bare skin making her almost dizzy with delight.

Finally he lifted his mouth, gasping for breath. She clung to him, bereft, needing more of those honey kisses. He rested his damp forehead against hers. "Miss Daisy," he murmured, "I really, *really* want to get naked with you."

Fifteen minutes ago—or maybe it was twenty—she would have told him in no uncertain terms that his attentions were unwelcome. Fifteen minutes ago, however, she hadn't known she was addicted to honey.

"Oh, this is bad," she said distractedly. The man was positively narcotic, and she had never suspected. No wonder so many of the women in town were nuts over him! They'd been tasting him, too. Suddenly she didn't like that idea at all.

"I thought it was damn good."

"It's totally ridiculous."

"But damn good."

"You aren't my type at all."

"Thank God for that. I'd never survive otherwise." He came back for another kiss, one that had her rising on tiptoe and straining to get closer. His right hand closed firmly over her breast, weighing and kneading, unerringly finding her nipple and rubbing it into a tight little point. The sensation splintered through her, making her moan. The sound of her own voice shocked her back into a small measure of sanity; she let herself revel in the feel of his hand on her breast for another few seconds, or twenty; then she dragged her hands from around his neck and braced them against his chest. Oh, goodness, even the feel of his chest was an enticement, so warm and hard with muscle, and with his heart thundering under her palm. Knowing he was just as excited as she, was as heady as her own arousal. She, Daisy Ann Minor, had done this to a man! And not just any man—Jack Russo, of all people!

He'd lifted his mouth as soon as she planted her hands against him. If his hand was slower to leave her breast, she didn't complain. As if every inch were agony, he eased away from her, putting a small space between them. Suddenly deprived of his heat, she felt as if the night had turned icy cold. It was a balmy summer night, but compared to Jack, the air felt almost wintry.

"You're ruining all my plans."

"What plans are those?" He bent his head and began nibbling at her jawline, quick little biting kisses, as if he had to taste her again. He didn't touch her in any other way. He didn't have to. She caught herself automatically leaning toward him, and jerked upright again.

She was distracted enough to say, "I'm hunting for a man."

"I'm a man," he muttered against her collarbone. "What's wrong with me?"

Her neck was getting weak, too weak to hold up her head. It was as if she were Superwoman and he was Kryptonite, robbing her of strength. Desperately she fought back. "I mean a *relationship* man."

"I'm single."

She burst out, "I want to get married and have babies!"

He straightened as if he'd been shot. "Whoa."

Now that he wasn't touching her, she could breathe more easily. "Yes, *whoa*. I'm husband-hunting, and you're getting in the way."

"Husband-hunting, huh?"

She didn't like his tone, but there was an oncoming car; she waited until it had passed before glaring up at him. "Thanks to you and your little show in the pharmacy, everyone in Hillsboro already thinks we have a—a thing, so no one there will ask me out. I *have* to go out to nightclubs now to find a man, but you're still doing the same thing, making people think we're together and keeping other men away from me."

"I've been keeping you out of trouble."

"Last week, yes, but this week I wasn't in any trouble, I wasn't causing any trouble, I wasn't even *near* any trouble. That man you ran off might have been the love of my life, but now I'll never know because you told him I was with you."

"He was wearing a 'Party Hearty' T-shirt, and you think he was the love of your life?"

"Of course not," she snapped. "That isn't the point, and you know it. He was just an example. At the rate you're going, you'll have every man in north Alabama thinking I'm spoken for. I'll have to drive to Atlanta to find someone."

"*Spoken for?*" he echoed, with enough incredulousness in his tone to make her want to smack him. "Do you know what century this is?"

She knew her speech patterns were a little archaic; that's what happened when you lived with your mother and aunt, who were darlings but were definitely old-fashioned. She tried not to use their more dated expressions, but that was what she'd heard most of her life, so that was what came out of her mouth more often than not. She did not, however, appreciate his pointing that out. "It's the twenty-first, smart ass!"

Silence.

"Oh, my goodness," she whispered, hand to her mouth. "I'm *so* sorry. I never say things like that."

"Well, yes, you do," he replied. His voice sounded strained. "I heard you. You just don't say them very often."

"I'm sorry," she said again. "I have no excuse."

"Not even that I made you mad as hell?"

"You did, but I'm still responsible for my own actions."

"God," he said, looking up at the heavens, "why can't all the bad guys be like her?"

God didn't answer, and Jack shrugged. "It was worth a try. C'mon, get back in your car before I kiss you again."

Unfortunately, that wasn't much of a threat. Daisy caught herself hesitating, then resolutely reached for the door handle, to find his hand there before hers. She seated herself, arranged her red skirt just so, buckled her seat belt, then remembered why they had stopped in the first place and narrowed her eyes at him. "Don't tailgate me again."

He leaned forward, his eyes heavy-lidded and his mouth slightly swollen, reminding her what they'd been doing just a few minutes before. "I won't. At least, not in a car."

Her heart skipped a beat, then raced into double time. She licked her lips, trying not to form that image in her mind. It formed anyway. Her nipples tightened and peaked.

"Go!" he said harshly, slamming the door and stepping back, and she went. After a moment his car pulled onto the road behind hers.

He stayed a very safe distance behind her, all the way back to Hillsboro.

FOURTEEN

The next morning Daisy went to church as usual. She knew there had been talk about her during the week, thanks to Jack and the condom episode, and in a small town the best thing to do under those circumstances was to follow her normal routine.

Because she knew people would be watching her, she took extra pains with her hair and makeup; it was funny how fast it had become routine. The Weather Channel said that the day would be hot and humid, with temperatures climbing toward the century mark, so she dressed as coolly as possible, even leaving off her panty hose and dusting the insides of her pumps with baby powder so her feet wouldn't stick to them.

It was already hot, probably almost ninety, at nine-forty-five when she left the house. She turned the air-conditioning in her car on "high," but the church was only two miles away, so the blast of air was just getting cold when she arrived. The church was nice and cool, though, and she heaved a sigh of relief as she entered the sanctuary and took her customary seat beside her mother and Aunt Jo, who both turned to her with beaming smiles. "You look great," Aunt Jo said, leaning over to pat Daisy's hand. "How did last night go?"

Daisy sighed. "I only danced three times," she whispered. "There was another fight. I didn't have anything to do with it," she hastily added when both women's eyes rounded. "But I think I may have to find some other club."

"I should hope so," said her mother. "All those fights!"

It wasn't the fights that disturbed Daisy, but the fact that the Buffalo Club seemed to be Jack's hangout. She was an intelligent woman; she knew better than to borrow trouble, and after last night it was obvious that being anywhere in his vicinity was a big problem. If he went to the Buffalo Club, she would go elsewhere. Period.

Someone slid into the pew beside her, and she automatically turned her head to smile a greeting. The smile froze on her face. "What are you doing here?" she hissed.

Jack looked around at the altar and choir loft, the stained-glass windows, and asked, "Attending church?" then leaned forward to say hello to Evelyn and Aunt Jo. Answering smiles came his way, and Evelyn asked him to come to dinner after services. He pleaded a prior engagement, which saved his toes, because Daisy had been prepared to grind her heel down on his foot if he'd accepted.

Daisy imagined she could feel the gaze of everyone in church centered on her back. "What are you doing here?" she whispered again, more fiercely this time.

He dipped his head closer to hers so he couldn't be overheard. "You didn't want everyone to think you bought condoms for a one-night stand, did you?"

Her eyes widened. He was right. By his coming to church and sitting beside her, everyone would assume there was a full-fledged romance between them, because a man just didn't go to a woman's church and sit beside her unless they were seriously involved. By giving up one morning of his time, he had changed her status from suspect to understandable. In this day and age, a sexual relationship between two romantically involved adults was the expected thing, even if organized religion did frown on it.

Two hours later, Daisy was a nervous wreck. Knowing that the chief of police wanted to get naked with her wasn't conducive to having a peaceful morning at church. She had tried her best to pay attention to the sermon, just in case it was aimed at her, but her attention had kept wandering. Specifically, it had wandered to the man sitting on her right.

Their intimacy of the night before had been startling. Even though they had done nothing more than kiss and a little light petting, it felt as if they had done so much more. She had felt almost incandescent in his arms, and there hadn't been anything halfhearted about his erection. She couldn't lie to herself; they had teetered on the brink of making love, and she had pulled back just in the nick of time.

She couldn't help wondering what would have happened if she'd forgotten her morals, forgotten that he wasn't her type, forgotten everything except satisfying herself. No, she didn't wonder what would have happened, she *knew*—she just wondered what it would have been like.

She couldn't get his taste out of her mind. Would the rest of his lovemaking have lived up to his kisses? He kissed like a dream, and tasted like a honeypot. Even if he were the world's worst lover, which she highly doubted, that would almost be worth putting up with just to get those kisses. On the other hand, going on the theory that a good kisser was also a good lover—she'd read it somewhere—then Jack Russo was something else between the sheets.

Those were not good thoughts to have during a church service. She fidgeted restlessly, and every time she moved, her leg seemed to brush against his. The air-conditioned church was very cool, but she was burning up again and she felt an almost overwhelming urge to kick off her shoes and tear off her dress. Either she was in premature menopause and having hot flashes, or she was hot in a far more basic sense.

She kept sneaking glances at him; she just couldn't help it. He dressed neatly, conservatively. His shoes were always polished, and that was important. After reading an article that said the state of a man's shoes reflected his general attitude about himself and others, she'd always looked at shoes and was careful to keep her own footwear clean and polished.

His graying hair was way too short, but it looked good on him. There was just a hint of curl on top, so she suspected he kept it short to keep that curl tamed. He was big, but there was nothing clumsy about him; he moved with a sort of controlled, animalistic grace. And there was no extra weight on him; she'd discovered that last night. He was all rock-solid muscle.

She was spending way too much time thinking about a man who wasn't her type.

He moved his hand, and the backs of his fingers subtly rubbed against her thigh. Daisy swallowed and stared hard at Reverend Bridges, trying to make sense of what he was saying, but the reverend might as well have been speaking a foreign language.

Jack was seducing her, right there in church, and she knew it. He wasn't doing anything much—though he was still rubbing her thigh—but then he didn't have to. He was there, and that was enough. She was doing a very good job of seducing herself, remembering last night and working herself into a lather.

She had to be blowing this all out of proportion, because logic told her no kiss could possibly be as potent as she'd thought last night. It was just that Jack was the first man to kiss her in . . . she couldn't remember exactly how long. Years. Which was entirely her fault, because she'd been sitting at home instead of getting out and doing something about her unkissed situation. But it had still been *years* since she'd been kissed, and the fact was, she had gone overboard in her reaction. It probably hadn't been nearly as exciting to him.

Then she remembered the way his heartbeat had thundered under her hand, and the only way he could have faked that erection was if he'd had a flashlight stuffed in his pants. A big flashlight.

Oh, dear. These were not good thoughts to be having during a sermon.

At last, at last, the sermon was over and the last hymn had been sung. People milled around, shaking hands, smiling and talking. Jack stood at the end of the pew, blocking her exit, while everyone in the church, it seemed, came over to greet him. Aunt Jo and Evelyn turned around and went out the other end of the pew and Daisy turned to do the same, but without looking Jack reached back and caught her arm. "Hold on a minute," he said, then returned to shaking hands. The men wanted to talk about the police force and feel macho by association; the women merely flirted, even the great-grandmothers. Jack just had that kind of effect on women. Daisy had used to think she was immune, but learned that feeling superior set you up for a big fall.

When the crowd had finally cleared out some and they could make their way out of the pew, Jack stepped aside and let Daisy exit in front of him, his hand going to her waist. Her heart jumped at his touch. He was really getting into the "we're a couple" act for everyone else's benefit, but his main objective was to get naked with her; forget the couple angle. He didn't want to get married and have children—come to think of it, he'd already been married, so he might already have children, too.

There was only one way to find out. She leaned forward and whispered, "Do you have any children?"

He gave her an appalled look. "Hell, no!" Then he remembered where he was and muttered, "Let's get out of here."

That was easier said than done. Reverend Bridges was still at the door, shaking hands and chatting with everyone as they left, and it seemed he had a lot to talk to Jack about. None of it seemed very important to Daisy as she patiently waited her turn, but the reverend was a man just like all the others, and he wanted to talk to the police chief. She wondered if it got on Jack's nerves. No one ever buttonholed her because of *her* job, and she was just as glad. Did all cops have to put up with this?

But at last her hand was shaken and small talk was made; Reverend Bridges gave her a speaking look, making her wonder if the sermon had been targeted toward her, which, after the talk of this past week, was certainly possible. She'd have to remember to ask her mother.

The heat was almost unbearable, rising off the street in waves. Men, Jack included, were shedding their coats and loosening their ties as soon as they left the church; the women, however, were stuck with bras and pantyhose, and Daisy was glad her legs were bare. The slight breeze was hot, but at least she could feel it.

He stripped his tie from around his neck and stuffed it in his coat pocket. "I'll follow you."

"Where are we going?" she asked in bewilderment.

"To your house."

Her heart jumped again. "I always eat Sunday dinner with Mother and Aunt Jo."

"Call them and cancel. You've just moved in; you have things to do."

And one of those things was him, if she was correctly reading the intent look in his eyes. She cleared her throat. "I don't think that would be a good idea."

"I think it's the best damn idea I've had in years."

Swiftly she looked around. The church parking lot was mostly deserted now, with no one wanting to linger in the heat. Still she leaned closer so there was no chance of being overheard. "You know what would happen!"

"I'm counting on it."

"I don't want an affair!" she hissed. "I want a relationship, and you're getting in the way!"

"So until a relationship comes along, have an affair with me." He moved closer, looming over her. As hot as the day was, he was hotter; his heat wrapped around her. His gray-green eyes burned. "I'm healthy. I'm normal, nothing too kinky. I'll try not to get you pregnant."

"*Try?*" she echoed, outraged.

He shrugged. "Things happen. Rubbers break."

That should have been an appalling thought. It wasn't. The fact that it wasn't told her how far gone she was, when not even the thought of an accidental pregnancy could cool her down. And what was—

"What's *too* kinky?" she whispered.

A grin flashed across his hard face. "I'll show you."

The old Daisy would have stormed off in a huff. Well, maybe not, because the old Daisy would have been as powerfully tempted as the new Daisy was. But the old Daisy wouldn't have had the nerve to go with a man for the express purpose of having sex, and the new Daisy couldn't seem to think of anything else. She wanted this man, and she was afraid that if anyone else came along, she wouldn't pay any attention to him because she was too busy obsessing about Jack.

"C'mon, try me on for size," he murmured. "I dare you."

It wasn't the dare that did it; it was the thought of trying him on.

"If you get me pregnant," she said, "you have to marry me."

"Deal," he said, and they got in their respective cars and drove to Lassiter Avenue, with him keeping a respectful distance between their bumpers.

She should have been shaking like a leaf, she thought a few minutes later as she put her key in the lock, but her hands were steady. She was only shaking on the inside, where it didn't count.

Jack stood in the middle of her cozy little living room, looking around, while she went to the phone and called her mother. As usual, she wasn't very good at lying, and when her mother asked her why she wasn't coming to dinner, all Daisy could do was look at him and blurt, "Jack's here."

He grinned.

"Oh!" said her mother, and giggled. Her mother giggled. "I understand completely. You two have fun."

Daisy desperately hoped her mother didn't understand completely, but the way things had been going lately, maybe she did. She put the phone down and said, "She told us to have fun."

"I intend to." He still stood in the middle of the room, making it look even smaller. "Are you hungry? For food," he added, feeling the need to be specific.

She shook her head.

"Good," he said, and reached for her.

She had almost convinced herself she'd imagined how good he tasted, until he kissed her again. She made a little humming sound and twined her arms around his neck, going up on tiptoe to press against him and meet his demanding mouth with demands of her own.

The peculiar melting sensation spread through her again, weakening her knees so that she had to lean against him, let him support all of her weight, and that made the melting spread even faster. Oh, God, he felt good. Her entire body throbbed from the contact. The incredible hardness of his muscles, the heat that practically glowed from him, wrapped her in a cocoon of physical delight that also robbed her of strength and left her totally pliable to his touch.

His arms tightened, and he pulled her even closer, fitting her soft curves to all the hard angles of his body, tilting her so that her pelvis cradled the hard bulge of his erection. She made another little sound, and he deepened the kiss until her breath was no longer her own, until it didn't matter if she breathed or not.

This was desire. This. The heat and need, the deep throb of emptiness, the tension and lassitude and sharp tingles. *This.*

She moaned, her head falling weakly back. He took the opportunity offered, his hot mouth trailing down her throat to close on the exquisitely sensitive juncture between neck and shoulder, scraping the tendon with his teeth, sucking her skin. Her entire body jolted at the wild, uncontained pleasure; her knees gave out completely, but it didn't matter, because he had her safe in his grasp.

His hands moved over her with slow, maddening purpose, stroking her breasts, unzipping her dress and pulling it down and off her arms, then unsnapping her bra and disposing of it. The dress bunched around her waist, unable to drop because there wasn't even a breath of space between their hips. At last his hands were on naked flesh, and he rubbed her nipples into hard, aching points, then tilted her back over his arm and bent his head to suck them. He wasn't gentle, but he didn't have to be. She clasped her hands around his head and held him there, gasping out cries of pleasure as the pressure of his mouth catapulted her to an even higher level of sensation.

She was desperate to feel his skin, and she jerked at his shirt, trying to get it off over his head without unbuttoning it. He raised his head long enough to help her, using only one hand because he didn't release her. They both fought the garment, and a couple of buttons fell to the rug; then it was off and both arms were around her again, her breasts crushed against the crisp hair that rasped her nipples almost as deliciously as his thumbs. She ached all over, the most heated, wonderful ache she'd ever felt in her life. She felt as if her entire body pulsed with need and excitement and desire, even between her legs.

"I thought they were lying," she gasped, barely aware that she was even speaking.

"Who?" he asked against her throat.

"Women. About this."

"This?" He didn't sound very interested. He found that sensitive place on her neck again, and held it with his teeth.

"The way it feels. This."

"How does it feel?" he whispered.

"I . . . throb." She could barely get the words out. "Between my legs."

A rough sound burst out of his throat and a shudder ran through him, his erection pulsing against her. "I'll make it stop," he said, his tone so low and rough the words were barely intelligible.

He slid his hands up her legs, tugging the close-fitting dress up as he went until the fabric was bunched over his forearms and his hands were inside her panties, his hot palms cupping her bottom for a moment, just a moment; then he moved them down, down, his fingers delving into her closed cleft and finding her opening. Daisy gasped, the sound strangling in her throat as her whole body seemed to seize, waiting, frozen in anticipation. Then he pushed two big fingers up into her and all her nerve endings rioted, arching her against him in a mindless search for more. Oh, God. She was stretched, penetrated—and it wasn't enough.

Her hips began to move, surging like the tide. "More," she managed to say, begging, whimpering the word. "More."

She couldn't seem to do anything except cling to him as he stripped her panties down and off, retrieved a condom from his pocket, then kicked off his shoes and fought his way out of the rest of his clothing. Naked, holding her to him, he stumbled back to sit on the couch and pull her over him, arranging her legs so that she straddled his lap. He put on the condom with quick, jerky movements, then grasped her hips and guided her into position.

Abruptly, time slowed. She gripped his shoulders at the feel of his penis probing between her legs, not inside her but nudging, as if enticing her to open and admit him.

Her breath came in quick little gasps; his bellowed out of his lungs. His jaw was set, his neck corded with strain, and yet he remained still and let her set the pace. The wonder of it suffused her. She moved back and forth in a subtle motion, caressing herself with the hard length, lifting and moving and—ah. He slipped into her, just a little, but enough to make him clench his teeth on another rough sound. His fingers bit into her buttocks, then relaxed.

Entranced, the expression in her eyes distant as she concentrated on the sensation of heat and stretching and fullness, Daisy lifted herself once more, settled, and took the broad head fully inside her. Jack groaned, his face twisted as if he were in pain. He shifted so his hips were on the edge of the cushion, stretching out his legs so she could take him at a deeper angle. She rose and fell, her eyes closing, savoring the slow, slow impalement as she squirmed and adjusted and finally, finally, he was completely inside her.

Magic.

That's what it felt like, her body not her own anymore but moving with a will of its own, twisting, seeking. She reveled in his size and nakedness, in the way she felt him deep inside where she had never been touched before. She loved the harsh sounds he made, loved the growing desperation of his grip, loved the increasing tension and heat of her own body as sensation wound tighter and tighter, and she leaned forward to kiss him, as everything suddenly reached critical mass and her senses exploded. The world dimmed around her. She heard herself shrieking and sobbing, felt her hips frantically surging against him; then abruptly she was on her back and he was pounding into her and she climaxed again just moments before he stiffened and heaved in his own orgasm.

In the aftermath she lay limply under his heavy body, comfortable on the overstuffed cabbage rose cushions. The cool air fanned against her sides, while perspiration glued their fronts together. She nuzzled her face against his throat, inhaling his heady, musky scent. He pressed a kiss to her temple.

"You had a condom in your pocket in church," she managed to say weakly, suddenly bemused by the thought.

"Yeah. I kept waiting for lightning to strike." His voice sounded hoarse, as if he could barely speak.

She smoothed her hand down his muscled back, over the coolness of his buttocks. "Did you just have one?" she whispered.

He lifted his head and smiled down at her, his eyes heavy-lidded, his hair dark with sweat. "You still have the PartyPak, don't you?"

FIFTEEN

The afternoon was her dream come true. First he decided he needed sustenance, so she slapped an ice cream bar into his hand and led him to the bedroom. He licked the last bit of vanilla off the stick while she turned back the covers. Then she pushed and he toppled and she jumped on top of him, rubbing herself like a cat against his strong, naked body. She felt his reaction twitching between her legs and curiosity overtook her. She rolled off and knelt beside him, wrapping both hands around his erection and studying it in delight.

Because the afternoon was her dream and she had always wondered, she leaned down and took him in her mouth. He tasted salty and smelled of musk, and she loved the way his penis pulsed and thickened. Entranced, she experimented with licks and swirls, then began investigating the underside leading down to his testicles.

Maybe she was going too fast, because he said, "My turn,"

and dumped her on her back. In a flash he was on her, pinning her down, settling between her thighs. Then he propped on his elbows and grinned down at her. "I'll let you have your way with me later, I promise. Just not right now."

The weight of him was delicious. She squirmed just a little, loving the way his hips fit between her legs and how naturally her thighs had parted for him. The position was wonderful and comfortable and exciting. "Why not right now?"

"Because I want to do it to you, and I'm bigger."

So he did, kissing his way down her body and lingering at all the right places. When he finally worked down to where she really wanted him, she thought she would die from the intensity of her climax. Oral sex was every bit as stupendous as an article in *Cosmo* had said it was, and Jack was very good at what he did. While she was still quivering in the aftermath, he crawled up so that his penis was nudging her again. "Where's the PartyPak? We need it *now.*"

"Let me up," she panted, both exhausted and eager. "I'll get it."

He rolled off, and she staggered to the closet, where she had put the PartyPak on the shelf under the box containing her sea shell collection. She pulled it free and began tearing at the cellophane wrapping. Without looking, she grabbed out a condom and handed it to him.

A peculiar expression crossed his face. "I'm not wearing a purple condom," he said, handing it back.

She looked down at the condom. "It's grape."

"I don't care if it's tutti-frutti; I'm not wearing a purple condom."

She dropped the offending condom on the rug and took out another one. Blueberry. She looked at it and wrinkled her nose, then dropped it.

"What's wrong with blue?"

"It would make you look . . . frozen."

"Trust me, it isn't frozen." But he didn't pick up the blue condom. She took out a cherry one, of a particularly violent shade of red, and shook her head.

"What's wrong with that one?"

"Nothing, if you want to look infected."

"Jesus." He flopped back on the bed and stared imploringly at the ceiling. "Isn't there a nice pink one in there? The bubble gum flavor?"

"I guess that would be the fuchsia," she said doubtfully, taking it out and examining it. She'd never seen any bubble gum that particular shade. She sniffed it; a faint scent came through the wrapper. Definitely not bubble gum, though she wasn't certain exactly what it was. Strawberry, maybe; whatever it was, she didn't care for it. She rooted around in the box, but couldn't find anything that could possibly be bubble gum flavored. "I've been stiffed. There's no bubble gum in here."

"Swear out a warrant tomorrow," he said in growing desperation. "Try the watermelon."

Sure enough, the watermelon condom was green. Daisy gave him an appalled look. "Gangrene."

He lunged off the bed, grabbed the purple condom from the floor, and tore off the clear wrapper. "If you ever tell anyone I wore a purple condom—"

"I won't," she promised, eyes wide; then he tossed her onto the bed and entered her with a quick, hard thrust, and they both forgot about colors.

It was so wonderful being naked with a man that she didn't even think of being modest. She simply enjoyed him and marveled at the pleasure she had been missing all these years, not just the intensity of making love but lying together afterward with her head cradled on his shoulder and his arms around her. She couldn't keep her hands off him; every time she tried, her palms started itching, so she just gave in and stroked him to her heart's content. "You're so hard," she marveled, sleeking her hand down his washboard stomach. "You must work out all the time."

"It gets to be a habit. When you're on the Teams, you have to stay in condition. And it isn't 'all the time'; I maintain with an hour a day."

" 'Teams'?"

"SWAT. In both Chicago and New York."

She propped up on an elbow. "SWAT? You mean the guys who wear black and carry big guns?"

He grinned. "Yeah, one of those."

"And you left that to come to a little town like Hillsboro?"

"I got tired of the pressure. Aunt Bessie died, I inherited her house, and I decided I wanted to try small-town life as an adult."

"No transition problems?"

"Just language problems," he said, and grinned again. "Now I can almost say 'y'all' like a native."

"Uh—no, you can't."

"What? Are you saying my 'y'all' isn't authentic?"

"I suppose it's an authentic Yankee trying to do a southern accent."

Just like that she found herself beneath him again; the man could move like a cat. "How about an authentic Yankee doing a southern woman?" he murmured against her throat.

She looped her arms around his neck. "You've got that down perfect."

He turned his head and looked at the "Froot Loops" array of condoms on the floor. "I don't want to wear purple again. How about the yellow? That would be banana flavored, wouldn't it?"

Daisy made a face. *"Euww. Not yellow."*

Exasperated, he said, "Why did you buy colored ones if you don't like the colors?"

"Oh, I never meant to *use* them," she said, blinking at him. "They were just for show. You know. For Mrs. Clud to tell her friends that I bought them, so they'd tell their friends, and some of the single men in town were bound to hear and be interested enough to ask me out. Then you ruined that by giving her the impression we were involved."

The expression on his face was indescribable. He coughed, strangled a little, and cleared his throat. "That was . . . ingenious."

"I thought so. It wouldn't have worked if I'd bought them at Wal-Mart or a chain pharmacy, but Barbara Clud is one of the biggest gossips in town, and she always tells what their customers bought. Did you know Mr. McGinnis takes Viagra?"

He coughed again, thinking of the bluff and hearty city councilman. "Uh, no, I didn't."

"Mrs. Clud told everyone. So I knew she'd tell about my condoms."

He buried his face against her shoulder, breathing deeply. He was shaking a little, and Daisy snuggled him close. "There, there. It's just small-town life. You'll adjust."

He lifted his head to see the humor sparkling in her eyes, and he gave up attempting to control his laughter. "If I ever need Viagra, remind me not to go to Clud's Pharmacy."

She considered the firmness pressed against her inner thigh. "I don't think you'll need it anytime soon. I didn't think you were supposed to be able to get hard again so fast. All the articles I read—"

He kissed her, and she stopped talking to taste the honey. His eyes were heavy-lidded when he lifted his head. "Maybe I've been inspired. Or provoked."

She took exception to that. "If anyone's been provoking, it's you—"

"*I* didn't buy seventy-two condoms."

She was silent a moment, digesting the meaning behind that;

then a satisfied smile broke across her face. "So my plan worked, didn't it? After a fashion."

"It worked," he said gruffly. "I kept thinking about the bubble gum flavor."

The phone rang, interrupting them. Daisy scowled; she didn't want to talk on the telephone; she wanted to play with Jack. She hesitated long enough that he said, "Answer it. It might be your mother, and we don't want them coming over to check on you."

She sighed and stretched beneath him, snagging the receiver and bringing it to her ear. "Daisy Minor."

"Hello, sweetie. How did the hunt go last night?"

It was Todd, and normally she loved gossiping with him, but not right now. "There was another fight, and I left early. I think I'll go to another club next time." Uh-oh; she hadn't meant to say that in front of Jack. She deliberately didn't look at him.

"I'll ask around, find out which places are best. So there weren't any prospects?"

"Not yet. I only got to dance three times." She turned her head away from the mouthpiece and said, as if she were talking to someone else in the room, "I won't be long. Y'all get started without me."

"I'm sorry, sweetie. I didn't mean to interrupt you while you have company," Todd said instantly. "I'll call back later."

"Oh, no, it's okay," Daisy said, feeling guilty about her little deception but definitely not wanting to talk on the telephone when she could be making love.

"Enjoy your company," he said gently. "Bye."

"Bye," she echoed, and fumbled the receiver back into place.

"Pretending to have company," Jack chided, propping himself on his elbows so he could look down at her. "Slick."

"I do have company. You."

"But you definitely don't want me to get started without you."

"Definitely not."

"So someone else is in on your husband-hunting scheme. Who is it?"

"Todd Lawrence," she said, stroking her hands over his arms and shoulders. "He helped me with my hair and makeup and clothes."

Jack lifted his eyebrows. "Todd."

If she wasn't mistaken, there was the slightest hint of jealousy in his tone. Daisy was thrilled, but at the same time she hastened to say, "Oh, he's gay."

"No he isn't," Jack said, startling her.

She blinked. "Of course he is."

"If it's the Todd Lawrence I know, lives in that big Victorian and owns an antiques store in Huntsville, he isn't gay."

"That's Todd," Daisy said, frowning. "But he's definitely gay."

"He's definitely not."

"How would you know?"

"Trust me. I know. And I don't care if he did pass the puce test."

"He's great at shopping," she said, defending her position.

"Hell, I'm great at shopping, too, so long as you're shopping for a car or a handgun, something like that."

"He's great at shopping for clothes. And he knows how to *accessorize*," she finished triumphantly.

"You've got me there," he admitted. "But he isn't gay."

"Yes, he is! What makes you think he isn't?"

Jack shrugged. "I saw him with a woman."

She was momentarily flabbergasted; then the explanation occurred to her. "He was probably going shopping with her. I'm a woman, and he spent the entire day with me."

"He had his tongue down her throat."

Her mouth fell open. "But—but why would he pretend to be gay if he isn't?"

"Beats me. He can pretend to be from Mars if he wants."

She shook her head, bewildered. "He even likes Barbra Streisand; I saw the CDs in his den."

"Straight guys can like Streisand."

"Really. What kind of music do *you* like?"

"Creedence Clearwater. Chicago. Three Dog Night. You know, the classics."

She buried her face against his shoulder and giggled. He smiled, liking the sound. "I'm a Golden Oldies kind of guy. What about you? No, let me guess: You like the *old* classics."

"No fair. You saw my music collection on the shelves in the living room."

"I was in there, what, a minute, while you called your mother? I didn't examine your music collection."

"You're a cop. You're trained to observe things."

"Give me a break. All I was thinking about was getting in your pants."

"What color is my couch?"

"Blue with big flowers on it. You think I wouldn't notice? We were naked on that couch."

She sighed blissfully. "I know."

"But you're right about one thing: because I'm a cop, I'm very observant. For instance, which club were you thinking about going to next time?"

Drat! He'd noticed. "I don't know," she said vaguely. "I haven't decided."

"Well, when you decide, I expect to know." There was a hard edge to his voice that she hadn't heard before. "I mean it, Daisy. If you're going out alone, I want to know where you are."

She chewed her bottom lip. What if he showed up wherever she went and scared off anyone who asked her to dance? On the other hand, he was right about the safety issue; she had to be intelligent about the matter. Besides, she was in a difficult position, literally: flat on her back, naked, pinned down.

"Promise me," he insisted.

"I promise."

He didn't ask if she would keep her promise; he knew she would. He pressed his forehead against hers. "I want you safe," he whispered, and kissed her.

As usual, one kiss led to another, and soon she was clinging to him, giddy with arousal. She wound her legs around his hips, and with a groan he sank into her, thrusting several times before suddenly cursing and pulling out. He leaned over the edge of the bed and blindly scrabbled for a condom. "I don't care what color it is," he said hoarsely.

Daisy didn't care either, didn't even look. She was shaken that they had almost made love without protection, that even those few thrusts carried a small amount of risk. Then he surged back into her, and she met his fierceness with her own, demanding everything he could give her.

Afterward, exhausted, Daisy dozed cuddled against his side while Jack stared at the ceiling and wondered what in hell Todd Lawrence was up to. Something was going on that made him feel antsy and he didn't like it worth a damn, especially when the uneasiness concerned Daisy. He had damn good ears, and Daisy had been lying under him at the time, the receiver only inches away; he'd heard every word of their telephone conversation. Maybe it was just the instincts of a cop prodding him, because there hadn't been anything he'd heard that he could honestly say struck him as suspicious, but it seemed to him that Daisy was being *guided* to certain clubs. He didn't like that scenario at all.

He'd been in bars and nightclubs every night except for Sundays since talking to Petersen. He'd seen one episode of a possible date-rape drugging—and that had been at the Buffalo Club on

Thursday night, so he'd gone back on both Friday and Saturday to see if he could spot something. As it was, the woman who had possibly been drugged had been with two female friends; Jack had discreetly questioned them, but they had not only allowed men to buy them drinks, they had also left the drinks unattended while they danced or went to the rest room, so there was no telling when or if the drinks had been drugged.

Both of the other women were sober enough to drive, which made him suspect the third woman had definitely been drugged. He helped them get their friend out to the car, quietly told them to get her to a hospital in case someone had put something in her drink, and saw them on their way before going back inside. Everything had been kept very low key; he didn't make a disturbance, didn't identify himself as a cop, because if some bastard was there slipping GHB or whatever into women's drinks, Jack didn't want to scare him off. He simply watched, trying to spot something or at least step in if another woman looked to be in trouble, and the next morning he'd called Petersen to tell him they maybe had a starting place.

Last night had been cut short by the fight, but his heart had almost stopped when he'd seen Daisy on the dance floor. She didn't seem to realize how she drew the eye with the contrast between her classy clothes and the way all the other women dressed; men watched her, and not just because she was a good dancer. They watched those legs, and the sparkling eyes that said she was having a ball. They noticed her breasts, and the way that red dress had clung to their shape. Even now, with her naked in his arms, just thinking about those breasts made his mouth water. His Miss Daisy was stacked; not overblown, but definitely stacked just right.

She wanted a husband and kids. He wasn't in the market for a wife, let alone kids, but he got a burning knot of what he recog-

nized as pure masculine possessiveness at the thought of her actually meeting someone she really liked at one of those clubs,
going out with him, sleeping with him, maybe even eventually
getting married. He didn't like that scenario at all. And when he'd
realized he had entered her without first putting on a condom, for
an earth-tilting moment he had continued thrusting, tempted almost past control at the thought of coming inside her. If he got
her pregnant—hey, he'd marry her. They'd made a deal. Being
married to Miss Daisy would be a hell of a lot more fun than
being married to Heather the Bitch, and look how long he'd stuck
that out.

He knew he was in deep trouble when the thought of getting
married didn't send him running. He glanced down at her sleeping face and gently stroked her bare back. So maybe he'd leave off
a condom and see what happened. Naw, he couldn't do that to
her—unless she showed signs of getting serious about someone
else, in which case he would fight as dirty as necessary to win.

SIXTEEN

The English setter bounded happily through the knee-high weeds, ignoring her owner's shouted commands. She was a young dog, and this was only her second time in the field. He'd been training her in his yard to retrieve, using a variety of lures, and her hunting instincts usually held sway there. In the field, though, her youthful exuberance sometimes got the best of her. There were so many interesting smells to be investigated, the heady scents of birds, mice, insects, snakes, things she didn't know and wanted to follow.

A particularly intriguing odor lingered on the morning air, leading her out of the field and into the woods that lined the field. Behind her, her owner cursed. "Goddammit, Lulu, *heel!*"

Lulu didn't heel, merely wagged her tail and plunged into some underbrush where the scent was stronger. Her sensitive nose quivered as she nosed the earth. Her owner yelled, "Lulu!

C'mere, girl! Where are you?" and she wagged her tail as she
began digging.

He saw the waving plume and fought his way through the
tangle of vines, briars, and bushes that grew under the trees, cursing with every breath.

Lulu grew more excited as the scent got stronger. She backed
up and barked to signal her agitation, then plunged into the
brush again. Her owner picked up his pace, suddenly alarmed, because she seldom barked. "What is it, girl? Is it a snake? Heel,
Lulu, heel."

Lulu grabbed something with her teeth and began tugging.
The thing was heavy and didn't want to move. She dug some
more, dirt flying behind her.

"Lulu!" Her owner reached her and grabbed her collar, pulling
her back, a broken limb in his hand in case he had to fend off a
rattler. He stared down at what she had unearthed and staggered
back a step, hauling her with him. "Jesus!"

He looked wildly around, afraid whoever had done this had
waited. But the woods were quiet except for the breeze rustling
the leaves; he and Lulu had disturbed the birds, and they had either flown off or fallen silent, but he could hear calls and singing
in the distance. No shots disturbed the quiet, and no maniac with
a big knife plunged out of the trees at him.

"Come on, girl. Come on," he said, snapping a leash to the
dog's collar and patting her flank. "You did good. Let's go find a
telephone."

Temple Nolan stared down at the piece of paper in his hand, at
the tag number written there. He could feel the icy finger of panic
tracing down his spine. Someone, a woman, had witnessed
Mitchell's death, though Sykes seemed to think she had either
not been paying attention at all or, in the dark, not understood

what she was seeing, because she had continued calmly into the Buffalo Club.

He tried to believe that Sykes was right, but his gut kept twisting. All it took was one loose thread and someone tugging on it to unravel the whole setup. Sykes should have handled Mitchell himself, instead of taking along those two yahoos for help. They should have waited until he wasn't in a public place before grabbing him. They should have—fuck!—they should have done a lot of things, but now it was too late and all they could do was contain the damage and hope it stopped there.

He picked up his office phone and dialed Chief Russo's extension. Eva Fay answered on the first ring. "Eva Fay, this is Temple. Is the chief in?" He always used his first name; for one thing, it made people feel more cooperative. For another, this was a small town and word would get around that he thought he was better than everyone else if he insisted on using his title. He lived in a big house, belonged to the country club in Huntsville and to Hillsboro's pitiful little excuse for one, he moved in a very exclusive circle, but as long as he still acted like a good old boy, they kept reelecting him.

"Sure thing, Mayor," said Eva Fay.

The chief picked up the line, his deep voice almost like a bark. "Russo."

"Jack, this is Temple." The first name business again. "Listen, on the way in this morning I spotted a car parked in the fire lane over at Dr. Bennett's office. I wrote down the tag number, but I didn't want to cause any trouble for any sick folks by calling a deputy to give them a ticket. If you'll run the tag number for me and give me a name, I thought I'd just give them a call and ask them not to park there again." No one could play the good old boy the way he could.

"Sure. Let me grab a pen." The chief didn't even sound surprised. He was becoming used to their little town. "Okay, shoot."

Temple read off the tag number.

Chief Russo said, "It won't take a minute. Do you want to hold on?"

"Sure."

When the information popped up on the computer screen, Jack stared at it in disbelief. He sat for a minute, his face set in a hard mask; then he printed out the screen and took the sheet of paper back to his office.

He didn't pick up the phone receiver, though. Let the mayor wait.

The car was registered to Dacinda Ann Minor, and the address was the one from which Daisy had just moved. The car was an eight-year-old Ford, so it was definitely her car. He hadn't known her given name was Dacinda instead of Daisy, but, hell, if anyone had named him Dacinda he'd go by Daisy, too.

He didn't know what was going on, but he knew one thing: the bastard was lying. His Daisy would no more park in a fire lane than she would run naked across the square. The woman didn't speed, didn't jaywalk, didn't even cuss.

Not only that, she hadn't been at Dr. Bennett's office this morning. He knew because he'd ended up spending the night, and she'd been fine. Glowing. A big smile on her face. He'd had to swing by his house for a change of clothes, but her car had been in its usual parking slot behind the library when he got to the office.

So who was running Daisy's tag, and why?

He thought fast. He could lie and say it was a stolen tag and did the mayor have a description of the car? Or he could tell the mayor it was Daisy's car and try to find out what was going on.

First Todd Lawrence, and now Temple Nolan. Way too much attention was being paid to one little librarian, and too many details weren't adding up. The niggling uneasiness had turned into a real itch between his shoulder blades.

What were the odds any of the town gossip about him and Daisy had reached the mayor's ears? They didn't move in the same circles. For all his comradery, the mayor didn't socialize much with the townsfolk. He did the official stuff, but not much else. He was good enough at the common touch that most people didn't notice, or they attributed the mayor's absence from certain functions to his wife, Jennifer, who evidently spent most of her time sloshed. Jack had noticed that the mayor used his wife as a convenient excuse a lot of the time.

Jack picked up the phone and went with his instinct. "Sorry to take so long, but the computer is slow today."

"That's all right; I'm in no hurry," the mayor said genially. "So who's the culprit?"

"The name doesn't strike a bell with me. Dacinda Ann Minor."

"*What?*" the mayor said, clearly stunned.

"Dacinda Minor—hey, I'll bet that's the librarian. Her name is Minor. Her name isn't Dacinda, though—"

"Daisy." Temple sounded as if he were strangling. "Everyone calls her Daisy. My God! She—"

"I guess even librarians can illegally park, huh?"

"Uh—yeah."

"Want me to call and give her hell? She's a city employee; she should know better."

"No, I'll call," the mayor quickly said.

"Okay," said Jack, knowing no such call would be made. "Let me know if I can help you with anything again, Mayor."

"Sure thing. Thanks."

As soon as the mayor hung up, Jack ran his finger down the list of city departments and located the library's number, then punched it in.

"Hillsboro Public Library," said Daisy's crisp voice.

"Hi, sweetheart, how are you feeling?"

"Just fine." Her tone changed, became warmer, more intimate. "And you?"

"A little beat, but I think I can make it through the day. Listen, someone said they saw your car at Dr. Bennett's office."

"I don't think so," she said. "That quack. He pushes diet pills."

Jack scribbled Dr. Bennett's name on a pad so he'd remember to do some checking into the good doctor's prescription-writing habits.

"I also heard that your name is Dacinda. True or false?"

"You're hearing a lot of things today. True, as you would know if you ever bothered to look over the list of city employees. I was named after Granny Minor."

"You've never been called Dacinda?"

She gave a ladylike snort. "I should hope not. Mother said they called me Dacey when I was a baby, but within just a month or two they were slurring it into Daisy, so I've been Daisy as long as I can remember. Why are you so curious about my name?"

"Just making small talk. It's been a while since I've heard your voice."

"Oh, at least an hour and a half," she said.

"Seems like longer. Are you going home for lunch?"

"No, I just talked to Aunt Jo, and she's found a dog for me. I'm going to see the people at lunch; she already has it arranged." Regret tinged her tone.

He wondered if she felt half as regretful as he did. But Daisy getting a dog was important, and he'd use the time nosing around, maybe shadowing the mayor for a while and seeing where he went.

"Listen, there are some things I have to check out tonight, but I'll come by if I can. What time do you usually go to bed?"

"Ten. But you—"

"I'll call if I can't make it."

"All right, but you don't have to—"

"Yes," he said, his tone more grim than he'd intended, "I do."

He didn't have to sound so glum about it, Daisy thought as she hung up. She wasn't clinging to him, demanding his time. She'd been very careful not to ask when she would see him again, though she'd been certain she would. A man didn't spend all afternoon and most of the night making love to a woman if he didn't really like what they had together.

One good thing about living on Lassiter Avenue: no one was likely to care who spent the night with her. Since she had just moved in, no one knew her, or knew which cars were normally in the driveway. For the first time in her life, she didn't feel as if a hundred pairs of eyes were on her. She had felt free with Jack, free to be as uninhibited as she liked, to make noise when she climaxed, to stand naked in the kitchen eating peanut butter and crackers for quick energy. She could carry on her affair with him without the entire neighborhood watching to see what time he left her house, or clucking their tongues if his car remained in her driveway all night.

All in all, she was very satisfied with the way things had turned out, though one of the things on her to-do list today was *buy more condoms*—regular ones, without a hint of flavor. She was tempted to go back to Clud's Pharmacy to buy them; let Barbara make what she liked of that! Jack's stock with the women in town would certainly go up when Barbara spread the word that he'd used up six dozen in one week.

At lunchtime, Daisy drove to her mother's house, picked up Evelyn and Aunt Jo; then they all went to Miley Park's house to pick out her dog.

Mrs. Park lived several miles outside of Hillsboro, on a pretty section of land with a huge fenced yard around her small frame house. She came out to greet them, wiping her hands on her apron and smiling, accompanied by a grinning, tail-wagging golden retriever bouncing along at her side.

"Sadie, sit," she said, and the dog obediently sat, but she quivered with eagerness to greet the visitors. Mrs. Park opened the gate and said, "Hurry, so I can close the gate before they get here."

"They?" asked Evelyn as they obediently hurried through the gate. Mrs. Park quickly closed it just as a tangle of puppies came bounding around the corner of the house.

"The little devils are fast as greased lightning," said Mrs. Park, bending to pat Sadie's head. "As soon as they hear the gate open, they come running."

Sadie got up to check her brood, nuzzling each of the puppies in turn as if counting noses. The puppies couldn't seem to decide what they wanted to do first, jump Mama and try to get some milk or check out the newcomers. They pounced and bounced back and forth, little tails wagging so hard their entire bodies seemed to be waving.

"Oh," said Daisy breathlessly, sinking onto the grass. "Oh!" There were only five of them, but they were so active it seemed as if there were a dozen. As soon as she sat down, they decided to check her out, and abruptly she had a lap full of puppies, puppies climbing over her legs and trying to lick her face, bite her hair, gnaw on her shoes.

Three of them were a mellow gold, and two were such a pale cream they were almost white. All of them were fat, bright-eyed balls of fur, with big, soft paws that seemed way too large for their bodies and baby fuzz so soft she just wanted to sink her hands in it.

"They'll be seven weeks old on Thursday," said Mrs. Park. "Sadie started weaning them two weeks ago; I've had them on just puppy food for a week now. They've had their first round of shots. That was a fun trip to the vet's, I can tell you!"

"They're beautiful," Daisy said, already in love. Her eyes were dazed. "I'll take them."

Everyone laughed, and she realized what she'd said. "Well, maybe just one would be better," she said, blushing and laughing at herself.

"I don't let Sadie's babies go unless I'm sure they'll have a good home," said Mrs. Parks. "Goldens are lively dogs and need a lot of exercise. If you don't have a safe place for it to run—"

"The backyard is fenced," said Daisy hastily, suddenly afraid she might not be allowed to buy one of these adorable babies.

"Is it a big yard?"

"Not huge, no."

"Well, that's fine for a puppy; when it grows, it'll need more exercise than it can get just playing in a small yard. Will you be able to take it for long walks, throw a ball for it, take it swimming?"

"Yes," promised Daisy, willing to promise anything and do anything.

"They like human companionship. No, they *love* human companionship. Will someone be home with it during the day, or were you planning on leaving it by itself in the yard all day while you're at work?"

Her thoughts hadn't gone that far at all; she turned a beseeching look on her mother.

"We can keep it during the day," said Evelyn.

"Do you have a lot of patience? The little devils can get into more mischief than you'd believe. If you leave something lying around, you can bet it'll be chewed on, especially during teething. On the other hand, they're eager to learn and please you, and I've never had one that was hard to house-train."

"I'm very patient." That was true, or she would never have waited thirty-four years to get a life. She picked up a puppy and laughed as its little pink tongue began madly licking in an effort to reach her face.

Mrs. Park smiled and folded her hands. "They're four hundred dollars each."

"Okay," said Daisy without pause. Mrs. Park could have said a thousand and she probably still wouldn't have hesitated.

Sadie came over and licked her baby while Daisy held it, then licked Daisy. She settled down beside Daisy's legs and was immediately swarmed, fat puppies trying to root under her in search of a teat, but Sadie had learned how to protect herself and they were frustrated in their efforts.

"Which one do you choose?"

All the other questions had been easy; this one was agonizing. She stared at them, trying to decide.

"There are three males and two females—"

"No, don't tell me," said Daisy. "I want to pick a personality, not a sex."

So she simply sat while puppies played around and over her. Then one of the pale-cream-colored ones yawned, its little mouth open wide, and its dark eyes with the absurdly long blond eyelashes began to close. Clumsily it climbed over her leg and turned around until it found a comfortable position on her lap, then settled down in a sleepy little ball.

"Well, I've been chosen," she said, picking up the puppy and cuddling it.

"That's one of the males. Take good care of him, now. I'll be calling and checking on him, and bring him back to see Sadie anytime you want. I'll just go get the paperwork to fill out so you can register him."

"What are you going to name him?" Evelyn asked as they

drove back to town. Jo was driving, while Daisy sat in back with the puppy asleep in her arms.

"I'll have to think about it. If the size of these feet are anything to go by, he's going to be huge, so I want something macho and tough."

Jo snorted. "He looks macho and tough. *Fuzzball* would be a good name."

"He won't be fuzzy forever." Already she felt sad at the thought of him growing out of his puppyhood. She stroked his little head and suddenly realized the enormity of the responsibility she had taken on. "My goodness, I haven't bought anything! We'll have to stop at Wal-Mart so I can get some puppy food, his food and water dishes, toys, a bed for him, and those house-training pads to put down. Am I forgetting anything?"

"Just double the supply," said Evelyn, "since we'll be keeping him during the day. There's no sense in carrying his things back and forth."

"I'll be late getting back to the library," said Daisy, and for the first time didn't care. She had a lover and a dog; could life get any better?

SEVENTEEN

Temple Nolan was more than stunned to find out the tag number belonged to Daisy Minor, he was disbelieving. Sykes had clearly said the woman was blonde, and Daisy's hair was brown. Moreover, he doubted she had ever seen the inside of a nightclub; she was the very stereotype of the community old maid who lived at home her entire life, was beloved by the neighborhood kids because she gave out the best candy at Halloween, and went to church three times a week.

But then a vague memory tickled, a snippet of conversation between two of the city clerks he'd overheard when he passed them in the hallway, about Daisy turning over a new leaf or getting her petals plucked, something with a horticultural flavor. Maybe Daisy was kicking up her heels a little. It still sounded so out of character for her he couldn't quite believe it, but it was worth checking out.

He could have asked Nadine, his secretary, if she'd heard any gossip about Daisy, but that icy finger of fear made him more cautious. If Daisy was indeed the woman Sykes had seen, Temple didn't want Nadine to remember that he had asked questions about her just before her death or disappearance, whatever Sykes arranged. So he told Nadine he was stepping out for a minute, then walked over to the library. He didn't even have to go inside; he looked through the glass door and saw Daisy seated behind the checkout desk, her head bent over some paperwork—her blond head. Daisy had lightened her hair.

He felt almost sick to his stomach.

He walked back to his office, his head down. When he entered, Nadine said in alarm, "Mayor, are you all right? You look pale."

"An upset stomach," he said, telling the truth. "I thought some fresh air might help."

"Maybe you should go home," she said, looking worried. Nadine was the maternal type, always baby-sitting her grandchildren, and she tended to dispense more medical advice than the doctors in town.

He had lunch scheduled with the mayor of Scottsboro, so he shook his head. "No, it's just indigestion. I had a glass of orange juice this morning."

"That'll do it," she said, opening a desk drawer and pulling out a bottle. "Here, have some Maalox."

Meekly he accepted two tablets and obediently chewed them. "Thanks," he said, and went back into his office. One of these days Nadine was going to diagnose indigestion in someone who was really having a heart attack, but at least in his case he knew exactly why he had a sour stomach.

He made sure his door was securely shut, then went to his private phone and called Sykes. What had to be done . . . had to be done.

Jack borrowed a pickup truck from one of his officers, pulled off his tie, put on sunglasses and a John Deere cap, and followed the mayor to his lunch with the mayor of Scottsboro. He saw nothing suspicious, but that didn't make him relax. Where Daisy was concerned, he *couldn't* relax. All his instincts, honed razor sharp by years in a dangerous job, were on the alert and scanning for a target.

Daisy, of course, was oblivious of the storm he could sense gathering around her. One of the things he enjoyed most about her was her absolute positiveness; it wasn't blindness to the bad things that could happen, just an acceptance that not everything was wonderful and a conviction that most things were. Look at her attitude toward Barbara Clud, the gossiping bitch: That was just the way Barbara was, so if you went to that pharmacy, you had to expect her to tell what you bought. Right now, however, he would have felt better if Daisy had a more suspicious view of the world; she might be a little more cautious. At least she was getting a dog for protection. If he couldn't be there at night, at least she'd have a sharp-toothed alarm system.

After lunch, the mayor went back to Hillsboro. Jack checked in with Eva Fay, then drove to Huntsville and located Todd Lawrence's antiques store, which was named, simply, *Lawrence's,* nothing cutesy. Jack went in still wearing the John Deere cap, which, judging from the cool look given him by an approaching salesman, marked him as the bull in the china shop.

The salesman was middle-aged, average in size, and disturbingly familiar. Jack seldom forgot a face; it came from years of studying everyone around him. This man had been at the Buffalo Club; in fact, if Jack wasn't mistaken, he had danced with Daisy on that first night. His suspicions kicked into overdrive.

"Is Mr. Lawrence in?"

"I'm sorry, he's occupied at the moment," said the salesman in smooth tones. "May I help you with something?"

"No." Jack took out his ID and flipped it open. "Mr. Lawrence. Now. And you'll need to sit in, too."

The salesman took the ID and studied it, then coolly returned it. "Chief of police of the Hillsboro Police Department," he said sarcastically. "Impressive."

"Not as impressive as a broken arm, but what the hell, I'll go with what works."

An unwilling smile touched the salesman's mouth. "Tough, too." He shifted his balance just a little, but the subtle changes in his stance made Jack's eyes sharpen.

"Salesman, my ass," he muttered. "This is about Daisy Minor."

There was another change in expression, a sort of rueful resignation. The salesman sighed and said, "Oh, hell. Todd's in his office."

Todd looked up when Jack and the salesman entered the small private office. His eyebrows rose as he recognized Jack, and he gave the other man a swift questioning glance before shifting into pleasant-businessman mode, rising to his feet and extending his hand. "Chief Russo, isn't it? The cap threw me off for a minute." He looked quizzically at the green cap with the yellow John Deere logo. "How . . . retro."

Jack shook his hand and said amiably, "How full of bullshit. Why don't we all sit down, and you and the martial arts salesman here can tell me how I'm jumping to all the wrong conclusions, that you aren't sending Daisy around to certain targeted night-clubs and bars, and that Bruce Lee really isn't shadowing her to—what? Catch her doing something illegal? Not likely."

"Howard," said the salesman, grinning. "Not Bruce."

Todd steepled his fingers and tapped them against his lips, watching Jack. "I really don't know what you're talking about."

"Fine." Jack didn't have time to bullshit around. "Then let's talk about what possible reason a straight man could have for trying to convince everyone he's gay, and what would happen if I blew his cover."

Todd gave a light laugh. "You really *are* reaching now, Chief."

"Am I? You know, when I first moved here, I rambled around a lot, learning the roads and the country, so I was in a lot of places where normally you wouldn't expect to see Hillsboro's chief. I was also paying a lot of attention to Hillsboro's citizens, asking who people were and learning their faces, so I knew you by sight."

"Your point?"

"My point is, if you're posing as gay, when you check into a motel with a woman, you shouldn't enter the room at the same time, and you really shouldn't try to suck her tonsils out while you're still trying to get the key card in the lock. Plays hell with the image. Want me to describe her?"

"Yes," said Howard, fascinated.

"Never mind," Todd said, his face suddenly impassive. "You get around to some out-of-the-way places, Chief."

"Don't I?" Jack agreed. "Let's get back to my original question: What in hell are you doing with Daisy?"

"I can tell you what I'm doing," said Howard. "I'm trying to make sure she doesn't get hurt in any way. The nightclub scene can be rough on women."

"Then why send her there? It's like sending a kitten into a bear cage."

"You make her sound totally helpless. She's an intelligent, observant woman who just wants to dance and meet men."

"Given what's out there in the bar scene these days, even intelligent women are ending up raped, maybe just by one man, maybe by all of his buddies, too—and that's if she's lucky and doesn't die. Did you warn Daisy about letting anyone buy her a drink? Or leaving a drink sitting on the table while she dances?"

Howard sighed. "That's where I come in. I keep an eye on her, watch to see if anyone salts her drink with something."

"So she's never out of your sight, right? You never go to the bathroom, or lose sight of her in the crowd."

"I do the best I can."

"Best isn't good enough, not when you're using her as some kind of shark bait." He leveled a hard stare at Todd. "So let's start hearing some details, and they'd better be good or you're outed."

Todd rubbed his jaw. "That threat usually works in reverse."

Jack merely waited. He had stated his intentions, and where Daisy was concerned, he didn't back down or negotiate. Her safety was too important.

Todd studied Jack's expression, evidently reading his determination. "It's personal, the reason I've been . . . working with Daisy."

Jack said softly, "I'm taking the whole thing personally."

"So she got to you, huh?" Todd smiled. "I knew, with just a little sprucing up, she'd turn heads. All she needed was a boost in her self-confidence. She's so damned charming, with that sparkle in her eyes like a kid on a roller coaster, I figured all she needed was more flattering clothes to really pull in the men."

"Let's get to the facts," Jack growled.

"Okay, in a nutshell: A friend of mine went to the Buffalo Club with a couple of friends. She was bummed out, not in the mood for dancing. While her friends were dancing, a guy came on to her, offered to buy her a drink. Because she was bummed out, she let him. The last thing she remembered is getting sleepy. She woke up the next morning in her own bed, naked, alone, and it was obvious something had happened. She'd been raped and sodomized. She did the smart thing, didn't shower, called the cops, went to the hospital.

"From the evidence, at least six different men raped her. She had only a hazy memory of the guy who bought her the drink. The cops had nothing to go on but some blurry fingerprints in her apartment, none of which showed up in the files, so the men have no priors. Dead end. Unsolvable crime, unless one of the bastards is caught for the rape of another woman and his DNA matches the DNA in the evidence samples of semen."

It was a far too familiar story. Date-rape cases were difficult to prosecute even when the victim knew her assailant. When it was a stranger whom she couldn't remember because she'd been drugged, catching the bastards was almost impossible.

Rage had him grinding his teeth. "So you decided to try catching them yourselves, by using Daisy as bait. Don't you think the cops could have handled it better, with a female police officer trained for such situations?"

"Sure, except they weren't doing it. Budget limitations, low-priority case. You know how it works. There's way too much crime and not enough money, not enough officers, not enough jails or prisons. Every department has to prioritize."

"I'm tempted to really hurt you," Jack said, keeping his voice even with an effort. "And I could, despite Howard here. What were you going to do if some asshole *did* drug Daisy? Go vigilante and shoot him in the parking lot?"

"The idea has merit."

"What are the odds it would even be the same guy? There's a lot of that shit out there."

"I know it would be a long shot. But it would be a beginning. Someone to talk, name some names, who would name other names." Todd spread his hands on the desk and stared at them, his face grim. "There's more to the story. My friend was the same woman you saw me with that day. She was at the Buffalo Club in the first place because we'd quarreled. She wanted to get married, I told her I couldn't because of . . . other things—"

"Like this assignment you're working."

Todd flashed a quick glance up at Jack. "Yeah," he said flatly. "Like this assignment. Besides, marriage is a big step. I was kind of glad to have the assignment as an excuse. I was crazy about her, but . . . hell, I guess I had cold feet. So that's why she was at the club."

Jack nodded, thinking he got the picture. Normal relationships were hard enough; when the woman had been raped, she understandably had a hard time trusting men again, or enjoying sex. "Did she get into therapy?"

"For a while. It didn't do any good. She killed herself."

The stark words fell like lead. All expression was gone from Todd's face, from his eyes.

Howard swore. "Jesus, man—you just said a friend was raped. God, I'm sorry."

"Yeah, so am I," said Jack. "You're grieving, you felt guilty, so you set Daisy up for exactly the same thing that happened to the woman you loved. You fucking bastard, I'd *enjoy* killing you." His clenched fists were shaking with the need to do just that.

"Don't go overboard with the sympathy, Russo," Howard said sarcastically.

Todd managed a faint smile, though there was no humor in it. "That was fast. You're in love with her; that's why you're so hot under the collar."

"Daisy doesn't deserve being used that way." Jack shoved away the comment about loving her. Whether or not he did was something he'd have to work out; he definitely cared about her and would do whatever it took to protect her. And whatever it took meant using whatever means necessary, with whatever weapons he had at hand. Something else was going on, something these two weren't involved in; alone, Jack would be hard-pressed to cover all the bases, but he figured he now had help.

"There's something else concerning Daisy, something I don't understand, but it's put me on edge."

A little expression filtered back into Todd's eyes. "What?"

"This assignment you're working . . . are you federal, local, or private?"

Todd and Howard exchanged a quick glance. "Federal. It involves interstate fraud."

"Fine. I don't need the details. I just need your help and I wanted to know what level I'll be dealing with."

"We can't compromise this setup—"

"You won't have to. Something peculiar happened this morning. The mayor called me, wanted me to run a license plate number, said he'd seen the car parked in the fire lane at a doctor's office. He gave me the small-town bullshit, how he didn't call a patrolman to write a ticket because he didn't want to upset someone who was sick—"

"Yeah, right, Temple Nolan with a big heart," Todd muttered.

"So I ran the number, and it was Daisy's. Not only would Daisy never park in a fire lane, she wasn't at the doctor's office. I know. So the mayor lied about where he got the number. If he'd seen the car himself, he'd have known it was Daisy's. Someone else wanted him to find out who the car belonged to."

"Maybe someone at the Buffalo Club saw her and was interested, wanted to find out where she lived and how to contact her."

"Someone who figured she'd never come back to the club and that was the only way he'd have of finding her? Someone who also happens to know the mayor?"

"Okay, so it's a thin idea. Do you have anything better?"

"No, all I have are the little hairs on the back of my neck, and they're standing straight up."

"That's good enough for me," said Howard. "From the accent, I know you're not from around here, but I can't quite place it. You're not just a small-town chief, though. What's your background?"

"SWAT, in Chicago and New York."

"Guess your little hairs have seen their share of action."

"They've never been wrong."

"So what do you want us to do?" asked Todd. "There's nothing to go on, no direction."

"Not yet. For now, I just want to make sure she's safe. The good news is, the address on the registration is for her mother's house. There's no official record now of her real address, unless someone has the strings to find out from the utilities—which the mayor does, with the city water department, but unless he knows she's moved, he has no reason to ask."

"Can you get into the files, take out that information?"

"The water bills are computerized. I'm no hacker, so I can't get into the system from outside, but maybe I can from the inside. What about the phone and electricity companies?"

"I'll see what I can do about blocking that information," Todd said. "And she needs to have her number unlisted, or any bozo can call information and get it."

"I'll handle that," said Jack. "I don't know what I'm looking for, I don't know why anyone would want to track her down, and until I do know, I want a shield around her."

"We've been working a situation for a couple of years now. If things come together, Howard and I will be busy and won't be able to help. You know how it works. But until and if the case breaks, we'll do what we can to help." Todd drummed his fingers on the desk. "Off the record, of course."

"Of course. Just friends helping friends."

EIGHTEEN

Jack drove back to Hillsboro, returned the truck to his officer, checked that Daisy was safe at the library, and filled the rest of the day handling the myriad details that cropped up every day in a police department, even a small one. He left the office at the usual time, drove home, cut his grass to kill some time, went in and showered, then called his office phone to make certain Eva Fay had gone home. Sometimes he thought she spent the night there, because she was always there when he arrived and no matter how late he stayed, she stayed later. As a secretary, she was damned intimidating. She was also so good at her job he'd have loved to see her transplanted to New York, to see what kind of miracle she could work on some of the precincts.

There was no answer at his office, so it was safe to go back. His car was in the driveway, plainly visible to anyone who looked. He left a bar light on in the kitchen, a lamp on in his bedroom upstairs, and one on in the living room. The television provided background noise, in case anyone listened. There was no reason for anyone to be watching his house, at least so long as whoever was after Daisy didn't find out about his involvement with her, but he wasn't taking chances.

At twilight, he got a few items he thought he might need and slipped them into his pockets. Wearing jeans, a black T-shirt, and another cap—this one plain black—he slipped out his back door and walked back to the police department. At this time of day almost everyone was inside for the night, having finished the chores around the house, eaten supper, and settled down in front of the tube. He could hear the high-pitched laughter of some youngsters chasing lightning bugs, but that was one street over. Maybe there were some folks sitting on their front porches, enjoying the fresh air now that it wasn't as hot, but Jack knew he was virtually unrecognizable in the deepening twilight.

His second-shift desk sergeant, Scott Wylie, looked up in surprise when Jack entered by the back door, which was the way all the officers came in. It was a quiet night, no one else around, so Wylie didn't even try to hide the fishing magazine he was reading. Jack had come up through the ranks, so he knew what it was like to work long, boring shifts, and he never gave his men grief about their reading material. "Chief! Is something wrong?"

Jack grinned. "I thought I'd spend the night here, so I can find out what time Eva Fay comes to work."

The sergeant laughed. "Good luck. She has a sixth sense about things like that; she'll probably call in sick."

"I'll be in my office for a while, clearing up some paperwork. I was going to do it tomorrow, but something else came up."

"Sure thing." Wylie went back to his magazine, and Jack went through the glass doors into the office part of the building. The police department was two-storied, built in a back-facing L, with the offices in the short leg facing the street, while the officers' lockers and showers and the evidence, booking, and interrogation rooms were on the first floor of the long section, with the cells on the top floor.

Jack's office was on the second floor, facing the street. He went in and turned on the lamp on his desk, scattered some papers around the desk so it would look as if he'd been working— just in case someone came up, which he doubted would happen— then he got a key from his desk and silently went down to the basement, where a short tunnel connected the P.D. to city hall. The tunnel was used to transport prisoners from the jail to court for their trials and was securely locked at both ends. Jack had a key, the desk sergeant had a key, and the city manager had once had a key, but it was taken from him when it was discovered he was giving his girlfriends tours of the place.

He unlocked the door on the P.D. side, then relocked it when he was in the tunnel—again, just in case. The place was dark as a tomb, but Jack had a pencil flashlight with a narrow, powerful beam. He unlocked the door on the other end, and left this one unlocked, because there wasn't supposed to be anyone in city hall after five P.M. The basement was silent and dark, just the way it should be.

He soundlessly climbed the stairs; the door at the top had no lock. He eased it open, listened, then put his eye to the crack and looked for light where there shouldn't be any. Nothing. The place was empty.

More relaxed now, he opened the flimsy lock on the water department door—the city really needed to replace its locks, it only took him a few seconds to get in—and booted up the computer. The system wasn't password protected, because it wasn't on-line. He clicked on Programs, found Billing, and opened the file. Bless their tidy little hearts, everything was cross-referenced between account numbers and names. He simply found Daisy's name, clicked on it, changed her address to his, saved the change, and closed the file. Bingo.

That taken care of, he backed out of the operating system and turned off the computer, relocked the door behind him, then made his way upstairs to the mayor's office. He had no idea what he was looking for, but he sure wanted to look around.

Like his own office, there were two entrances to the mayor's: one through Nadine's outer sanctum, and a private, unmarked door a little farther down the hallway. The locks here were much better than the locks on the door at the water department.

Jack decided to use Nadine's door, on the theory that she might think she'd accidentally left it unlocked. Repeating the process he'd used at the water department, he took a small set of probes and picks from his pocket, then put the penlight in his mouth, crouched down, and went to work. He was good at picking locks, though until tonight he hadn't been called upon to do so since moving to Hillsboro. When people asked him about his SWAT training or any of the action he'd seen, they never asked about any specialty training he might have had on the side. He always downplayed the action part—hell, he wasn't a Rambo, none of them were, though there were always a few who let their heads get too far into the mystique—and kept quiet about some of the training, because it seemed smart to keep something in reserve.

The lock yielded in about thirty seconds. Normal citizens would be alarmed at how easy it was to open locked doors; they thought all they had to do was turn the key and they were safe. Unfortunately, the only people they were safe from were the people who obeyed laws and respected locked doors. A lowlife would break a window, kick in a door; Jack had even known them to crawl under houses and saw holes in the floor. Alarm systems and burglar bars were good, but if someone was determined to get inside, he'd find a way.

Witness himself, breaking into the mayor's office. Jack grinned as he slipped through Nadine's office, holding the penlight down so the beam wouldn't flash across the windows, and tried the door into the mayor's office. It was unlocked; that meant one of three things: Either Temple had nothing to hide, he was so careless he didn't deserve to live, or he made certain there was nothing suspicious here to see. Jack hoped it was the first but figured it was the third.

Working fast but systematically, he went through the trash and found a wadded piece of paper with Daisy's tag number scribbled on it, but nothing else interesting. He smoothed out the paper; it was a sheet from the memo pad printed with *Temple Nolan* at the top, the same memo pad that now rested on top of Temple's desk. It followed, then, that the mayor had been here in his office when someone called asking him to run that tag number.

A quick search of the mayor's desk turned up nothing. Jack surveyed the office, but there were no file cabinets, just furniture. All the files were in Nadine's office. There were, however, two phones on Temple's desk. One was the office phone, with a list of extension numbers beside it. The other had to be a private line, so Temple could make and receive calls without Nadine knowing.

It was a long shot, but Jack took a tiny recorder out of his pocket, hit *redial* on the private phone, then held the recorder to the earpiece, recorded the tones, and quickly hung up. He had a pal who could listen to the tones and tell him what number had been dialed. Next he hit *69, and scribbled down the number the computer provided. It wasn't a local exchange, so the last call Temple had received had not been from his wife asking when he'd be home for supper. Jack tore off a few extra pages of the memo pad to make certain no impression was left behind, wadded up the extras, and dropped them into the wastebasket. The trash would be emptied before Nolan came to work, not that he was likely to go through his own trash, considering there was nothing interesting in there except Daisy's tag number, which Jack also dropped back in the trash.

That was all he could do tonight. Taking out a handkerchief, he carefully wiped all the surfaces he had touched; then let himself out through Nadine's office. He went back through the basement tunnel, up to his office, where he restacked all the papers he'd scattered on his desk so Eva Fay wouldn't realize he'd been here when she wasn't, turned out the light, and locked up. Everything was just the way he'd found it.

He went out through the back; things were a little busier now than they had been before; an officer had brought in a drunk driver, a big guy who stood about six-six and weighed at least three-fifty. When Jack came through the doors, both Sergeant Wylie and the officer glanced at him, their attention momentarily distracted, and the drunk saw his chance for an escape, ramming his shoulder into the officer and sending him flying, then lowering his head and charging straight into Wylie's stomach.

It had been a while since Jack had seen any action. With a whoop of sheer joy, he joined the melee.

It took all three of them to subdue the big guy, and they had to resort to some rough stuff before they got him down. It was a good thing the guy had been cuffed, or someone would have been really hurt. As it was, once they had him down and hog-tied, Sergeant Wylie felt his ribs and winced.

"Anything broken?" Jack asked, wiping blood from his nose.

"I don't think so. Just bruised." But he winced again when he touched them.

"Go get them checked out. I'll handle things here."

The officer, Enoch Stanfield, had a fat lip and a rapidly swelling eye. He was trembling slightly from adrenaline overload as he soaked his handkerchief at the watercooler and held the cold cloth to his eye. "God, I love this job," he said in an exhausted voice. "Nowhere else would I have the opportunity to get the shit kicked out of me every day." He eyed Jack. "You sounded like you were having fun, Chief."

Jack looked down at the big drunk, who had gone to sleep almost as soon as they got him hog-tied. Gargantuan snores issued from his open mouth. "I live for days like this." Jack was abruptly exhausted, too, though he wasn't shaking like Stanfield.

He had to call in another officer to help them drag the drunk into the tank to sleep it off. He also called in one of the medics to check him and make sure he was okay, that the big guy wasn't in insulin shock, or something like that, even though the Breathalyzer indicated that he was simply piss-assed drunk, a diagnosis with which the medic concurred. A cold pack was put on Stanfield's eye, a stitch in his lip, and another cold pack on Jack's left hand, which was beginning to swell. He had no idea what exactly had happened to hurt his hand, but that's the way it was with fights: you just threw yourself in and took stock afterward. By the time he had everything organized, including a replacement for Wylie for the rest of the shift, it was almost ten-thirty; the third-shift officers were there to take over, the second-shift officers were all there except for Wylie, and a couple of the first-shift guys had heard the excitement on their scanners and had come over to take a look. After all, it wasn't every day the chief got involved in taking down a D and D, drunk and disorderly.

"There's no way Eva Fay won't hear about this," he said glumly, causing general laughter.

"She'll raise hell, you being here without her on duty," Officer Markham, a twenty-year veteran with the force, said tongue-in-cheek.

The men, Jack realized, were thoroughly enjoying the situation. It wasn't often the rank and file got to see their chief get down and dirty. There had always been a hint of reserve in them that wasn't due just to difference in rank; the biggest part had been that he was an outsider. His wrestling with a big drunk had made them feel he was one of them, a regular cop despite his rank.

To top it all off, he had to walk back home. He could have had one of the guys drive him home, but then he'd have had to come up with a reasonable explanation for why he'd walked over in the first place, and he didn't want to deal with it.

The house was just as he'd left it. Nothing seemed disturbed or out of place. He went straight to the phone and called information, to see if he could get the number of the mayor's private line in city hall. There was no such listing, which didn't surprise him. Next he called Todd Lawrence, who answered on the third ring with a sleepy "Hello."

"I got the address changed," he said. "And I used call return on the mayor's private line to get the number of the last call to him, and *redial* to record the tones of the last call he made."

"You've been a busy little boy." Todd sounded more alert.

"This gives us two numbers to check out. Think you can find out what the mayor's private number is and get those records, too?"

"Too? You want me to get telephone records on three numbers." It was stated as fact.

"What else are federal friends for?"

"You're going to get your federal friend's ass fired."

"I figure my federal friend owes it to Daisy."

Todd sighed. "You're right. Okay. I'll see what I can do, maybe call in some favors. This is completely off-record, though."

Next Jack called Daisy, though a quick look at his watch told him it was just after eleven. She'd probably gone to bed at ten on the dot, but after all his efforts on her behalf that day, he thought he deserved at least a brief chat.

"Hello." She didn't sound sleepy; she sounded tired, but not sleepy.

"Are you already in bed?"

"Not yet. It's been an . . . eventful night."

"Why? What's happened?" He was instantly on alert.

"I can't turn my back on him for a second, or he's tearing something up."

" 'Him?' "

"The dog."

The dog. Jack heaved a sigh of relief. "He doesn't sound very well trained."

"He isn't trained at all. Killer, no! Put that down! I have to go," she said hurriedly.

"I'll be right over," he said, just before she hung up, and didn't know if she heard him or not. He didn't care. He grabbed his keys, turned off the lights, and went out the door.

Daisy was exhausted. Her mother had called her at three P.M. and said tiredly, "Jo and I are taking the puppy over to your house. At least the yard is fenced in and he can run there. We'll stay there with him until you get home."

"Oh, dear." That didn't bode well. "What has he done?"

"What *hasn't* the little devil done? We're run ragged just trying to keep up with him. Anyway, we'll see you in a couple of hours."

When she got home at ten after five, both her mother and Aunt Jo were dozing in the living room, while the puppy slept between her mother's feet. He looked so adorable, lying on his belly with his back legs stretched out behind him, like a little bearskin rug, that her heart melted.

"Hello, sweetheart," she crooned. One heavy eyelid lifted, his little tail wagged; then he went back to sleep.

Aunt Jo roused. "Thank God you're home. Good luck; you'll need it with this little devil. Come on, Evelyn, let's git while the gitting's good."

Evelyn sat up and looked ruefully at the puppy between her feet. "We called Miley Park to see if maybe there was something wrong. She just laughed and said he might be a little excited at being in a new place, but that golden retriever puppies are nonstop mischief until they're about four months old. Well, he does stop when he's sleepy."

"He has two speeds," said Aunt Jo. "He's either at a dead run, or he's asleep. That's it. Have fun. Come on, Evelyn."

"I think we'll go by Wal-Mart and buy some baby gates so we can at least hem him up in one room. Do you want us to pick up some for you, too?"

"We'll buy what they have in stock," said Aunt Jo. "Come on, Evelyn."

"Oh, dear, is he that bad?" Daisy asked, dismayed. He looked like such a little angel, lying there asleep.

"He seems to be mostly house-trained," said her mother. "But he needs to go outside every two hours, as regular as clockwork. He did piddle on the puppy pads—"

"When he wasn't tearing them to shreds," interrupted Aunt Jo. "Evelyn, come on."

"He likes his stuffed toys—"

"He likes everything, including his water dish. Evelyn, if you don't come on, I'll leave without you. He might wake up any minute."

The puppy lifted his head and yawned, his little pink tongue stretching out. Within ten seconds, her mother and aunt had their purses and were out the door. Daisy put her hands on her hips and looked at the little fluff ball. "Okay, mister, just what have you done?"

He rolled over on his back, stretching. She was unable to resist rubbing the warm little tummy, which he took as an invitation to begin licking her everywhere that pink, eager tongue could reach. She picked him up and cuddled him, loving the warmth and smallness of him under all that fuzz. His big, soft feet batted at her, and he wiggled, signaling that he wanted down. She set him down, then broke into a sprint when he darted for the kitchen.

All he wanted was some water. He lapped eagerly, then all of a sudden pounced into the bowl with both front feet, sending water flying.

She got the kitchen floor mopped up—which he thought was a great game, because he kept pouncing on the mop—fed him, and took him outside to do his business. He squatted as soon as his feet touched the grass; then he attacked a bush. Worried that the leaves might be poisonous to him, or at least upset his little tummy, she got him away from the bush and used the hose pipe to run water in the kids' wading pool she'd bought for him.

He was too little to climb over the rim of the pool, so she helped him in and watched him run and slide in the two inches of water until he was drenched, she was drenched, and her sides ached from laughing so much. Lifting him out of the pool, she wrapped him in a towel and carried him inside, hoping he'd take another nap so she could eat.

He pounced into his water bowl again. While she was mopping, he chased the mop. Then he grabbed the kitchen towel and made a run for it. She caught him as he dove under the bed, and hauled him out. Her efforts to take the towel away from him evidently convinced him she wanted to play tug-of-war and he pulled on the towel for all he was worth, emitting baby growls while his whole body quivered with effort.

She distracted him with a little stuffed duck. He threw the duck over his head, pounced on it, and managed to stuff it under the couch where he couldn't reach it. Then he stood there and yapped until she got down on her hands and knees and retrieved the duck. He immediately stuffed it under the couch again.

Next she tried a rubber chew toy as a distraction, and it worked for about ten minutes. He lay on his belly and held the chew toy between his front paws, gnawing with fierce concentration. Daisy took the opportunity to get out of her work clothes and begin making herself a sandwich. She heard a crash from the living room and ran in barefoot to find he'd somehow dislodged the television remote control from the lamp table and was busy trying to kill it. She took the remote away and put it in a safe place.

He loved her red toenails. He pounced on her bare feet. He kept jumping at her, trying to catch her fingers in his mouth; startled, she would jerk her hand back, and his sharp little baby teeth *hurt*. Finally, she just held her hand down and he mouthed her fingers as if tasting her, then, satisfied, released her.

At last, he got sleepy. He stopped practically in mid-run and collapsed on his belly, heaving a huge sigh as his eyes closed.

"I guess it was a big day for you, little guy," she murmured. "Do you miss your mama, and your brothers and sisters? You've always had someone to play with, haven't you? And now you're all by yourself."

It was after seven o'clock by then, and she was starving. She finished making her sandwich and ate it standing where she could keep an eye on him. He looked so sweet and tiny while he was asleep, but as soon as his eyes opened, he would be full speed again.

He slept on, with the absolute obliviousness of a baby. She decided to take a quick shower and left the bathroom door open so he could come in if he woke up. She undressed, dropping her clothes on the floor, and stepped into the tub. She had just gotten soaped when she heard something and parted the curtain to see a pale fuzz ball darting into the hall with her panties in his mouth.

Daisy leaped out of the tub and ran in naked, sliding pursuit. He somehow squeezed behind the couch with his captured treasure. She pulled the couch away from the wall and retrieved her panties. There was, of course, a hole in them. He wagged his tail.

"You little demon," she said, picking him up and carrying him into the bathroom with her. She closed the door so he couldn't get out, put her clothes on the back of the toilet where he couldn't reach them, and got back into the shower. He spent the whole time yapping and standing on his back legs, trying to crawl over into the tub with her.

She had learned from the mop episode; instead of stepping out onto the bath mat to towel off, she stood in the tub. He eyed the towel with longing, sitting on his haunches and looking angelic.

His little face was so happy, she thought, his mouth open in a perpetual smile. His dark eyes, the rims dark, as if someone had lined his eyes with kohl, were very exotic with his pale fur and long blond lashes. He was so curious and enthused about everything that his tail wagged nonstop, like a souped-up metronome.

"So what if you're a little devil," she said. "You're *my* little devil, and I fell in love with you when you climbed in my lap." His tail wagged even faster as he listened to her voice and the crooning note in it.

"I have to come up with a good name for you, something that sounds big and tough. You're supposed to protect me, you know. I don't think it would scare many burglars if I yelled, 'Sic 'im, Fluffy,' do you? How about *Brutus?*"

He yawned.

"You're right; you aren't a *Brutus.* You're too pretty. How about *Devil?*" After a moment, watching him, she vetoed that choice herself. "No, I don't like that, because I just know you're going to be a sweetheart when you grow up."

She tried out names on him for the rest of the evening: Conan, Duke, King, Rambo, Rocky, Samson, Thor, Wolf. None of them were right. She just couldn't look at that smiling little face and make a macho name fit.

She learned not to leave water in his water bowl, or it ended up on the kitchen floor. When he went to his bowl, she poured a little water in, and after he'd lapped that up, she poured some more, until he quit lapping. Unfortunately, there was usually some water left in the bowl when he finished, and he pounced into it. Daisy mopped up water seven times that night, with him in fierce pursuit of the mop head.

He was so intelligent she was amazed; in just that afternoon and night he had learned to go to the back door when he needed to go outside. Finally he seemed to be winding down, so Daisy introduced him to his dog bed, which she had placed in her bedroom so he wouldn't be lonely and cry at night. She closed the bedroom door to keep him corralled for the night, placed the stuffed duck in the bed with him, and wearily crawled into bed. She turned out the lamp, and exactly two seconds later he started whimpering.

Fifteen minutes later she gave up and lifted him into the bed with her. He was almost hysterical with joy, jumping and tugging at the covers and licking her in the face. She had just gotten him settled down when the phone rang. It was Jack. While he was talking, the puppy found her robe, which she'd tossed across the foot of the bed, and began tugging at the sleeve. She said, "Killer, no! Put that down! I have to go," and hung up to lunge across the bed and grab him just before he tumbled backward to the floor.

Not five minutes later, the doorbell rang. Sighing in fatigue, she got out of bed, picked up the puppy, and carried him with her to the door. That seemed the safest thing to do. A quick peek revealed Jack standing impatiently on the porch. She turned on the light and with one hand unlocked the dead bolt and let him in.

He stepped inside and froze, staring at the puppy. "That's a puppy," he said in almost stunned astonishment, which was really observant of him considering she'd already told him she had a dog.

"No!" she said, pretending shock. "That lady lied to me."

"That's a *golden retriever* puppy."

She cuddled the baby to her. "So?"

With measured movements, Jack closed the door, locked it, then rhythmically beat his head against the frame.

"What's wrong with my puppy?" Daisy demanded.

In a strained voice he said, "The whole idea was to get a dog for *protection.*"

"He'll grow," she said. "Look at the size of his feet. He's going to be huge."

"He'll still be a golden retriever."

"What's wrong with that? I think he's beautiful."

"He is. He's gorgeous. But goldens are so friendly they're no protection at all. They think everyone is their friend, placed on earth just to pet them. He might bark to let you know when someone comes up, but that's about it."

"That's okay. He's perfect for me." She kissed the top of the puppy's head. He was squirming, trying to get down so he could investigate this new human.

Sighing, Jack reached out and took the little guy in his big hands. The puppy began licking madly at every inch of skin he could reach. "So his name's Killer?"

"No, I've just been trying out names. Nothing seems to fit."

"Not if they're like *Killer*, they won't. You name goldens something like *Lucky*, or *Fuzzbutt*." He lifted the puppy until they were nose to nose. "How about *Midas?* Or *Riley?* Or—"

"Midas!" Daisy said, her eyes lighting as she stared from him to the puppy. "That's perfect!" She threw her arms around him, stretching up on tiptoe in an effort to kiss him, but the newly named Midas got there first and licked her on the mouth. She sputtered and wiped her mouth. "Thanks, sweetie, but you aren't half the kisser the guy is."

"Thanks," Jack said, holding Midas at a safe distance as he leaned down and their lips met. And clung. The kiss deepened. The melting started again.

"Do you mind if I spend the night?" he murmured, trailing his kisses down her throat.

"I'd love it," she said, and was overtaken by a huge, jaw-breaking yawn.

Jack gave a crack of laughter. "Liar. You're dead on your feet."

Daisy blushed. "I had a very active day yesterday. And last night." She glanced at Midas. "And tonight. I can't turn my back on him for a minute."

"How about if I stay and we do nothing but sleep?"

Blinking in astonishment, she said, "Why would you want to do that?"

"Just to make sure you're all right."

"I think you're going overboard with this protection business."

"Maybe, maybe not. Today the mayor got me to run a tag number; he said he'd seen the car parked in the fire lane at Dr. Bennett's office. Guess whose tag it was?"

"Whose?"

"Yours."

"Mine!" she said indignantly. "I've never parked in a fire lane in my life!"

He hid a grin as he set Midas down. "I didn't think so. Do you have any idea why the mayor would want me to run your tag number?"

Slowly she shook her head.

"If he had seen your car, he'd have known it was you, so obviously someone else got him to do it. That has me a little worried. The good thing is, you've moved, so your address isn't the same as what's on your registration."

She gasped. "My goodness, I totally forgot about that! I'll go to the courthouse and change—"

"No, you will not," he said sternly. "Not until I find out what's going on."

"Why don't you just ask Temple?"

"Because I feel uneasy about the whole thing. Until I'm satisfied nothing suspicious is going on, I don't want you to give out your new address to anyone. Tell your family to keep it quiet, too."

"But if anyone wants to know where I live, all he has to do is follow me home from work—"

"After today, I'll handle that. I'll drive you home, and I guarantee no one will be able to tail us."

She stared up at him, at the hard cast of his expression, and realized he was deadly serious. For the first time, a frisson of alarm skittered up her spine. Jack was worried, and that worried her.

Midas scampered into the kitchen, and she heard the splat as he landed in his water bowl. "Get the puppy and take him out in the backyard while I mop up the water," she said, sighing. "Then we'll go to bed."

"With him?"

"He's a baby. You don't want him to cry all night, do you?"

"Better him than me," Jack muttered, but he obediently took Midas outside and was back in five minutes with a sleepy puppy in his arms.

"I suppose he sleeps in the middle," he said, grumbling.

Daisy sighed. "At this point, I'll let him sleep wherever he wants. And we have to take him out every two hours."

"Do what?" he said in disbelief.

"I told you, he's a baby. Babies can't hold it."

"I can tell this is going to be a great night."

NINETEEN

If the blonde lived at the address Nolan had given him, Glenn Sykes had yet to see her today. Two older women had come and gone, but not the blonde. In that kind of residential neighborhood, it was difficult to keep watch without being spotted himself, because old folks sat out on their porches and watched everyone who went by.

He got a phone book and looked up *Minor.* There was only one listing, and that gave the same address the mayor had given him, so the blonde had to live there. Maybe she was off on a business trip or something. He was both worried and relieved: relieved because the woman evidently hadn't been paying much attention to them, and worried because it was on the news that a man's body had been found in the woods by a hunter—it was always those damned hunters—and if the newspaper ran a picture of Mitchell, the lady just might remember that she'd seen him Saturday night.

The mayor seemed unusually shaken by the whole situation, which also worried Sykes. He thought everything could be managed if no one lost his cool, but the mayor's hold seemed to be slipping a little. Because of that, he was reluctant to call Nolan and tell him the Minor woman hadn't shown up. He didn't want to send the mayor off the deep end, but neither did he want to just let the situation languish. He needed to find her and get things taken care of so that that loose end was tied off and the mayor would settle down. They had another shipment of girls coming in, Russians, and Sykes wanted everything handled before they arrived. They stood to make some big money off this batch; one was supposed to be only thirteen, and as pretty as a doll.

He drove by the Minor house several times after dark that night, when he wasn't as likely to be noticed, but the beige Ford still hadn't showed up. Finally it occurred to him to go to the Buffalo Club. *Duh!* He felt like smacking himself in the head. This Minor babe was into partying, not sitting at home nights with two old women. Feeling certain he'd find her there, Sykes made the drive to Madison County.

But when he scouted out the parking lot, the beige Ford wasn't there. The traffic was lighter on Mondays than it was on the weekend, so he was certain he hadn't missed it. Either she had already hooked up with some guy and gone home with him, or she had gone to some other club.

Okay, it was beginning to look as if the best way to find her was to stake out where she worked. That should be easy to find out, in a small town like Hillsboro. Hell, the mayor might even know her. Come to think of it, he'd sounded unusually subdued when he'd called and given Sykes her name and address; maybe he *did* know her, and his conscience was acting up.

Sykes couldn't find the woman now, but he was damn sure where she'd be tomorrow: at work. He figured he might as well go home and get a good night's sleep, then call the mayor in the morning on the chance he knew the woman and knew where she worked—she was such a classy-looking babe, the mayor might even have the hots for her. Sykes hoped not. The mayor had become skittish enough already without Sykes's having to eliminate one of his playmates.

But everything would work out tomorrow. Tuesday looked like a busy day.

Daisy and Jack took turns getting up every two hours and taking Midas out. Like a little trooper, he did exactly what he was supposed to every time. Unfortunately, every time they brought him back in, he thought it was playtime and it took another half hour or so before he cuddled up and went back to sleep.

"This is like having a newborn," Jack said at seven o'clock, sitting at the table and sipping his second cup of coffee. His face was rough with stubble and his eyes had dark circles under them. Daisy lacked the stubble, but her eyes matched his.

She looked down at Midas, who was lying on his back with all four paws in the air, and the stuffed duck in his mouth. "Except you don't have to chase down newborns," she said. "They pretty much stay where you put them."

"I'll get him a ball. Chasing it should wear him out, so he'll nap longer—and more often."

Despite her fatigue, Daisy beamed at him. That was so sweet, buying her puppy a toy. He'd been very good natured about the whole thing last night, but then he *had* volunteered to stay. She would have loved to have made love with him, but at the same time, sleeping together and not having sex had been . . . kind of wonderful. They had even managed to cuddle, though Midas had been right there, squeezing his fat little body between them as if that was his natural place.

"Since you got a welcome mat instead of a guard dog," he said, with a pointed look at the puppy, "I want you to be especially careful until I satisfy myself there's nothing to worry about with this tag-number deal. There are a few things I want to check out. Until then, I'll drive you to and from work, and stay here at night."

"Okay," she said, a little astonished. It sounded as if he planned to move in, at least for the short term. What astonished her was how pleased she felt. She should be out trying to find a husband, but she didn't feel as enthusiastic about it as she had just a few days before. Of course, a few days before, she hadn't had a lover, and she hadn't watched him cradle her puppy in his strong arms to carry it out for a nature call in the middle of the night. Just remembering that made her feel squishy, as if she had turned to mush inside.

Maybe Jack wasn't her type, but somehow she didn't much care.

"The city council meets tonight," he continued, "so I'll bring you home, then go to my house to shower and change clothes, and come back here when the meeting's over."

"Should I wait with supper?" she asked, just as if they did this all the time.

"No, go ahead and eat. If you have the chance." He gave Midas a wry glance, then began chuckling. The puppy had dozed off, still on his back with his feet in the air.

While she was thinking of it, she called her mother to see if she was still willing to puppy-sit.

"I'll come over there," Evelyn said. "As far as I'm concerned, that fenced back yard is priceless. I'll be over about eight-thirty, so you'll have plenty of time to get to work."

That taken care of, Daisy hung up the phone and immediately began to worry about how she would explain to her mother why Jack was driving her to work. As for explaining his presence—she was, after all, a thirty-four-year-old woman—she didn't owe explanations about her love life to anyone.

"You have to leave," she said. "My mother's coming over."

He seemed to be fighting a grin. "If you feed me breakfast, I'll be out of here by eight o'clock. I'll go home, shave and change clothes, and be back here in plenty of time to get you to the library."

"It's a deal," she said promptly. "It doesn't take long to whip up a bowl of cereal."

"Biscuits," he wheedled.

Exasperated, she turned on the oven.

"And eggs and bacon."

What was a home-cooked meal, compared to the trouble he was going to on her behalf? He was just lucky she had stocked up on all the necessary things out of habit before she realized she wouldn't be doing much cooking for herself. Cereal in the morning and a sandwich at night was much more practical when there was only one sitting down at the table.

She put the bacon in the frying pan, covered it with a screen so the grease wouldn't splatter all over her new stove, then got out the flour, oil, and milk and began mixing up the biscuit dough. Jack watched in amazement. "I thought you would use the canned kind."

"I don't have any."

"You actually know how to make homemade biscuits?"

"Of course I do." She stopped to take out her new biscuit pan and coat it with nonstick cooking spray. She didn't roll out the dough, but did it the way her mother had taught her: she pinched off a certain amount of dough, rolled it into a ball, flattened the ball with a quick pat, and placed it in the pan.

"Aunt Bessie did it that way," he said, fascinated. "She called them choke biscuits, because she choked off the dough instead of using a biscuit cutter."

"Biscuit cutters are for sissies." She had made as many biscuits as she, her mother, and Aunt Jo usually ate, but she figured

Jack would eat as much as two of them put together. The oven was still heating, so she checked on the bacon and turned it.

Jack got up and poured himself another cup of coffee, grabbed the Huntsville morning paper off the counter, and went back to the table. Daisy hadn't had time to even glance at the paper the day before, because of Midas, but she could always read it at the library.

The oven beeped as it reached the pre-set temperature. Daisy put the biscuits in to bake and turned to get the eggs out of the refrigerator. As she did, a picture on the front page caught her eye. The man looked familiar, though she couldn't quite place him.

"Who's that?" she said, frowning a little as she pointed.

Jack read the caption. "His name was Chad Mitchell. A hunter found his body Sunday morning."

"I know him," she said.

He put down the paper, his gray-green eyes suddenly sharp. "How?"

"I don't know. I can't quite remember." She got out the eggs. "How do you want them, scrambled or fried?"

"Scrambled."

She cracked four eggs into a bowl, added a little milk, and beat them with a fork. "Set the table, please."

He got up and began opening cabinet doors and drawers until he found the plates and silverware. Daisy stared absently at the bacon as she turned it one last time.

"Oh, I know!" she said suddenly.

"He was a library patron?"

"No, he was at the Buffalo Club. He tried to dance with me, that first night, and wanted to buy me a Coke, but the fight started before he could get back."

Jack set the plates down and gave her his full attention. "That was the only time you saw him?"

She cocked her head as if studying a scene in her memory. "I don't think so."

"What do you mean? It either was or wasn't."

"I'm not certain," she said slowly, "but I think I saw him in the parking lot of the club on Saturday night, before I went inside. He was with two other men; then a third one got out of a car and joined them. He didn't seem all that drunk when he came out of the club, but then he passed out and they put him in the bed of a pickup."

Jack rubbed the back of his neck in an almost angry gesture. "Jesus," he muttered.

She stared at him, her cheeks a little pale. "Do you think I was the last person to see him alive?"

"I think you saw him get killed," he said harshly.

"But—but there wasn't a shot or anything. . . ." Her voice trailed off, and she sagged against the cabinet.

Jack looked at the article, checking his facts. "He was stabbed."

She swallowed and turned even whiter. Jack started to reach for her, but she suddenly gathered herself and did what women have done for centuries when they were upset: they busied themselves doing normal stuff. She tore off a paper towel and lined a plate with it, then took up the bacon, placing it on the paper towel to drain.

Moving that frying pan out of the way, she took out a smaller one, sprayed it with cooking spray, then poured the beaten eggs into it and set it on the hot eye. She checked the biscuits, then got the butter and jam out of the refrigerator and set them on the table.

Jack looked around. "I don't want to use the cordless. Do you have a land line?"

"In the bedroom."

He got up and went into the bedroom. Daisy busied herself stirring the eggs and watching the biscuits as they rose and began to brown. After a minute he came back into the kitchen and said,

"I have some people checking into some things, but I'm afraid one of the men in the parking lot saw you, and got your tag number."

She stirred the eggs even harder. "Then call the mayor and ask him who gave him the number."

"There's a slight problem with that."

"What?"

"The mayor lied to me when he asked me to run the number. He may be involved." Jack paused. "He's *probably* involved."

"What do we do?"

"I've already taken steps to make sure no one can find you. Don't tell anyone you've moved; tell your mother and aunt not to mention it—in fact, call your mother back and tell her to make certain no one follows her when she comes over here."

She gaped at him. "This is my mother, not James Bond!"

"Then tell her to let your aunt drive. I think that woman could outdo Bond."

In the end, he was the one who called her mother, and in a calm tone told her what he wanted her to do. Daisy concentrated on breakfast, which was about all she could handle right then. "Another thing," she heard him say, "do you have Caller ID? Then erase it. I don't want Daisy's number showing up anywhere."

"I need to give a statement," she said when he hung up. "Don't I?"

"As fast as possible." He picked up the phone again and hit *re-dial*. When her mother answered, he said, "Daisy won't be at work today. Call—"

He glanced at Daisy, who said, "Kendra."

"—Kendra and tell her to handle things. Make something up. Tell her Daisy has a toothache."

When he hung up again, he said, "If this guy is trying to get to you before you can give a statement and description, possibly even make a positive i.d. from police photos, then the thing to do is give it as fast as possible so he won't have anything to gain."

"Don't I have to be alive to testify?" she asked, and was proud her voice was so steady. She raked the fluffy scrambled eggs into a bowl, took the perfectly browned biscuits out of the oven and dumped them in a bread basket, then set everything on the table.

"You will be," he said. "That's a promise."

TWENTY

Sykes did something he'd never done before: he called Temple Nolan at home, bright and early Tuesday morning. Wherever the blonde worked, he wanted to be there in plenty of time to intercept her if possible, or in place to follow her home when she left. It would make for a long day, but he was a patient man.

Temple answered on the third ring, his voice fogged with sleep. "Y'ello?"

"It's me."

"Sykes!" Instantly, Temple sounded more alert. "For God's sake, what are you doing calling me here?"

"The Minor woman never showed up at the address you gave me. You sure she lives there?"

"I'm positive. She's lived there her whole life."

That answered one question, Sykes thought; the mayor definitely knew the woman personally.

"Then she stayed somewhere else last night. Maybe she has a boyfriend."

"Daisy Minor? Not likely," Temple scoffed.

"Hey, if she's hanging out at the Buffalo Club, she isn't Mother Teresa."

"I guess so," Temple said reluctantly. "And she's bleached her hair. Damn!"

"The good news is, she seems to be clueless."

"Then maybe we could forget about—"

"No." Sykes was decisive. "She's a loose end. The shipment of Russians will be here soon; do you want to take the chance this Minor woman doesn't screw up things? I don't think Phillips would take kindly to losing that much money. The Russians are worth three times any of our other shipments."

"Shit."

Hearing acceptance, Sykes said, "So where does she work? If I can, I'll grab her this morning, maybe at lunch. If not, I'll follow her this afternoon when she gets off and get her then."

"She's the damn librarian," Temple said.

"Librarian?"

"Hillsboro Public Library. She works next door to city hall. She opens the library at nine and she's the only one working until lunch, I think, but you can't grab her there. There are too many people going and coming from city hall and the police department, and you can see the library parking lot from both places."

"Then I'll follow her at lunch, see if I get a chance. Don't worry. One way or another, I'll get her today."

As the two men hung up, in her bedroom Jennifer Nolan quietly depressed the disconnect button and held it as she settled the receiver back into place. She had been listening in on Temple's calls for years now, a sick compulsion she couldn't resist. She had heard him make assignations with so many different women she had long since lost count, and yet every time he did, a little part of her still died. Over the years she had tried to muster enough self-respect to divorce him, but it was always easier to dull things with alcohol and other men. Sometimes she had even been able to drink enough that she could pretend the other men hurt him the way his women hurt her, but she had lost even that forlorn hope when he began asking her to sleep with men to whom he owed favors.

Elton Phillips was one of those men, and since then Jennifer had actively hated her husband, hated him with a fierceness that ate at her like acid. He *knew*, he had to have known, what Elton Phillips was like, and still Temple had sent her to him. In the privacy of Phillips's bedroom she had screamed and cried and begged, and in the end merely endured, praying that she wouldn't die—until she reached the point that she prayed she *would* die.

But he hadn't intended to kill her; there was no need. He trusted Temple to keep her under control, not that she would have gone to the cops anyway. She never wanted her children to find out what had been done to her, or what part their father had played in it. Jason and Paige barely tolerated her anyway, because of the alcohol; they would turn their backs on her forever if they knew about all the other men, and Jennifer had no doubt Temple would make certain they knew.

Had Temple even noticed that she hadn't willingly had sex since she'd recovered from Phillips's assault? She could barely tolerate it now, and only if she'd had enough to drink beforehand. Temple had even stolen that pleasure, sordid as it had been, from her. She had nothing left now except her children.

And maybe Temple had just given her the means to get rid of him and keep Jason and Paige.

She struggled to remember all she'd heard. Temple had said the man's name, something like *Lykes.* No—it was *Sykes.* And something about a shipment of Russians, which didn't make sense. She couldn't imagine Temple being involved in bringing in illegal aliens; he was vociferous in his opinion about what the country needed to do to beef up its borders to stop the flow of wetbacks. She knew one thing, though: if Elton Phillips was involved, then it was nasty.

But that about Daisy Minor—Jennifer was certain she hadn't misunderstood that. Daisy was a "loose end," and loose ends were tied up. Jennifer knew what that meant, though how Daisy could be involved with Temple was also something that didn't make sense; Temple went for glossy women who knew the rules and never gave him any trouble. It sounded as if Daisy was causing a lot of trouble. That man, Sykes, was going to "get" her. He'd meant *kill* her.

She needed to tell someone about this, but who? The local police department would be the logical choice, but how likely were they to take her seriously? Their mayor was planning to kill the librarian? Plus he's smuggling in Russians? Sure. Very believable.

At the very least she needed to warn Daisy. Jennifer reached for the bedside phone, but stopped before lifting the receiver. If she could listen in on Temple's calls, he could listen in on hers.

She had until lunchtime; that was when Sykes was going to try to grab Daisy.

Whom to call? The Jackson County Sheriff's Department? The FBI in Huntsville? Or Immigration? Not the sheriff's department, she thought; with the kind of network Temple had built, they were too close for comfort. Temple spent a lot of time in Huntsville, though; could he have any influence on the federal level? Surely not. Still, the last thing she wanted to do was underestimate him; she'd have this one chance, and one chance only, to get away from him and not completely lose what little affection her children had left for her.

She tried to think, something she hadn't let herself do in far too long. She had no friends whom she could call for help or advice. Her parents had moved to Florida, and her one brother hadn't spoken to her in years; she didn't think she even had his phone number. When had she become so isolated?

She had to do something, even if it was nothing more than drive to the library and warn Daisy. She wouldn't even have to do that. She could just wait until Temple left the house, so he couldn't overhear her, and then call to warn Daisy. That was okay for the short term, but she had to figure out something that would stop Elton Phillips and her husband, once and for all.

Evelyn dropped what she was doing, got dressed, and came right over. As soon as she arrived at Daisy's house, she fixed Jack with a mother's gimlet stare and said, "What's going on that you thought I might be followed, why shouldn't we tell anyone where Daisy's moved to, and why did I have to erase her number off my Caller ID?"

"It's possible she witnessed a murder," Jack said as he took his plate to the sink.

"My goodness," Evelyn said weakly, sinking down into the chair he had vacated. Midas bounced around her feet in exuberant greeting, and she automatically leaned down to pet him.

"The body was found in Madison County, so I'm taking her to Huntsville to give a statement. What has me worried is that someone got her tag number and had it traced, so someone may be trying to find her. I might be overreacting, but until this is settled, I'm keeping her hidden."

"This is my daughter you're talking about. You aren't overreacting. Do whatever you have to do to keep her safe, you hear me?"

"Yes, ma'am. In the meantime, warn everyone in your family not to answer any questions about her. Don't give anyone any information, not even the mayor. He may be involved."

"My goodness," Evelyn said again. "Temple Nolan?"

"He's the one who had me trace the tag number."

"There's probably a perfectly good explanation—"

"Would you risk Daisy's life on that possibility?"

"No, of course not."

While they had been talking, Daisy had been methodically cleaning up the kitchen, her brow furrowed with thought. "If Mayor Nolan's involved, then he knows all of us: Mother, Aunt Jo, Beth, me. None of them are safe, either, if the object is to get to me. He'd know I would do anything to protect them." She looked at Jack; the colors of her eyes intensified in her pale face. "Can you protect all of them? Not just Beth but Nathan and the boys, too?"

He hesitated, then told her the truth. "For a while. Then money problems start kicking in. Deputies can't be indefinitely assigned to guard duty."

"Then unless I can make a positive identification of one of the three men from police photos, or they happen to solve the crime and it was someone else entirely, we're looking at a long-term situation."

He nodded, his gaze holding hers. He wished she hadn't made such an accurate assessment, but she was too intelligent and well read not to have eventually figured it out anyway. Watching her expressive face, he could practically read the thoughts chasing through her mind.

"Don't borrow trouble; we've got enough to handle right now. We'll do this one step at the time. You make the statement, give them descriptions of the three men, and we'll take it from there."

"All right, but for now, I don't just want my family guarded, I want them *gone.*" She turned to Evelyn. "How about a week in the Smokies? You and Aunt Jo, and Beth's entire family."

"I'm not leaving you with this going on!" Evelyn said fiercely.

"I'll be safer if you do," Daisy pointed out, with irrefutable logic.

Evelyn hesitated, torn between common sense and a mother's instinct to fight for her child.

"For one thing," Daisy continued, "guarding one person would be much easier for the police than guarding seven. For another, I won't be distracted if I know you're safe, so I won't be as likely to make any mistakes."

"She's right," Jack said, throwing his weight behind her arguments. "Pack up and leave town as fast as you can. I can assign a couple of officers to guard you until you do, and have the Huntsville department do the same for Beth's family."

"What about the puppy?" Evelyn looked down at Midas, who was gnawing on one of the chair legs. "Who will take care of him?"

Daisy followed her gaze and swooped down on him. "Midas, no, no," she said sternly, picking him up. If her tone of voice registered with him, it wasn't evident from the joyous wiggling, tail-wagging, and licking with which he welcomed her attention. "I'm obviously not going to work for the duration, so I'll take care of him."

Evelyn said, "Midas, huh?" in a tone that said she had accepted, however reluctantly, the need to leave her daughter in Jack's care.

Daisy brushed her nose against the plush fur to hide the sudden tears that welled in her eyes. "Jack named him. It was either that or *Fuzzbutt.*"

Jack moved forward before the scene got uncomfortably emotional. "Ladies, you have a lot of preparations to make. I'll make some calls; Mrs. Minor, two of my officers will be waiting for you when you get home."

"Goodness," she said, reaching for the phone. "I'd better warn Jo."

Thirty seconds later, she was heading out the door. Jack said, "Call Beth and tell her to start packing. Would Nathan already be at work?"

"No, he's on second shift."

"Good. I'll call Huntsville and get some protection on them right away. If he has any problems reporting off with his employer, let me know and I'll get the okay."

Evelyn was nodding as she went down the porch steps. She suddenly stopped and turned back to him. "There's one thing I want you to know."

"What?" he asked warily, put on guard by the narrowing of her eyes.

"I make a darn good mother-in-law, if I do say so myself. But I'll make an even better enemy, if you let anything happen to my daughter."

"Yes, ma'am," he said, understanding completely.

Daisy stared after her mother, her eyes round with surprise. "She just threatened you," she said incredulously.

"And very well, too."

"Um . . . that thing about a mother-in-law—"

"We'll talk about it later. Go get ready." He rubbed a rough hand over his jaw, making a rasping sound. "Mind if I borrow your razor? I don't want to leave you to go home and shave."

Daisy got ready while he was on the phone in her bedroom. She kept leaning out of the bathroom trying to hear what he was saying, but couldn't make out many of the words. Finally she gave up and concentrated on what she was doing, staring at herself in the mirror and feeling as if none of this was real. She was ordinary Daisy Minor, a librarian who had lived her whole life in this little town. People like her didn't expect things like this to ever happen to them. But she had decided to go husband-hunting, and now someone was hunting her. It was open season all around.

Jack came into the bathroom. "Okay, everything's set with your family. My officers will escort your mother and aunt to Beth's house. They should all be out of reach within a couple of hours."

"Good." She leaned forward and applied some lip gloss, then stepped back. "The bathroom's yours. The razor's in the medicine cabinet."

He looked down at Midas, who of course had followed them and was now plopped on his belly, chewing on Jack's shoelaces. "You have a crate to put him in while we're gone, don't you?"

"No, but that's okay." She bent down to separate puppy and shoes. "We're taking him with us," she said as she left to get dressed.

Temple lingered over his breakfast of freshly squeezed orange juice and a bagel with cream cheese. Usually he left the house by eight-thirty, but by eight-forty-five he still hadn't left. Patricia, their cook and housekeeper, left the kitchen to tidy the bedrooms and do the laundry.

Jennifer didn't eat; she seldom did, but usually it was because her stomach was too queasy from her drinking the day before. Today the queasiness was caused by jagged nerves. She sat silently, drinking a cup of coffee and wishing she could add just a dash of whiskey to it, but she didn't dare. If she added one dash, she'd add two, and soon she'd leave out the coffee altogether. Her hands were shaking, and she clasped them around her cup, willing the shakes to stop, praying Temple would leave soon because she didn't know how much longer she could last.

He didn't speak to her, but then he seldom did. They lived in the same house, but their lives were almost completely separate. He no longer told her when there were social functions she might have been expected to attend as the mayor's wife; he no longer told her anything, not where he was going or when she could expect him back. He didn't tell her the details of his day; if one of the kids called him, he didn't even tell her that, though she knew from things they had said that they called him regularly. They must be calling him at work, she thought, because they never called here.

She might already have lost them beyond recovery, she thought, and swallowed the nausea that welled up on a bubble of pain. Her babies . . . they were grown, now, but part of a mother always remembered that time when they had just come from her body, when they were so tiny and helpless and she was their entire world, and they were hers.

Her children were ashamed of her. They didn't want to talk to her, didn't want to be around her. Temple had done this, but he'd done it with her help. She had sought refuge in a bottle instead of facing the truth: the man she loved didn't love her, had never loved her, would never love her. She was a means to an end for him. She should have taken the children and left him, and no matter how nasty the divorce got—and it would have gotten nasty, she trusted Temple on that—at least she would have had her pride, and her children wouldn't look at her with contempt.

Jennifer looked at the clock. Five till nine. Why was he staying so long?

The phone rang, startling her. Temple got up and answered it on the cordless, taking it with him into his office and shutting the door.

So that was why: he'd been waiting for a phone call.

Shakily she took her cup of coffee upstairs to her bedroom, closing and locking the door. Patricia had already made the bed and tidied her bathroom. Jennifer sat down on the bed and looked at the telephone. If she picked up now, Temple would hear the click; when she listened in, she always picked up just as he did, and she covered the mouthpiece with her hand so no noise would leak through.

Her heart pounded. She lifted the receiver and started punching buttons, as if she were making a call. She didn't even put the receiver to her ear, and she heard Temple shouting, "Jennifer! Damn it, I'm already on the phone."

"W-what?" she stammered, slurring her voice just a little. Maybe he'd think she had started drinking before she came downstairs. "S-sorry. I was just calling—"

"I don't give a damn. Get off the line."

She heard a chuckle on the other end, a deep laugh that made her go cold and every hair on her body lift in alarm. Elton Phillips.

"Sorry," she said again, then placed her hand over the mouthpiece and quickly clicked the button to make it sound as if she'd hung up.

"The stupid bitch," Temple muttered. "Sorry about that."

"That's all right," Phillips said, and laughed again. "You didn't marry her for her brain."

"That's for damn sure. If I had, I'd be shit out of luck, because she doesn't have one."

"I'm beginning to wonder if she's the only one whose bulb doesn't glow all that brightly. You've made several mistakes lately yourself."

"I know. I apologize, Mr. Phillips. Sykes has everything under control."

"That remains to be seen. The Russian girls will be here tomorrow morning, and I want Mr. Sykes's full attention on handling the shipment. If he doesn't take care of this librarian problem before then, I'll be very unhappy."

Belatedly, Jennifer remembered that the answering machine function built into the phone included a "call record." She blinked at the base unit, looking for the correct button. It had to be with the other function buttons. PLAY, DELETE, PAUSE—there it was: CALL RECORD. She depressed the little red button and prayed that it didn't make a noise or beep a warning.

"He'll grab her when she leaves the library for lunch, or when she goes home this afternoon. She'll just disappear. When Sykes handles something personally, there aren't any problems."

"Really? Then why was Mitchell's body found so fast?"

"Sykes didn't handle it. He stayed behind at the club to find out who had seen them in the parking lot. The other two were the ones who handled the body."

"A mistake on Mr. Sykes's part."

"Yes."

"Then this is his last chance. And yours."

Phillips abruptly hung up, and Jennifer almost cut the connection on her end. She waited, though, waited for a couple of long seconds. Why didn't Temple hang up? She sat with her finger poised on the button. Was he waiting to see if he heard a betraying click? Cold sweat trickled down her spine.

Finally the line clicked, and in the next split second she disconnected, too, returning the receiver to the hook. She dashed across the room to unlock her door, then ran into the bathroom and quickly squeezed some toothpaste on her toothbrush, turned on the water, and began brushing for all she was worth. Temple never came to her bedroom; she was panicking for no reason—

The bathroom door opened and Temple said, "What in hell—"

She jumped and shrieked, spewing toothpaste all over the sink. She was so shaky that she lost her balance and stumbled backward, colliding with the toilet and almost falling over it, but she managed to grab the tank and steady herself, sitting down hard on the lid.

Temple eyed her with disgust. "For God's sake, you haven't even had breakfast and already you're drinking."

With a trembling hand she wiped the toothpaste off her mouth and didn't say anything. Let him think she was drunk; that was safer.

"Who were you calling?"

She indicated her hair, accidentally swiping the toothbrush against the side of her head. "I need my hair done."

"No joke. Next time, make sure I'm not using the phone before you pick up and just start punching numbers." He didn't wait to see if she agreed; he just turned around and left. Jennifer rested her head against the sink, taking deep breaths and trying to slow her pulse rate. When she felt steady enough, she got up and washed her face, rinsed out her mouth, then used a washcloth to wipe the toothpaste out of her hair.

She hadn't turned off the answering machine recorder. She went back into her bedroom; Temple had left the door open, so she went over and closed it again, then went to the phone and stopped the recording.

That little tape was golden. The question was, what did she do with it? Who could she take it to? Temple had often said that the new police chief, Russo, was "his" boy, meaning he had Russo in his pocket. He'd been glad when old Chief Beason retired, because Beason had been around a long time and had his nose poked into too many things, knew too many secrets. It remained to be seen if Russo was as blind as Temple thought him to be, but Jennifer couldn't take the chance right now. It was too important that she get this right.

She stayed in her room another half hour, then went downstairs to see if Temple had left. He wasn't in his office, so she checked the garage; his car was gone.

Finally! Seating herself at his desk, she looked up the number for the library and quickly dialed it.

"Hillsboro Public Library."

Jennifer took a calming breath. "May I speak to Daisy Minor, please? This is Jennifer Nolan."

"I'm sorry, but Daisy isn't working today. This is Kendra Owens; may I help you with something?"

Dear Lord, now what? "Is she at home? Can I reach her there?"

"Well, I don't know. Her mother said she had a toothache, so she's probably at the dentist's office."

"Do you know which dentist she uses?" Jennifer felt her control slipping. She needed a drink so bad. No. No, she did *not* need a drink; she needed to concentrate on what she was doing.

"No, I don't."

"This is important, damn it! Think! I need to get in touch with her immediately; someone is going to try to kill her."

"Excuse me? Ma'am? What did you say?"

"You heard me!" Jennifer clenched the receiver so tightly her knuckles turned white. "You have to find her! I heard my husband on the phone talking to a man named Sykes who's going to kill her, unless I can warn her first."

"Maybe you'd better call the police—"

Jennifer slammed down the phone and buried her face in her hands. Now what? Dentists. How many dentists could there by in Hillsboro? Not many, but what if Daisy went to a dentist in, say, Fort Payne? Or Scottsboro?

No, wait. Call Daisy's mother and find out which dentist she used.

She looked up that number, but the phone rang and rang, and no one answered.

Jennifer flipped to the Yellow Pages, located *Dentists-Dentistry,* and began dialing. She couldn't give up now. She'd failed at a lot in her life, but she couldn't fail at this.

TWENTY-ONE

Dogs aren't allowed in public buildings unless they're service dogs," he said for the fifth time when they were on their way to Huntsville.

Daisy looked over her shoulder at Midas, who was asleep on his blanket in the backseat. "They'll let him in unless they want to take my statement in the parking lot."

Jack had argued the whole time she was putting Midas's dishes in his car, along with a supply of food and water. He had argued when she clipped the leash to the puppy's tiny collar. He had argued when she spread the blanket on the backseat and deposited Midas on it, along with his stuffed duck and rubber chew toy. He had argued until she got into the passenger seat and fastened her seat belt, and then he'd gotten behind the wheel without another word.

As far as Daisy was concerned, the subject of Midas was

closed. Anyone who would kill another human being wouldn't hesitate to kill a dog; Midas was under her guardianship now, and she wouldn't leave him in the house alone, helpless and unprotected.

"I've been thinking about that night," she said, absently watching the mountains as they drove. "I saw their faces when they came out of the club, because the neon sign was shining down on them. There were two of the men, with Mitchell between them. The third man was waiting in the parking lot. Then a car pulled in and the headlights caught them, and I saw the faces of all three because they looked at the car. I didn't know any of them, but I can describe them."

"Just get the details straight in your mind, and hold them there." He reached over and took her hand. "Everything will be all right."

"I know." She managed a smile. "You promised my mother."

They reached the building that housed the Madison County Sheriff's Investigation and Patrol offices at nine-thirty. It was a two-story sixties-type building, yellow brick on bottom and pebbled concrete on top, with long, narrow, vertical windows. The sign on top said *Forensic Sciences Building*. The departments of forensic sciences and public safety were also in the building.

"Huh," said Daisy. "I might have known it would be here."

He looked puzzled. "Why?"

She turned and pointed. "Because you just passed a Krispy Kreme doughnut shop."

"Do me a favor," he said. "Don't mention it to them."

He put his cell phone in his pocket, then gathered Midas's paraphernalia while Daisy got the puppy out of the car and carried him to a little patch of grass. He obediently squatted, she praised him, and he pranced at her heels as if he knew he'd been a very good boy. He didn't like the leash, though, and caught it in

249

his mouth. Every few steps he'd stop and bat at it. Finally she picked him up, cradling him on her shoulder as if he were a baby. Content, he licked her chin.

No sooner had they stepped inside the building than a female deputy said, "You can't bring the dog in here."

Daisy immediately stepped back outside and waited. Unwilling to leave her out there by herself even though he was certain they hadn't been followed, Jack said to the deputy, "Please call Detective Morrison and tell him Chief Russo is here with the witness," and went back outside himself to wait with her.

The summer heat was already broiling, and the humidity was so high the air felt thick and heavy. Daisy lifted her face to the sunshine anyway, as if she needed the light. They didn't say anything, just waited until Detective Morrison came outside with a quizzical expression on his dark face. "Deputy Sasnett said you brought your dog—" He broke off when he saw the puppy, his expression changing to a grin. "That isn't a dog. That's a ball of fluff."

Jack offered his hand. "I'm Jack Russo, Hillsboro's chief. This is Daisy Minor, the witness I told you about. Where she goes, the ball of fluff goes."

He shook Jack's hand, scratched his head, and said, "I'll be right back." Five minutes later, having cleared the way, he led Jack, Daisy, and Midas to his office.

Midas was an angel, sitting on Daisy's lap while she calmly told the detective what she'd seen Saturday night. Yes, she was certain the man in the middle was the man who had introduced himself to her the week before as Mitchell, and, yes, she was certain that was his photograph in the paper. She described what he'd been wearing, to the best of her memory: jeans, boots, and a light-colored western-style shirt. Detective Morrison quietly passed Jack the crime scene photos. The clothes were dirty, since the body had been buried, but they were as Daisy had described them. That meant Mitchell hadn't changed clothes from the time Daisy saw him in the Buffalo Club parking lot, which definitely upped the chances that he had been killed that night.

"Do you want to see them?" Jack asked Daisy.

She shook her head, and he passed the photos back to Detective Morrison.

Jack's cell phone rang. He took it out of his pocket, looked at the number showing in the window, and said, "It's the office. I'll take it outside."

He stepped out into the hall before hitting the *talk* button. "Russo."

"Chief, this is Marvin." Tony Marvin was the first-shift desk sergeant. He sounded uneasy, as if he wasn't certain he should be calling. "Kendra Owens just called from the library. Jennifer Nolan, the mayor's wife, called wanting to speak to Miss Minor, and when Kendra told her she wasn't there, Mrs. Nolan became very agitated. She said Miss Minor's life was in danger, that she'd overheard the mayor on the phone with a man named Sykes. Mrs. Owens said Mrs. Nolan seemed convinced they intended to kill Miss Minor. Since you had us put that protective detail on Miss Minor's mother and aunt this morning, I thought you should know about this."

The little hairs on the back of Jack's neck stood up. "You're exactly right, Tony. It's looking like the mayor's in trouble up to his ass. Have Mrs. Nolan picked up; take her statement." He paused, thinking. "Keep her there. Put her in one of the interview rooms and hold her."

"Mrs. Nolan, Chief?"

"Her life could be in danger, too."

"You mean this isn't just a case of Mrs. Nolan hitting the bottle way too early?"

"I wish it was. Get a deputy out to the Nolan house as fast as possible."

"Yes, sir," said the sergeant. "Uh, what do you want me to do when the mayor hears about this?" Tony said "when," not "if," because in a small town there was no "if."

"Stall him. Blow him off. Make it sound as if she's drunk and you don't believe a word she's said. I don't want to spook him until we have her statement."

"Okay, Chief."

"And don't put anything on the radio about it; telephone contact only. That'll buy us some time."

Jack disconnected and called Todd, and brought him up to speed. "Jennifer Nolan's statement will give us reasonable grounds for getting a court order on those phone records, so if you don't already have them, now we can get them legally. She gave us a name, too: *Sykes.*"

"It's always nice to do it legally," Todd said dryly.

"Before, I was just curious and uneasy. It's different now." Now that he knew there was a crime involved, everything had to be by the book. He didn't mind bending the rules—or outright breaking them—when it was personal, but it was more than personal now. He didn't want this case thrown out of court because of a technicality.

"I'll see what I can find on Sykes. If he's had so much as a speeding ticket, I'll find him."

Jack stepped back into the detective's office and told them what was going on. Detective Morrison made quick notes, his left hand bent in that peculiar position so many lefties used. "If your mayor was involved with Chad Mitchell, he isn't particular about his friends. Mitchell was a bottom-feeder; we've had him on resisting, possession, attempted rape, theft, B and E. We got him last year on date rape, but the prosecutor couldn't make it stick. He never did any major time, six months here, a year there."

"Possession," said Jack. "Of what, exactly?"

Morrison consulted his file. "Marijuana, mostly. A small amount of cocaine. Rohypnol, clonazepam, GHB."

"He was big on the date-rape drugs."

"How does Mayor Nolan fit in with this?" Daisy asked. "He wasn't one of the three men I saw with Mitchell, but he has to be involved somehow."

"My guess is Sykes was one of the three, though, and Sykes is tied to the mayor in some shady deal they're working."

"That's the most logical scenario," said Morrison, getting to his feet. "Miss Minor, you said you saw them briefly, but clearly. I know it'll take a lot of time, but I'd like you to look at our mug shots, see if you recognize anybody. Don't guess; be *sure,* because if you aren't, the defense lawyer will tear the case apart."

Midas had been an angel the whole time, sitting in Daisy's lap, but when she stood up to follow Detective Morrison, he decided it was time to do some exploring and began wriggling madly in his effort to get down. Daisy set him on his feet, and he immediately made a dive for the detective's shoes. "Quick, where's his duck?" she said as she rescued shoelaces, which was more difficult than it should have been because Detective Morrison started laughing and shuffling his feet, sending Midas into a spasm of joy at the new game.

"Here." Jack separated the duck from the rest of puppy things he'd brought in with him, and tossed the duck across the floor. Seeing a new target, and one that was evidently running from him, Midas abandoned Morrison's shoes and bounced after the duck. When he captured the escapee, he gave it a hard shake, then tossed it over his head and pounced again.

"I'm sorry," Daisy apologized. "I just got him yesterday, and he's only six weeks old, so I couldn't leave him alone, especially not knowing if whoever was looking for me might hurt Midas if he couldn't find me."

"Yes, ma'am, some folks are mean," the detective agreed. "It's best to be safe. Tell you what; since you have the puppy, I'll bring the mug shots in here for you to look at. That way he won't get too excited, seeing a lot of people at once."

"That's a *real* good idea," Jack said, grabbing the duck before Midas could get to it, and tossing it again. His black eyes bright with glee, Midas bounced and pounced, then dragged the duck back to Jack and dropped it at his feet.

"Well, look at that," said Morrison, marveling. "Didn't take him long to catch on, did it?"

Jack was still throwing the duck when the detective came back, his arms laden with pages of mugshots. Entranced with the game, Midas ignored Morrison's return.

Daisy settled at the desk with the photographs in front her, for the first time realizing the enormity of the task. This wasn't a matter of looking at fifty pictures, or even a few hundred. There had to be *thousands* of them, and the photographer seemed to be particularly unskilled, because the photographs could scarcely have been more unflattering to the subjects.

She closed her eyes and pictured the three men she'd seen, then picked out the most distinctive face: long, narrow, with prominent brow ridges. He'd had long, dirty blond hair and long sideburns, a distinctly unappealing style. Hair could be changed, though—she was an expert on that—so she disregarded that and concentrated on face shapes. She could also automatically disregard anyone in a minority. By adapting the system she'd learned in a speed-reading course, she began skimming pages and turning them at a faster clip, occasionally pausing to study a face and then move on.

After fifteen minutes, Midas lay down on her feet to take a nap. Daisy stopped to glance down at him, and Jack used the opportunity to ask, "Do you want something to drink? Coffee? A soft drink?"

"I don't recommend the coffee," said Morrison.

Daisy shook her head. "I'm fine."

Morrison said, "Then I'll leave you to it. I have some calls to make, so I'll borrow an office and check back when I'm finished."

Minutes ticked by, marked only by the soft swish of the pages as she turned them. Midas eventually roused, and Jack took him outside. When he came back, with the puppy prancing on the end of the leash as if he'd done something wonderful, Jack said, "It's time for lunch. You need to take a break."

"I'm not hungry," she said absently.

"*I* am."

She looked up in amusement. "You ate four times what I did at breakfast."

"Which is why you need to eat. If I'm hungry, you have to be."

"In a little while." She turned her attention back to the pages, blinked, put her finger on a photo, and said in a positive tone, "That's one of the men."

The man's hair was shorter in the photo, but his sleazy sideburns were still long, the color was still dirty blond, and the Neanderthal brow ridges hadn't changed.

Jack briefly studied the photograph, said, "I'll get Morrison," and disappeared out the door.

Daisy sighed and gently rubbed her eyes. One down and two to go. The other two wouldn't be as easy as this one, either, since he was the most distinctive of the three.

Morrison came back on the double and looked at the photograph Daisy pointed out. "George 'Buddy' Lemmons. I know this joker. We've had him on B and E, assault, robbery, vandalism. He's another bottom-feeder. He usually pairs with . . . ah, hell, what's his name?" He went out of the office and they heard him call down the hall, "Hey, Banjo, you remember Buddy Lemmons?

We got him for wrecking that old lady's house over on Bob Wallace last year. What was the name of the other perp?"

"Calvin . . . something Calvin."

"Yeah, that's right." Morrison came back into the office muttering, "Calvin, Calvin." He sat down at his computer and typed in the name. "Here he is. Dwight Calvin. Is he one of the other men?"

Daisy went around and looked at the photograph on the computer screen. "Yes," she said positively, studying the slight, dark-haired, big-nosed man.

"You're sure?"

"I'm sure. I haven't seen anyone who looks like the third man, though."

"It would help if we had Sykes's first name, but we'll pick up these two birds and my guess is they'll start singing. Buddy and Dwight aren't big on taking the fall for anyone else. In the meantime, Miss Minor, where will you be?"

"At home," she began, but Jack shook his head.

"Until this is settled, I'm checking her into a hotel, and I'm not telling anyone where she is—not even you, Morrison. If you want to get in touch with her, call my cell phone, because that will be the only contact."

TWENTY-TWO

Just where are you planning on stashing me?" Daisy asked when they were in the car. "I have the puppy with me, re-member?"

"Like I could forget," Jack muttered. "I don't like the idea of stashing you anywhere, but it's the only logical thing to do. Some motels take pets; I'll call the local Triple A and find one."

"I don't have any clothes with me," she pointed out. "Or books."

"I'll send someone by your house to pack some things for you."

She thought about that. "Send Todd. He'll know what to get."

"I told you, Todd isn't gay."

"That doesn't matter. He knows what separates go together, and what makeup to bring."

"Eva Fay—"

"Todd."

"All right," he said under his breath. "I'll send Todd."

In the end, he didn't have to call Triple A to locate a motel that accepted pets; they drove by a new place that had just been built off I-565, pulled in, and checked, and it did have two rooms allocated for people with small pets. Both rooms were empty at the time, so Jack chose the one that faced the rear. He checked her in under a false name—she was now Julia Patrick, he informed her when he got back into the car and drove around the building to her assigned room.

He unlocked the door and carried in Midas's things while Daisy let the puppy investigate a patch of grass and chase a butterfly. He was too young to do much chasing; after a few minutes, he flopped on his belly to rest. The heat was almost searing, too hot to let him play outside without any shade to shelter him. She carried him inside the blessedly cool room and gave him some water, and with a tired sigh he settled down on his blanket.

"I'll be back tonight with your things," he said. "I don't know what time, but I'll call first. Don't open the door to anyone except me."

She sat down on the king-size bed. "All right." She wouldn't beg him to stay, though she wanted to. She had been leaning on those strong shoulders all day long, she realized, letting him handle everything. Of course, murder *was* his field of expertise, so to speak; he knew exactly what to do.

She wanted to ask him how long she'd have to stay here, but that was a silly question: he had no real idea. Morrison might locate Lemmons and Calvin right away, or the two might have left town. They might locate Sykes, or they might not. Jennifer Nolan's testimony might be reliable, but everyone in town knew she was an alcoholic; if she'd been drinking this morning, that had to call her statement into question. Everything was up in the air.

Jack had been a rock. Daisy knew she would have managed

without him, but it had been nice to have him planning the course of action, taking care of her family, even keeping Midas occupied while she looked through the mountain of mug shots.

He sat down beside her and put his arm around her, hugging her close to his side. "Are you all right?"

"I'm still feeling a little stunned," she admitted. "This is so . . . unreal. I watched a man die, and I didn't even realize."

"You don't expect to see a murder. Unless there's a shot or a big fight, most people wouldn't notice. It's too far outside their experience." He tilted her chin up and kissed her. "I'm glad it was outside your experience," he murmured.

Until he kissed her, she hadn't realized how much she had been craving him, his taste and touch, the hot male scent. She put her arms around his neck and whispered, "Don't go just yet."

"I need to," he said, but he didn't get up from the bed. Instead his arm tightened about her and his other hand slid down to her breasts, stroking over them before beginning to unbutton her blouse. Daisy closed her eyes as bliss began unfurling inside her, made all the stronger by the stress of the day. For a little while, so long as he touched her, she could forget and relax.

She tugged his T-shirt free and slid her hands under it, flattening her palms against the heavy muscles of his back.

"All right, you convinced me," he said, shucking the shirt off over his head and standing to unfasten his belt. Jeans, underwear, socks, and shoes came off in one rough motion, and he left them on the floor, tumbling to the big bed and taking her with him. Her sandals dropped to the carpet. He wrestled her out of her blouse and bra, tossing both garments toward the dresser on the other side of the room.

He pressed kisses to her stomach as he unzipped her denim skirt and peeled it down, then trailed up to her breasts and sucked her nipples until they were hard and flushed with color, sticking out like raspberries. She felt dizzy, but was ravenous for more. She couldn't get enough of him, couldn't satisfy the urge to touch him, because every texture made her want more.

"It's my turn," she said, pushing on his shoulders.

He obediently rolled over onto his back and covered his eyes with a forearm. "This is going to kill me," he muttered.

"Maybe not."

Thoroughly delighted with this opportunity, she cupped his testicles in both hands, feeling the weight and softness of his scrotum, the hardness within. She buried her face against him, inhaling the musty scent, darting her tongue out to taste. His penis jerked against her cheek, enticing her, so she turned her head and took him in.

He groaned and his hands fisted in the bedspread.

She had no mercy, not that he asked for any. She tasted and licked and stroked until his powerful body was drawn like a bow, arching on the bed. Then she stopped, sat back, and said, "I think that's enough."

An almost inhuman sound rumbled in his chest and he jackknifed, grabbing her and twisting and coming down on top of her. She laughed as he fiercely stripped her panties down and pushed her legs apart, settling between them and positioning himself for the strong, single thrust that took him to the hilt and changed her laughter to a groan. She drew her legs up, clasping them around his hips, trying to contain both the depth of his strokes and the wildness of her response. She wanted to savor every moment, not rush headlong into climax, but already she could feel the tension building.

He stopped, his muscles flexing with tension. "Fuck," he said between gritted teeth. "I don't have a condom."

Their eyes met, his narrowed with the savagery of the control he was trying to retain over his body, hers wide with sudden awareness.

His hips rocked as if he couldn't hold still another moment. "Do you want me to stop?" His face was grim with the effort it took him to make the offer. Sweat gleamed on his forehead and shoulders, despite the air conditioner blowing directly on the bed.

Common sense said yes. A lifetime of responsible behavior said yes. They shouldn't take the risk, or any more risk than they already had just in his unprotected penetration. Some deep, primitive instinct, however, craved the feel of him inside her, and her lips moved, forming the word *No.*

His control broke, and he began thrusting deep and hard, over and over, and what had begun as simple pleasure became something more, something wrenching and powerful. Daisy clung to him because she could do nothing else, because with that one word she had demanded everything he could give her and could hold back none of herself. She arched in climax, her heels digging into his thighs, the shuddering starting deep and spreading out in convulsive waves. For a long moment she stopped breathing, stopped thinking, caught on a peak of sensation so sharp it blurred the world around her. Then it faded and slowly she went limp, muscle by muscle, legs and arms falling open and releasing him to move fast and strong in his own orgasm.

His heavy weight crushed her into the mattress, but she couldn't find either the strength or the will to protest. He was utterly limp, his heartbeat slamming against his rib cage, his breath rushing in and out of his heaving lungs. Maybe they dozed; time certainly seemed to disappear.

After a while, groaning with the effort, he withdrew and moved off her to lie on his side and hold her close. Daisy buried her face against his throat, acutely aware of the wetness between her legs. This could be a disaster. But it didn't feel like a disaster; it felt . . . right.

Gently he stroked her. She tried to think of something to say, but there didn't seem to be anything *to* say, nothing that needed saying. All she needed to do was come to terms with what lay between them a sudden awareness that this was much more than an affair.

It couldn't be. Could it?

"God, I've got to get back to the office," he muttered. "I can't believe I let myself get sidetracked like this."

"I'm sure five minutes one way or another won't make much difference," she consoled.

He opened one eye and glared at her. "Five minutes? I beg your pardon. I've been better than five minutes since I was sixteen."

She twisted around to look at the clock on the bedside table. The problem was, she didn't know if they had dozed, or for how long. She decided to give him the benefit of the doubt. "Then I'm sure an hour one way or another—"

"An hour! Shit!"

He bolted out of bed and went into the bathroom. She heard the sound of water running, the toilet flushed, then he came back out and went to the foot of the bed, where he'd left his clothes on the floor. He looked down and froze.

Alarmed by his expression, Daisy struggled up on her elbows.

He looked up then, and in a very even tone said, "Your dog ate my shorts."

She tried not to laugh; she really did. She managed to hold it in for about one second; then giggles started shaking her like little earthquakes. Once one erupted, they immediately morphed into a belly laugh that rolled her onto her side, holding her stomach as if she could contain them that way.

He bent down and picked up the puppy, holding him at eye level. It was impossible to deny Midas's guilt, because shreds of the dark green boxers were hanging from his mouth. He seemed very happy about it, too, wagging his tail at a frantic beat, paddling his feet as he tried to get within licking distance.

Jack said, "Fuzzbutt, you're a pain in the ass." But he said it in an almost crooning tone, and he cuddled the puppy to him as he removed the shreds from the little mouth.

Daisy looked at the fuzzy puppy and the big, naked man holding him so gently, and she thought her heart would leap right out of her chest. She had already been halfway there, but in that moment she fell completely, irrevocably in love.

No, this wasn't an affair, at least not on her part. It was much, much more.

He put Midas on the bed, leaving Daisy to deal with the puppy while he got dressed. As she fended off big feet and a madly licking tongue, Daisy watched the jeans slide up over his naked butt and had some very lascivious thoughts.

When he was dressed, he leaned over her and kissed her, and the kiss became longer and deeper than either of them had intended. Spots of color burned high on his cheekbones when he pulled back, and his eyes were narrowed again. "You're dangerous," he muttered.

"All I'm doing is lying here." She caught Midas as he began pulling on the bedspread, told him no, and removed the fabric from his mouth.

"That's what I said. A naked woman and a fuzzy puppy: what more can a man want? Well, maybe a beer. And a good ball game on the tube. And—"

She grabbed one of the pillows and threw it at him. "Go!"

"I'm going. Remember, don't open the door—"

"—to anyone but you," she finished.

"I don't know what time I'll be back. There's a Huddle House next door if you get hungry." He scribbled some numbers on the notepad by the bed. "This is my cell number, the number of my office, and Todd's numbers here and at home. Call any or all of them if you need anything."

"Why do you have Todd's numbers?" she asked curiously.

"I might have known you'd ask," he muttered.

"Well, why do you?"

"Because he's helping us locate Sykes. He has some good contacts we're using." He kissed her again, scratched Midas behind the ears, then was out the door and gone.

Daisy climbed slowly out of bed, her legs protesting. Midas went over to examine the big wet spot on the bedspread, and she hastily grabbed him, setting him on the carpet. He followed her to the bathroom, nosily sniffing around as she washed off.

Embarrassed by the thought of the motel maids finding the bedspread in that condition, Daisy industriously worked at the spot with a wet washcloth and a hand towel until she was certain nothing would show when the spot was dry.

Her first wet spot, she thought, staring at the dark circle. She hoped it was the first of many, because she wanted Jack Russo to be the father of her children.

It remained to be seen whether or not he wanted the same thing. He hadn't run when her mother had made that pointed comment about the kind of mother-in-law she was, but then he wouldn't, not with a murder investigation going on and her to protect. He wasn't a man who shirked his responsibilities.

She really should have made him stop, she thought as she dressed. She didn't want him to marry her because she got pregnant; she wanted him to love her. This time it would probably be okay—the timing wasn't right—but Mother Nature had a way of playing tricks and she wouldn't breathe easy until she got her period.

She sat down and looked around the motel room. As motel rooms went, she supposed, it was nice. It was larger than normal, maybe because it was one of the rooms for people with pets. There was a recliner for sitting, a round table with two chairs, and a tiny refrigerator with a four-cup coffeemaker sitting on top. The bathroom was functional but unremarkable.

Now what?

On impulse, she got out the phone book and looked up *Sykes.* She didn't know this particular Sykes's first name or where he lived, so there was no point in the exercise, but she looked at the list of Sykeses and thought about calling each one. She could say something like, "Mr. Sykes, this is Daisy Minor. I hear you're try-ing to kill me."

Not a great idea. What if he had Caller ID? That would tell him where she was.

She didn't normally watch much television, but there was nothing else to do. Midas had decided to have another snooze; when he woke, she would carry him out again, but how much time would that occupy? She picked up the remote, settled in the recliner, and turned on the television.

She didn't like waiting and doing nothing. She didn't like it at all.

At least her family was out of reach. Daisy knew she would have been a nervous wreck if Jack hadn't gotten them out of town. Her mother was sure to call this evening to reassure herself Daisy was all right, and she'd be worried when there was no answer. On the other hand, Jack seemed to think of everything, so he had probably given her mother his cell phone number or another way she could check.

But what about Jack? She went cold. It was no secret they were involved, not after the way he had sat beside her in church. What if Mayor Nolan heard the gossip and told this Sykes to go after Jack as a way of flushing her out of hiding?

She made a dive for the telephone and called Jack's cell phone. He answered after one ring. "Russo."

"You have to be careful, too," she said fiercely.

"What?"

"If the mayor finds out we're involved, that makes you a target just the way my family was."

"There's a difference between your family and me."

She loved them all, so she couldn't see this difference. "Such as?"

"I'm armed."

"Just be careful. Promise me."

"I promise." He paused. "Are you all right?"

"Bored. Hurry back with those books."

Daisy fretted after she hung up, pacing around the room. She hated being stashed here out of the way, not knowing what was going on, not being able to help. It wasn't in her nature to just sit and wait. Once she identified a chore or a problem, she couldn't rest until it was handled.

Something had to happen soon, or she'd go crazy.

Jack frowned as he broke the connection. Daisy already sounded restless, which wasn't good. He needed to know she was doing exactly as he'd told her; he needed to know she was safe so he could concentrate on finding Sykes.

The call he had received right before Daisy's had him worried, though. One of his detectives had gone out to the Nolan place, but Mrs. Nolan hadn't been there. They hadn't located her yet. If Kendra Owens had gossiped about that phone call, it could already have gotten back to the mayor.

The little hairs on the back of his neck were standing up again.

TWENTY-THREE

Nadine hesitated in the doorway of Temple's office, her indecision plain on her face. He looked up, irritated. He'd been on edge all day, waiting to hear from Sykes, wondering if he'd already accomplished the mission. The phone call from Mr. Phillips hadn't been a joy, either. People who disappointed or ran afoul of Elton Phillips wound up dead. If Sykes didn't succeed this time, Temple knew he'd have to do something to placate Phillips. Kill Sykes, maybe. The prospect of killing Sykes worried him, because Glenn Sykes wasn't a fool and he wouldn't be an easy man to kill.

Nadine still lingered in the doorway and Temple snapped, "For God's sake, Nadine, what is it?"

She looked taken aback at his unusual irritability. Temple almost never let himself show temper; it wasn't good for the image. Today, though, he had other things besides his damn image to worry about.

Nadine wrung her hands. "I've never said anything before. I think people's private lives are just that, private. But I think you should know what Mrs. Nolan did today."

Jesus, not now. Temple covered his eyes, massaging the ache that ran under his eyebrows. "Jennifer has . . . problems," he managed to say, the way he had so many times in the past when he wanted to elicit sympathy. It was his pat answer, one he didn't have to think about.

"Yes, sir, I know."

When she didn't continue, Temple sighed, realizing he'd have to prompt her rather than say what he really wanted to say—that he didn't give a good goddamn what the bitch did, he hoped she'd T-boned a power pole and killed herself.

"What has she done this time?" That was another pat response, showing his patience and weariness.

Now that he had asked, Nadine spat the words out as if she couldn't hold them in any longer. "She called the library and told Kendra Owens you were trying to have Daisy Minor killed."

"*What?*" Temple shot up from his chair, color leeching out of his face. His knees wobbled in shock, and he had to grab the edge of his desk. My God. Oh, my God. He remembered the sudden uneasy feeling he'd had this morning, the one that had made him check to see what Jennifer was doing. The bitch had been listening in on her bedroom extension. Mr. Phillips would kill him. Literally.

"Kendra didn't take her seriously, of course, but she was worried in case Mrs. Nolan did something, you know, sort of foolish, so she called the police department and reported it."

"The fucking *bitch!*" Temple said fiercely, and he didn't know if he meant Jennifer or Kendra, or both.

Nadine stepped back, more than a little affronted by his language. "I thought you ought to know," she said stiffly, and closed the connecting door with a bang.

With a shaking hand Temple picked up his private line and called Sykes's number. After the sixth ring, he replaced the receiver. Sykes wasn't at home, of course; he was waiting to follow Daisy home from work. After Jennifer's stupid call, if Daisy had disappeared after lunch, the police department would have been on full alert, hunting for her, so the lack of action meant nothing had happened yet. He had to find Sykes and tell him to call off the whole thing. If anything happened to Daisy now, he, Temple, would be number one on the list of suspects.

Something had to be done about Jennifer. With her drinking history, though, it would be easy to set up an "accident." Bash her in the head, run her car into the river, and be done with it.

But not right away. Anything done right now would be too suspicious. They couldn't do anything to jeopardize the shipment of Russians.

First thing, though, he had to mend fences with Nadine. It wouldn't do to have her bad-mouthing him to her little circle of friends. Gossip like that had a way of spreading like kudzu vines.

He opened the door, mustered the charm, and said, "I'm sorry, Nadine. I had no right using language like that. Jennifer and I had an argument this morning, and I'm still on edge. Then to find out she did something like that . . ." He let his shoulders slump.

Nadine's expression softened a little. "That's all right. I understand."

He rubbed his forehead again. "Was Daisy upset when Kendra told her about the call?"

"Daisy isn't working today. Her mother called in and said she had a toothache. I have my own suspicions, but that's the story." She waggled her eyebrows, looking arch.

Nadine should never try to look arch, Temple thought; she resembled a flirtatious frog. "What do you mean, 'suspicions'?"

"About where she is. Well, I don't know where she is, but I doubt she has a toothache."

"Why do you say that?"

"Because I had to call over to the police department right before lunch, and Eva Fay said Chief Russo hadn't been in all day either."

The throb behind Temple's eyebrows worsened. "What does that have to do with Daisy?"

"You mean you haven't heard? They're seeing each other." For Nadine her satisfaction at being the first to impart this news more than made up for his rudeness and bad language.

Temple felt as if he'd been hit between the eyes with a two-by-four. "What? Seeing each other?" He could barely say the words, the shock was so great. Disaster yawned at his feet.

"Barbara Clud said they bought—well, they bought intimate articles together. Chief Russo sat with her at church on Sunday, too."

"Then it has to be serious." His voice sounded hoarse, and he made a show of clearing his throat. "Got a tickle in my throat."

Nadine fished a cough drop out of her desk and gave it to him. "I'd say it's serious, him going to church with her."

Temple nodded and escaped back into his office, trying to grasp all the ramifications of what he'd just learned. Damn it! When Russo had run that tag number for him, he'd pretended not to know whose it was. Why would he do that? What had made him hide the fact that he knew Daisy? There was no reason to unless . . . unless he knew damn well Daisy hadn't been parked in a fire lane at Dr. Bennett's office, and the only way he could know that was if he'd been with her during the time in question.

The "intimate articles" bought at Clud's Pharmacy had to be condoms, which meant they were sleeping together. Russo obviously wouldn't have spent the night with Daisy at her mother's house, but he had his own house to which he could take her. Temple had never thought Daisy Minor would spend the night with a man, but then he'd never thought she'd bleach her hair and go to the Buffalo Club, either. Daisy had evidently run wild.

So Russo knew he'd been lying about seeing the car. Russo wasn't a fool; he'd figure out real quick that someone else had asked Temple to find out who the car belonged to. That wasn't so bad, except for the lie. That was suspicious; Russo would wonder what was going on, and Temple didn't want a man like Russo wondering about anything he did.

Right now he had to do damage control. He had to find Sykes and call him off, he had to do something about Jennifer, and he had to make certain the shipment of Russians was handled smoothly, because the least hint of trouble at this point would be more than Mr. Phillips would tolerate.

Jennifer drove aimlessly, afraid to go home because surely Temple would have heard by now what she'd done. You couldn't keep things like that quiet in a small town. She couldn't stop crying, though she didn't know why she was crying at all, unless she was having a nervous breakdown and just didn't realize it. She couldn't do that, she thought; that would give Temple the chance to put her in a mental ward somewhere.

She had removed the little tape from the answering machine and dropped it in her purse. She would get someone to listen to it; she just didn't know who. Part of her wanted to just drive to the police department, walk in making as much noise and fuss as she could, and get someone to play the tape right there in front of everyone. That way it couldn't be disregarded, and no one would think she was drunk and imagining things. That would be the smart thing to do, but she couldn't seem to get her act together enough to do it.

She felt as if she were shaking apart on the inside; she needed a drink, needed one worse than she had ever needed one before in her life, and for the first time in her life, she was afraid to take one. Once she did, she wouldn't stop, and then she would be helpless. Her life depended on staying sober. She couldn't seem to think straight now, but she wouldn't be able to think at all if she drank.

Finally, almost automatically, she found herself on the road to Huntsville. It was the road she took to go shopping, to have her hair done. Whenever she left the house, it was to go to Huntsville. The road was nice and familiar. Twice she stopped and threw up, though she hadn't eaten anything and it was mostly dry heaves. Withdrawal symptoms, she thought; her body was rebelling against not having its accustomed alcohol. She had been dried out before, but always in a clinic, where she'd been given drugs to ease the way.

Maybe that's what she should do. Maybe she should check herself into a clinic, if she could manage to get herself all the way to Huntsville. She had done what she could, tried to warn Daisy; if she checked into a clinic, when she got out in a month, everything would be all over and she wouldn't have to deal with it.

Except she would have to deal with her conscience if anything happened to Daisy and she hadn't done everything she could to stop it.

She drove with both hands locked on the steering wheel, but still she couldn't seem to keep the car in the right lane. The dotted line seemed to wiggle back and forth, and she kept swerving, trying to stay on the right side of it. A big white car blew past, horn blaring, and she said, "I'm sorry, I'm sorry." She was doing the best she could. That had never been good enough, though, not for Temple, not for Jason or Paige, not even for herself.

A horn kept blowing. She checked to make certain she wasn't accidentally leaning on her own horn, but her hands were nowhere near it. The white car had gone past, she hadn't hit it, so where was that horn coming from? Her vision swam and she wanted to lie down, but if she did, she might not be able to get up.

Where was that damn horn?

Then she saw a flash of blue, the strobe effect making her even dizzier, and the big white car was on her left, coming closer and closer, crowding her off the road. Desperately she stomped the brakes to keep from colliding with the white car, and the steering wheel jerked in her hands, tearing free of her grip. She screamed as her car began a sickening spin and her seat belt tightened with an almost brutal jerk, holding her as she left the road; the front axle plowed into a shallow ditch, and something hit her in the face, hard.

Haze filled the car, and in panic she began fighting to get free of the seat belt. The car was on fire, and she was going to die.

Then the car door was wrenched open and a big, olive-skinned man leaned in. "It's okay," he said in a calm tone. "That isn't smoke; it's just the dust from the air bag."

Jennifer stared at him, weeping, torn between despair and relief that it was all over. Now she wouldn't have to decide anything. If Chief Russo was working in cahoots with Temple, there was nothing she could do about it.

"Are you hurt anywhere?" he asked, squatting in the open door and examining her for any obvious injuries. "Other than your bloody nose."

Her nose was bleeding? She looked down and saw red drops splattering all over her clothing. "What caused that?" she asked, bewildered, as if there was nothing more important than finding out why she had a bloody nose.

"Air bags pack a strong wallop." He had a yellow first-aid kit in his hand and he opened it, took out a thick pad of gauze. "Here, hold it to your nose. It'll stop in a minute."

Obediently she held the pad to her nose, pinching her nostrils.

"You called the library this morning and reported a threat you overheard your husband making," Chief Russo continued, his voice still as calm as if they were discussing the weather. "I'd like you to make a statement about what you heard, if you feel like it."

Jennifer tiredly let her head fall back against the headrest. "Are you working with him?" she asked, all nasally. What did it matter? There was nothing she could do even if he said yes.

"No, ma'am, I'm not," he replied. "Maybe you haven't heard, but Daisy Minor is a special friend of mine. I take threats against her very seriously."

He could be lying. She knew that, but she didn't think so. She'd suffered too much pain at a man's hands not to notice the complete absence of threat from Chief Russo. Her purse had spilled all its contents on the floorboard when she hit the ditch; she unfastened her seat belt and slowly leaned forward, scrabbling through the mess until she found the tiny cassette tape. "I didn't just hear it," she said. "I taped it."

TWENTY-FOUR

Mrs. Nolan was very shaky, but she was coherent. To cover all bases, Jack insisted she take a Breathalyzer test; nothing registered. She not only wasn't drunk, she hadn't had any alcohol that day. One of his investigators took her statement; then several of them listened to the answering machine tape. The mayor's voice sounded a little tinny, but recognizable.

"—*grab her when she leaves the library for lunch, or when she goes home this afternoon. She'll just disappear. When Sykes handles something personally, there aren't any problems.*"

"*Really?*" That was the second man, the one Mrs. Nolan identified as Elton Phillips, a wealthy businessman in Scottsboro. "*Then why was Mitchell's body found so fast?*"

"*Sykes didn't handle it. He stayed behind at the club to find out who had seen them in the parking lot. The other two were the ones who handled the body.*"

"A mistake on Mr. Sykes's part."

"Yes."

"Then this is his last chance. And yours."

Daisy hadn't been mentioned specifically, but with the mention of the library and Mrs. Nolan's testimony about the part of the conversation she hadn't taped, it wasn't necessary. Mitchell had been mentioned, and someone's seeing them in the parking lot of the club. With Daisy's testimony and identification of two of the men who had killed Mitchell and Temple's own voice on this tape, the mayor was firmly implicated in a murder. Mrs. Nolan didn't understand the reference she'd overheard about a shipment of Russians, but Jack was beginning to have nasty suspicions.

Regardless, the mayor and his friend were nailed.

Eva Fay was one of the people gathered around listening to the tape. She put her hands on her hips. "Why, that snake."

His people were angry, Jack saw. Investigators, patrol officers, and office personnel alike were incensed. He was no longer the outsider, but one of them, and his woman had been threatened. Not just any woman, but Daisy Minor, whom most of them had known for years. The bad thing about living in a small town was that everything became a personal issue. The good thing about living in a small town was that everything became a personal issue. During times of trouble, the support system was massive.

"Let's bring the mayor in for questioning," he said quietly, keeping a firm lid on his own anger. Daisy was safe; that was the important thing. "Contact the Scottsboro P.D. and have Mr. Phillips picked up, too." He would have liked to have thrown up a net to catch this Mr. Sykes, but he didn't have the manpower to block every street in town to check licenses. Sykes worried him, but as long as Daisy stayed put, Sykes couldn't find her.

"I've kept everything off radio," said Tony Marvin. "He won't have a clue we're on to him."

"Sure he will. Remember Kendra Owens? Do you think she's gone all day without mentioning Mrs. Nolan's call to anyone else?"

"Not Kendra," said Eva Fay. "She's sweet, but she loves to talk."

"Then we have to assume the mayor knows Mrs. Nolan called us. He'll be on guard, but he doesn't know about the tape, so he may not have bolted. C'mon, let's get this ball rolling."

The damn Minor woman wasn't anywhere in town, which made Sykes very nervous. She hadn't shown up at work; she hadn't been at home. She simply wasn't there. When people veered so far out of their normal routine, something was up.

He even called the library, taking care to use a pay phone in case they had Caller ID—not likely in a municipal building, but possible, and that damn call-return service meant he had to be cautious all the time anyway—and asked for Miss Minor. The woman who answered gave him no information other than that Miss Minor wasn't in that day, but there was an underlying tension, a stiffness, in her voice that worried him even more.

Okay, he wasn't going to get the Minor woman today. That was a setback, not a catastrophe.

But what had the woman at the library so on edge?

It was a small detail, the nervousness in a woman's voice, but it was the little details that would jump up and bite you on the ass when you least expected it, if you didn't pay attention and take care of them. His instinct told him it was time to pay attention.

He called the mayor on his private line, but there was no answer. That was another worrisome detail. If he knew the mayor, he'd planned to stay in his office all day long, providing himself with an airtight alibi in regard to Miss Minor's disappearance, just in case.

His next call was to the mayor's cell phone. No answer. Really uneasy now, Sykes called the mayor's house. Nolan himself picked up on the second ring.

"The Minor woman isn't working today," Sykes said. "I'm calling it a day."

"Sykes! Thank God!"

The mayor sounded winded and on the verge of losing control, which wasn't good at all.

"Listen, we're in trouble. We have to get our stories straight, back each other up. All we have to do is lie low for a while and I think it'll blow over."

"Trouble? How?" Sykes kept his voice mild.

"Jennifer overheard me talking to Mr. Phillips this morning, and the drunk bitch called the library, asking for Daisy. She wasn't there, so Jennifer told Kendra Owens that I was plotting to have Daisy Minor killed."

Jesus. Sykes pinched the bridge of his nose between his eyes. If the mayor had just used an ounce of caution in his telephone conversation—

"What did Kendra Owens do?" His question was just a matter of form. He knew damn well what Kendra Owens had done.

"She called the police department. It's a good thing Jennifer's a drunk, because I don't think anyone believed her, but if you'd grabbed Daisy today, it would have raised all sorts of questions."

Great. Now the Hillsboro cops were alerted.

"There's one other thing."

With an effort, Sykes remained calm. "What else?"

"Chief Russo and Daisy are romantically involved."

"And this interests me, how?"

"Russo is the one I called to run the tag number for you yesterday. I told him I'd seen the car parked in a fire lane at a doctor's office. He knows I lied, because he knew she wasn't sick.

And when he gave me the information, he pretended not to know her."

Okay, so now we had a suspicious chief of police. It was those damn details again; Nolan had added too many, and they'd tripped him up. If he'd just asked the chief to run the license plate, without explanation, then the chief would want to know why the mayor was running his girlfriend's tag number, but he wouldn't know Nolan had lied. For that matter, why did Nolan have to get the damn chief of police to run a simple tag number? But, no, Nolan couldn't use a lowly peon; he had to get the head man, just to show his power.

"I came home to find Jennifer, shut her up, but the bitch isn't here."

"That's good. Her turning up dead after making a call like that wouldn't look good."

"She's a drunk," said Nolan dismissively. "Drunks have wrecks all the time."

"Maybe they do, but the timing would still be suspicious. Just lay low."

Nolan didn't seem to hear him. "Maybe I'll take her for another visit to Mr. Phillips. He'd like that, but she wouldn't." The thought pleased him, because he laughed.

He was dealing with idiots. Sykes closed his eyes. "The police might be keeping an eye on her, so Phillips wouldn't like it if you led them straight to him."

"No. You're right. I have to find her, anyway. She said something about having her hair done, and she's just stupid enough to make a call like that, then toddle off to the beauty salon."

Or the police had brought her in to make a statement, which was the most likely thing. Didn't Nolan know a damn thing about police procedure? They didn't just blow off a call like that, especially when the subject was the chief's squeeze. Miss Minor had conveniently disappeared, Mrs. Nolan was also missing and probably at the police department, and the next step was to pick up the mayor for questioning.

This wasn't good at all. After Nolan's performance yesterday and today, Sykes had drastically revised downward his opinion of the mayor. He was cold-blooded, but he didn't hold up under pressure, and he let his ego get in the way of clear thinking. What would happen when the cops started asking him questions? Nolan might hold the line, but if he got rattled, Sykes figured he'd try to cut a deal and roll over on everyone else.

Well, he couldn't let that happen.

"How good a cop is the chief?" he asked.

"Damn good. He was a SWAT team member in Chicago, then in New York. I was lucky to get him for a small town like Hillsboro."

Yeah, lucky the way a turtle crossing a busy highway was lucky: it took a miracle to get him across unsquashed. Sykes didn't figure Nolan had any miracles coming. He'd picked a chief who was at home on the front lines, one who would act aggressively in dealing with a threat to his woman. The only thing working in their favor at this point, as far as he could see, was that Mitchell's death and the discovery of his body hadn't happened in Russo's jurisdiction.

Then a thought occurred to him. "Did you mention Mitchell this morning when you were talking to Mr. Phillips?"

"That was why Mr. Phillips called. He wasn't happy that the body had been found so fast, and I explained to him that it was because you hadn't handled it yourself."

So Nolan had mentioned not only Mitchell, but Sykes's name as well. Mrs. Nolan didn't know them, but now she had their names. This whole thing was unraveling so fast Sykes couldn't even begin to catch the threads.

"Tell you what," said Sykes. "Just sit tight, pretend nothing unusual is going on, and they can't touch us." *Yeah, right.* "Nothing has happened, no attempts have been made against Miss Minor, so no crime has been committed. Russo might wonder why you lied about her tag number, but so what? Stick to your story. Maybe you wrote the number down wrong, transposed some numbers or something."

"Good idea."

"If they question you about Mrs. Nolan's telephone call, tell them you have no idea what she's talking about. Was she drinking this morning?"

"She's always drinking," said Nolan.

"Did you see her have a drink?"

"No, but she was clumsy, falling over stuff."

The way things were going, if Nolan thought his wife was drunk, Sykes was willing to bet she'd been stone-cold sober.

"Do you think Russo will ask me any questions?"

Is the sun coming up tomorrow? "Probably. Don't sweat it; just follow the plan."

"Should I warn Mr. Phillips?"

"I wouldn't. Let this blow over, and he'll never know anything about it. We'll handle this shipment of Russians and he'll be happy as a clam."

"Shit, I forgot about the shipment."

"No problem. I've got it covered," said Sykes, and disconnected.

What he had here, he thought, was a major fuckup. The mayor's wife had his, Sykes's, name, and Mitchell's. If Russo was half the cop Nolan thought he was, he had Mrs. Nolan's statement and was checking out everything she said. Mitchell hadn't been found in his jurisdiction, but with goddamn computers everywhere, all Russo had to do was a search and, lo and behold, there was a dead man named Mitchell. That would really get things stirred up, and when they began wondering what a dead man named Mitchell had to do with Daisy Minor, they'd show her Mitchell's photograph and she just might remember where she'd seen him—and the three men who had been with him.

There were times when there was nothing else to do but cut your losses and do damage control. This was one of those times.

Sykes pondered his options. He could cut out; he had his alternate identity in place. But he'd always thought he'd save the alternate identity for a life-and-death situation, and this didn't qualify. He'd have to take a hit, maybe do a year or so of hard time, but maybe not even that. He hadn't been the guy with the knife; they could get him for conspiracy to commit, obstruction, things like that, but not murder one.

Besides, he had a powerful weapon to use: information. Information was what made the world go round, and prosecutors make deals.

He had no faith in Temple Nolan; the man would roll over on a dime. Within a few hours, Glenn Sykes would be a wanted man.

But not if he rolled first.

Calmly, the way he did everything, Sykes drove to the Hillsboro Police Department. For a P.D. in a sleepy little town, the place looked unusually busy; there were a lot of cars in the parking lot. He walked in through the automatic glass doors, noting the officers standing in clumps talking in low voices, the air of tension. Patrol officers should be out in their cars, patrolling, so these guys were probably the first shift, hanging around. Again, a telling detail.

He went up to the desk sergeant, his hands at his sides, obviously empty. "I'd like to speak to Chief Russo, please."

"The chief's busy. What can I help you with?"

Sykes looked to his left, down a long hall. He briefly saw a very pretty woman, distraught, accepting a cup of coffee from a plainclothes guy, probably an investigator. Because he'd made it his business to know things about Temple Nolan, he recognized Mrs. Nolan right off. She certainly didn't look or act drunk; so much for Nolan's theory.

He turned back to the desk sergeant. "I'm Glenn Sykes. I think y'all are looking for me."

TWENTY-FIVE

Of all the things Jack had never expected to happen, having Glenn Sykes walk into the station, introduce himself, and ask to speak to him was number two on the list. Number one was his reaction every time he got close to Miss Daisy, but he was learning to live with that. He was also beginning to think nothing was impossible.

Sykes was of average height, a little stocky, and neatly dressed. His sandy hair was short and neat; he was clean-shaven, his nails pared and clean, clothes pressed. He didn't look like anyone's version of a hit man, but then Ted Bundy hadn't looked like a monster, either. Criminals came in all shapes, sizes, colors, and could be wearing rags or diamonds. The smart ones wore diamonds. The really smart ones looked like this man.

Sykes was also very calm, and certain of what he wanted. "I want to cut a deal," he said. "I can give you Mayor Nolan, the man who stabbed Chad Mitchell, a man named Elton Phillips, and a lot more. Let's get the D.A. in here and talk."

"We know who stabbed Mitchell," Jack said, leaning back in his chair. "Buddy Lemmons."

Sykes didn't even blink. "Miss Minor identified him, didn't she?"

"She got a good look at all three of you."

"So you've got her stashed someplace safe."

Jack didn't respond, just watched Sykes. The man had an excellent poker face, giving away nothing.

"There's something a lot bigger than just a stupid piece of trash getting offed." Sykes leaned back, too, as relaxed as Jack.

"I was wondering how the mayor is tied in."

"There's a lot of money in the sex trade," Sykes said obliquely. "You going to call the D.A. or not? You need to move fast; there's something big going down tonight."

"The Russians," said Jack.

Sykes whistled softly through his teeth, not even trying to hide his surprise. "Guess you know a lot more than I thought. But you don't know where and you don't know who."

"I'm guessing Mayor Nolan does, though."

"He'll sing like Tweety Bird," Sykes agreed.

"So why would the D.A. want to deal with you?"

"Because trust is a rare commodity, and I don't have much of it."

Jack studied the sandy-haired man, the clear, cold eyes and utter calm of his manner. "You've got the goods on all of them, don't you? You documented everything."

"That's right." Sykes gave a thin smile. "Just in case. I like having a little leverage when things go wrong. And sooner or later, they always go wrong. You just gotta learn when to get out."

Jack left the room and placed the call to the district attorney in Scottsboro. If a deal had to be made, he thought Sykes would be a better state witness than Mayor Nolan, simply because Sykes struck him as more ruthless and organized. Sometimes you had to deal with the devil, and this was one of those times.

Then he called the motel where he'd left Daisy, wanting to give her the word that she was safe. The front desk switched him through to her room, and he listened to the ringing. Four rings. Five. Six. He began to sweat.

Maybe the front desk had put him through to the wrong room; mistakes happened. He disconnected, called back, and asked for her room again. One ring. *Two.* A cold fist knotted in his chest. She should be there. *Three.* Maybe she was getting something to eat at the Huddle House. *Four.*

Sykes was here. There was no way Daisy was in any danger now. *Five.*

She wouldn't have left for any reason, would she? She was safe there. But what if she'd come up with one of her off-the-wall plans and thought she could trap Sykes or the mayor?

Six.

Logic told him she was okay. The worst fear he'd ever known, however, whispered all sorts of scenarios to him, scenarios that ended with Daisy—

Seven.

He tried to imagine a life without Daisy in it, and it was like hitting a stone wall. Full stop. Nothing.

Eigh—

"Hello?" Her voice was a little breathless, as if she'd been running.

The relief that poured through him was almost as shattering as the fear had been. His hand tightened on the receiver, and he briefly closed his eyes, "What took you so long?" he growled.

"I was outside with Midas. Actually, the leash slipped out of my hand and I've been chasing him."

He hadn't meant to say anything, but he was still so shaken from those few moments of terror that the words slipped out. "I thought you'd left."

She paused. "Left? As in *left* left, rather than just stepped outside for a minute or gone to get something to eat?"

"I was afraid you'd come up with one of your plans—"

"Have I ever given you any reason to think I'm stupid?" she demanded angrily. "I'm safe here; why would I leave? That's what always happens in movies; either the woman or the kid disobeys instructions and does exactly what they've been told not to do, thereby putting both themselves and everyone else in danger. I've always thought that if they were that stupid, then let them die before they have a chance to breed. My goodness, you'd think I make a habit of—"

"Daisy," he said softly.

She paused in her tirade. "Are you about to apologize?"

Maybe that would speed things up. "Yeah. I'm sorry. I panicked."

"Apology accepted," she said in that prim voice that made him want to grin.

"I called with some good news, sweetheart. Sykes walked into the station a little while ago and gave himself up, wanting to make a deal. You're safe."

"You mean it's all over?"

"There's some mopping up to do. I've been in contact with Morrison, and they haven't found Lemmons and Calvin yet, but they will. The mayor's wife got him on tape making threats against you, and Sykes is ready to roll over on everybody. I don't know what time I'll get back to pick you up."

"So I don't have to stay here tonight?"

"You might. This could go on all night."

"When Todd brings my things, I'll just have him drive me home instead."

Guiltily, Jack glanced at his watch. It was after six, and he hadn't remembered to call Todd at all. "I'll try to catch him at his store, save him a trip."

"You forgot to call him, didn't you?"

He sighed. "Busted."

"Under the circumstances, you're forgiven. Has my mother called?"

He'd had his cell phone with him all day, even carrying it into the john with him, so he knew he hadn't missed any calls. "Not yet." Mrs. Minor wouldn't wait too much longer before checking on Daisy, though.

"Just get her number, and I'll call her back when I get home. Call Todd now," she reminded him.

"I will." He did, and luck was with him; Todd was still in Huntsville. Jack brought him up to date and asked him to pick up Daisy.

"Sure, no problem." Todd paused. "Sykes mentioned the sex trade. He may have some information on the men I'm looking for, or on the dealers who sell the date-rape drugs."

"The way this thing's spreading out, anything's possible. If you want to ask him some questions yourself, I can swing it."

Another pause. "I can't get officially involved."

"I know. I'll get the D.A. to question him about drugs, but if you want to talk to him personally later, just let me know."

"For now, I'll stay behind the scenes and see what the D.A. comes up with."

"It's your call. Just don't forget to pick up Daisy. By the way, she has her puppy with her."

Todd said warily, "You said that like you're warning me about something."

"You haven't met Midas, have you?"

"What is he, a half-grown Great Dane?"

"He's a six-week-old golden retriever. A ball of fuzz. Dogs don't come any cuter. He melts hearts left and right."

"And?"

"And don't turn your back on him."

Smiling, Jack hung up and went back into the room where his investigators were taking Sykes's statement. Another investigator and a patrol officer were on their way to pick up Mayor Nolan and bring him in for questioning. They had gone from not knowing anything that morning to pretty much having things sewn up tonight. Some of it had been pure luck, such as his noticing Mrs. Nolan on the road back from Huntsville because she was driving erratically, but most of the events had been the direct result of someone doing something stupid. Even Glenn Sykes, who was pretty damn sharp, had been stupid to get involved in the first place. It all came down to the choices they made, and criminals in general made stupid choices.

When the D.A. and his assistant got there from Scottsboro, the D.A. was noticeably upset. He took Jack aside and said, "Elton Phillips is a very respected member of the community. We have to be very sure of what we have before I'm going to proceed an inch with this."

"We have him on tape, and we have corroborating testimony from Mr. Sykes. I'm pretty damn sure."

"Was the tape legally obtained?"

"Mayor Nolan's wife taped it with the answering machine on her bedroom extension."

The D.A. considered that. It was Mrs. Nolan's own phone, and the mayor obviously knew there were extension phones in his house, therefore he couldn't argue that he had an expectation of privacy concerning his telephone conversations. The legal ground seemed pretty solid.

"Okay, let's see what Mr. Sykes has to tell us."

When Temple Nolan saw the white city-owned car turn into his driveway, he took a deep breath and forced himself to remain calm. Everything would be all right. Sykes's suggestions had been reasonable; Jennifer's wild telephone call could be explained away, as could his asking Russo to run a tag number for him. As Sykes had pointed out, since he hadn't been able to find Daisy, no crime had been committed. If Daisy had realized she'd seen anything important in the parking lot of the Buffalo Club, she'd have already told someone. They were clear.

His doorbell rang. Quickly he took off his tie and rolled up his shirtsleeves, to give himself a casual, unworried look. Picking up a section of the Huntsville newspaper, he took it with him to answer the door; he looked like a man who had been reading the newspaper and unwinding, a man with nothing to hide.

He affected a look of mild surprise when he opened the door. "Richard," he said to the investigator. "What's up?"

"We'd like to ask you some questions about an allegation your wife made this morning," Investigator Richard Hill said, and he didn't sound apologetic, either. That was a little worrisome, Nolan thought.

"Sure. Come on in. Nadine told me about Jennifer calling the library, but I didn't think anyone would take it seriously. Jennifer . . . has a little problem with alcohol, you know."

"Yes, sir," said Investigator Hill. He eyed the newspaper, the rolled-up sleeves. "Settling down for the evening, sir?"

"It was an upsetting day. I brought some paperwork home with me; after I finish the paper and have supper, I'll work on that for a while. Is something wrong?"

Hill looked at his wristwatch. "I'm just surprised you didn't remember the city council meeting tonight," he said calmly. "It started five minutes ago."

The mayor froze, aghast. He'd never, in nine years, missed a city council meeting. Richard Hill knew something drastic would have to be wrong for him to totally forget about it. "I remembered," he said, trying to cover himself. "But it seemed best to stay home with Jennifer tonight." Thank God he'd lowered the garage doors, so they couldn't see that Jennifer's car wasn't in the bay.

"Mrs. Nolan is at the station," said Investigator Hill, still very calm and polite. "If you'll come with us, sir, we'll drive you there."

"Jennifer's at the station?" God, what should he say now? How could he explain not knowing where she was? "Is she all right?" Good. A touch of concern. That was inspired.

"Mrs. Nolan's just fine, sir."

"That's a relief, because she was . . . over the top this morning, if you know what I mean."

"Please come with us."

"Sure. I'll take my car and follow you—"

"No, sir, I'd prefer you ride with us."

Nolan stepped back, but Hill and the patrol officer smoothly flanked him and grasped his arms, forcing them behind his back. Handcuffs were quickly snapped around his wrists.

Outraged, he stared at the two men. "Get these cuffs off me! What do you think you're doing? I'm not a criminal, and I refuse to be treated like one."

"It's procedure, sir, for your safety and ours. They'll be re-moved at the station." They physically shepherded him from the house, their grasps on his arms propelling him forward.

"You're fired!" he ground out, his face turning dark red. "Both of you. There's no excuse for this kind of treatment."

"Yes, sir," said Hill as they put him in the backseat of the car and closed the door.

Nolan could barely breathe, he was so furious. Jack Russo had to have instigated this, to get back at him for . . . surely not be-cause he'd asked him to run Daisy's tag number; that was ludi-crous. But what else could it be? Maybe Russo was the insanely jealous type who went off the deep end at the least attention any-one paid to his girlfriend.

The only other explanation was that they believed Jennifer.

He began hyperventilating and forced himself to slow his breathing. He could handle this; all he had to do was stay calm. No matter what Jennifer said, he could put a spin on it that threw everything she said into doubt. After all, she was a drunk, and the whole town knew it. She had no proof, just one side of a tele-phone conversation that she'd overheard, and she was bound to have garbled it.

When they reached the police department, he was aston-ished at the number of cars there. Something was going on, something more than the city council meeting. Then he saw three of the city councilmen standing outside the glass doors leading into the station, and his stomach knotted. The sun was going down and the fierce heat had abated, but sweat adhered his shirt to his back as Hill opened the car door and assisted him from the backseat.

The city councilmen looked at him, but they didn't make eye contact. It was as if they were watching an animal in a zoo, noth-ing more than a matter of curiosity.

"Take these cuffs off!" he said to Hill in a fierce undertone. "Goddamn it, the city council is watching."

"I'll take them off when we're inside, sir," said Hill, catching his arm.

Meaning when they had him where he couldn't get away. Dizzily he looked around, and a familiar-looking car caught his eye. It was a gray Dodge, and it was parked in one of the slots reserved for the patrol cars, but no one seemed to care.

Sykes drove a gray Dodge, an ordinary car that he said no one ever noticed. This car had a Madison County tag on it; Sykes lived in Madison County, just outside Huntsville.

Why was Sykes here? If they had arrested him, they wouldn't have let him drive here any more than they'd let Nolan. How had they even located him? There was no reason for Sykes to be here, unless—

Unless Sykes had turned on them.

He was hyperventilating again, colors running together in his vision. "Sykes!" he roared, lowering his shoulder and ramming it into Investigator Hill, breaking his hold. *"Sykes!"* He began running toward the station. "You bastard, Sykes! You motherfucking bastard, *I'll kill you!"*

Investigator Hill and the patrol officer chased him, and the patrol officer made a diving tackle, wrapping both arms around the mayor's knees and bringing him down. With his hands cuffed behind him, Nolan couldn't catch himself, and he skidded face-first along the rough asphalt of the parking lot, leaving skin and blood behind. Mucus and blood poured from his broken nose as they hauled him to his feet. "Sykes," he said again, but his mouth was full of blood and the word was unintelligible.

The city councilmen stepped to the side as they half-carried him through the doors, the councilmen's expressions disgusted, as if they'd seen something nasty. Temple Nolan tried to think of something to say that would reassure them, some pat answer he'd rehearsed and used a hundred times before and which never failed to elicit the response he wanted, but nothing came to mind.

Nothing came to mind at all.

TWENTY-SIX

It was almost three o'clock in the morning. A multi-department task force waited in the night for the delivery of the Russian girls. Members of the Hillsboro Police Department, Jackson County Sheriff's Department, Madison County Sheriff's Department, the FBI, and the INS had hidden themselves behind trees, bushes, the propane gas tank, and anything else they could find. They had parked their vehicles on another road and trekked over a mile across a field to reach the trailer.

Glenn Sykes was there, to fulfill his usual role. If anyone else had shown up to accept the shipment, the driver of the truck would have been spooked; since he was armed, no one wanted him spooked. The girls in the back of the truck had been through enough, without risking getting them killed by ricochets.

Jack lay under a big pine tree, his black clothing blending into the night shadows. The chief of any department seldom saw any action, but it had been decided that his expertise would be welcome. According to Sykes, usually there was only the driver to contend with, but the Russians were so expensive that Phillips had wanted an extra guard to make sure nothing went wrong. The two men were outnumbered fifteen to one, but there was always the chance that one of them would try something stupid; hell, it was almost a given, unless everything worked perfectly and the lawmen had the two overwhelmed before they knew anything was happening.

A black rifle lay cradled in Jack's arms. He knew exactly how much pressure was needed to pull the trigger and how much kick to expect. He'd burned thousands of rounds of ammunition in this weapon; he knew its every idiosyncrasy, the smell and feel and weight of it. It was an old friend, one he hadn't realized he'd missed until he had taken it from the cabinet in his house and felt the way it settled in his arms.

Sykes was inside the trailer, the lights on, watching television. They had carefully searched the trailer to make sure he had no means of contacting the driver, but Jack thought that even if they'd had a dozen telephones lined up for him to use, Sykes wouldn't have made the call. He had coolly decided to cut his losses by cooperating fully, and he'd keep to his bargain. The D.A. had almost wept with joy at the wealth of evidence Sykes offered him and had given him a real sweetheart deal. He wouldn't even do time; five years' probation, but that was nothing to a man like Sykes.

In the distance they heard the whine of a motor, rising above the nighttime cacophony of frogs, crickets, and night birds. Jack felt the kick of adrenaline and got a firm grip on his reactions. It wouldn't be smart to get too excited.

The truck, a Ford extended cab pickup with a camper on the back, turned into the gravel driveway, and the driver immediately killed the lights. There was no signal of any kind, no tapping of the horn or flashing of the headlights. Instead, Sykes turned on the porch light and opened the trailer door, stepping out to stand on the highest of the three wooden steps leading up to the door.

The driver turned off the motor and climbed out. "Hey, Sykes." The guard stayed in the cab.

"Have any trouble?" Sykes asked.

"One of the girls got sick, puked a couple of times, but I figure it was just from riding in the back. Stunk, though. I had to stop and hose out the back, to keep the other girls from puking."

"Let's get 'em inside, then, so they can clean up. Mr. Phillips is anxious to see this bunch."

"He's waiting on the young one, right? She's a pretty little thing, but she's the one been puking so much, so she's not real spry right now."

In the distance came the sound of another car, and everyone in hiding froze. The driver looked alarmed, and Sykes made a staying motion with his hand. "Hold what you got," he said softly. "It's nothing to worry about, just a car passing."

But the car seemed to be slowing. The driver stepped back toward the truck cab and opened the door, sliding half inside with one leg still on the ground, and the men under the trees knew he'd just armed himself. They all held their fire, though, waiting to see what happened.

The car turned into the driveway, headlights on bright. Glenn Sykes immediately turned to the side to save his night vision, his hand up to shield his eyes even more.

The car, a white Lexus, pulled up right behind the truck, and the headlights were turned off. A man got out from behind the wheel, a tall man with graying blond hair brushed straight back. He wore a suit, though the night was muggy, and who wore a suit at three o'clock in the morning, anyway?

"Mr. Sykes," said a smooth voice, with the hammy kind of

southern accent that actors always used. After two years in the south, Jack could pick up some of the nuances now, and he knew that wasn't a north Alabama accent. Something about it struck him as fake; it was just too exaggerated.

"Mr. Phillips," Sykes said, surprised. "We didn't know to expect you."

That was true. The Scottsboro police hadn't been able to locate Mr. Phillips, though they'd been very low-key about their search. Until he was in custody, everything was being kept as quiet as possible, because they didn't want him forewarned and perhaps able to destroy evidence, or even skip town completely. He had enough money to live very comfortably in Europe or the Caribbean, if he wanted.

Sykes glanced at the driver and guard. "It's all right. Mr. Phillips owns the operation." The two relaxed, getting out of the truck. Their hands were empty; both of them had left their weapons in the cab.

"There've been a series of mistakes lately," said Phillips, walking toward Sykes. "I wanted to personally supervise this shipment to make certain nothing went wrong."

Meaning he couldn't wait to get his hands on the thirteen-year-old girl in the back of the truck, Jack thought, and disgust curdled his stomach. Slowly he centered his sights on Phillips, because his presence was unexpected and in Jack's experience the unexpected meant trouble.

"Nothing will go wrong this time," said Sykes, his voice calm.

"I'm sure it won't," Phillips purred, and pulled a pistol from the right pocket of his suit jacket. He aimed and fired at Sykes before any of the men surrounding them could react; Sykes slammed back against the trailer, then toppled off the steps.

Jack's finger gently squeezed the trigger. His shot took

Phillips exactly where he'd wanted it to, and Phillips went down screaming.

All hell broke loose.

To the uninitiated, the explosion of noise, lights, and motion as black-clad, heavily armed men burst from their hiding places, all shouting, "Police! Get your hands up!" or identifying themselves as FBI—whichever the case might be—would be nothing more than terrifying confusion. To Jack, it was a well-oiled operation, practiced over and over until each man knew what to do and what to expect. The two men still standing knew the drill: they froze, their arms automatically going up to lock their hands behind their heads.

The Russian girls inside the camper went into hysterics, screaming and crying and trying to escape, beating against the locked camper door. The INS agents got the key from the driver and opened the door, reeling back at the stench. The hysterical girls erupted from their prison, kicking and scratching as they were caught and held.

One girl managed to slip past everyone and run full speed down the dark country road before sheer exhaustion made her stumble and fall; the INS agent who gave chase picked her up and carried her like a baby in his arms, while she sobbed and made hysterical exclamations in her own language. The INS, forewarned, had a Russian-speaking agent on hand, and she began trying to calm the girls, saying the same phrases over and over until they actually began to listen.

There were seven of them, none older than fifteen. They were thin, filthy, and exhausted. According to Sykes, though, none of them had been sexually assaulted; they were all virgins, and were to be sold for ridiculously high prices to gangs who would then charge wealthy, depraved men even more for the privilege of being the first to rape the girls. After that, they would be used as prostitutes, and sold over and over among gangs who would work them for a while, then sell them off. None of them spoke English; all of them had been told that if they didn't cooperate, their families in Russia would be shot.

The INS translator told them over and over that their families wouldn't be harmed, that they would be able to go home. Finally they calmed enough that, warily, they began to think she might be telling the truth. Their ordeal, the long trip from Russia and the brutal conditions they had endured, made it difficult for them to trust anyone right now. They huddled together, watching the black-clad people move around them, frightened by the flashing lights of the emergency vehicles as they arrived, but making no further effort to escape.

Jack stood over Sykes as the medics evaluated the wounded men. Blood from the chest wound soaked the entire left side of his body, but Sykes was conscious, his face ashen as the medics worked to stabilize him. In the background, Phillips's screams had deteriorated to guttural moans. Sykes looked up at Jack, his gaze vague with shock. "Will . . . he live?"

Jack glanced over his shoulder at the second knot of medics. "Maybe. If he doesn't die of sepsis. I didn't nick the femoral artery, but groin wounds can be a bitch when the colon is involved."

"Groin . . ." Sykes almost managed a grin. "You shot . . . his balls off."

"I haven't checked. If there's anything left, though, it won't be in good working order."

Sykes gasped for breath, and the medic said, "We've radioed for a helicopter to transport him," meaning every minute counted if Sykes was to survive.

"I'll . . . come out . . . on top yet," said Sykes, and looking down at him, Jack figured that if sheer willpower could keep the man alive, then Sykes would be testifying at Nolan's and Phillips's trials.

* * *

At six-thirteen, Jack trudged into his office. He hadn't been home, hadn't showered, and still carried his black rifle. He was more tired than he'd been since . . . hell, since the last time he'd carried the rifle, but he felt good, too. All he wanted to do was take care of some details and go home to Daisy.

Both Sykes and Phillips were in surgery at a hospital in Huntsville, but even if Sykes died, they had more than enough to prosecute.

Sykes had been a regular fountain of information. Mitchell had been killed because of his habit of dosing the girls with GHB; he'd killed two of them, so Nolan had decided he had to be dealt with. When questioned about the date-rape drugs, Sykes had rattled off the names of the dealers he knew. A dozen different investigations had been launched as a result of what Glenn Sykes had to say.

Having been given all the details by Todd, Jack had personally asked Sykes if he knew anything about the woman who had been given GHB at the Buffalo Club and raped by at least six men. That was one question for which Sykes didn't have any answers, though; Jack didn't think there ever would be any answers.

When he opened the office door, he stared in disbelief at Eva Fay, sitting at her desk. She looked up and held out a cup of fresh, hot coffee. "Here, you look like you need this."

He took the coffee and sipped it. Yep, it was so fresh he could still smell the coffee beans. He eyed her over the cup. "All right, Eva Fay, tell me how you do it."

"Do what?" she asked, a look of astonishment on her face.

"How do you know when I'm coming in? How do you always have hot coffee waiting for me? And what in hell are you doing here at six-fifteen in the morning?"

"Yesterday was a busy day," she said. "I had a lot of stuff I didn't get done, so I came in early to handle it."

"Explain the coffee."

She looked at him and smiled. "No."

" 'No'? What do you mean, 'No'? I'm your boss, and I want to know."

"Tough," she said, and swiveled back to her computer screen.

He knew he should go home and clean up first. He knew he desperately needed some sleep. But what he needed most was to see Daisy, to be in the company of a woman who would never park in a fire lane or even jaywalk. After the filth and sordidness he'd seen, he needed her cleanness, her simple good-heartedness. And even though he knew she was all right, he needed to *see* her, to let his eyes reassure his brain. He wasn't sure exactly when she'd become so important to him, but there were some things a man couldn't fight. Besides, she'd let him use her shower.

She opened the door almost as soon as he knocked. "I heard you drive up," she said, then got a good look at him. "Goodness."

"It'll wash off," he said, swiping at the remnants of black face paint. He'd done a halfhearted job using paper towels in the men's rest room at the station, but there hadn't been any soap, and the job definitely called for soap.

She eyed him dubiously. "I hope so."

She was carrying Midas, and the puppy struggled madly to reach him. Midas didn't care what he looked like, Jack thought, reaching out to take the fuzzbutt in his arms. Midas began his frantic licking ritual, and Daisy frowned at him. "I don't know if you should let him do that," she said.

"Why not? He always does this."

"Yes, but you usually aren't covered with . . . stuff. I don't want him to get sick."

Jack thought about grabbing her and getting some of that stuff on her, but she'd probably smack him. She looked good enough to eat, he thought, with her blond hair tousled and her odd-colored eyes sleepy. Her skin was fresh and clear, and the thin pink robe she wore was almost thick enough to keep him from being able to tell she wore only a pair of panties underneath.

"I thought you'd like to know it's all wrapped up."

"I know. Todd called me."

"Todd." He growled the name. He liked Todd, even trusted him, but suddenly he felt the hot bite of jealousy. He didn't like Daisy's easy friendship with the man, because even if she still had doubts about Todd's sexual orientation, *he* didn't.

"Don't just stand there, come in," she said, taking Midas from him and setting the puppy on the floor, where he bounced off in search of recreation. "Go take a shower while I cook breakfast."

That sounded like heaven. He was already pulling off his clothes as he left the room, though he still had enough wit about him to take everything with him and not leave it on the floor for sharp puppy teeth to shred. Something, a sudden sharp need to get everything in order and nailed down, stopped him in the doorway. He looked back at her. "Daisy."

She paused at the kitchen door. "Yes?"

"Remember the deal we made?"

"Which deal?"

"That I'd marry you if you got pregnant."

Her cheeks got pink. He loved it that she could still blush. "Of course I remember. I wouldn't have begun this affair with you if you'd said no. People have to be responsible, and if you think you can weasel out of the deal now—"

"Let's go to Gatlinburg this weekend and get married."

Her eyes rounded and her lips parted in surprise. "But I'm not pregnant. At least, I don't think . . . It was just that once, and—"

"So we try again," he said, shrugging. "If you insist on being pregnant before we get married."

"My goodness, of course not! You mean you actually want—"

"Oh, yeah," he said softly. "I want."

Midas pranced back into the living room, a dishcloth trailing from his mouth. Daisy stooped and caught him, and took the dishcloth away. "You don't mind having children? Because I really do want at least a couple of kids, and you seemed horrified when I asked you if you had any."

"I was horrified at the thought that I might have had any kids with my ex."

"Oh. That's good."

But she didn't give him a definite answer, just stood there looking preoccupied, and he began to get worried. He dropped his shirt to the floor and crossed the room to her. Wrapping one arm around her waist, he pulled her against him and put his other hand on her throat, using his thumb to tilt her chin up. "I know I'm dirty and smelly," he said, "but I'm not letting you go until I get the answer I want."

"Not just an answer, but the answer you want, hmm?"

"You got it."

"I have a question."

"Ask it."

"Do you love me?" She immediately blushed again. "I didn't think you were my type at all, but it didn't seem to matter. The more I was around you the more I wanted to be with you, and I'd love to marry you, but if you don't feel the same way I feel, then I don't think we should get married."

"I love you," he said clearly. "That's as plain as I can make it. Now, will you marry me?"

She beamed at him, the million-watt smile he'd noticed the first time he'd ever spoken to her, when he'd gone to the library to sign up for the virtual library. That smile did more for him than blond hair and makeup ever could. "Yes, thank you."

Then he had to kiss her, and when he stopped, he didn't feel nearly as tired as he had when he'd arrived. He began dragging her toward the hall. "Forget about breakfast. Take a shower with me."

"Midas—" she began, looking around for the little demon.

"We'll take him with us." Jack scooped him up and removed his shirt from the puppy's mouth. "He needs a bath, too."

"He does not, and besides, I don't think I can do it with him in the tub with us, watching."

"I'll blindfold him." He tugged her into the bathroom.

"You'll do no such thing!"

"Then we'll close the door and let him play on the floor." He suited action to words and decided the sacrifice of a shirt was worth it for the peace. He dropped the shirt, and Midas pounced on it.

Daisy immediately leaned down to take it away from him, but Jack stopped her and efficiently stripped her out of her robe and panties, then bundled her into the tub. He shucked off the rest of his clothes and let them drop, too. Let Midas have a field day.

He got into the tub with her and turned on the water, then when it was hot, turned on the shower, shielding her with his body until the initial icy blast turned warm. As he lifted her, she put both arms around his neck, her expression serious. "Could we start trying right away?"

Maybe he was too tired to think clearly, or maybe he just had other things on his mind. "Trying what?"

"To have a baby," she said, exasperated, then gasped as he slipped into her. Her gaze immediately unfocused and her head drooped back as if it were suddenly too heavy for her neck.

"Sweetheart," he promised, "you'll never have to buy another PartyPak."

EPILOGUE

Evelyn and Aunt Jo had outdone themselves with Sunday dinner, a sort of celebration for Daisy and Jack. There had been a dinner in Gatlinburg the week before, right after their wedding, but that had been at a restaurant and didn't count. Now the table fairly groaned under the weight of all the food. The whole family was there, as well as Todd and his friend Howard, whom Daisy had been astonished to recognize. She hadn't thought Howard was gay, because why would he have been at the Buffalo Club if he was? Of course, Jack was still adamant that Todd was straight, so maybe she wasn't a good judge of such matters.

Midas prowled under the table, unerringly locating her by her scent, and plopped down on her feet. His little tongue lapped at her ankles, and she peeked under the tablecloth to check on him. He had that sleepy look that meant he was settling down for a nap. He'd worn himself out, greeting so many different people, and of course each had to be played with before he moved on to the next.

Only a few short weeks ago she'd been agonized by how empty her life was, and now it was brimming over. Her family had always been there, of course, but she had found some very dear friends, she now had Midas—and then there was Jack.

How could she ever have thought jocks weren't her type? This particular jock was just what she needed. He always looked so tough, with his short-cropped graying hair and his broad shoulders and thick neck, and the cocky way he had of walking, like a man who took up all of his allotted space and then some. He still crowded her, in bed and out, but she had learned to adjust. If he took up more than his half of the bed, then she had no where else to sleep but on top of him, so if he wasn't getting enough sleep these days, it was his own fault.

She felt almost incandescent with joy; so far her period was four days late. She was stunned by the possibility that she might have gotten pregnant so fast, but then Jack had certainly worked at his appointed duty. She had kept waiting for her period to start, but this morning hope had suddenly overwhelmed common sense and she was almost certain. When they left her mother's, they were going to buy a pregnancy test kit. Tomorrow morning, they would know for sure.

She couldn't decide which she wanted most, a son or a daughter. She thought of Jack throwing a football with a tough little guy, and her heart melted. Then she imagined a little girl, all dimples and ringlets, cradled in her daddy's muscular arms, and she shivered with delight. No matter which she had, though, she'd ask Todd to help her decorate the nursery, because he had such wonderful taste in interior decorating. And she wanted to ask him if he would be the baby's godfather, though she'd have to talk that over with Jack first because he might have another friend in mind.

Todd commented on the lace tablecloth, asking her mother if she knew how old it was. Daisy tilted her head, studying him. He was as neatly dressed as always, today wearing a white silk shirt and pleated forest green trousers with a narrow black belt cinched around his waist.

Under the table, Jack's leg nudged hers, as if he couldn't bear not touching her any longer. She ignored him, her gaze locked on Todd.

Jack realized whom she was watching, and he suddenly shifted restlessly. "Daisy—" he began, but he was too late. Her voice rang out, clear and crisp.

"Todd, do you know what color puce is?"

Caught off-guard, Todd turned to her with a startled look. "You're making that up, right?" he blurted.

Glenn Sykes had been out of the hospital for almost a month when he drove up to Temple Nolan's house, though the former mayor no longer lived there. He was out on bail and supposedly living in Scottsboro until his trial, but Sykes hadn't made any effort to find out where. For now, he was just concentrating on being alive and getting his strength back.

He'd been in an odd mood since getting shot, though maybe it wasn't so odd. Almost dying tended to change your outlook, at least temporarily. He still figured he'd handled things the best way possible for himself, even though it had gone bad there at the end, with Phillips showing up. He allowed himself a cold smile; he still enjoyed thinking about Russo's well-placed shot.

There was one other person who probably enjoyed thinking about that shot just as much as he did, and that was why he was here.

He rang the doorbell and waited. He heard footsteps; then Jennifer Nolan opened the door. She didn't know him, though, so she didn't unlatch the storm door. "Yes?"

She was a beautiful woman, he thought, more than merely pretty. He'd heard she had stopped drinking; maybe she had, maybe she hadn't, but today her eyes were clear, if full of shadows.

"I'm Glenn Sykes," he said.

She stared at him through the screen, and he knew what she was thinking. He had been in her husband's employ, privy to all the dirty secrets; he probably knew about Temple giving her to Phillips.

"Go away," she said, and started to shut the door.

"It doesn't matter," he said softly, and she froze, her hand still on the door.

"What . . . what doesn't matter?" Her voice was low and strained.

"What Phillips did. It doesn't matter. He didn't touch *you,* just your body."

She whirled, her eyes full of rage. "Yes, he *did* touch me! He killed part of me, so don't come here telling me what he did or didn't do."

He put his hands in his pockets. "Are you going to let him win?"

"He didn't win. I did. I'm here, and what's left of him will go to prison, where I'm sure he'll be very popular."

"Are you going to let him win?" Sykes repeated, his cool gaze locked on hers, and she hesitated.

The moment drew out, as if she was helpless to close the door and bring an end to it. Her breath came fast and shallow. "Why are you here?" she whispered.

"Because you need me," he said, and Jennifer opened the door.